Lords
of
the
Seventh
Swarm

Tor Books by Dave Wolverton

The Golden Queen
Beyond the Gate
Lords of the Seventh Swarm

Lords
of the
Seventh Swarm

Dave Wolverton

TOR®

A Tom Doherty Associates Book / New York

LORDS OF THE SEVENTH SWARM

Copyright © 1997 by Dave Wolverton

Edited by David G. Hartwell

A Tor Book
Published by Tom Doherty Associates, Inc.
175 Fifth Avenue
New York, NY 10010

Tor Books on the World Wide Web: http://www.tor.com

Tor® is a registered trademark of Tom Doherty Associates, Inc.

Library of Congress Cataloging-in-Publication Data

Wolverton, Dave.
    Lords of the Seventh Swarm / Dave Wolverton.—1st ed.
        p. cm.—(The Golden queen ; bk. 3)
    ISBN 0-312-85771-3
    I. Title. II. Series: Wolverton, Dave. Golden queen ; bk. 3.
PS3573.O572L67   1997
813'.54—dc20   96-32446
                                                      CIP

First Edition: January 1997

Printed in the United States of America

0 9 8 7 6 5 4 3 2 1

Lords
of
the
Seventh
Swarm

O n e

When Thomas Flynn deserted his niece in her hour of need, he did it with the best intentions. Oh, he knew Maggie would damn him for the deed and curse him till the day he died—and beyond. But he'd won the contempt of better people. So he deserted her.

The truth was that, though Gallen and Maggie determined to run off to Tremonthin to fight the Inhuman, Thomas knew he shouldn't go. He felt a deep warning in his heart—"It's a hero they want, someone to brandish a sword, not a minstrel with an overlarge gut and gaudy attire." Some folks might ascribe such misgivings to cowardice, but Thomas held with certain sects of priests who would called it "inspiration." You should always listen to that inner voice, they'd say, and this time Thomas agreed.

He'd never been one to face danger. A good pair of legs and a keen eye for the nearest thicket could extricate a man from most situations. So when Gallen told Thomas that he *had* to come to Tremonthin with him and Maggie, Thomas's first inclination, and last, was to run.

As he packed his bags, he wondered if he was doing right. He didn't understand life here on Fale. He'd seen wondrous things—men flying on mechanical wings, doors that let you walk from one world to another. But this world held dangers as great as its wonders.

So far, Thomas hadn't met the Dronon monsters. His kin on Tihrglas thought them to be demons. But Thomas knew better. He understood why the

Dronon sought to conquer mankind. Folks here had more food than they could eat, comfortable homes, the promise of lives extended for thousands of years. Thomas understood why the Dronon would want to seize these things.

But he couldn't understand why some humans sympathized with the Dronon. As he slipped from his room, Thomas considered the rose they'd found outside Maggie's room a few hours ago—a delicate thing, lustrous as pearl—until the petals on it began spinning like a pinwheel, slicing open the Lord Mayor of Toohkansay. An odd trap that Maggie's enemies had left for her.

'Tis a strange and dangerous world, Thomas told himself as he slipped down the city's darkened corridors. I don't know what dangers to watch for, much less how to fight them. If I go with Gallen to Tremonthin, I'll be a burden. I can't hobble so far and fast as I used to.

He imagined how Maggie would curse him when she found that he'd run out. She'd say he only thought of himself, that he was a mercenary. Well, damn her for her judgments. At fifty years of age, Thomas knew that "Few vices will destroy a man quicker than the craving to own all virtues."

I'm doing what's best—not just best for me, best for Maggie and Gallen, Thomas told himself. He met some guards in the corridor who had been posted to protect him.

One tall, wiry man who cradled a rifle, asked Thomas, "Would you like an escort?"

Thomas said, "No, I'm just after a stroll in the moonlight, and a little fooling about on the mandolin." Thomas patted his instrument cases as if they were lovers, then passed down the corridor, dimly lit with fixtures that shone from the ceiling like jewels. He'd left his mandolin in his room and filled the case with spare clothes. He'd kept his lute for sentimental reasons, but neither instrument was valuable. His mantle—the headpiece he wore that held knowledge of all things musical—told him that far better instruments could easily be purchased.

On his way out of Toohkansay, Thomas stopped at the cantina, which had emptied at this time of night of everyone but the golden serving droids who scampered about, preparing the morning meal. Since the food was both free and excellent, Thomas took enough for several days—bread and cheese, wine, ham, chicken, and fruit. Then Thomas ambled outside and stood in the open, staring over the river.

The night was warm; the stars in the sky burned with unnatural brightness. Maggie had said it was because they were so close here. Thomas didn't quite understand such talk. Something about the galactic center. Out on the edge of the river, bullfrogs croaked from the rushes, competing with soft music that played from speakers beside him.

It truly was a lovely night, a great night for travel, but Thomas would not walk. Gallen and Orick were excellent trackers, so Thomas cast his eyes about, searching for a vehicle of some sort, or an animal to ride.

At the docks, just beneath the cantina, lay some small boats shaped like white swans, with wings spread wide.

Thomas carried his bags to the docks, stepped into the nearest boat, then looked for the ties that held it to the dock. He couldn't see any, and he attributed that failing to the poor light. The shadows made it painfully dark.

By accident, Thomas pushed his hand against the dock; the boat drifted a few feet into the depths.

He cast his eyes about for oars; found none.

So he sat in the boat, fuming. No oars, he thought. No damned oars. Nothing to row with but his mandolin case. True, I could use my lute, it would make a better oar, but I dare not ruin it.

He considered just drifting the river, but as the boat drew away from the dock, it just sat, as stationary as if it wallowed on the beach.

"Damn," he cursed, "how am I supposed to go anywhere?" The head of the swan boat turned; its dark eyes blinked, startling Thomas. He leapt back, tripping over his seat.

"Where would you like to go?" the swan asked. "I'll take you."

Thomas didn't know what to answer. He stammered, "Downstream." The swan boat moved. Thomas felt its legs kick, paddling, as if it were a living creature.

Thomas rested on the cushioned seats and watched the stars burn overhead. The boat moved slowly. It was a pleasure craft. Thomas found himself fighting tiredness as the boat carried him away.

He roused a little when distant sirens wailed back at the city; he'd gone far downriver. He'd never before heard a siren, did not know that it warned of a Dronon invasion. He simply wondered why someone played such loud squawking horns at night; he closed his eyes and slept.

When he woke, the boat was still heading downstream. Thomas judged he'd gone far enough. He planned to wait three days until Gallen had left the planet, hide in some thicket.

Strange trees with long drooping stems and dark trunks lined the river. Thomas watched till a wide tributary opened between trees, then told the swan to go in. The swan swam up a small river for a mile, then Thomas set camp and ate a heavy breakfast, drank half a bottle of wine.

The next two days came warm and sunny, the nights pleasant; Thomas felt at peace. After the first day, when Gallen didn't catch him, Thomas suspected his nephew and niece had left Fale. By the third day he felt certain of it.

On that day he'd have taken the swan back to Toohkansay, but instead, while exploring the shoreline, he found a trail by the river, a graveled walk. There, he sat on the banks and played his lute. There he met the Lady Wimisonne, a woman past her prime who enjoyed Thomas's company so much that he found himself sharing her bed for the next month.

From her he learned of the invasion, of the Dronon's search for Gallen and Maggie. During days "The Lady" worked in town. To keep Thomas entertained, she showed him how to run the holo.

From it, Thomas learned more about the Dronon than he'd ever wanted to know: On the first night of the invasion, while Thomas floated lazily down the river, a human Lord Protector had challenged the Lords of the Seventh Swarm to a ceremony called "Right of Charn," in which the man fought the Dronon in an effort to turn them back from the planet.

It was then that mankind got its first glimpse of the Lords of the Seventh Swarm—the Golden Queen Cintkin and her Lord Escort Kintiniklintit.

The Lords terrified Thomas. He understood why his kin back home had thought them demons, had mistaken a Dronon Vanquisher for Satan, "Lord of the Flies." Though Thomas had seen a dead Dronon, he'd never watched a live one, a Lord Vanquisher, move. He hadn't imagined the way it would bounce on its hind legs, with a rhythmic grace. He hadn't imagined the power of the beast. Kintiniklintit looked like some horrific wasp or mantis—with his pee-colored wings and huge battle arms held out dangerously. He seemed enormous.

Though his size was attributed to a natural mutation, holovid commentators speculated that Kintiniklintit was a product of eugenics, that human engineers had gifted him beyond other Vanquishers. He'd been sired by the Lords of the Sixth Swarm, who had conquered mankind. That meant that humans *could* have boosted this young prince.

But there was other evidence of an unholy alliance. The Lords of the Seventh Swarm seemed to have embraced human technology more than anyone would have thought possible: They were traveling through the world gates, technology forbidden to all but the Tharrin and their representatives.

Until he learned all this, Thomas hadn't recognized just how dangerous the Dronon were. Until he saw Kintiniklintit in battle, he had no idea why Gallen fled from the Dronon.

The Lord Protector who challenged the Kintiniklintit was a huge man, a full head taller than Gallen O'Day. The fellow had enough muscle on him, he could have auctioned it off to blacksmiths.

Even more fascinating to Thomas was that a woman stood beside the Lord Protector. In order to make the ceremony complete, the man had to risk not only his life, but the life of his wife. Thomas wondered at the woman's nerve. My Maggie has done that, he reminded himself.

The holovision didn't show the Lord Protector's battle against Kintiniklintit. Witnesses said it was too gruesome to display. The beginning of the battle was unspectacular—photos showed the Lord Escort clocking record wing-speeds, computer graphics projected his mass to be one-third larger than any other Vanquisher ever encountered. The holos showed the Dronon flying toward the human Lord Protector, an enormous man all in black, who leapt and kicked as Kintiniklintit approached. Then the screens blanked, denying Thomas a view of the poor man's fate.

It was said that in one blow, Kintiniklintit slashed the Lord Protector with a heavy, serrated battle arm, slicing him into ragged halves. Kintiniklintit spared the man's wife. That was something, Thomas considered.

Despite the images on the holo, as Thomas stayed with Lady Wimisonne, she filled his nights with such diversion he did not worry much about rumors of Dronon searches.

Even when the Dronon left the planet Fale, Thomas remained with "The Lady" for a few days.

For weeks, she'd told Thomas that if he wanted some fun, he should go to the "recreation center." Thomas felt his face burn with embarrassment at such words. Though the folks on Fale spoke the same tongue as Thomas, they spoke with an odd accent, and Thomas sometimes found that the way they combined words varied from his custom. Back on Tihrglas, the term *recreation center* was a euphemism he would not have used in front of a lady. It referred to the secluded homes of single women notorious for letting any man into their beds. For a traveling man, the name of such a woman was worth gold, for such a woman not only would feed a man for a day or two, but provided some good sport. So Thomas often traded names of such women with minstrels, saying, "I'll be wandering down Gort Ard way. You would not have the name of a recreation center, would you?" To which the minstrel would reply, "There's always Mary Mimsey O'Keefe."

It caused Thomas no little embarrassment that Lady Wimisonne urged him to go to another "recreation center." Each time she did, Thomas asked if she'd tired of his company. Always she laughed his question away, but finally Thomas feared she really must be weary of him, so while she stepped out for an afternoon, he packed his bags and went to the *recreation center*, only to discover it was just a pub.

Strange place, Fale. Strange and wonderful, Thomas decided for the hundredth time.

There, he drank his fill, sang to an appreciative audience, and laughed the night away. The Dronon were gone, Fale was his once more, and back at home, Lady Wimisonne would welcome him back to her bed energetically.

But when he stepped from the pub, clothes and instrument cases in hand, he was surprised by a shadowy figure who stepped up behind him. "Thomas Flynn?" a man asked.

"Yes?" Thomas turned to confront the fellow. Thomas never made it. A light flashed, and a sharp pain erupted in his shoulder, and he fell.

Three months later, Thomas Flynn sat slumped in a chair, a black blindfold covering his eyes, hands chained behind his back. His stomach cramped painfully.

Thomas felt a fool. It didn't matter if his captors were Dronon or their lackeys. Bagged is bagged.

So he sat chained to a chair in some financial minister's basement.

Thomas had resolved never to speak. But resolutions didn't matter. On the very first night of his capture, Thomas's interrogator simply placed a circlet on Thomas's head. Thomas had felt a prick at the back of his neck as the machine sent tendrils to infiltrate his brain, then Thomas listened as he told his interrogators everything.

Ignorance, that's what did Thomas in. Who ever heard of Guides and nanoware and all the interrogator's nasty tricks?

Of course, Thomas told the interrogator that Gallen and Maggie had gone to Tremonthin. He'd told them where Maggie had lived for seventeen years—even naming the room where she slept at Mahoney's Inn, in the city Clere, of County Morgan, on Tihrglas.

As he betrayed his niece over the weeks, Thomas became weighed down with guilt. He hoped his answers would do no harm. What did the Dronon care where Maggie was born? She'd never return home. As for her destination, Thomas could only hope that the young folks had accomplished their mission on Tremonthin and escaped.

Yet it rankled Thomas. Treachery. Treachery. Thomas's body betrayed him by speaking. The Dronon collaborators wrenched Maggie's secrets from him.

I *am* a fool, Thomas had thought bitterly a thousand times in the past weeks. Dying a brave death on Tremonthin would have been infinitely preferable to this.

Three times now I have betrayed Maggie. I betrayed her in her youth when her mother died, by leaving her in the care of strangers. As her only living relative, I only came to claim her when she won an inheritance.

I betrayed her again when I refused to join her quest to Tremonthin. In my naïveté, I imagined I knew more than she.

And I betrayed her at last by answering every question the Dronon's interrogator put to me.

Over and over, Thomas considered his betrayal, until he imagined that if the Dronon ever unchained his hands, he would strangle himself.

But for now he only sat, starving, choking on the scent of his own excrement—for the interrogator left him in filth.

Until, finally, he heard the door open to his cell. Briefly, Thomas hoped his captors would finally kill him.

His head hung sideways, and though his tongue felt swollen dry, Thomas Flynn began to sing the words to an aria written by an ancient composer named Acuon of Freewater. It was a haunting melody with intricate musical phrases that seemed to meander then would thunder back to their major themes clothed in new majesty, having accrued power in their travels. It was a song of defiance.

A person walked in, stirring the air, padding on soft feet. It did not sound like the heavy boots of his interrogator. Thomas heard a lighter tread.

A scent filled the room, a restrained sweetness. The intruder tiptoed around Thomas, never speaking. Thomas took a deep breath.

It was Maggie, his niece—he felt sure. He could smell her wool shawl, the scent of her dark red hair, all mingled with a rich fragrance of perfume she'd got off-world.

The sense of smell is such a strange thing. Most people hardly notice how much they rely on it, how easily a scent is remembered.

After all these weeks, all the answers the Dronon had forced from him, Maggie was here.

Thomas's heart sank. Captured. She'd been captured; held prisoner with him. The Dronon would kill her. The Lords of the Seventh Swarm would force

Gallen to fight, for Gallen and Maggie held the title of "Lords of the Sixth Swarm." The Dronon imagined that by winning this title, they would gain legal claim to the worlds of man.

Of course when Gallen lost the battle, the Dronon would also kill Maggie. Thomas's ignorance would lead to the death of his only kin.

"Maggie?" Thomas cried, straining against his blindfold. "I'm sorry! They made me tell. I tried to hold back. I tried to be quiet! Can you forgive me, lass?"

She did not answer. Only circled him, lightly brushing his shoulder with her woolen shawl, padding around him.

"Maggie?" he pleaded once again.

She reached out, tugged vainly for a moment at his blindfold, then pulled it away, raking the skin around his eyes with her long nails.

The figure standing before Thomas was not Maggie. Instead, a man all dressed in black robes stood, a man in a golden mask. It was the kind of mask common on Fale, a thin film of incandescent material. Behind the mask were deep brown eyes. Thomas's interrogator, Lord Karthenor.

"Forgive the minor deception," Karthenor said. "The Lords of the Seventh Swarm wanted assurance that they had Maggie's scent right."

Karthenor raised a small perfume bottle, then sprayed it on his wrist, held it up for Thomas. It smelled like Maggie, as true and clear as if she were in the room.

"A person's scent is marvelous," Karthenor said, "as distinctive as a retinal scan, as individual as genetic mapping. Yet we leave it wherever we go."

"How, how did you do this?" Thomas asked.

"*You* did it," Karthenor laughed. "We had only to send emissaries to Tihrglas, to collect samples of her body oils from the comforter on her bed. Recreating her scent is a minor thing.

"For this, I thank you. Now our Dronon Seekers will be able to track Maggie across the worlds."

"Och, damn your sorry hide!" Thomas shouted. "I hope you never catch her. If I were free, I'd break your spine!"

Karthenor smiled benignly, glanced up to the silver circlet weighing on Thomas's head. With the Guide on, Thomas could not fight, could not flee. Yet Karthenor still kept Thomas chained. Thomas could only imagine one reason for the shackles: meanness. A minor torture.

Karthenor mused, "If you were free, I'm sure you would do more than merely break my spine. But you will never be free again."

T w o

"Och, this is no proper place for a bear," Orick growled. He sniffed at the dead monster at his feet.

The creature looked like some huge gray slime mold. It had just come slithering out of the stream not forty feet distant, and Gallen had been forced to fry it with his incendiary rifle. Now it lay, burned and quivering, just outside camp. It was the third monster Gallen had killed in the past three hours.

Orick shook his head, wondering if the slime was edible. "My mother always said that you'd bring me to Ruin, Gallen, and here we are."

"It's just the name for the planet—because of all the alien ruins hereabouts," Gallen said. He grunted, pulling at some vines near the edge of camp, trying to get them from the ground so that he could burn them for a campfire. The little bear, Tallea, went to his side and began pulling with her teeth, trying to help Gallen out.

Orick glanced off at the skyline. Ruin was a strange world—too far from its primary sun, which sat directly overhead like a child's purple ball. It gave the landscape a violet hue.

Here, strewn across the desert, were huge red boulders, shaped like eggs, lying in the sand, and farther in the distance, a wind-sculpted sandstone mesa rose above the desert floor like some castle. Odd bushes grew all around— some sprouting like hair, others all thick and rubbery. The plants filled the air with alien scents.

Only the sound of the stream, burbling as brooks will, reminded Orick of home. No, Ruin was no proper place for a bear. Still, Orick wouldn't have minded it so much if he could actually *see* some of these famous ruins that the planet was named after, but Orick had no such luck. It was, after all, just another alien landscape.

The gray mold at Orick's feet quivered, whether in dying throes or in an attempt to escape, he didn't know.

"Maybe we should move the camp away from the brook," Orick said. "I think it attracts predators."

Gallen didn't answer. He'd got some of the dead vines over in front of the spaceship and was trying to set them afire. Tallea was out looking for more wood. Perhaps Gallen was building a fire in the hope of scaring off predators. Perhaps he did it because they planned on camping here, next to this stream, and Gallen was just used to having a campfire. They didn't really *need* a fire, as far as Orick could tell. Though he'd grown sick of riding in a spaceship this past few weeks, he still thought it safer to sleep in there than to sleep out here in the open, on an alien world.

Why couldn't Gallen find some nicer planet to camp on? Surely there were worlds in the process of being terraformed hereabouts, places where forests grew and the grass was green. Proper places for a bear. But, no, Maggie wanted this planet because it wasn't listed as inhabitable on the star charts: "A good place to hide from the Dronon," she said. They were already well quit of the Milky Way. Here in the Carina Galaxy, they'd come to the fringe worlds, on the edge of civilization.

Gallen quit fiddling with the wood, looked up at the ship. The *Nightswift*'s landing lights blinked violet and ivory. It was a sleek ship, some sixty meters long and thirty wide.

The headdress of black ringlets that Gallen wore over his long hair glittered in the soft lights, the crystal disks of memory for his mantle jiggling as he drew ragged breaths. A single sapphire gem began to glow in the center of Gallen's mantle. Gallen had just chosen that moment to download his memories into his mantle so that if he died, his memories could be placed into a clone.

After a few heartbeats, the gem quit blazing so fiercely. Maggie was still in the ship, resting. Being nearly five months pregnant was taking its toll on her energy levels.

Gallen gazed down at Orick. "I've been thinking," he said softly, so as not to be heard through the ship's open door. "We could move this ship to another camp—or maybe we could go back the way we came. It's time to quit running from the Dronon. I have to fight them sometime."

Orick had been Gallen's friend for years, yet he felt no less loyal to Maggie. He didn't like having to side with one or the other.

Orick said, "Fighting is too risky. For every minute you keep running, that's another moment of freedom you give to every man and woman in the galaxy."

"That's where Maggie is wrong!" Gallen said, voicing an argument that had been going on for weeks. "The Dronon are setting outposts on every world, searching for us. They're killing those who help hide us. The very threat of invasion keeps our people in fear: what kind of freedom is that?"

"It's a devil's bargain," Orick agreed, "but you have to admit, Gallen, *you* don't have an answer to this problem." He looked down at the quivering mold, pondering.

"What do you mean, I have no answer?" Gallen said. "I just told you my answer."

"I know, I heard you. Kill Kintiniklintit. But you've been killing outlaws and usurpers ever since we met," Orick grumbled. "And what has it got you? You killed the Lords of the Sixth Swarm, and now you want to face the Lords of the Seventh Swarm. And when you beat them, maybe you'll have to fight some more, or maybe you can go back to killing folks who are no better than Dronon, though they have human shapes. And do you know what it's got you, Gallen: you're a slave. You're a miserable slave!"

"A slave?" Gallen said, amused by Orick's tirade. "Maybe so, but . . . I was *born* to be a Lord Protector."

"Yeah, so you're a clone of some famous Lord Protector," Orick grumbled. "That doesn't mean you have to follow in his footsteps. As I remember the story, didn't he eventually get martyred? Are you going to follow in his footsteps? Are you going to let somebody else decide how you'll live your life."

"What else can I do?" Gallen said. He began pacing, hardly daring to look at Orick.

And at that moment, the answer came to Orick, an answer he had felt in the depths of his soul but never had been quite able to voice to Gallen. "Ignore evil," Orick said. "Jesus said to forgive others. If a man comes to you, though he has sinned seventy times seven, and asks forgiveness, then you forgive. Ignore evil."

Gallen shook his head angrily. "I disagree! 'Resist Satan, and he will flee from you'! God strengthened David so he could slay Goliath. God ordered Joshua to destroy the Hittites and the Jebusites."

Orick grinned, a glint in his eye. "The devil quotes Scripture, too. You're not a religious man, Gallen. When did you start quoting Scripture?"

Gallen laughed. "I warmed my share of pews as a kid. You forget, I've got more than one priest in my family."

Orick felt chagrined. He said softly, "Sometimes, sometimes God has commanded men to fight. But I'd like to know Gallen, are you so eager to fight because that's what God wants of you, or is it just in your nature? Sometimes God tells people to run, too. Moses took the children of Israel and fled from Pharaoh. Joseph and Mary were told to flee Israel when Herod sent his soldiers to slaughter the babes. Sometimes you should run from evil. Maggie's right in this, in asking you to run. Her life is at risk as much as your own. And there's the babe to worry about. She has to make the choice for her own life."

Gallen opened his mouth to argue, yet nothing came out.

Orick looked up at Gallen, then shook his head in despair. "Gallen, my oldest and dearest friend, I think it's time for me to leave you."

There, he'd said it. He'd been thinking it for months, and now he'd finally said it.

"Leave?" Gallen asked, astonished. "Where would you go?"

"Anywhere. We've been on a dozen fine planets. Home, maybe. Back to Tihrglas."

Gallen's mouth just worked of its own accord, as if he would speak but couldn't find the words. He'd been totally unprepared.

Orick felt—weary, sick at heart. "Oh, don't you see it, Gallen? I've been thinking about this for months. The night the Dronon came to Tihrglas, I almost left you for good. You know I've always wanted to be a priest. I wanted to serve God, but you've become a slave to evil, and I can't watch it anymore. You sicken me, my friend. You're destroying yourself!"

Orick's eyes watered with tears. It hurt to say these things.

"What do you mean, I sicken you?" Gallen asked. "I haven't changed."

"Oh yes you have!" Orick said. "Remember the day we first met?"

Gallen looked at Orick, confused, and shook his head.

Orick reminded him. "We were on that hot August road that runs through the hills by the mill outside Gort Ard, and you was hunting for that killer, Dan'l O'Leary?"

"You mean the *very* first time we met?" Gallen asked. "You were with that friar, what's-his-name."

"Friar Bannon," Orick said, remembering the thin old fellow with the rotting teeth, his head shaved bald. "A godly man—one of the best there has ever been."

It had been a scorcher of a day, and Gallen was tracking a murderer and had lost the boy's trail somewhere along the road. Dan'l O'Leary had managed to leap off the margin of the highway into some brush. Gallen could not discover his trail. Yet Gallen also knew the general area where the boy had vanished, and he'd asked Orick to sniff the killer out.

Now, Friar Bannon had known the killer. Dan'l O'Leary was only fifteen, but he was a big kid, and dumb. The kind who figured it was easier to make it as a highwayman than as a farmer. So one summer's night he waylaid a wealthy traveler, brandishing a cudgel. When the fellow was slow to get his purse open, Dan'l hit him in the head, hoping to subdue him, but in his excitement he hit the fellow too hard, knocking his brains all over the dirt road.

While Dan'l stood over the corpse, looking for coins hidden in the man's boots, his own mother rounded the bend in the road and discovered her son was a murderer.

In her shame, she ran into town and told everyone what had happened. Dan'l took off into the woods, where he foraged off the land and sometimes visited Friar Bannon, telling how he was torn by the desire to return home, wanting to repent, knowing he'd hang if he did, suffering from the pain of a damned soul.

So it was that Orick came upon Gallen, hunting for the killer, and Gallen asked Orick to sniff the boy out.

"What will you do to him if you catch him?" Orick had asked, for Orick was a young bear, and having heard of the boy's grief from Friar Bannon, he was not sure if it would be appropriate to help apprehend the youngster. Friar Bannon felt convinced that the boy would repent, and he hoped that the law would be lenient with the child—perhaps give him a good beating rather than a hanging. The murder was a youthful mistake, after all, not the act of a hardened criminal.

Yet the boy compounded his crimes by not turning himself in. Friar Bannon had said that given one winter in the wild, this boy *would* become a hardened highwayman—or the weather would break him, and he'd come to his senses. Friar Bannon hoped for the latter.

"I don't know what I'll do with this one," Gallen had answered Orick thoughtfully, sitting down on the roadside. "It's been bothering me. Gut him, maybe. I don't want to put the kid through a hanging. The wait and embarrassment. His poor mother is beside herself already. He isn't a mean lad. So I think I'll kill him swiftly. Looks like that would be about best for everyone."

"Not for Dan'l," Friar Bannon had said quickly.

"Maybe not," Gallen had agreed. "But I can't just let him go free."

"No, the best thing for the boy would be to make his peace with God and man," Friar Bannon had said. "If only he would run far away and start his life over, but I think the lad is sort of like a dumb calf that hasn't realized it's time to wean from his mother. He still wants to go home, and there's no telling him otherwise."

Gallen had looked the friar in the eye, just held his gaze for a moment.

"I helped you hunt Dan'l, for three days," Orick said, wondering if his message would get though, "and when you caught him, what did you do? You gave him some money from your own purse, pointed him toward the border, and kicked him in the pants as you sent him on his way."

Gallen's face took on a closed look. "It was the best thing I could do, it seemed. Like Friar Bannon, I hoped he would change."

"A devil's bargain," Orick intoned. "A year later, Dan'l became a highwayman, and we had to track him down all over again, and that time you gutted the lad."

"I thought he'd go straight," Gallen whispered. "But he murdered three more people. Do you think I did wrong letting him go the first time?"

"No, you idiot. Don't you see it? You did *exactly* right." Orick replied. "You exercised compassion. You hoped for the best. It wasn't our fault the lad didn't live up to our expectations. It was his fault. He deserved what you gave him—both the forgiveness *and* the punishment."

"So what is your point?"

Orick grunted and frowned as he considered. "My point is this: when I first helped you catch that boy, I almost didn't do it. I only came with you that day because you were trying to do what was best for everyone. Sometimes, we have to make a choice, and hope that it's best for everyone, and offer no blame to ourselves or others if we're wrong."

"That's what I've been trying to do," Gallen said.

"No. Ever since Dan'l let you down, you've found it harder and harder to exercise common sense. Jesus said that 'In the last days, because wickedness shall abound, the love of many will wax cold.' Well, Gallen, your heart has been waxing colder and colder ever since I met you. You're a hard man now, hot for vengeance, hot to kill the Dronon. You're willing to go die under a tide of your enemies, while your sweet, sensible wife just wants to get away from this mess."

"Sensible? We have a duty," Gallen said. "She isn't thinking of other people, her obligation to humanity. She's afraid for herself."

Orick countered, "She has a duty to her child, too. And she has more brains in her right ear than you have in your whole head! Gallen, I know you have faith in yourself, but that first win against the Dronon was a fluke. The Dronon know how you beat them, and Kintiniklintit won't make that same mistake again. Maggie's right to ask you to run. If you had any sense, you wouldn't be talking like this!"

"But I've been exercising," Gallen said. "I'm stronger now. I think I've got a kick that will pierce a Dronon's exoskeleton. I could win this fight!"

"Och, maybe," Orick said, unwilling to let him pursue this line of thought, "but in the long run, your tenacity will only plant you in an early grave!"

"Maybe that is exactly what he wants," Tallea said. The little she-bear had just pulled another vine over to the fire and hunkered on the ground, her paws down under her nose.

"What?" Orick asked the she-bear, his voice betraying his surprise at the remark.

"Maybe he wants to die," Tallea said. "It's what I'd do. Just as the Lords of Tremonthin transferred my memories, my dreams, into this body, they can design a new body for Gallen, one with the speed and strength of a Tekkar, the size of a Rodim. That's what he wants. What does he care if the Dronon slay him, so long as the Lords of Tremonthin bring him back stronger."

"I wish it were so simple." Gallen sighed. "Download my memories into a more fearsome body. If I could do it, I would slough off this flesh in a heart-beat."

"Then why don't you?" Orick asked.

Gallen looked to Tallea. "I think Tallea can tell you part of the answer. . . ."

Tallea scratched her snout with a paw and said, "A new body is clumsy. Arms and legs are shorter or longer than you remember. Muscles don't work as you think." Orick had noticed that Tallea was rather bumbling, even for an adolescent she-bear. He'd hoped she would grow out of it, but he hadn't dared say anything. Tallea, after having been a human in her last life, had enough difficulty trying to acclimatize herself to being a bear without worrying about the fact that she was a hopelessly clumsy bear.

"Exactly," Gallen said. "When you switch bodies, every muscle and bone is different in size and shape. It takes years for your brain to acclimate to those changes. I don't have years. If I got myself downloaded into a clone tomorrow, I'd just get killed.

"But even if I could get a new body, I doubt that if I made such a major change, the Dronon would allow me to fight. Veriasse considered rebuilding himself, but my mantle tells me he wisely chose against it. The Dronon might see my genetic enhancements as weapons, unlawful for use in unarmed combat."

"But that hasn't stopped Kintiniklintit from fighting in the arena," Orick countered.

"Kintiniklintit isn't human," Gallen said. "You know how reluctant the Dronon were to let me fight in the first place. The same rules don't apply to us that apply to them."

Orick lay on the sandy ground and put his chin on his paws. He had never even imagined downloading Gallen into another body, yet everyone else around him had given the plan considerable deliberation.

"So there's nothing you can do to better your odds," Orick grumbled in such a tone that he let Gallen recognize that he, too, could see the futility of this plan.

"No," Gallen said. "No stratagem I can come up with. Their exoskeletons are too thick. They fly too quickly. But, Orick, Orick, before you argue too strongly against fighting back, consider this: right now, I have defeated only the Lords of the Sixth Swarm. Six other lords want to fight me, but you also must recognize that they almost never challenge one another. Have you asked yourself why?"

"It's not worth the trouble," Orick said. "You don't fight someone that tough if you don't have to."

"Precisely," Gallen said. "I beat the Lords of the Sixth Swarm, but I didn't do the job convincingly. The other Dronon Lords see my victory as a fluke, a performance that is not likely to be repeated. But what if I did win again? What if I killed Kintiniklintit, and I did it convincingly?"

"So you think that if you kill him, the rest of the Dronon Lords will shy away from fighting you in the future?"

"Exactly," Gallen said. "The Dronon have chosen this form of succession by nature. It seems right to them to fight for control. Their inherited behaviors, their sense of what is right, won't allow them to explore any other method of succession. But the Dronon aren't stupid. The young Golden Queens don't simply rush into battle when they attain their mature colors. They watch the Lords of the Swarm and consider and plot, often for decades. So long as the Lords of the Swarm appear strong, younger goldens don't attack. According to my mantle, some Golden Queens live their entire lives without seeking to take control of the hive."

"So you hope that if you can beat Kintiniklintit, the Dronon might leave you alone?" Orick said, warily.

"I hope so," Gallen said. "I *have* to believe there is something we can do. I have to believe that through strength and speed, and wit, and skill, and sheer force of will I can transcend this problem. The Dronon are beatable. I've proven that. But even Maggie doesn't really believe I can whip them a second time. I know I can. I can, and I will. But I can't discuss this with Maggie now. She's not ready to fight. She's too frightened—she can't even sleep because of the nightmares." He looked off toward the ship, and there was worry in Gallen's eye. Maggie was falling apart.

"Transcend the Dronon then—" Orick said, "transcend your enemies. But don't play their game. Don't think that just because you learn to toss them two throws out of three, that you've won the war. They'll come back and kill you for it. Even if you could beat Kintiniklintit, even if you killed every one of them, you'd lose your decency. Forget about them. You've fought them all you can, Gallen. Let someone else take up the sword. Forgive the Dronon and everyone like them."

"Orick," Gallen said, shaking his head, "what does that accomplish? If we ignore evil, it will simply thump us on the head until we pay attention to it."

Orick said, "I have a question for you: did David slay Goliath, or did God?"

Gallen considered a long moment. "Are you saying that if I ignore the Dronon, God will fight them? Even you don't believe that!"

"Is anything too hard for the Lord?" Orick whispered, and he knew in that moment, though for his whole life he had fought the doubts, he did believe it.

Gallen drew a surprised breath and stepped back. "Orick, I think maybe you should become a priest after all."

Orick wasn't sure what Gallen meant by that. Orick had considered leaving Gallen to study for the priesthood many times. Perhaps, Orick thought, this was a fight—the first fight they'd had—and Gallen was telling Orick that the time *had* come for Orick to leave. But no, Gallen spoke with a tone of both surprise and reverence. In the past, he'd always seemed *amused* by Orick's interest in the priesthood. Now Gallen seemed astonished by it, and he took it seriously. Gallen was simply acknowledging a side of Orick that he'd never really appreciated. Orick said softly, "I would that all men were priests, devoting themselves to God."

Gallen studied Orick, perplexed. "I . . . I'll consider what you've said."

Gallen reached down absently and ruffled Tallea's fur, patting her snout. He was lost in thought as he stalked off back into the ship, his black robes flowing out behind him, his head bent. The doors to the ship closed off quickly as he entered, swallowing him.

Tallea watched him leave, then grumbled, "I wish he wouldn't do that!"

"Do what?" Orick asked.

"Pat my nose like I was some damned hunting hound!"

Orick stared at her, his mouth opened in surprise. He always liked it when humans patted his snout or scratched behind his ear.

"I was a grown woman, swinging a sword in battle, before he ever got out of diapers!" Tallea said, then she growled in disgust, a throaty rumble.

"Gallen's a good lad. It's not disrespect he's showing you," Orick apologized.

Tallea shook her dark head, wagging it broadly from side to side, and she was so angry that tears formed in her eyes. She turned and began heading into the ship.

"Really," Orick said, "he's just being affectionate!"

"Well maybe I don't want *his* affection!" Tallea said, turning on him so fast that Orick thought she'd bite him.

"Halloo there," Orick said. "You don't have to act like you've got a tick on your butt. What's eating you?"

"What's eating me?" Tallea asked. "Nothing—Everything!"

"Everything? Really? Everything?" Orick said. It was true that they didn't have a home, that the Dronon were chasing them, that they were camped for the night on an alien world filled with monsters. But far from everything was wrong. At least they were alive.

"You—this is not what I had planned . . ." Tallea said in exasperation. "I didn't come here to be patted like a dog, and have people making fun of my clumsiness!"

She spun and bolted for the ship; the door hardly had time to whisk open before she reached it. Orick hurried after her, unsure why she'd broken into tears.

Tallea ran into her stateroom, jumped up on the bed. The door to her room began to slide closed in front of Orick's nose. Tallea shouted, "Lock!" but Orick leapt through before the door shut. The lock snicked into place behind him.

Tallea made whining noises, little barks, as bears will when they cry, and she turned her back.

"Well now," Orick said, climbing up on the bed, nuzzling her ear with his snout. He licked it just a bit. "Sure, it must be hard to go from being human to being a bear, but you always struck me as a woman who was mostly gristle and sinew. All good things have their price. At least you're not one of those funny-looking human varmints without any hair anymore. . . ." He hoped she'd laugh, but Tallea just sniffled.

Orick let the silence stretch uncomfortably, until at last Tallea said, "Did I make a mistake, Orick?"

"A mistake? How could it be wrong for a human to finally get a pelt like the rest of the mammals?"

Tallea snickered, turned her brown eyes to him. There were tears in them. "Did I misunderstand something, Orick? I thought you loved me."

"Well . . . I do!" Orick protested. "How could I not love you?"

"I thought you would love me—in the same way a man loves his wife." The sentence was clipped, the words uninflected, yet Orick knew there was a depth of emotion hidden beneath those words. He licked her ears gently with his broad tongue.

"Is it a formal proposal of marriage you're wanting?" Orick asked. He knew she did. It wasn't decent to keep a woman waiting—especially when it was obvious she loved him, that she'd chosen to live as a bear solely so they could be together. It was a strange alliance they had formed on Tremonthin— the Caldurian warrior and the bear, fighting in the caverns beneath the Hollow Hills. By nature Caldurians bonded to those they protected, and that bonding was arguably a form of love. But Orick had never imagined she would bond to him, nor that after she gave her life in his service, she would ask the Lords of Tremonthin to place her memories into the flesh of a bear. Such a sacrifice.

Orick had always wished to find a she-bear who would love him as truly as he could love her—a she-bear whose affections would remain steady even after she was no longer in heat. Tallea had asked the Lords of Tremonthin to tailor her body so she could fulfill Orick's dream.

The thing is, that while Orick had always dreamed of love, he didn't quite know how to manage the little things—like how to talk about all the important things he and Tallea needed to discuss.

Tallea sighed. "I don't need a marriage proposal. By becoming a bear, I think I've already made the proposal myself. I just need to know if you accept me."

Orick's heart pounded. This was the moment he'd feared. He didn't quite know how to tell her that he'd long considered a career in the priesthood, that her show of devotion was both totally unexpected and somewhat troubling. "I care for you . . ." he tried to ease into the topic.

"If you love me, then why don't you make love to me?" Tallea said. "I've been a bear for months!"

Orick gaped in surprise, then sniffed the air. "You . . . are you in heat?" he gawked, wondering if his nose was plugged.

"No!" Tallea said, perhaps even more shocked than Orick. "Is *that* what you've been waiting for?"

"You mean—you would do it even when you're not in heat?" Orick shouted. He'd never heard such an outrageous proposal, never even considered the possibility. Sure, humans did it that way, but they were an aberration in the animal kingdom. Right-thinking bears would never—

"Yes," Tallea said, turning suddenly to face him full. "Yes, please, yes! Take me now!" she growled with such desire in that throaty rumbling that Orick could hardly imagine it.

"But . . . but I've taken a vow of chastity!" Orick said, blurting the first objection that came to mind. It was true. Though he'd never made the vow to proper priesthood authorities, he had indeed made that vow to God in his heart.

Tallea cried, "Why would you do a stupid thing like that?"

"I promised myself to God's service," Orick said. "Never thinking—I mean it was before I met you."

Orick looked at the poor she-bear. If he kept to this course, it would prove a tragedy for Tallea of epic consequences. He didn't want to hurt her, but for now, he was still unresolved as to his course of action. He wanted to serve God, but to be truthful, in the past he had found that when a she-bear was in heat, the temptation had been more than he could easily endure. He wasn't good at maintaining his vow of chastity, but with each successive failure, he became more determined to keep to it.

"So you can't serve God and me?" Tallea asked.

"No man can serve two masters," Orick said, and then suddenly realized that she would not understand the allusion. Tallea was a heathen who'd never heard of Christ or his gospel. "The Son of God said that."

Tallea studied him. "He was right. Every Caldurian warrior knows that he or she can only be bound to one master." Tallea considered his words. "So you've decided? You will not bind yourself to me?"

Orick had seldom found himself wedged into so tight a crevice. If he told her that he was undecided, that during every passing hour of the past few months that question had been foremost in his mind, yet he was still vacillating, then he might find himself voicing words that would only give her unrealistic hopes. At the same time, it would be equally unfair to the both of them if he told her that he had decided against her. For it was untrue. "Give me some time. I love you as a friend already, a true friend. But you chose me without warning. This all came so suddenly."

"I see." The warmth had all gone from her voice. After a long moment, she whispered, "Orick, as far as bears go, am I attractive?"

Orick looked into her eyes, which sparkled under the ship's lights. Her fur was dark and glossy, her nails long and black. She was, in fact, one of the most beautiful she-bears he'd ever met, and once she went into heat, Orick imagined that every bear on Tihrglas would fight for the chance to be her mate. What she did not know was that as a juvenile, those looks did not matter. It was scent that excited Orick, not her lusty appearance.

"Indeed, you are fair, my love, more beautiful than the mountains of Tirzah."

"Good," Tallea said, then she yawned and stretched, lowering her head, arching her back so that her tail raised seductively in the air. Orick doubted that she had ever seen a female take the mating position, but she did it now quite naturally, then came and licked Orick once on the mouth. "Very good," she whispered, "and good night to you." Though it was not yet dark here on Ruin, Orick and the others were still running on ship time, and he indeed felt weary. Apparently Tallea, like Maggie, had decided to keep to the ship's schedule.

She sent him from her room. Orick padded back outside, somewhat glad for the fresh air, where he lay on the ground thinking of that last inviting look she'd given him. For a moment, when speaking to Gallen, he'd felt as if he were truly a priest, speaking under the power of inspiration. Now he felt miserable, and he lay wondering how he would ever be able to spurn such a lovely creature once she went into estrus.

It was with these thoughts in mind that Orick was disturbed by the sound of flapping wings. He looked up to see the oddest creature soaring over the desert—a winged man, who soon landed at Orick's feet, with a fascinating invitation for dinner.

T h r e e

L ord Felph found himself muttering under his breath as he made his way down a long stone staircase to a tiny room on the lower levels of his palace.

Felph's heavy robes dragged behind him on the staircase as he walked, and the cool air here in the tunnels chilled the bald spot on his head and his long, pale fingers. The dark sun shone thin and red through the oval, open windows along the staircase, windows that had long ago been carved by Qualeewoohs while digging their cloo holes.

Indeed, the lower lip of each window was worn from the feet of Qualeewoohs who had nested here over the millennia, wearing the oval portals into irregular shapes. Felph had had his droids clear away all the old nesting sites centuries ago, convert the nesting cells into passageways and chambers for his citadel. Most of the palace now showed no sign that Qualeewoohs had ever lived in this mountain. Only here, in the very western wing, did the anachronistic sites still exist.

Felph hated the old reminders. Perhaps that is why his daughter chose to live down here.

Once, Felph stopped to rest, breathing raggedly from exertion, and stared out one crumbled window to the sheer cliffs of the redrock mountains stretching out around him. The sky above held no clouds, yet the distant dark sun gave only muted light. In the valleys far below, at the base of the slopes, peculiar oily gray trees grew in an impenetrable tangle, and, as Felph watched, a flock of a dozen black-winged *skogs* leapt from the brush and began winging their way with bulletlike speed toward one of the garden ponds on the palace grounds.

Felph finished resting, but his heart still raced as he reached the bottom of the stairs, then knocked timidly at a wooden door which swung halfway open at his touch.

The weaver woman was inside, as usual, sitting before her great loom in a rocking chair that tilted away from the window. The frame of the loom was massive, spanning floor to ceiling along the far wall. The left wall was covered with bobbins of narrow yarn in a thousand colors of the rainbow, each in its place, each in a hue so subtly different that Felph could hardly distinguish one bobbin's shade from its neighbor's. The beveled glass from the window, which was cut in a starburst pattern, cast fractured rays of red light over the room, limning the weaver's silver hair, illuminating her work. She wore her hair in small braids that cascaded casually down her back. A twisted net of gold chains, like a crown, gleamed dully on her brow, and she wore a simple but elegant shift of purest white. Over her bosom was a small vest of twisted wheat-colored fiber, a pretty thing woven by her own strong fingers.

Her back was turned to him, and she sat at her loom working the treadle with eyes closed, as always, weaving colorful scenes into a great tapestry. Her hands moved reverently through the wool as she worked a reed, beating the filling yarns into place to create her tapestry, yet the tapestry lay sprawled upon the floor near her feet, as if discarded. It was the making of the thing, not the completed product, that the woman enjoyed, for she was weaving images of things that would shortly come to pass, and the tapestry held the only record she kept of her prophecies.

Felph's mouth felt dry; his hands trembled as he held the door to keep it from swinging all the way inward, and he did not want to look at the tapestry, did not want to be here speaking to the weaver now, but the sunlight shone upon the scarlet scene she was creating, and woven onto a colorful background patina of stones was an image of Felph himself, lying in a puddle of his own gore, his throat slashed, while over him stood his glorious son Zeus—a young man of stocky build and gray, brooding eyes—exultant as he held a bloodied knife up toward the dark sun.

Arachne tensed, listening to Felph without glancing. "What is it, Lord Felph?" she asked. He did not answer. Instead, Felph stared at the scene of his own murder and wondered at the weaver's prophetic abilities. If you are as wise as I think you are, then you already will know why I have come, he told himself.

"You test me?" Arachne asked when he didn't reply. "All right, then." She took a deep breath, stopped as if listening to the air. . . . "There has been a change in the population," she guessed, or seemed to guess, but she said the last word with conviction. Could someone have told her? Was she playing with him? Not likely, though his children enjoyed such mind games. Still, he could not fathom how she'd guessed. "Not a birth—Shira is not due yet for two weeks. A death?" she hazarded. Felph knew she wasn't prophetic, that she was taking subtle clues from him, from the way he breathed, the intonation of his words, the position of his body relative to hers. She had sensitive hearing, could probably measure the beats of his heart. He wanted to give her no clues, so he tried to control his breathing perfectly, to maintain a steady rhythm, say nothing. "No . . . not a death, then." She turned to him suddenly; a smile warmed her face. She was beautiful, young in spite of her silver hair, and she had penetrating black eyes that stared through him. She knew he did not like gazing into her eyes—they were too wise, too probing—and he glanced away. "Visitors!" she said with delight. "We have visitors to our world. Tell me, Felph, who are they?"

"They're landing now, out near Devil's Bunghole. Four people, according to the ship's logs, milady," Felph said, smiling broadly in spite of his nervousness. Though he was her lord and her creator, Felph stood in awe of Arachne. The weaver woman had been made for this purpose, to comprehend mankind better than they comprehended themselves, to sift through subtle clues to the motivations and desires of others, then predict what they would do. Yet even as he'd designed her mind, trained and nurtured his creation, Felph had never imagined that Arachne would become what she had become. Felph felt immensely gratified with his creation. At the same time, he was humbled by her, frightened of her abilities. "Two-two of them are humans, a young man and a pregnant woman. The other two are genetically enhanced bears."

"What class of starship do they command?" she asked.

"A TechKing Fleet Courier."

"A fast ship. Expensive . . ." the weaver mumbled. "They must be rich. But why would they come to Ruin? You say they're landing at Devil's Bunghole?"

She thought a moment. If they were tourists, they'd land at the salt pillars of Kloowee, or at the twelve towers of Sandomoon Breeze, or perhaps at the opal plains. If they were here to study Qualeewooh ruins, they'd have contacted Felph before landing. He was the foremost authority on such ruins.

Felph wondered what the weaver might be thinking. He enjoyed watching Arachne solve puzzles. "They are fugitives," she said with finality, turning back to her loom.

"I don't know. They could be so many things—explorers, entrepreneurs, settlers," Felph said. "Why do you imagine them fugitives?"

She did not bother to reply. She absently gazed at the tapestry taking shape on her loom. "There is something you're not telling me?" she accused.

Had she heard an unusual silence after his last question, an expectant undertone?

"There is one thing," Felph admitted. "According to his ship's log, the man is a Lord Protector, and his wife is a Lord Technologist. I'm thinking of hiring them. The Lord Protector could teach Herm and Zeus a few things—tactics and self-defense—"

"—And you hope he can find the Waters for you . . ."

"Well, yes," Felph said. "I'd thought of that."

"And little else," Arachne said. "Certainly you've considered little else." The damning tone of her voice said that she was already considering ramifications that were far beyond Felph's ability to comprehend.

"I—I thought the woman might help in my creations," Felph said, to prove that he'd indeed been considering the possibilities. "Hephaestus is coming along fine."

"It's Aphrodite you want to make next. Why don't you just finish her?" It was not really a question. The weaver's tone suggested dismissal. Felph stood, stroking his short gray beard. Arachne was lost in her own thoughts, but mumbled, "So, a Lord Protector. . . . We have powerful refugees then. Running from the Dronon."

"I doubt it. The Dronon have been vanquished—"

"Temporarily!" Arachne sighed, as if weary of Felph's stupidity. I must seem simpleminded to her, Felph thought for the thousandth time. She turned at her work. "Have you considered the danger in bringing them here?"

"Danger?" Felph asked. "What danger? They won't harm us."

"I'm not afraid of what they'd do to us. It's what we'll do to *them*."

Arachne turned to Felph, head cocked toward the sunlight, as if straining to hear distant music from outside the window. Suddenly she grunted in surprise at a thought that occurred to her. "I want to meet them, immediately," she said, ordering him to fetch the off-worlders.

"Well, uh, yes. Of course," Felph said. "I'll plan a dinner party, tonight. I'll invite the whole planet."

The whole planet wasn't many. A few odd hermits, a couple of xenobiologists, five dozen ill-bred refugees who performed various odd jobs for Felph.

"Perfect." The weaver woman took a small pick from the workbench beside her chair and began plucking yarn from her tapestry, destroying the image of Felph's murder. She muttered under her breath, "New people on the planet. This changes the weave, this changes everything. . . ."

It had annoyed Felph that Arachne prophesied his demise. If he were to be murdered, it would be a nuisance—having his memories downloaded into a new body, making all those minor adjustments that come with your unanticipated death.

But somehow it annoyed him that the murder was off. "Wait," Felph shook a finger at her. "Are you telling me that a dinner party is all it will take to win this reprieve? You think Zeus won't kill me, if I arrange a *party?*"

"At least for now," she said. "Zeus is easily distracted. A young woman to ogle, especially a pregnant one, will intrigue him. I assume she is pretty— a Lord Protector would not likely marry an ugly woman. Go tell Zeus to help prepare for the party, and it will drive all thoughts of murder from his mind— for two or three days, at least."

Felph chuckled softly, shaking his head. "So, Zeus plots against me, and *you* would do nothing to stop him?"

"Zeus takes no counsel from me—or anyone else," Arachne said. "He's stubborn."

Felph considered. His son, Zeus, was a brilliant young man, prone to ruthlessness. The young man wore a Guide that was supposed to control him, keep him from acting on his violent impulses. But Zeus had managed to remove the Guide three years past, and might do so once again. On that occasion, Zeus *had* tried to murder Felph. He'd first crept into the revivification chamber and tried to erase all records of Felph's genetic mapping, along with certain other security programs. Only a minor error had kept Zeus's plot from reaching fruition.

Felph nodded slightly to Arachne, thinking, Well, if my son plots against me, perhaps I *need* a Lord Protector at my side.

M aggie was not impressed by Felph's palace, nor was she impressed by the local mode of travel. The florafeem she, Gallen, and the bears rode thundered over a redrock ridge the color of flame; the roaring clack of the thousands of fanlike wings on the florafeem's underbelly had dulled her hearing. The beast handler, who rode beside her, was a man named Dooring. He spoke loudly.

Dooring had explained to her that the florafeems were native to Ruin, strange creatures that sucked nectar from the dew trees out in the tangles. Big animals. In shape they resembled some strange flower, with four "wings" shaped like petals, but the wings did not flap. Instead, thousands of bony fanlike appendages under the creature's rigid surface fluttered at a tremendous speed, creating enough upward force to keep a florafeem aloft. On top, the creature's skin seemed to be only a thick membrane over an upper frame of cartilaginous bone. That membrane was covered over by grasslike purple hairs, and small creatures lived on it.

The florafeem measured some fifty meters in diameter. This beast had a saffron-colored silk pavilion erected on its back.

Dozens of blue-scaled birds swooped and dived around the florafeem, feeding off insects that lived on its back, giving high, croaking calls. In the pavilion behind her, Maggie was vaguely aware of Gallen, resting his hand on her back, sometimes massaging her weary muscles.

The bears, Orick and Tallea, both lay on their paws, staring ahead, tired.

The journey to Felph's palace had taken nearly three hours, and Maggie's back felt stiff from sitting. Though she was past the point in her pregnancy where she should have felt morning sickness, she'd been fighting nausea for the past two hours. A dozen times she wished that she and Gallen had refused to travel by florafeem. The idea had seemed quaint upon invitation, yet she hadn't known how unbearable the journey might be. Still it was not the discomfort of the journey that unsettled her on the final approach. It was Felph's palace.

As she topped the cliff, she saw it shining among the fields ahead like something from a fairy tale, yet utterly unlike anything so . . . insignificant. Felph's palace was enormous—all carved from rose-colored sandstone on three sides of a mountain. The palace gleamed like a moon, for all along the base of it, thousands of brilliant lights shone, illuminating even the dusty skies above. The walls of the palace rose perhaps a thousand meters high, and it was impossible to imagine how thick they might be. The walls weren't perpendicular, for stone piled so high could not have supported the structure; instead the walls climbed at a steep slope, and every fifty meters would be a small road or trail carved along the exterior of the castle.

An ornate fence made of stone pillars bordered each road. On the walls above each road, gargoyles and angels were carved in bas-relief, engaging in scenes hellish and heavenly. Water cascaded over the walls in dozens of places—from a pot held by a gaggle of demons, from a cloud that served as a stool for a thoughtful angel. The water was captured and reused hundreds of times to utterly astonishing effect, for as the lights shone on the palace, the falling waters cloaked the stone in shimmering wonder.

The beast handler next to her, Dooring, had been talking almost nonstop until a few moments earlier. She almost thought of him as some artificial intelligence, its processors broken, verbally spewing out everything it knew. Maggie realized he had quit speaking so she wouldn't be distracted by his voice on first sight of Felph's palace. Now he stood, gesticulating wildly at the pillars and verandas, the glorious towers and the glittering stained windows.

"Look at that! They've got the lights on for you—and even the waterfalls. What a treat! Have you ever seen anything like it? Look at that statue! *In*credible!"

"How many people live in the palace?" Maggie asked. She imagined that this palace could easily house a million souls.

"Six," Dooring shouted. "And a handful of us servants. Felph hardly ever sleeps in the same room twice! Oh, would you just look at that! And here comes Brightstar over the mountains behind it. Incredible!" He slapped his forehead, continuing his monologue.

Indeed, Ruin's small dark sun was setting, and its twin star, which the locals called Brightstar, was rising gloriously over the hills.

At the base of the mountain Maggie spotted a cloud of dust. Golden worker droids shone among the dust like beetles, scurrying about. Maggie counted hundreds of droids that must have been carving these rocks for centuries.

Dooring the beast handler kicked the creature with his heels, just above its huge central eye. The florafeem thundered down. A single vaulted opening at the base of the mountain provided an entrance hundreds of meters high and at least three hundred wide.

There, in the sky, flapping his wings, was Felph's handsome son Herm, who had come personally to Maggie's camp to invite them to dinner, giving vague hints of a possible offer of employment. He hadn't said what the job would consist of. Apparently to discuss such matters prematurely would flout local customs.

Herm flew just ahead of the florafeem, a brilliant glow globe in hand, and led them through the air.

Maggie felt . . . annoyed. All this ostentation. All this waste. On the two dozen worlds she'd visited, Maggie had never seen anything like it.

Felph was obviously vain, possibly mad. Dooring had told Maggie that Felph relied almost solely on droids for servants. Though Dooring worked for the old man, he hadn't personally seen Felph in a dozen years. Instead, Felph's passions in life seemed to be the study of history, and engineering his own genetically upgraded children.

If Herm, with his wings, was an example of Felph's handiwork, she wondered at his purposes. Herm, a painfully thin man, had hair of darkest brown that framed a handsome face, and his eyes were like twin pieces of palest green ice. But most curious about him was the enormous wings, sweeping up from his back, all feathered in beer brown with splotches of white. He wore a pair of clean blue tights, and had on a nice white tunic, stiff with embroidery about the neck, cuffs, and waist. Herm seemed bright, energetic, intelligent, and he affected a slightly superior smile. He seemed to be only a slightly altered human.

But from her work with the aberlains of Fale, Maggie knew better. He'd have to be incredibly strong to fly with such mass. His bones would have to be hollow, which meant that his immune system might be vastly different from a human's. She suspected that Felph would have simply resorted to a nanotech analog for that immune system, but she didn't know.

More troubling than Felph's engineering his own children was the fact that Lord Felph made Herm wear a Guide.

Maggie had worn one once, only for a few days; the memory horrified her. The artificial intelligence in the Guide linked directly to the brain, so that when Maggie wore one, she could not control her own muscles. The Guide even controlled her desires, at times, when her master wanted.

Maggie could imagine nothing a father could do that would be more cruel than to enslave his children in their own bodies.

Maggie suspected she would detest Felph. The vanity of such a man.

Yet as they thundered through the first set of walls, then rose up to one of perhaps a hundred gorgeous verandas where the spraying fountains shone, Maggie recognized one important fact: Lord Felph had money, enough money to ensure that she got the best medical help possible when she delivered her child.

So she had to wonder. Could she endure working for a man she would hate?

The florafeem thundered to the ground in a broad veranda, settling next to four other florafeems. Apparently some other guests had already arrived.

Maggie dismounted shakily, walking to the edge of the creature's broad, gravelly back, then glancing down. It was a good three-foot drop, and in her tender condition she didn't want to jump. She looked over her shoulder, saw half a dozen other florafeems floating over the valley. They looked like giant flowers blown on the wind, the tall pavilions gleaming like crimson and golden stamens at their centers.

Herm himself walked up and took Maggie's hand, helped her from the beast.

Herm spoke a gracious welcome and bid the guests enter, waving under the wide stone arches toward a glittering chamber. Enormous tables held piles of food among dozens of candelabras, and several other guests had begun snacking near those tables.

Herm guided Maggie, Gallen, Orick, and Tallea to the center of the great hall, nodding as he walked toward various small knots of people. A ragged foursome of men appeared, from their dirty and tattered tan outfits and numerous weapons, to be soldiers fresh from the tangle. The group looked toward Maggie, and she inwardly cringed. Something about their eyes, their unblinking eyes, unsettled her.

"Poachers," Herm whispered.

"What do they poach?" Maggie asked.

"Qualeewoohs," Herm said. Maggie thought it repugnant that anyone would resort to eating a sentient alien species. As if reading her thoughts, Herm whispered. "They kill them for their spirit masks—and for any artifacts they might be carrying."

He nodded toward a knot of men and women talking at another table, people who looked almost as dirty as the poachers. "Xenobiologists and paleontologists."

Most of the rest of the people milling about—perhaps a dozen or two—all wore the same black tights and golden tunics that Dooring wore. Maggie recognized it as something of a servant's uniform.

"How many people on planet?" Gallen asked.

"Maybe a hundred," Herm answered. "At least it was close to that at last count, though doubtless some have died. Most are like those you see. Lord Felph employs a few workers, and we have some scientists and treasure hunters. Some are just recluses and madmen."

Maggie hadn't imagined that so few people would live on a whole planet. True, they were in the Carina Galaxy now, having fled the Milky Way, and true, Ruin was on the far frontiers even of the Carina Galaxy. But a hundred people?

Outside, the other florafeems began to land, and people off-loaded. Most were dirty hunters and field scientists. Maggie took a quick guess, and imagined that eighty or ninety people must have already arrived.

A small gaggle of locals crowded around to meet Gallen's group. The four were, apparently, the first strangers to visit Ruin in several years. Their appearance caused a stir.

Maggie took a place to one side of the great hall, waiting for locals to come by so Herm could make introductions. Here, in this stately palace, the crowds looked out of place. They were a sweaty, begrimed lot. No charitable sentiment on Maggie's part could disguise the fact that most of these folks didn't need introductions to Maggie so much as they needed introductions to a bar of soap.

Tentatively, the people of Ruin introduced themselves. From the far side of the room Herm spotted a fellow and waited for him to approach. "I fear," Herm whispered, "that you're about to discover why my father doesn't appreciate visitors."

No sooner had he whispered these words than a smelly man with unblinking eyes came and took her hand, bowed low, and kissed it. "Rame Onowa," he said in a high voice, "at your service, ma'am."

He glanced up to Herm, waiting for the winged man to make a more formal introduction. "Rame is an itinerant cave dweller-cum-philosopher," Herm said, "who lives in the ruins near the Yesterday Hills."

Rame was suitably attired in a hooded robe of moldy blue hair. His narrow hatchet face was covered with a beard and grime. His teeth were more orange than yellow. "So pleased to meet you," Rame said, now pumping her hand vigorously. "So pleased to meet such a beautiful, beautiful woman. You'd . . . you'd certainly make a fine decoration for any man's cave Miss, uh Miss . . ."

"Maggie O'Day," Maggie answered, trying to pull her hand away.

"Ah! A beautiful name," Rame said, then glanced toward Gallen and the bears. "So tell me, Maggie, what brings you to Ruin?"

Rame stood close and peered into her eyes, unblinking, as if trying to peer beneath any layers of deceit, and Maggie tried to pull her hand back. Suddenly, a memory but two weeks old flashed through her mind, terrifying her.

Never before had Maggie heard a war band of Vanquishers in flight: now she understood why men called these aliens *Dronon.*

The falling sun of Avendon lay on the ragged gray hills, creating a cold silver blade of light on the horizon. In that blade of light, Vanquishers flew in such vast numbers they looked like a row of thunderheads stretching over the hills, their black carapaces glinting in the dying sun. Their flashing amber wings limned the clouds with a sickly yellow hue; even kilometers away, the beating of their wings created a deep moaning that was not quite song, not quite a sound of pain. Almost mechanical.

Machines. They were as mindless and unyielding as machines.

The Lords of the Seventh Swarm. Maggie took one last glance at the Dronon over her shoulder. The cloud of warriors sped forward. So close. So close. Out over the prairie, wind stirred clouds of pollen from the purple sage.

Maggie ducked into a gully, gasping, the scent of sage and dust thick in her throat. She put a hand on her swollen belly, holding the son who waited to be born. Behind her, Gallen stopped. He raised a hand to shade his eyes, half clutched it into a fist, shielding his eyes, then just held it for several seconds, so it became a gesture of denial, as if with one hand he could hope to hold the swarm at bay.

Sweat streamed down Maggie's face. Her heart pounded. Her mind was numb from too many sleepless nights, from hours of running. Maggie couldn't imagine the Vanquishers being more than ten kilometers out, flying fast. Maybe closer.

After months of nightmares in which the Dronon caught her in darkness, then tore off her arms, it looked as if Maggie's worst fears would come to pass. She fought her panic, but she was too battered to be tough anymore. She looked frantically for a place to hide.

"Hurry, my love," Gallen urged, trying to steer her downhill. Maggie stumbled with weariness. "The gate must be here. The map says we're right on top of it." He clutched a map in one hand.

In the shadows of a creosote bush, a sparrow peeped querulously.

A whining sound approached overhead, the hum of a Dronon antigravity drive. Maggie glanced up. A bullet-shaped vessel hurtled over the rise, its fore-end cluttered with sensor arrays. It was a Dronon Seeker, a machine that hunted by scent.

A Vanquisher straddled the Seeker, hugging the vessel. The Dronon's wings were folded back, its head low against the frame of the Seeker.

It was the demon that haunted Maggie's dreams, hurtling toward them in the darkness like the angel of death. Its huge front arms, its battle arms with their serrated edges, were poised above its head, ready to chop down. The Vanquisher shouted in its own language. Maggie could not understand it, but dozens of mouthfingers beneath its jaws thumped loudly over the thin membrane of its voicedrum; the banging of its voice echoed over the gully, a sound of warning. Maggie looked for her reflection in its faceted eyes. Its translucent wings buzzed in a blur.

Beside her, there was a movement and a flash as Gallen spun and fired his pulp pistol. . . .

Maggie pulled her hand from Rame's, lurched back, blinking tears, trying to recall what question the madman had asked her. The fear of the Dronon weighed heavily on her, as heavily as it had two weeks earlier when they'd finally escaped Avedon only to find that the world gate they'd walked through led to a planet in the Carina Galaxy. The Lords of the Seventh Swarm had been so close on Maggie's trail, had come so close to blocking all their exits, that Maggie convinced Gallen to borrow a space cruiser from the Tharrin governors on Certes, fly off into the frontier worlds of the Carina Galaxy, where Maggie hoped to give birth to her child in safety. Out here, there were no world gates. Travel between worlds might be more difficult, but at least, Maggie hoped, the Dronon would not be able to track her so easily.

Indeed, they'd come to Ruin at the behest of the governors of Certes. The planet was not listed on any official star charts.

"I, uh, I uh, didn't mean to frighten you," Rame said as Maggie backed away. "I'm sorry."

"We're just here for a visit," Gallen interrupted the two, taking Maggie's hand, holding it, so that Rame would quit pawing at her. "We wanted to see the ruins."

But Rame looked at the fear on Maggie's face, and it seemed that he knew better.

"I'd take care of you," Rame said. "If you were my woman, I'd take care of you." He reached up with one grubby hand, as if to run his fingers over the smooth skin at the hollow of her throat. "Come see my cave," he whispered urgently. "You'll like my cave. It's peaceful there. Got a waterfall in the back of it. There, in the dark places, I could teach you the secrets of the Qualee-woohs." He stared at her, unblinking.

Gallen edged forward, almost blocking Rame with his own body. Maggie was not afraid of the man, not really.

There was a look of . . . peace in Rame's dark eyes. A look of total contentment and surrender. Almost, Maggie wanted to fall forward into those eyes, to feel what Rame felt. She caught herself and pulled away, wondering if Rame had some odd power, wondering if he'd purposely triggered those dark memories in her.

But she couldn't imagine such a thing. No. She'd been having anxiety attacks like this for the past several weeks. It was the stress that caused her agitated state. The constant fear and running.

Herm pushed himself between Rame and Maggie, disposed of the man by saying, "Rame, would you be so kind as to wait on the veranda? The High Confab is coming, and we need someone to offer the proper greetings when she lands."

"The High Confab? Here? Tonight?" Rame asked, his eyes growing impossibly more and more huge under his hooded cloak.

Herm said, "Yes, her attendants said she would come tonight, and she'll need a proper escort."

With a throaty cry of astonishment, Rame turned and trundled toward the veranda, to a set of stone perches where visiting Qualeewoohs might land.

"Who is this High Confab?" Orick the bear asked. For the past several minutes, he'd been sniffing around, watching the folks. No one had spoken to him, and he'd seemed more interested in food than conversation anyway.

"A figment of Rame's hallucinations," Herm told Orick, "a Qualeewooh who visits him in his dreams. Like many of the mad folks around here, Rame sleeps with a Qualeewooh's spirit mask over his face. If you aren't mad already, such things will drive you that way soon enough."

A moment later, a beautiful woman appeared through the crowd, as brilliant and extraordinary in her brown silks and diamonds as the other folk were plain.

She must be one of Felph's children, Maggie realized. No one else looked a thousandth so elegant. She appeared to be no more than twenty, yet her eyes spoke of wisdom beyond her years. Auburn hair cascaded down her back to her waist, and her eyes were clear light brown.

Maggie realized that Herm had disposed of the madman just in time for this woman to make her appearance. Herm introduced her, with a slight, mocking smile, "May I present Hera, Felph's fourth."

"Fourth?" Gallen and Maggie said, confused.

"Fourth created being," Herm said. "Informally, we call Lord Felph our 'father,' but I didn't want to confuse you. We're his creations, we have no mother or father in the common sense of the word."

Maggie looked up to the Guide that Hera wore in her hair, a simple circlet of silver. "He calls you his daughter, yet he makes you wear a Guide?" Maggie said, disapproval giving an edge to her voice.

"What loving father wouldn't want to control his child's thoughts?" Hera said. "It keeps me pure."

Maggie grimaced, "It keeps you bobbing like a marionette on your strings, you mean."

Hera fidgeted with the diamond rings on her fingers. "My father has our best interests at heart. He desires good for all people."

I'm sure, Maggie almost said. But showing such sentiments would accomplish nothing. Felph's children were his creations, mere things. Perhaps the girl was so naive, she believed the propaganda Felph fed her.

Or perhaps I'm wrong about him, Maggie wondered. Perhaps a loving but misguided father might seek to control his children this way.

"Maggie meant no disrespect," Gallen said. Hera studied his blue eyes, long golden hair, broad shoulders. Maggie had seen that spark of interest in other women.

At that moment, Hera's eyes went unfocused, and she immediately turned and marched toward a graceful staircase near the middle of the room.

"You must forgive us," Herm apologized. "Lord Felph has sent word that he desires our presence. He wishes us to make an appearance en masse. Apparently he did not know Hera had already come down to the party. Please, forgive us."

The winged man flushed in embarrassment, then flew swiftly up to the top of the staircase and waited for Hera to join him.

Then they disappeared into a door that opened seamlessly from the wall.

Somehow, Maggie was horrified by this. The poor girl, she thought. Lord Felph didn't bother to ask her to come to him, simply ordered her Guide to bring her, so that in the midst of a conversation, Hera abandoned her guests.

Yet either Hera was too dumb to know how Felph abused her, or she wasn't able to voice her own pain.

Lord Felph and his children did not come down immediately. For ten minutes Maggie waited.

Then suddenly music swelled all through the great hall—a stately march with many ringing bells. At the top of the grand staircase, white lights shone brilliantly, and the seamless hole opened once again.

Lord Felph came out. He was an old man, Maggie saw at once, stooped and graying. With rejuvenations and life extensions, the body he wore could easily have been a thousand years old. Maggie doubted it was his first. He wore no mantle of authority, made no show of ostentation in clothing. He wore only a simple frock of dark gray, much as if he were a monk back on Maggie's home world. He wore no jewelry. The only glimmer came from his dark blue eyes, which glanced out over the crowd knowingly.

Yet as his children came out behind, each one shone. Though he lacked ornamentation, he lavished it upon his creations. A woman came to his beckoning arm, a woman with silver hair—not the silvering of hair gone gray with age, but rather a genuine silver sheen, as if it had been spun of metal. She wore a stunning dress of turquoise blue that flashed as she moved, yet Maggie's gaze was drawn more toward the woman's eyes. She studied Maggie and Gallen frankly as she descended the staircase.

Maggie felt a physical wrenching. Turn away, something in her mind told her. Turn away. Don't let her see you.

For the woman's eyes pierced Maggie, inspected her, and dismissed her all in a glance.

"Felph and Arachne, hooray for Felph and Arachne!" the employees cheered, shouting and clapping. Their jubilant cheers were answered by more subdued clapping from the scientists and poachers and eccentrics in the crowd. Maggie thought the employees' level of enthusiasm sounded odd, strained. Perhaps Felph expected such accolades from them.

Behind them marched Herm, all dressed in a new outfit of elegant black, looking debonair.

Following him came Hera, and on her arm a tall man with a broad chest, incredibly handsome, with long flowing hair, a beardless face with strong jaws, and eyes of such a piercing black that they seemed to glitter like jewels. His light gray jacket and white pants all somehow worked together so that as Maggie looked at him, her gaze riveted to those dark and disturbing eyes.

"Hooray, hooray for Zeus and Hera," the people all shouted, and Maggie had an odd sinking feeling. She knew little of mythology, only what her mantle downloaded to her, and she was disturbed by the naming scheme Lord Felph had chosen for his children.

Last of all, came a young girl, no more than twelve or thirteen. She was both lithe and strong, with a very athletic build. Yet, apparently without her even knowing, she was the most beautiful woman Maggie had ever seen. Her long amber hair fell in a casual braid over her left shoulder, and her eyes were of the deepest gray. She was more full-bodied than a Tharrin, physically stronger and more sensual. Indeed, she seemed the perfect combination of strength, grace, and sensuality, though she was not even well into her teens. Maggie watched Gallen's eyes: he seemed riveted by her face, the astonishing sweetness of her smile.

Her appearance brought an enthusiastic explosion of shouts from the townsfolk. "Athena! Yay for Athena!" they cheered.

The people of Ruin all continued applauding Lord Felph and his creations. Audio recordings played the sounds of thousands more people cheering and clapping, so that the walls fairly shook with the tumult, though fewer than a hundred guests had gathered.

Suddenly, out through the east windows on the veranda, fireworks began to explode, shooting high into the air, forming brightly colored rainbows that whistled over the verandas and waterfalls.

Lord Felph descended.

Maggie found it hard to look at Felph's children. She found she was shaking, and her breath came ragged. Slaves. They were all slaves, wearing their silver Guides.

As Felph and his creations reached the bottom of the stairs, Felph raised his hands, and the people of Ruin quieted their cheering. Felph stood nodding and blinking pleasantly in the bright lights, while his servants circled him and continued clapping, shouting, "Jolly good! Well-done! Hurrah for Lord Felph!"

Felph held his hands higher, begging them to quiet.

"I hope you have all had an opportunity to eat, and to meet the newest additions to our planet—our guests!" Felph waved toward Gallen, Maggie, and the bears. His voice came out somewhat weak and raspy.

This was followed by more enthusiastic cheering and much nodding of heads, including a few calls for a toast.

But Lord Felph would have none of that.

"And now, my good friends, my employees," Felph called, raising his hands for silence, "I would like you all to *leave!*" This last word he shouted, so that it echoed from the ceiling of the room. The music had just stopped, and the echoing booms of the fireworks died away in Maggie's ears.

Moreover, the cheering died on the lips of the planet's people, and all of them stared, gawking at Lord Felph.

One flabby fellow called into the silence, "But ah haven't 'ad a chance for a bite, yet!" though he stood with both fists holding a silver platter generously filled with cakes and meat.

"I brought you here to meet my guests, nothing more," Lord Felph said with a flourish of his hand, waving the people all away. "I gave you ample time for that task, and if you squandered it, it's your own damned fault. As for food, if you like, you may each grab a plate as you depart, and drain a mug, too. The florafeems are still on the terrace, and they'll depart in a few minutes. It has been so nice of you to come. But really, you must leave, *now!*"

The guests stared in dismay, unwilling to believe Lord Felph would throw them out.

Felph hunched, alone in the spotlight. All around the room, it began to grow ominously dark as lights dimmed, so that only the old man could be seen. He eyed the guests, chin thrust out, glaring as if in mute rage, till at last he could hold still no longer.

He stomped his foot on the floor with all his might, so that the sound of it rang out. Then he bent forward and began howling, a strange, inhuman shout that sounded of genuine pain. "Noowwwww!" he cried, stomping again. "Get out nowwww! I can't bear your presence any longer. I can't tolerate it! Get out while you still can! Nowwwww!"

As the old man bent low, his face twisted in pain, his eyes stared out accusingly on the people of Ruin.

Maggie's heart began pounding in fear. Lord Felph panted, and slobber dripped down his chin.

"Careful, careful," someone whispered in the crowd behind Maggie, "he's in one of 'is moods!"

Those closest to Felph began backing away slowly, raising their hands as if to prove that they weren't armed. Perhaps they imagined he had a weapon and would begin shooting. Those near the tables of food each grabbed plates, while some of those closest to the doors actually took off sprinting for the terrace. One woman fell and shrieked as a heavy man trampled her, then several other people began screaming, perhaps believing that Felph had unleashed some security droids on the crowd with orders to shoot.

In moments the room emptied of all but Maggie, Gallen, the bears, and Felph's children. Even of Felph's servants, only the faithful Dooring remained, smiling broadly.

In the sudden silence, Felph began chuckling under his breath, the sound reverberating from the high walls. He then stared at the retreating figures, who turned to shadows out on the veranda.

He eyed them not with the lack of composure typical of madness, but instead with the steady and calculating gaze of a stage performer gauging his audience.

He glanced at the tables filled with refreshments—tumbled in disarray. Then he gazed back at the fleeing people and murmured, "So go the gray masses, marshaled alternately by gluttony and terror. Pity the weak."

F elph turned back to Gallen and Maggie, marched boldly up to them, and bowed so low his wispy hair nearly scraped the floor. Gallen had thought he would wear a crown of some type, a Controller to order the Guides his children wore, but he wore only a small device mounted into his skull, behind his right ear.

"I'm very pleased to make your acquaintance, Gallen, Maggie," Felph said, nodding to each in turn, smiling pleasantly. "May I introduce you to my beloved children—Arachne, Hera, Zeus, Hermes, and little Athena."

Felph's children each bowed in turn, none of them speaking a word. Apparently Felph had forbidden them to speak. And yet, and yet, can eyes not sometimes speak as loudly as words?

Gallen knew how much wearing a Guide, even for a few days, had pained Maggie. Now he looked into the eyes of Felph's creations. The oldest, Arachne, smiled weakly; everything about her posture, her trembling smile, begged, "Please, free us."

The children—for though some were older than Gallen, he still saw them as children—hovered behind Felph, bright, intelligent, eager for attention.

Lord Felph finished his introductions, and said, "I hope you enjoy my hospitality."

"As do I," Gallen said, cautiously. "Are you certain you want us to stay the evening?"

"Indeed, of course." Felph chuckled. "Don't fear. I play the eccentric only for the sake of the locals. It keeps them away. So you see, there is nothing to worry about, really. Besides, we haven't had dinner yet, nor have we discussed my proposed terms of employment. I'm very wealthy. I'm sure you'll find the terms . . . fascinating."

Felph stood taller, then gazed fixedly at the bears. "I see you also brought your *pets?*"

"Orick and Tallea are my friends, not my pets," Gallen said. "They do talk."

"Talking pets?" Felph murmured, intrigued. "Like parrots and macaws and whatnot?"

"I'm very pleased to make your acquaintance," Orick blurted, rising on his hind legs, trying to ease Gallen's obvious distress at Felph's comments. "Your palace is remarkable!"

"Well, yes, thank you," Felph said, somehow delighted that the bear would speak to him. He reached out and pinched the fur above Orick's left paw. "Isn't it a bit warm in there?"

"Only when I build a fire," Orick jested, then laughed, as did Lord Felph.

"Well, I'm very happy to meet you," Felph told Orick once again, and Felph graciously took both of Orick's paws in his hand at once, then shook lightly, as if with a dear friend. Felph glanced at Gallen. "Charming bear—a talking bear, really. Now, to dinner."

As the people of Ruin mounted the florafeems outside, Felph led Maggie and the others through the great hall to a wide corridor that opened into a spacious formal dining room. An enormous table carved of a single slab of white marble sat in the center of the room. The walls had been covered in dark rosewood and inlaid with gold. A single chandelier lit the center of the room, a chandelier with tiny glow globes hidden in a golden net, hung with huge cut diamonds that glittered brilliantly.

Twenty server droids lined the walls. A sumptuous feast was set, with six main meat dishes, several types of bread and rolls, and a dozen dishes of vegetables and fruits, not to mention desserts and liqueurs. Maggie had dined at state banquets on half a dozen worlds, but nothing compared to Lord Felph's table.

The servant Dooring went to the table, pulled out Felph's chair, then seated the others in turn. Orick and Tallea could not properly sit at a table, so Dooring removed the chairs, letting the bears stand.

Felph let his guests eat their repast in silence, careful to avoid any talk of business, for to do so was taboo in many cultures. It was an odd and eerie meal, for Felph talked casually of many things—the great drought which would end in a few weeks as Ruin neared Brightstar and the polar caps began to melt, the commercial value of various relics found on Ruin, the outrageous excesses of the governor in a nearby star system who wanted to annex Ruin, and so on. But it was not Felph's choice of topics that Gallen found to be eerie, it was simply that his children did not speak. Obviously, Lord Felph had forbidden them.

Gallen felt suspicious of his motives.

When the last dessert was finished an hour later, Felph pushed his chair from the table a foot, a formal sign that dinner had ended. Gallen did the same.

"Now to business," Felph said, folding his hands over his belly, "unless you are still hungry?"

"No," everyone said in unison, including Orick. It was a rare meal that served enough even for that bear.

"Good, good." Felph nodded thoughtfully. He stared at Gallen. "As you may have noticed, I keep very few human retainers. My droids handle the vast bulk of my work—cultivating the fields, mining the hills. They work as technicians and factory workers, servants and cleaners—all here in the depths, under the palace. I reserve humans only because of their versatility. It is rare that I seek to hire a human. The palace is self-sufficient. I even export some small items. Yet—I need your services, Gallen O'Day."

Gallen nodded. "Is it a criminal you want to apprehend? If so, this fine dinner, though much appreciated, was hardly necessary. Tracking criminals is what I do."

Felph smiled and shook his head. "It is not a criminal I seek. It is a deed I want done, an artifact—an ancient Qualeewooh artifact—that I would like you to acquire." Felph folded his hands and raised them to his chin, watching Gallen's face. "You have seen the jungles of Ruin from space? We call them the *tangles*, for the trees of Ruin become tangled together into such strange and impenetrable masses, that the word 'jungle' somehow does not do them justice. At the base of every tangle is a lake or sea, and the native dew trees float on these waters, spreading broad floating leaves that cover the water completely. The dew trees themselves are enormous, sometimes fifty meters wide, and their roots may anchor a thousand meters deep into the ocean, while the trunks rise fifteen hundred meters in the air. On these dew trees, parasitic plants grow— ribbon trees and fire brush and a thousand forms of fungus, until all of them twist into an impenetrable mass."

"I've seen them from space, but not close up," Gallen said. Indeed, when Gallen had landed, it seemed that he had little choice of spots to set camp. The land that was not desert on Ruin seemed to be the impenetrable tangle, and so Gallen had landed in a clear desert, where native predators might not prove too bothersome.

"The tangles are filled with wildlife. Florafeems, like the ones you rode here, feed in the foliage at the top, and thousands of other species of animals live in the canopy, some of them hundreds of meters into the growth, where perpetual darkness reigns.

"The predators in the tangle are—unusually nasty, let us say. Evolution has given them certain advantages over the human form. Their nervous systems give them superior reflexes—which let them react about twice as fast as humans do, and their muscles process energy at a more rapid rate."

Gallen smiled wryly. "So they are nasty enough to keep you from your artifact?"

"Other men have gone searching for it. I've sent killer droids into the tangle, trying to recover the object of my desires—I've even sent in a dozen of my own clones. No one has managed to retrieve it for me."

"So, you are saying it's dangerous?" Gallen asked.

"For normal men. Perhaps even for you. No Lord Protector has ever tried the deed. I would, of course, provide droid escorts, the finest military weaponry—"

"Yet even then, you don't expect me to succeed."

"Why would you say that?" Felph asked.

Gallen nodded toward Felph's children—to Arachne and Hera, Athena. "You don't let them speak. You're afraid they'll ruin the deal, talk me out of it."

Felph grinned. "Very perceptive. I should have known that a Lord Protector would be so perceptive. To put it candidly, I am unsure of your chances. If I thought the venture fruitless, I wouldn't even entertain this notion."

"You told me that I would find your offer interesting," Gallen said. "I'm not exactly interested in dying."

"Of course not," Felph said.

"So what do you offer?" Gallen asked. "I assume the reward justifies the risks?"

"I would, of course, take precautions before sending you in. I'd clone you, download your memories, so that should you fail, you will have lost nothing. Beyond that . . ." Felph spread his hands wide, indicating his palace, "whatever you want."

Orick gasped, and even Gallen sat back in surprise. Gallen could imagine a lot. As he gazed at the opulence around him, he realized that Felph really would make good on his offer.

"That's right," Felph said. "I am four thousand years old, and in my youth I inherited more money than I could ever spend. That has been invested and accruing interest for ages. I control the economies of fifty worlds. If you acquire the artifact I desire, I will give you," he shrugged, "half."

Gallen's heart pounded. Maggie reached over, clutched his arm under the table. A warning? Did she want him to jump at the offer, or back away from it. He glanced at her, and her face was set, wary. She was telling him only to be careful, he suspected.

But he couldn't be careful. Only days ago she'd begged him to flee the civilized worlds, get her away from the Dronon. Government officials, sympathetic to Gallen's plight, had loaned Gallen a ship.

"What would be worth so much?" Gallen asked.

"The Waters of Strength," Felph said.

Gallen asked, "What makes them so valuable?"

Felph shrugged. "I'm not certain that they are. At the very least, they intrigue me. That intrigue has held me here on this planet for six hundred years.

But if the legends are true, then it is said that in ancient times the Qualeewoohs brewed the Waters of Strength, and those who drank them made four great conquests." He raised one hand and counted off on four fingers, "Self. Nature. Time. And Space."

Gallen shook his head. "That seems a bit much to expect from a potion. What proof do you have that it exists?"

"There are many accounts of it in Qualeewooh histories. It was brewed some thirty millennia ago, at the dawn of the Age of Man," Felph said. "As for evidence of its continued existence, there is ample evidence. What evidence would you have?"

Gallen shrugged. "A thirty-thousand-year-old Qualeewooh, telling me where to find it."

Lord Felph raised a brow. "All right," he said. "Fair enough. Follow me."

He got up from the table, and Gallen followed him out the corridor, back into the great hall, and out another passageway. Maggie followed at Gallen's back, along with the bears, Felph's children, and Dooring.

The passageways led to a road that wound outside the palace itself, and Gallen saw that night was full upon them, but though the stars dusted a cloud-less sky, Brightstar outshone them all, more like a brilliant moon than a star. Gallen could see quite well, and indeed felt the heat of the star. He followed Felph through a garden of dahlias in shades of white and black, then down into a great chamber, an ancient chamber carved by the Qualeewoohs.

Felph reached into his pocket, pulled out a glow globe, and held it aloft. "If you look up here, you can see writing on the walls, most of it in a tempera made from colored clays mixed with pulp from bark." There was indeed writing on the ceiling, intricate designs of stylized Qualeewoohs painted in vivid reds, blues, yellows, and greens. There was a queer feeling to the place. Strange scenes on the ceiling depicted birdlike creatures in armored helms, who carried knives on their wing tips, battling beasts in the heavens. The hall was ten meters across, but less than two meters high. By the odd proportions, one sensed it had not been burrowed by human hands. The symbols were obviously stylized, yet there were intricacies in the work that astonished Gallen. It was like nothing ever painted by a human. On one wall was a set of symbols that gave off ominous overtones. They depicted yellowish fanged beasts, like upright jackals with large ears, apparently dancing in a green mist.

"What do these symbols mean?" Maggie asked.

"No one knows," Felph said. "Each mating pair of Qualeewoohs writes in their own private language, which they teach their children, but the children themselves create their own version of that language at adolescence. The result is that after a few generations, even the Qualeewoohs can't decipher the family writings. But Qualeewoohs tell me that the private languages tell mostly of common things—nearby nesting sites, feeding grounds, and the attendant dan-gers at each. But there is much more personal information that the Qualeewoohs don't share with us—mystic teachings and magical rites."

"You mean that the Qualeewoohs are still alive?" Orick asked. "I thought that they were all killed or something. That's why the planet is called Ruin."

"Not killed," Felph said. "They are rare, but not extinct. We're in a period called 'the bone years,' when their members become quite few. It's a planetwide drought. And of course, over the past few centuries, their numbers have dwindled lower than ever. Poachers, you know."

"I still cannot believe people would kill them," Gallen said, not bothering to conceal his outrage.

"Perhaps if you'd met a Qualeewooh, you'd understand," Felph answered. "They are feral. Their ancestors reached great heights of civilization, but the descendants—are poor representatives of their species."

He brought the light to a corner, where a glass case had been built into one wall. "Here you can see some spirit masks—Qualeewooh masks made of lacquered leather, with some inlaid silver fangs, and writing painted on the masks. The Qualeewoohs make these when they reach adolescence, then have them permanently glued to their faces. The masks cannot be removed. When a Qualeewooh dies, its body is left behind as being nothing, something merely cast off. But the dead Qualeewooh's mate will bring the mask back to one of its favorite aeries." He raised the globe toward the wall. The birdlike masks were about three feet from nose to head, and just the width of a human face. Gallen got the distinct impression that the empty eye sockets on the gray-blue masks were gazing out at him. "You said you wanted to speak to a dead Qualeewooh. Open the case. Put on a mask. As I remember, the center one there is quite well-made."

Gallen looked at Felph suspiciously. The hair rose on the back of Gallen's neck. On Tremonthin, the Inhuman had downloaded memories of past lives into Gallen. And somewhere, Gallen felt he had lost a bit of himself in a sea of otherness. He dared not put on the mask.

"What do the masks do?" Gallen said.

Felph frowned in thought. "The methods for making a spirit mask are kept secret from humans, so it is difficult to explain precisely how they work. The means for producing them is taught by the 'ancestors,' the Qualeewoohs' word for gods. I cannot explain it any better than to say this: you and I would say that these masks are receivers. The masks let the Qualeewoohs' dead ancestors speak to them."

Gallen said, "But earlier tonight, Herm said that wearing the masks drives you insane."

Felph smiled secretively. "Some would say that it drives you *divine*. It is true that long-term exposure to alien thoughts might . . . confuse some. But there is little harm in short-term exposure. Please. You said you wanted proof of the Waters. This is part of the evidence."

Gallen immediately stiffened. Felph seemed more than a bit mad himself. He had worn the masks, of that Gallen felt certain. Perhaps the mask had made him insane. Certainly a normal man would not have howled for his guests to leave his party, would not have bayed like a wounded hound almost as soon as they entered his home. Felph was insane, and possibly dangerous. Gallen didn't trust his judgment, didn't want to don the mask. Yet a certain morbid fascination gripped him. Gallen wanted to know for certain that Felph spoke the truth.

Gallen went to the case, pulled out the mask that Felph had indicated—a mask of deep purples with threads of red among the silver writing. He took a deep breath, then held the strange birdlike mask up to his face with both hands. Almost immediately he stiffened, as if bracing himself for a blow. Wearing the mask somehow seemed suffocating—though Gallen could breathe easily enough. It was an odd sensation. He felt as if—his head had elongated, as if it were pulled into a far place.

Almost immediately he saw something—a vision one might call it, and the oddity of it repelled him. At first, his mind could not make sense of what he saw. A world as flat and featureless as a sea of molten lead, skies in banded shades of yellow and crimson, and green birds of light wheeling through the skies. One of the birds was flying toward him, growing larger and larger in his field of vision, and its thoughts seemed to pummel Gallen. Half-formed questions formed in Gallen's mind—questions that he felt, curiously, must be answered once posed.

He choked back a sob, then drew the mask away, shoving it toward Felph. He found that he had dropped protectively to one knee.

He blinked rapidly and shook his head, as if trying to wake from a disturbing dream, then said weakly. "All right. I believe you."

"What, what did you see?" Orick nearly shouted.

"It is not so much what you see," Felph said. "It was what you think and feel. The ancestors speak to your whole soul—your hopes and desires and dreams."

Orick asked, "What did they say?"

Gallen shook his head. "They asked me . . ." he struggled for words, "if I could seek for the Waters of Strength. To seek with my whole being. They told me to find . . . peace?" He frowned, as if uncertain of the message.

Maggie looked to Gallen, then to Felph, incredulous.

Felph said, "Would you like to try it, Maggie, Orick? Do you want to hear the voices of the ancestors?"

Maggie shook her head vigorously. Orick and Tallea declined the offer.

"Such a shame," Felph said. "Perhaps you'll change your mind. Here: this mask is for you, Gallen, since you had the courage to wear it. It's quite valuable. It dates to the thirty-third ascendancy, a historical period that ended about three thousand years ago. The finest masks were made then." He presented the mask to Gallen with a bow. Gallen took it, gingerly, put it under his arm.

"I—I don't get it," Orick said. "You said that the Qualeewoohs had conquered time and space. If that's true, why don't you bring us one."

Felph smiled broadly. "Well, Orick, that is hard to explain, and I don't know the answer for sure myself. The Qualeewoohs say that the ancestors are 'flying between the stars.' I think that phrase means, quite frankly, that they do not exist in the physical universe. They have been transformed into something else, something that travels to another dimension, where time and space as we know them no longer exist."

Maggie seemed astonished at this. She pushed up at her mantle, as if to shove it from her head. She did that at times when it was downloading too much information to her. "That would require a more sophisticated level of technology than even *we* have!" she said. "We've never crossed dimensional boundaries."

Felph shrugged. "Qualeewooh technology differs from ours, yet I doubt it is 'more sophisticated.' "

Maggie said, "This is incredible. My mantle has no information on these masks; as a Lord of Technology, I should know something of them."

Gallen's own mantle whispered to him. "The nature of the artifacts discovered here has been classified as secret. It is vital that such technology not fall into Dronon hands."

Until now, Gallen had thought it exceedingly odd that the government would conspire to hide an entire world. Now he got an uneasy feeling that they had stumbled onto something darker and more important than he ever would have imagined.

Softly, Maggie asked, "What proof do you have of such a level of technology?"

"Ah," Felph smiled. "I see your reservations. A technologist doesn't want dreams and alien voices whispering in her ear. She wants hardware." He bent his head. "Unfortunately, not much has survived the past twenty thousand years. You can search the aeries—the Qualeewoohs call them *cloo* holes, but all you will find are cave paintings. But some evidence exists. Come back here, into this passage."

Felph hobbled to a hole that had been excavated in the back of the chamber, then led them through a corridor that sloped down, then suddenly opened into a far larger chamber, an almost perfect oval.

Here, things were far different from the room above. Felph had installed a very dim continual light on one wall. Mounted on the wall opposite from the light was bolted a metal panel with graceful lines etched deeply into it. Whereas the previous walls had all been covered with exotic pictographs, these loops and whorls were clearly different. They didn't seem to be writing. They didn't represent anything.

"Can you guess what this is?" Felph asked.

Maggie drew close and studied the metal panel. "This isn't the low-quality silver we've seen on Qualeewooh spirit masks. This is a solid sheet of platinum." The panel was nearly two meters tall and ten long. "Something this big had to have been milled in a foundry." She studied the grooves in the metal. They followed two separate tracks, mirror images of one another, that led from the floor to the ceiling and back down again in graceful sweeps. "It looks like writing etched into the metal," Maggie said, uncertain. But even Gallen guessed that these weren't pictographs, not representational characters at all. "These etched tracks are so narrow and deep: the grooves must have been cut with a laser."

When she examined the etchings closely, she suddenly bolted backward in surprise.

"A recording?" Maggie said, astonished. "These grooves are an audio recording?"

"More than just audio!" Felph said. "It's an audiovisual recording from the second expansion, approximately thirty thousand years ago. This predates nearly every civilization on Earth. Our ancestors were just learning to shape stone, while these people were developing laser technology and recording studios, performing brain surgeries and actively terraforming their own planet to make it more suitable. You should see the stone aqueducts on Fire River—over four thousand miles of covered aqueducts in all—and most of it is still usable."

Felph brought a small device from the pocket of his robe, something that looked like a high-tech top—a spindle on a round spool with a thin, curved handle. He placed it in one of the grooves on the lower right-hand corner of the metal plate, and twisted. There was a snapping sound as a lock snicked open. A heavy rumbling followed.

A hole opened in the stone floor, and a statue began rising up, revealing the shape of a birdlike creature sculpted from colored glass. The figure was corroding, miserable in appearance, but Gallen could sense the general appearance of the being.

The Qualeewooh had light-colored feathers on its chest, while the longer plumage on its wings was mostly tan with some green tips at its wings. The statue showed the creature with its wings upraised, and Gallen could distinctly see the tiny hands—each with four long fingers, at the apex of each wing. The Qualeewooh's brownish neck was long and slender, with a blaze of white at the throat, and its head held a large beaklike snout, with many teeth that were needle-sharp, including two large pairs of upper fangs that reminded Gallen of a boar's tusks. As with any bird, the eyes were set on each side of its head, so that the Qualeewooh could see in any direction above, below, or to either side. Somehow, even from only this crude icon, Gallen would have recognized that this creature was sentient.

But this creature seemed more than intelligent. It carried itself with a pride, with a majesty, few humans could have aspired to. Perhaps it was the spirit mask that the statue wore. This particular mask was formed of platinum, inlaid with cabochons of dark blue azurite. The spirit mask flamed up and outward into some mystical crown, and the glass eyes of the statue stared deeply from this mask, secretive, wise—but mostly, most frighteningly, malevolent.

There were other oddities about the statue. On its fingers the Qualeewooh wore heavy rings, each shaped like a long, raking claw. On its chest it wore a bandolier with many tiny implements that might have been tools or keys.

There, in the dark room, gazing at this ancient glass statue that barely caught the light in the darkness, Gallen felt a primal, palpable fear. Something about this creature made him step back. He suspected this was no representation of a Qualeewooh lord or philosopher. This was a demon.

The sight of the statue affected the others in the same way. Everyone had moved back from it. Felph appeared not to notice. He still had his little device in the track on the platinum wall, and now he placed an identical device into a groove on the lower right side. "These are models of the spindles a Qualee-wooh used. I've motorized these, so that they'll play over the recording. In ancient times, there were no motors. A nest mother would have stood here, a spindle in each claw, flapping her wings to play the recording. You can imagine what it would look like."

He pretended to grab both implements and begin running them through the narrow grooves, pulling them toward him, raising them slightly, then pushing them back out along their tracks, then pulling them back in.

The result of his odd motions was that Felph suddenly looked as if he were a bird, mimicking the motions of flight, flapping his wings.

When he finished his demonstration, he reached down to the spindles, pushed a button on each one, and the spindles actually began to move.

A quavering sound issued from the spindles, remarkably loud. It was a song—reed pipes, thunderous drums, some strange instrument that might have been a wood paddle scraping over stone.

It was a marvelous melody—rich, exotic, completely alien and yet immediately recognizable as music. One could hear high winds whistling through crevices, the music of flapping wings and beating hearts.

Qualeewoohs were singing in that song, too.

The ancient Qualeewooh language was raucous, with many squawks among its frantic whistling. It was a dramatic weaving of sound, like voices crying in a jungle over the peeping of frogs. The Qualeewoohs' cries reverberated throughout the chamber—a challenging tone that might have been voicing curses or deprecations.

Orick shouted in astonishment, "Look in its eyes!"

Gallen stared into the eyes of the statue, and saw that somehow—he could not see the source—an image was being projected through the statue. In the black depths of the statue's eyes Gallen could discern five Qualeewoohs winging over the red deserts of Ruin, soaring over rocky bluffs. From overhead, a second flock of Qualeewoohs plummeted with deadly grace from cloudy skies, diving into their fellows, talons stretched out, apparently fitted with metal spurs. The attackers slashed the necks and wings of their adversaries. A squawking roar filled the room, as if a hundred Qualeewoohs shrieked in pain and terror, then the image focused on two Qualeewoohs who soared and dived, battling in the sky.

The sounds softened, almost breathless, and Gallen suspected this recording recounted the tale of these two Qualeewoohs. It must have been an epic battle, for it lasted more than ten minutes, and Gallen was astonished at what he saw—Qualeewoohs flying in complex loops, twisting dives, terrifying strikes and heroic dodges.

In the end, one Qualeewooh plummeted in a dazzling pattern, as if trapped in a whirlwind, spiraling down. In the last second of its attack, it reached out with one wing, where its tiny hand carried a thin blade, and smote off the head of its adversary.

Thus the adversary tumbled to earth, end over end, its head somersaulting in the air.

The vanquishing Qualeewooh soared on over the plains, master of all it surveyed.

For the next several minutes of the recording, all one could see was a lone Qualeewooh flying through endless empty skies, accompanied by a ringing song that could only have come from some type of pipes or whistles, unaccompanied by other instruments, until at last the remaining Qualeewooh reached a mountain aerie and entered a cave.

In the back of the cave, Qualeewooh chicks huddled in downy feathers, shaking amid the shells of their eggs, making querulous peeps as the dark lord approached, beak open, displaying his razor-sharp teeth.

There the tale ended.

Gallen's logic told him that this recording showed a major battle between good and evil. If so, something was certainly amiss. This was not a heroic tale as he understood it: of the Qualeewoohs who had fought, the loser was not the aggressor, but the defender.

The defender, a smaller Qualeewooh, had worn a simple spirit mask of bright silver, unadorned with any gaudy stones. In all the encounters, it had wheeled away, retreating with great speed and desperation toward a distant line of hills. True, it did rake its attacker on occasions, but only in self-defense.

And the song, the strange song at the end that sounded like reed pipes, seemed to Gallen not to be trumpeting victory, nor sounding an anthem of peace.

Instead, it was a bewailing tune, a howling. I am the dark god of the skies, the icon had cried. Through victory I am diminished.

When Felph's spindles reached the lowest bottom corners of the panel, the song ended. The glass statue receded down into the floor, where the stone doors slid back in place with a snick.

Felph turned around, pocketed the devices that let him play the recording.

Gallen stood in the solemn chamber, with his friends around him. Beside him he could feel Maggie standing close, shivering from fear. Gallen remained utterly silent, the alien music ringing through his head. No one spoke. No one wanted to be the first to break the spell the Qualeewooh music had woven. The whole battle, the symbolism, was utterly alien. But Gallen felt that, somehow, he understood.

He wondered how this cave had appeared to the Qualeewoohs, thirty thousand years ago: many nesting sites had probably been here in the cliffs. The chicks would have come into this cave, in the darkness, Gallen imagined. Perhaps the chicks would have been small, so young they hadn't grown their adult plumage. So they would have been ugly, gangling things with small wings and large heads.

A priestess would have stood before the platinum panel and waved her wings, as if taking flight. Immediately the dark god would rise behind her, its malevolent intent glowing in its eyes.

Each chick would have had its head turned to the side, gazing at the dark god with one eye only. Perhaps the victim of the murder symbolized the priestess in her flight. That sounded somehow right.

Gallen realized that the defender in the battle had been lighter of color. Female, perhaps? The death of virtue, the end of civilization. That's what the dark god brought.

He stared at the scene in his imagination, lost in thought, until Felph said quietly, "I first came to Ruin nearly seven hundred years ago, as an archaeologist. I was part of a team that discovered this site. All the others, they've moved on to other worlds, other ruins. But I've stayed to study the Qualeewoohs and their civilization.

"You see, they are not unlike us. Their ancestors were violent hunters, lords of the skies. They traveled in great flocks that darkened the heavens. When they descended on the twisted jungles, they carried off what they desired.

"And like our ancestors, they grew to be too numerous, and began to war.

"But they were not really like us," Felph mused, and his tone was somber. He stared at the floor, his dark eyes unfocused, his gaze directed inward.

"Man was content to live with war, and even gloried in it. But the Qualeewoohs never romanticized it, never saw it as a necessity, nor even really tolerated it."

"What happened to them, then?" Orick asked, his deep voice full of awe. "Why did they die out?"

"They haven't, as I said," Felph answered. "But if our astrophysical models are correct, things here changed about thirty thousand years ago, during the fourth expansion. Ruin circles a small sun, as you can see—one too small to regularly burn away the planet's polar ice caps. Darksun drew close to its larger sister every six years in a very elliptical orbit, and when the suns reached perigee, the combined light provided enough heat to melt the polar caps here on Ruin. With this melting, water would fill the shallow seas, and as the tangles enlarged, the local flora and fauna populations would explode for a few years.

"But about twenty-eight thousand years ago, something changed the orbits. It may have been that a large planetary body passed through the system, or even hit Darksun, skewing its orbit, making it more and more elliptical. On a cosmic scale, the variations in orbit appear minor, but the changes here on Ruin have been dramatic.

"The result has been that the six-year cycle now takes three hundred years to complete. The free water here on Ruin is becoming more and more concentrated at the poles, and now, even when the ice caps do melt, they can't melt completely."

"So the Qualeewoohs died out?" Maggie asked.

"No, not exactly," Felph said.

"Their numbers were on the decline even before this tragedy. That is what intrigued me about them. You see, Qualeewoohs are intelligent creatures—smarter than the average human who isn't genetically enhanced.

"No, they weren't dying out. What happened is this: in the early days of human technology, our ancestors' innovations concentrated in several areas—the production of shelter, transportation, food, and weapons of war.

"But the Qualeewoohs never needed these. They needed no transportation. Because they were winged creatures, they were free to hunt and move at will. Indeed, I can find no evidence that, outside of litters for carrying their sick, the Qualeewooh ever created any kind of vehicle.

"As far as shelter goes, their needs seemed minimal. The Qualeewoohs, unlike humans, cannot live in extreme cold. Their wings and necks dissipate too much heat, so they were never free to expand beyond their lower temperate regions. Nor can they nest near the tangles, where predators steal their eggs. So they nest in mountainous areas above the tangles—and there were plenty of nesting sites.

"Also, the Qualeewoohs, unlike humans, are pure carnivores. The ancients did develop methods of ranching—controlling predators and unwanted herbivores. The tangles provided them with hundreds of different natural pesticides and whatnot. But because the Qualeewooh are carnivores, their numbers naturally stabilized at smaller populations than human populations would. Indeed, food became the predominant limiting factor in their expansion.

"But war, of course, was their big problem. When driven by hunger, Qualeewoohs engaged in the worst sort of cannibalism. A well-fed Qualeewooh is a magnificently moral creature, but when a Qualeewooh starves, when its brain suffers from a lack of sugars, it enters a dark state that the Qualeewoohs call 'The Voracion.' A Qualeewooh so afflicted becomes a terrible, mindless predator—slaying anything but its own mate in an effort to survive. Thus, starving adults would forage into the nesting territories of enemy flocks, slaying the females, eating eggs and chicks. In lean years, terrible things happened.

"In an effort to abolish the slaughter, the Qualeewoohs focused their research efforts. The Qualeewoohs did not seek to *protect* themselves from their neighbors, as humans did. Mankind developed all sorts of fascinating myths about how other tribes of humans were 'evil' and inferior so we could continue to justify our war efforts.

"But among Qualeewoohs, who could fly, there was no boundary between peoples. A global language developed early in their civilization, along with two or three very similar global cosmologies, and everyone understood one another. One Qualeewooh could join with any flock he or she chose, and, it appears to me, the Qualeewoohs' territorial instinct never developed as strongly as did mankind's.

"And there is one more thing you must understand: the Qualeewoohs were brilliant mathematicians. They could estimate populations of animals, count their citizens, study the prevailing weather, then calculate accurately how many of their own people they could supply with food and water.

"So when the Qualeewoohs turned to the problem of war, they took a pragmatic approach. Instead of trying to search endlessly for new sources of food and water, instead of trying to defend themselves from the inevitable depredations of others—their technology focused on self-control."

"You mean to limiting their numbers?" Gallen asked.

"No," Felph said. "That was but a small part of their program. I mean that they turned toward social and genetic manipulation. That they practiced genetic manipulation is obvious. We've found fossilized plants from the tangle and compared their DNA to that in current samples. The dew trees, which serve as the platform for all other life here on Ruin, show a common pattern of genetic manipulation across twenty-three separate species. The Qualeewoohs inserted the instructions for a common root and hibernation system through all those species. It is only because of these genetic manipulations that any life at all still thrives on this planet.

"But even more importantly than their manipulations of the flora and fauna, they developed a genetic upgrade which they spread among their own kind. They inserted a gene into their thirty-second chromosome that makes it terrifying, utterly intolerable, for one Qualeewooh to be near another adult of the same sex. The very sight of an adult Qualeewooh of the same sex sends both individuals into flight."

Gallen considered. The Qualeewoohs had not been territorial, but by assuring that any two Qualeewoohs of the same sex who saw each other would immediately flee, you created a tremendous buffer zone between territories. Yet something more happened.

You dismantled society. The Qualeewoohs who had developed the technology he'd seen here had been flock animals, nesting together. Social, communicative. But they'd doomed their descendants to become solitary hunters, living in exile.

To Gallen the implications seemed horrifying.

Felph looked up at him, a gleam in his dark blue eyes, and stroked his beard. "Mankind chose to tolerate violence, to seek eternal expansion in the hopes of outrunning his own overpopulation. But the Qualeewoohs, in spite of the fact that they are raptors, could not live with such a choice. For them, the only purpose civilization ever served was to find the root of their own violent nature, then destroy it. Better to end civilization, they decided, than to live with the madness."

Tallea said, "How sad. Think of all they lost!"

But Orick simply shook his head. "How noble. Think of all they gained!"

"Indeed!" Felph said. "You see it. The Qualeewoohs are utterly unlike us in so many ways. With mankind, *our* whole system of values is incongruous, illogical. But the Qualeewoohs' society works for them—in many ways far better than ours ever worked for us.

"That is why I've stayed here for so long. I've studied their social relations, considered the implications in our own society, weighing them against the Dronon threat."

Gallen found Felph's tone very disturbing, incongruous. Half an hour ago, he'd talked casually about how humans slaughtered modern Qualeewoohs. Now he spoke reverently of their respect for life. Gallen recognized that Felph's respect for the Qualeewoohs was directed toward "the ancestors," the Qualeewooh gods, as he'd called them earlier. Modern Qualeewoohs, in spite of the fact that they were kindly philosophers, in spite of the fact that they glued spirit masks to their faces in order always to be guided by their ancestors, were somehow not worthy of Felph's respect. He saw them as creatures, not creators.

His position annoyed Gallen. Felph seemed to have an almost schizophrenic attitude about the creatures.

"What conclusions have you reached?" Maggie asked, and there was an edge to her voice, a threat. She, too, was perturbed by Felph's attitudes.

Gallen recognized the source of Maggie's concern. Felph's genetic experiments, the way he treated the people above, the way he enslaved his own children—all suggested Felph was involved in something sinister. Could he be an aberlain, Gallen wondered—altering the human genome to fit his own whims, seeking to modify his own children as the Qualeewoohs had done? Gallen glanced at Felph's beautiful, silent children. His slaves.

"Conclusions? None, for certain," Felph said. "I suspect the Qualeewoohs' solution was at once noble and desperate beyond anything I could condone. They doomed their descendants to lives of isolation. They doomed their species to eventual extinction. And they lost too much in their quest for peace—the opportunity for social discourse that we as humans take for granted.

"Still, I could almost congratulate them for the devil's bargain they made, if not for the Dronon. In time, the Qualeewoohs' shortsightedness will condemn this world. The Qualeewoohs never anticipated alien invaders, either human or Dronon. This world, with its dull red sun, is a perfect habitat for the Dronon. When the Lords of the Swarms discover this place, as they surely will, the Qualeewoohs won't be able to defend themselves."

"Perhaps that won't happen for a long time," Gallen said.

"One could only hope," Felph replied. "Unfortunately, what seems long to us is actually a short time on a cosmic scale. Five hundred years, a thousand? The Qualeewoohs don't have that long."

Gallen said, "Don't you think mankind can find an answer to the problem?"

"No," Felph answered. "What answer could we come up with? The Dronon have had plenty of time to duplicate most of our higher technology in the past eighty years. A full-fledged war is almost too horrific for either species to consider, not when entire worlds would burn to ash.

"Mankind, I think, would gladly strike up negotiations for treaties with the Dronon, but the Dronon psyche does not allow for such things. They seek dominion above all, while mankind putters about, trying to find peaceful solutions to the problem.

"I hear—I hear," Felph continued, "that some humans back in the Milky Way have finally won the title Lords of the Sixth Swarm. But what will they do with it?"

"I couldn't say," Gallen answered, stifling the urge to laugh at the irony.

What would Felph think if he knew that at this very moment he was entertaining the Lords of the Sixth Swarm?

"I'll tell you what they should do," Felph said emphatically. "They should go to each Dronon queen in each hive of the Sixth Swarm and sterilize them. Then let it be known to the lords of the other swarms that if they challenge mankind again, and mankind wins, this will happen to their swarms. That's what we should do! With the extinction of their swarms as a threat, the Dronon would never dare challenge us again."

Maggie said, "But, if you destroyed the Sixth Swarm, you would be committing genocide against Dronon on hundreds of worlds."

"Not genocide—" Felph argued, "sterilization. Those living on such worlds could continue to live out their natural life spans."

Orick shook his head. "I don't think that will happen. I don't see how we could do it."

"Certainly the Tharrin will never do it," Felph said. "But I suspect that many of our *human* leaders throughout history might have done it. Unfortunately, we've given over our free agency to a pack of sniveling aliens who haven't got the fortitude to do what needs to be done."

"The Tharrin aren't aliens," Orick said.

"Of course they are—aliens of our own creation." Felph considered for a moment. "What we need is a new kind of civilization, with leaders strong enough to meet the challenge imposed by nonhuman sentients."

This is what Gallen had been waiting for. Felph hadn't admitted to being an aberlain. On most worlds throughout the universe, the work of aberlains was strictly illegal. Only on Tremonthin did mankind work assiduously to create new subspecies of humans to populate new worlds.

Maggie said, "And is this the work you've chosen for yourself, to create this new society?"

"Of course," Felph said. "Someone must rise to the challenge."

"Isn't it illegal to engage in genetic manipulations on humans?"

"Ruin doesn't belong to the Unity of Planets, so of course none of their laws apply. We're sovereign here."

"What of your local laws?" Gallen asked.

Felph seemed astonished by the question. "I really haven't made up any, yet." He studied their faces, saw their surprise. "You see, Ruin's constitution was written several hundred years ago by me and two colleagues. As a jest, we decided to form a monarchy. With only three of us on the planet at the time, it seemed a simple solution to any political problems. We drew straws, and I won. As an independent world recognized by the Unity, anyone who wants to settle here must swear to obey the laws of our constitution—and accept me as sovereign. As a result, I've retained my title of 'Lord Felph.' "

"What of the people who live on your world. Don't any of them object?" Gallen asked in astonishment.

"Object? Why would they object?" Felph asked. "People only object to government when it makes demands of them. I make no laws, levy no taxes. With the excess supplies I generate, I feed and clothe anyone who wants. No, no one objects to my reign. How could they?"

In the moment of silence that followed, Gallen furrowed his brow, then said. "Lord Felph, you've supported your view that the ancient Qualeewoohs created the Waters of Strength, and you've argued persuasively that they had at least some fairly high levels of technology. But one concern nags me. What makes you think the Waters of Strength still exist?"

Felph shot Gallen a knowing smile. "There are those who have tasted it. They bear witness."

"But you said no one has reached it!" Orick blurted.

"No *human*," Felph corrected. "There are creatures, animals in the tangle, with curious traits."

"Such as?" Gallen asked.

"They are nearly immortal," Felph said. "Oh, you can slay them, but they regenerate in a few hours. They attack as dumb animals do, with cunning, but lacking foresight. Come into the tangle with me, Gallen, on a small excursion, and I'll show you what you're faced with."

This seemed so improbable that even Gallen dared not speak for a moment. "Predators?" Gallen asked. "These are the predators you want me to fight?"

"I did not say it would be easy," Lord Felph answered. "It might take you a few trips. But you, or one of your clones, could make it."

Gallen shook his head thoughtfully. This would take some consideration.

Maggie said, "I understand that you want to hire *me* for something?"

"Possibly," Felph said. "At the very least, I would like to download the memory crystals from your mantle, particularly with emphasis on nanotech modifications to human life-forms. I can pay well, say a thousand credits per gig of nonduplicatory information?"

Maggie said, "I won't give you information as an aberlain unless you are forthright with me. I won't do anything immoral. I must know exactly what you are creating." She glanced up at the beautiful children that hovered around Felph, mute witnesses to the conversation. Felph was controlling them through their Guides, forcing them to keep silent during this entire evening. It was an eerie, ghastly thing to behold.

Felph folded his hands together, put them up to his chin, and gazed at Maggie. "Indeed, I suppose you must know, mustn't you?"

He cleared his throat. "You saw the people of Ruin, tonight, didn't you? Scholars, eccentrics, poachers—they are all much alike, ragged creatures who live only to fill their bellies, procreate, entertain themselves. And occasionally scratch where it itches.

"The universe is filled with such people. They do nothing of import, think nothing of import, say nothing remarkable. They are of no more consequence than the beasts of the field. They take up space on a planet, nothing more. Their whole lives are wasted."

"They're important in the eyes of God," Orick said. "No one is a waste. Christ said that God sees even the falling of a sparrow, and we are far more important than a sparrow!"

"You are a Christ worshiper?" Felph asked.

"Aye," Orick said.

"If man is more important than the sparrows, then why does your God promise us a hell? I'll tell you:"—Felph gazed fiercely at Orick—"your God's hell is nothing more than a dumping ground for human waste. That is why your Scriptures tell us that it will be so full. Few will make the grade. It has always been so, in any theology.

"You've seen the filthy people of my world? Once every generation, some young child will come to me, asking to learn, asking for a way off this world. I have teaching machines here, free for the asking. There are ways to improve one's self. I take such children as servants, have them work a few years, then arrange for their transport off this rock, if that is what they want. But so few make the grade, so few want to be anything more than human waste."

Orick was becoming furious at Felph's words. "I can't believe that!" he roared.

"Alas, I wish it were not so," Felph grunted. "We fear the Dronon. We fear that they will enslave us. But what value is our freedom, I beg to know, if we do nothing with it? What value are our lives if they pass by, as unremarked as a breeze?"

"A good life is its own reward," Orick said.

Felph peered out at him from bushy eyebrows, his eyes amused and glittering. "I would say that any life—good or bad—is its own reward. A gluttonous life may seem fine and pleasant to a glutton, but I doubt that your Christ would say that such a life is a good, or that it is a reward."

"A sinless life leads to greater reward," Orick said.

"Then by all means, let us all lead sinless lives," Felph said. "But if I understand aright, it is not enough just to avoid sin. One must openly wage a war for good—wield the vibro-blade of chastity, et cetera?"

"The sword of truth," Orick corrected.

"Whatever. You get the idea."

Felph's argument with Orick had run its course. Maggie said, "So, you are trying to create people who are not part of the dirty masses? How, exactly, do you plan to do this."

"The answer is simple," Felph said. "I've created children who *crave*."

"Crave what?" Gallen asked.

"You seem angry with me," Felph said. "Why?"

Gallen said, "I don't believe we should meddle with our children in this way."

Felph pointed accusingly at Maggie's belly, at the swell of a child in her womb. "Isn't *that* meddling? Aren't you taking this life lightly? If you give birth naturally, you have no idea what will be born, what you are giving life to. Would you not want your own children to crave to be something more than—than some twenty meters of gut with attached gonads?"

"Of course," Gallen said. "We all want our children to excel. But I don't experiment on the unborn! I prefer to have my children naturally."

"Experiment? Why damn you, you ignorant ass!" Felph shouted. "What is that thing in Maggie's belly but an experiment! You merely hope for the best. You create it, you let it grow, you nurture it. But it is nothing more than an experiment concocted by two foolish children who have no grasp of the responsibilities they're accepting. Giving birth naturally is no great virtue. Dogs do the same! Nature does not care one whit for your child. It doesn't mind if your son is born a monstrosity with two heads and no heart. It takes no pity when your child whines in the night from hunger, or when it shivers from cold. It does not hope and dream and work for your child. Nature is so . . . arbitrary. Damn you, to trust your child into the benevolent care of an uncaring nature, then to berate me with such a tone!" Felph clenched his fists and glared at Gallen, his head shaking from side to side in his rage.

Instead of becoming more angry at Felph's arguments, Gallen actually grinned. Perhaps it was Felph's courage, his stubbornness. In the past several years, Gallen had gained such a reputation as a bodyguard—and then as a Lord Protector of entire worlds—that no one outside of Orick dared berate him. Yet here this old man, someone Gallen could knock over as easily as if he were a cornstalk, was shouting at Gallen like a maniac.

"Forgive me," Gallen said, with a nod of deference. "I'd never considered genetic engineering as an obligation, rather than a choice. Still, I worry at what you are doing to your own children."

"They *crave*," Felph said, "as I told you!"

"But what do they crave?" Orick asked. Of them all, the bear seemed most horrified by Felph. Maggie seemed to be reserving judgment. Gallen now found himself favorably disposed toward Felph. The little bear Tallea had been quiet, nonjudgmental. As a refugee from Tremonthin, she had seen thousands of subspecies of mankind. The idea of engineering one's offspring perhaps did not seem so horrific to her.

Felph told Orick, "My children crave everything: glory, honor, power, knowledge, carnality. They seethe with it, more than you will ever imagine! So I have given them what they need to attain the heights they desire—strength, cunning, beauty!"

"A new race of leaders? That is what you want?" Maggie asked, suspicious.

"Precisely! We will no longer be led by alien Tharrin," Felph exulted. "I'm creating new leaders, with all the attributes that mankind revels in!"

Orick growled, "With all of mankind's weaknesses? You say they crave honor and power? Won't this lead to jealousies and corruption? You want to rid us of the compassionate Tharrin and put *these* in their place?"

"We are at war! We are at war!" Felph shouted.

Gallen was disappointed by this. Felph was just another crackpot out to create a race of supermen. It seemed that everywhere he went, someone was trying to define what mankind ought to become. Perhaps it was merely the age he lived in. With the Dronon threatening the very existence of mankind, every aberlain in the galaxy was concocting some scheme to overcome the threat. As a species, mankind would have to grow or die.

"I don't think that either my wife or I will work for you, sir," Gallen said, finally. He turned away, began walking toward the stairs that led up out of the darkened cavern. He expected the others to follow. Orick hurried after him, and Tallea followed.

But Maggie hesitated, as if still lost in thought.

"Wait!" Felph shouted. "Where are you going? I didn't give you permission to leave yet! You haven't given my offer proper consideration! At least think about it!"

Maggie turned to Gallen. "Wait a minute."

Gallen looked down the stairs at her. She gazed up at him, confusion showing in her face

"Gallen, he's right."

"Right?" Gallen asked. "To be manipulating his children this way?"

"No, he's right . . . to be fighting. Maybe his work won't do any good. Maybe it will come to nothing. But at least he is trying, and if we stayed here to work with him, we would be fighting the Dronon. You're the one who always wants to fight."

She let the words hang in the air. For weeks they had been arguing this point. Gallen was tired of running. He wanted to fight the Lords of the Seventh Swarm. But he couldn't challenge them without Maggie at his side. If such a fight would risk only their own lives against the Dronon, Gallen suspected that Maggie would stand beside him in such a battle, and they'd live free—or die together. But Maggie had a child in her belly. They couldn't jeopardize the babe. So Gallen had agreed to run with her, to hide, until after the child was born.

But now she was telling him that they could make a stand here. They could fight the Dronon from here. She wanted to accept Felph's offer.

She touched her own belly, feeling the heaviness of the child growing in her. From the top of the stone stairway, Gallen looked down into the dark hole, the ancient stone Qualeewooh ruins, where Felph stood in the darkness holding a glow globe, the light faintly playing upon the gloriously beautiful faces of his children.

Maggie said softly, "I have one more question before we decide whether to accept employment. Lord Felph, why do your children all wear Guides. Why do you keep them enslaved?"

Felph stammered, "Freedom is such an important thing, a tool that is used for ill as often as good. I want them to value it, to learn to use it correctly. So I give them only as much as I am certain they can handle. In time, when I trust them, I will remove all restraints."

Gallen considered this. Maggie abhorred the Guides. She'd lived with their restraints under Lord Karthenor.

"Freedom is such an important thing," she said, "that I fear even *you* should not be its arbiter. How can they learn to use a tool they do not hold? Give your children their freedom, and perhaps they will learn as much from its misuse as they will from its proper use."

Her words seemed to stun Felph, for he stood gaping at her, considering her proposal. Maggie continued, "You told Gallen that he could name any price for his labor. Here is the coin I desire: I can persuade Gallen to stay and work for you on one condition. So long as we choose to remain here, you will remove the Guides from your children."

"In time—in a hundred years or so they may be ready—" Felph stammered.

"We don't have a hundred years for them to learn!" Maggie said. "You imagine that the Dronon will be here in five hundred years, but the Dronon have built keys for the world gates. They're here in the Carina Galaxy now."

Lord Felph, master of Ruin, gave a strangled little cry of astonishment, then dropped his glow globe so that it clattered on the stones as its light grew dim.

Dooring never got much respect from Lord Felph. Ignored half the time, worked like a slave the rest. But today . . . today had been a nightmare—organizing a sumptuous dinner for the entire planet, one that Lord Felph promptly sabotaged, followed by a trip to chauffeur the new employees via florafeem, followed by a late night of minor surgeries to remove Felph's children's Guides. Afterward he'd had to clean the dining halls, and, last of all, he now stood before Gallen's ship, the *Nightswift*, which only moments before had been flown to Felph's hangars on autopilot.

It wasn't enough to be Felph's personal valet; Dooring had the misfortune of being the planet's official dockmaster. As such, his obligations were simple. He had to verify that the ship didn't carry any contraband, and that it was properly registered.

The job only took a few minutes.

Using a keycard, he verified to the ship's AI that he was the dockmaster, then entered the ship. The *Nightswift* was a fast little personnel ship. The kind of thing that only the very wealthiest people could afford.

The inside was plush—plump couches, a fashionable flower arrangement on a small table, large staterooms.

No one on Ruin lived in such luxury. Indeed, most folks on planet couldn't dream of ever buying passage off-world. Dooring wondered. Gallen and Maggie were seeking jobs with old mad Felph when, if they had half the brains of a wetland mudsucker, they'd hop in their ship and fly off.

Dooring nosed around through the staterooms for a few minutes, studying the few possessions Gallen and the others had brought.

He checked the cargo hold; it was nearly empty.

He went to the ship's registry terminal and requested information on the ship's registration and passenger logs.

He discovered that the ship was registered as a government-owned vehicle. Not a private ship at all. That was odd.

The news sent a little flutter in Dooring's stomach. For a long moment, he wondered what to do. Gallen hadn't identified himself as a government agent. As a Lord Protector, it was quite possible that he would be a government agent, but then he would be assigned a post.

Was he traveling undercover?

Yet he seemed to have no destination in mind, not if he were willing to stay here and work for Felph.

No, there was something curious about Gallen. Dooring had seen the fear in Maggie's face earlier in the evening, when Rame had asked what brought them all to Ruin. She'd been terrified to the core of her soul.

She's running from something, Dooring decided. Perhaps they were all running from something. Maybe this Gallen wasn't even a Lord Protector, but only wore the stolen mantle of some dead man.

Dooring wondered: could the ship be stolen?

There was no ansible available on planet, but this ship had one. Dooring went to the ansible, requested a "security priority one" transmission, so that the ship's AI would automatically delete any record of his call after it was made, then sent a broadband message across the cosmos, alerting authorities in the Milky Way that here on Ruin, a world in the Carina Galaxy, he had discovered a certain Lord Protector named Gallen O'Day flying what appeared to be a stolen spaceship. He sent the ship's registration numbers along with the planetary coordinates, and sat back. Even at speeds much faster than light, the message would take a couple hours to reach the Milky Way.

Dooring didn't want to wait for a reply. It was late, late, and his sweet wife Keri waited in bed.

Still, Dooring felt satisfied. If Gallen was hiding from someone, for whatever reason, Dooring had just blown the lad's cover.

Wouldn't it be grand, Dooring thought, if I caught this fellow in some scheme. Perhaps then Lord Felph would give me some respect.

Dooring smiled to himself, satisfied, as he exited the ship.

*T*he night Lord Felph released her, Hera shook from head to toe in anticipation. The heavens did not thunder, the rocks did not cry out. Yet it was such a momentous event in her life, it seemed odd to Hera that all nature did not take notice.

Felph and Dooring had come to her room, and, with Zeus at her side, Felph had Hera sit in a chair before her vanity. Chandeliers of green brass hung above Lord Felph like vines, and the glow globes in them suspended in the air like pale lavender honeysuckle. The walls in this room tonight all displayed three-dimensional images of a tropical glade in shades of deep green, as if they stood in a vast garden of mangrove under the moonlight, with water glinting from distant pools.

Hera felt as if she were in an enchanted forest, then Dooring brought out the Guide extractor from its case. The device was a simple rod in shape—thin, like a long splinter of silver. A magic wand.

With this Felph touched her Guide on the central gem, on her forehead, and the AI quit sending its pulses through Hera's nervous system, released control of her muscles. She seemed to relax more deeply than ever before. It was as if all her life she'd been tense, expectant, and now she eased totally into a plush, soothing couch.

After he'd freed Hera, Felph then freed Zeus. There was fear in Felph's eyes as he did so, yet Zeus only smiled when the deed was finished.

Yet if the heavens did not thunder at her release, certainly the world changed profoundly. Hera did not notice it all at once. The first clues came as she and Zeus undressed, prepared for bed.

Zeus stood before the mirror on his vanity, removing his dinner jacket, putting away the platinum and Tanzanite pin he'd worn in his lapel. He'd been prattling, and Hera had been so preoccupied with her thoughts as she took off her makeup that she didn't notice the turn in the conversation.

Zeus said, "I don't know why father insists on hiring these off-worlders. It's their mantles he wants, not the people under them, eh? Put on a Lord Protector's mantle, and I'd be a Lord Protector myself."

Hera said, between wiping off her eye shadow, "I doubt he'd sell it. You can't buy a Lord Protector's mantle."

"If he didn't sell, we could always take off his head. The mantle would make a fine little basket to hold it in, don't you think?"

Hera turned and stared at him. He'd never made such a tasteless jest, never spoken that way before. But then, perhaps he'd never been free to do so. Her husband had worn a Guide all his life, and until this moment, Hera had believed that she loved him, that she loved Zeus desperately despite his penchant for adultery. Now she just stared at him in wonder, not knowing what to say.

Zeus was gazing into the mirror, his long dark hair swept back over his muscular shoulders, staring intently at his own reflection, at eyes so dark and penetrating that it was like gazing at holes in the sky. He stared through the mirror, into some scene imagined; his lips curled in a sardonic grin.

Who are we? Hera wondered, suddenly feeling odd. The room was familiar, with its separate vanities and wardrobes, the enormous bed where they'd made love so many thousands of times. But the people in the room, Zeus and herself, were not familiar.

When she was a child, Hera had once asked Felph why she wore a Guide. He'd told her that all princes and princesses wore crowns. For years after, she'd always wanted to believe that the Guide made her special. But she never felt special. The Guide had only made her a slave, controlled her thoughts, ordered her perceptions, stimulated her emotions. It had made her a stranger to herself.

Hera had not chosen to marry Zeus, not really. As a child, she'd been enamored of him, and once when she was twelve, he'd lured her to a garden, and there he'd raped her. Afterward, she felt it was her fault. She forgave him, and in time grew to love him inestimably.

Lord Felph had created her to be Zeus's wife, had given her to him. Her Guide had not allowed her to love another, to think wantonly of another man.

So Hera loved Zeus as perfectly as one person could love another. She craved his presence. She admired his strength. She ignored his faults. She forgave his infidelities.

And Zeus loved her in return, in his way. It was true that Lord Felph, acting from some motive Hera did not understand, had given Zeus more freedom than he allowed his other creations. Zeus's Guide had let him lust after other women. Indeed, Hera wondered if his Guide had not even encouraged him to seek their affections.

While Hera's Guide held her prisoner in her rooms, Zeus would sneak from the palace to visit his paramours.

Yet Zeus always returned. Lord Felph had given Hera a special beauty that had always drawn Zeus back no matter how many times he loved other women. Perhaps it was her beauty. Perhaps his Guide had made him return. Hera wanted to believe he would have come back to her in any event.

I should test him, Hera thought. This stranger, my husband. Now that he does not wear a Guide, I should test him.

Hera got up from her vanity, turned her back so that Zeus would not see her face, and stood looking out the high, arched window. Brightstar sailed over the deep valleys, falling like an enormous diamond through sapphire skies. Hera's tower looked down seven hundred meters to a lower level of the palace and the fields beyond.

She opened the window. Secreted in terrace gardens two hundred meters below were beds that teemed with roses and orchids, Japanese plum and lavender. A gust of cool wind brought the fragrance to her window.

Hera tasted the scent of flowers on the wind. Smiled. This is a fertile place in the desert, she thought. Fertile lands, fertile minds plotting about how to be more fertile. She did not have to reflect to discern the source of Zeus's anxiousness. "You looked . . . irresistible, tonight."

He shot her a brief but fetching smile in the mirror, used his toes to push his shoes off his feet.

"You did not need to impress me. Was it Maggie you were after?"

"You know I love only you," Zeus protested. He stood before the mirror, naked now, and began cleaning off his own makeup. "Maggie . . . sounds too much like *maggot.* Who would want to make love to a maggot? Besides, she is pregnant." Hera knew he wanted Maggie by the way he heaped on insults.

"I don't know," Hera demurred. "She has red hair. No one else on Ruin has red hair. . . . That would be enchanting, and she is only a few months along. Not overly large yet. Do not think of her as pregnant, think of her as fertile, a ripe melon full of sweet fruit, ready to burst. Perhaps she is lusty, too, a woman of passion. She is not from this world. Who can guess what secrets she knows for pleasing a man?"

"Yes, well apparently she pleases one man," Zeus said. "What of him?"

"A husband is but a nuisance. Perhaps while you divert yourself with Maggie, he would be entertained by me?" Zeus knew Hera had never hungered for another man, not so long as she'd worn her Guide, so she was quick to add, "Gallen seems very bold, and handsome."

Zeus turned, raised his right brow. "Do I hear lust in your voice?" He affected concern, but his voice hinted at eagerness, as if she would agree to a swap.

Tonight, he was saying, perhaps we could put off our long feud, our petty rivalries? Tonight, perhaps, you will let me enjoy my decadence?

Of course, Hera could not agree to that. It was a game to him, chasing other women. He, Herm, and Arachne all played the "Great and Dreadful Game," a contest where points were awarded for various feats of manipulation. Zeus's philandering was part of the Game to him.

But it was not a game to Hera. It seemed a matter of life and death. If Zeus bedded a woman, for a moment he would be able to celebrate the points he scored. But if Hera blocked his tryst, she not only robbed him of his damnable points, she won a reprieve from the ache his infidelities caused.

I can't let him enjoy his decadence, but at least I can *feign* to do so, she thought. Tonight I'll unbalance Zeus. "Perhaps, now that we no longer wear our Guides, we will be free to put aside our jealousies?" she said with a hint of petulance. Zeus's expression of pleasant surprise gratified her no end, encouraged her a bit more. After all, if he was a stranger to her now, she was as much one to him. Hera affected a breathless, pleading tone. "You've sported with enough women; certainly you cannot object if I choose a man?"

Zeus put a hand on his hip, suddenly tense. He was possessive and would not like the idea of her sleeping with another. Yet the idea of truce tempted him. "So, you want to sleep with this Milk?" He snorted the term "Milk" in derision, as locals often did when speaking of people from the Milky Way. "That . . . would be your affair," he said, turning away, feigning disinterest. "I would not come between you. In fact, it could be entertaining to see if you can lure him to your bed."

Hera laughed. "If? You wonder *if* I can do so? I have my attractions." He watched her in the mirror. She smiled at him, pulling at the vee in the neck of her low-cut evening gown. Hera was beautiful. How could she not be? The greatest body sculptors in the universe had designed her.

"Seduction is an art"—Zeus shrugged—"one you have not bothered to acquire."

His condescending tone hurt her. You lout, she thought. You have no idea how I play you! How many times have I had to draw you back into my arms?

"Then you don't mind if I bed the Lord Protector?" she said flatly.

"Ah, you don't have to be hurt," Zeus soothed. "I mean no disrespect. You're lovely beyond all women, Hera. How could this cretin not be allured by your"—he waved toward her chest—"obvious charms." He added, "Besides, if you have difficulty attracting the prey, I can advise you."

"Thank you. I'm sure I don't need a coach."

Zeus glanced at her, a puzzled expression. "Sport with him if you like, but don't become attached. Skills are so . . . easily learned. If he does something you like, you will, of course, teach me?"

"As surely as you have taught me the things you've learned abroad," Hera responded. She went to the window, gazed out. She did not want Zeus to see her face, red with anger. She wanted him to imagine she was anxious for the escapades to begin. She'd known all along that Zeus would try to seduce Maggie. It really did not matter whether Maggie was married or not, pretty or not, pregnant or not—Zeus collected lovers the way settlers on Ruin collected spirit masks from dead Qualeewoohs.

For years now, Hera had suffered humiliation at Zeus's hands. Seldom had she been able to take much vengeance. Now Zeus would pay. He could not suspect the humiliation she would heap on him. Hera almost felt sorry for Zeus, so handsome, with eyes smoldering from his desire. Almost she felt sorry.

E i g h t

*T*en weeks after he'd confirmed Maggie's scent to Lord Karthenor, Thomas's captors roused him from sleep and hustled him outside. He stood blinking in the cool morning sunlight. The day looked different than he remembered, the skies too purple. Such was the atmosphere of Fale. Thomas felt surprise at his surroundings—palm trees and groves of strange fruits. Bright parrots squawked among the green shadows. Nothing like the landscape where he'd been abducted months before. Nothing like home.

Lord Karthenor was nowhere to be seen, but two of his men had prepared airbikes and packs out behind the house, in a green glade. Three bikes sat by, slick silver things with winglike stabilizers front and back.

Thomas wanted to run, struggled to run, but the Guide affixed to the base of his skull kept him in place. Still, he was relieved when his captors removed his shackles and handcuffs. They did not speak to him. They treated him as a *thing* to be prodded and moved about, much as any other piece of equipment.

Lord Karthenor appeared from a door at the back of the house. He and his men wore dark robes of brown, faces hidden by the golden masks of Fale, which gave off their own dim light. Karthenor addressed Thomas, "Greetings. The sunlight should do you some good, don't you think? You're looking rather pale after months in the basement."

Thomas could not answer. His Guide did not permit him to speak. Karthenor's questions were not meant to elicit a response, only to torment.

"Perhaps you are curious where we're going? We've located Maggie. She's jumped off the gated worlds, and we've run her aground in the Carina Galaxy. She believes she is safe, beyond the range of Dronon ships. But we have a surprise for her."

Karthenor smiled. "Here, have a seat on the airbike, in back. You can ride with me."

Thomas could think about running, could dream of knocking his captors in the head and darting into the jungle, but the Guide would not let him. He could not move a muscle without Karthenor's command.

So he mounted the bike behind Karthenor and sat like a bag of parsnips on the airbike as it skipped along the ground to a distant world gate.

So, Thomas's betrayal would bear fruit. Thomas abhorred the thought. He wished he could kill Karthenor. Running from the man would do no good. He had to fight.

Yet the Guide held Thomas prisoner in his own body. Perhaps that was the greatest torture of all, to sit behind Karthenor, smelling the scent of the man's dark robes, while Thomas imagined how he could unclasp his hands, reach up, and throttle Karthenor.

Thomas struggled to control one hand; he needed but squeeze with two fingers. He concentrated till sweat poured from his brow, and his whole body trembled. All during the two-hour trip to the world gate, he fought, then wrestled even harder as the airbikes carried them through the portal between worlds.

Thomas did not understand the gates. He knew that for a moment he became incorporeal. The tiniest fragments of his body were somehow tossed through a hole in time and space, so they landed on a far world.

Thomas hoped that in that moment of travel, he would be free, he would be able to lift his hands and strangle Karthenor. Or perhaps he would stick his hand in Karthenor's robe and draw the weapon this evil lord had secreted there. Thomas knew little about guns, but he had no doubt that the bulge he felt in Karthenor's chest holster carried something deadly.

Still, when they passed between worlds, Thomas could not move.

On Tremonthin they zipped over hills green with a stubby growth of spring grass, a dismal land of rain and clouds. Oak trees sat in groves in the distance, until at last Karthenor found some muddy roads, rutted from carriage tracks.

Karthenor and his cohorts seemed pleased by this discovery, and they followed the course of the road, whipping past carriages and oxcarts. The locals were much like people from Thomas's home—plain folks in simple cloth of their own making, many wearing swords. They passed stone houses with thatched roofs, screamed through the narrow streets of towns.

For hours their journey dragged, as daylight waned.

The locals were shocked at the sight of the airbikes, and many shouted and pointed.

It was not the ignorant wailing of those who believed they saw de-mons—as would have accompanied their appearance on Thomas's own home world. Instead, the airbikes caused outrage. By riding them, Thomas's captors proved they were criminals, and many shouted, "Out, get out of here with those things!"

Some locals tossed rocks as Karthenor passed, and late in the evening, when a rock finally connected lightly with Karthenor's shoulder, the Lord spun his airbike around and confronted the man, a simple farmer with long yellow hair who'd been herding a flock of sheep down a narrow mountain road. Up above them, a tiny stone home sat, smoke curling up from its chimney.

The man stood his ground, holding a shepherd's crook up as if it were a quarterstaff. "Off with you, man!" the shepherd yelled, but fear showed in his eyes. "Look what you've done! Your damned machines have scattered my sheep!" Indeed, a dozen muddy ewes leapt up the hillside, running even now.

Karthenor offered no word of apology. Instead, he simply breathed angrily, "You *hit* me!"

The shepherd looked away guiltily. "Sorry," came a lame apology.

"Indeed, you shall be," Karthenor raged, his voice suddenly loud. He reached into his robe, pulled his gun. Thomas could not stop him. As Karthenor drew his weapon and aimed, Thomas struggled to move his hand, to unclasp his fingers and spoil the man's aim. But Karthenor had ordered Thomas to hold on earlier in the day. The Guide allowed nothing more.

As Karthenor took aim, the shepherd's mouth opened in an O of surprise, and his eyes grew wide. Perhaps he was too frightened to run, for he merely stood.

Thomas trembled with the effort to unlock his fingers. His chest heaved, and his breath came ragged.

Almost, Thomas imagined he was able to unlock his fingers; almost he thought he'd managed to open them.

Then the weapon discharged. It made an odd plunking noise, like a stone dropping cleanly into water, and the shepherd's right leg collapsed. Thomas saw no blood, heard no cracking of bones. Yet it seemed obvious the bones of the shepherd's legs had shattered in a dozen places, for when the shepherd fell, the leg twisted grotesquely.

The shepherd cried out in pain and dropped faceup in the muddy road. Karthenor whispered to Thomas, "Let go of me, I have a matter to attend."

Thomas released his grip, sat astride the airbike. By now, Karthenor's cronies, who had fallen behind, suddenly rounded a bend a quarter mile back.

Up a couple hundred yards ahead, at the little farmhouse, a young woman opened the door, stood looking down the hill, a wailing child in her arms. She bounced the toddler on one hip, gazing down at Karthenor curiously.

Thomas realized that from her vantage, she could not see the farmer lying in the road. A small slope obscured her view.

Karthenor stood, stretched his muscles, looked about. This was a lonely stretch of road, miles from the nearest town. The sun was nearly down, and shadows crept along the hillside.

"Madam, could we trouble you for some hospitality, tonight?" Karthenor called up the hill. "We need a place to sleep."

The woman was obviously frightened. Her face paled, and she looked about. "I—I suppose I could get you some food. There's room in the shed out back. Have you seen my husband? I thought I heard him yell."

Karthenor pointed over the ridge. "Your husband is chasing sheep. Seems they got away."

She nodded uncertainly. She had full breasts, a narrow waist. Her thin yellow cotton dress was worn from too much use. The child screamed and twisted in her arms, leaning his head back to nurse.

Karthenor studied her approvingly, licked his lips, then he and his men advanced.

Thomas was not shocked at what happened next. Dismayed, yes, but not shocked. It was to be expected from men like Karthenor.

Thomas had heard of such evils in his lifetime.

Karthenor showed him nothing new.

Yet afterward, Thomas was horrified to the core of his soul. He was not horrified by what Karthenor did, but by the way that Karthenor used him— Thomas—used his hands to do his dirty work.

When Karthenor and his men raped the young mother, Karthenor ordered Thomas first to hold her down. She submitted to the indignities Karthenor heaped upon her, biding her time, hoping her husband would save her.

But just as the first of Karthenor's men nearly finished, the woman's wounded husband began to scratch at the door and call for help. He must have regained consciousness, dragged himself uphill on his elbows.

Karthenor opened the door, pulled the shepherd in, and propped him in a corner. The fellow's face was a mask of pain and horror, scratched by briars, smeared with grime. He lay, breathing shallowly, unable to move or fight, and his mind retreated from the scene before him, till sometime in the night, he died.

That was the worst of it, how a husband paid for his meager attack by watching Karthenor's men rape his wife. Thomas wished to God that Karthenor would just kill the man quickly. Thomas could do nothing to help these people. He struggled to cry out, to run. The Guide would not let him.

As Karthenor's men came back to finish raping the woman, she decided to struggle. She now knew her husband could not save her; perhaps she believed Karthenor would kill her in any event.

Thomas had been holding her wrists, and he tussled with her. Her hands were thin, but strong from hard labor, and Thomas had been weakened by sitting imprisoned so long. She broke free for a moment, scratched at the eyes of her rapist, and Karthenor's man responded with a vicious uppercut to the jaw, bouncing the back of her head against the floor, hard.

At the far side of the room, Karthenor sat near the fireplace, holding the woman's child in his lap. The babe was oblivious to the struggle and the scene of horror going on around him, and instead seemed fascinated by Karthenor's golden mask. The lad kept touching Karthenor's chin and laughing.

Karthenor had not seen the woman go limp. He said softly, "If she will not give it to you, just take it. Thomas, strangle her for me."

All day, Thomas had worked to free his fingers, had wanted to strangle Karthenor. Now, despite his deepest hopes, the fingers seemed to work with a will of their own.

When the woman went limp in his hands, Thomas could not release her neck. Karthenor had ordered him to strangle her, and the Guide forced Thomas to continue the work until ordered to stop.

Karthenor came and sat beside Thomas at that moment, sat down, holding the babe, who in the silence, in the warmth of the fire, simply lay back and studied Karthenor's glowing face, like a pale moon in the darkness.

Karthenor watched Thomas with a furrowed brow. "Do you know why I hate you, why I make you do these things?" Karthenor said at last.

"No," Thomas answered, surprised his Guide left him free enough to speak. Perhaps the Guide considered the question to be more than rhetorical.

"I hate you . . . because you are Maggie's uncle, and she has undone me. I was a powerful man under the Dronon's rule, one of their most trusted servants. They made me wealthy and came to my call. But Maggie tried to take that from me when she killed the Lords of the Sixth Swarm.

"Now I am a hunted man."

Karthenor stared at the dead woman's face. A bit of spittle had escaped her lips—Thomas was still choking her—and Karthenor wiped it off with his finger. "She was such a sweet girl. Her husband shouldn't have angered me. I have no patience with such.

"May I tell you a secret, Thomas?"

Thomas did not answer. His Guide saw no need for it.

"This woman, this child, this man"—Karthenor waved expansively, the folds of his dark robe billowing out as if he wore priest's garb—"they don't matter. They don't matter in the least. And the worst of it is, they have chosen not to matter."

He waited, as if for Thomas to argue, but the Guide would not let Thomas speak.

"You see," Karthenor said, "this man and woman are what we call Backwards. They have rejected technology. They're doubling back on the path of evolution. They live here in this . . . house of stone and twigs, and they've chosen to do nothing with their lives. In two hundred years, no one will remember their names. They have taken their free agency, and they've chosen oblivion. It makes no difference whether they live or die. So, I've chosen to kill them. But this child—this sweet child shall live. In the morning, when we leave, I'll take it with us, and we'll dispose of it on some other world, where its life *might* take on meaning.

"You can let the woman go now, Thomas. She's quite dead."

Thomas released the woman's neck, and she fell back to the dirt floor of her home. Thomas wanted to beg her forgiveness, tell her he was sorry. But it would not matter.

"Let me see your hands," Karthenor whispered. Thomas held them up for inspection.

"Would you look at that? Months of incarceration, and still you have calluses on your fingers. You must be quite the musician, Thomas Flynn. Did you see the lute hanging from the rafters? Do you know how to play it?"

Thomas looked up. Indeed, he hadn't seen it. "No. Yes," he answered both questions in turn, as his Guide demanded.

"Calluses," Karthenor whispered. "You see, Thomas, that's why I like you so much better than I like *them*." The barest nod indicated the dead shepherd and his wife. "You are a man who works, who strives to attain. I've heard you singing. You've a fine voice, a great talent. The universe is a better place because you are here.

"You could have stayed in your own world. You could have lived happily in Tihrglas. A talented man like you could have retired in some style. But you chose to leave that all behind, to grasp for something more. I like that in you, Thomas."

Thomas wanted to spit in Karthenor's face. The applause of this monster was an outrage.

"I see by your grimace that you do not care for me," Karthenor said. "It does not matter. You and I are not so unalike, regardless of what you think. After all, I have questioned you under the influence of my Guide. I know your secret heart. You are a man who uses people, then discards them. You care nothing for your fellowmen. You hold them in low regard. Perhaps not to the degree that I do, but you are not much better.

"Still, you make the unimportant ones serve you. You're smart enough to do that, at least, but I fear, Thomas, that you lack vision.

"So I'll teach you what the Dronon have taught me. You see . . . this farmer, his wife—they served no purpose. But you and I are people who matter. We are the dreamers, the achievers, those who grasp. And by letting them serve us"—he waved at the corpse of the dead woman—"in however small a manner, we suddenly have given meaning to their meaningless existence."

Karthenor looked into Thomas's eyes and said, "Tell me all that you are thinking. Speak the truth, Thomas."

"You're a monster! You're a monster to use such cold logic against me!"

"Yes?" Karthenor said.

Then, against every inclination Thomas had toward decency, he confessed, for his Guide uttered words he would never dare, "And yet, and yet, in one thing—you are right. We are much alike. Both of us take what we want from the world, in an effort to live our dreams. I debauch women and leave them alive to face their guilt. Perhaps, once, because of my callousness, I left a woman to die. . . ." Even with the Guide on, Thomas could speak no more.

"Often farmers will plow a field, then leave it fallow after," Karthenor said. "To leave behind the women you have debauched makes sense, for one might always return and gain more service from them.

"But let me enlarge your vision," Karthenor said. "You are a simple man, from a backward planet, so I will try to speak in analogies you can comprehend: when a man owns a pig on your world, does he not use the whole creature? It is true that he feeds it, and cleans its pens, and gives it water—so that the casual bystander might be led to believe that he is a servant to his hog.

"But such a bystander would be shortsighted, wouldn't he? No, the farmer has a greater goal. As the pig matures, he uses its dung to enrich his fields. He might let it root in stony ground, so that later it is easier to plant in that field. And when the pig is ready to slaughter, the farmer takes its flesh to eat, its skin to wear, its intestines to make casings for his sausage. He will eat the pig's stomach, heart, liver, kidneys, brain, ears, blood. He will boil the bones to make soap, and feed scraps of the hog to his dogs. Those parts he does not find a use for, he will bury in the ground to fertilize his fields. Nothing is wasted. Do you understand? Nothing!"

Thomas nodded in answer to the question.

"Now, the Dronon are wise in this respect. They use their own people, use them as efficiently as we use hogs. They put them to work, demanding their time, talent, and effort. No Dronon life is wasted, no moment left unaccounted for. And because of this, this great secret, the Dronon as a species shall outmatch mankind. We are ephemeral. We are fog that they shall pass through on their way to glory. So, unless you wish to be destroyed, this is the lesson you must learn from the Dronon: the proper *use* of mankind!"

Even had Thomas been able to respond, he would have been unable to speak. Karthenor's cold wisdom astonished and horrified him. It was not the ruthlessness of his logic: it was the honesty of it, the simplicity. He had never considered mankind in such a light, and Karthenor's vision seemed to pierce a veil of darkness in Thomas's mind. Yes, he almost wanted to say, yes, that is how it should be. A life should not be wasted. Yes, I want to live in a world where life has meaning.

Yet he could not. He could not look down upon man as such an ignoble thing.

Karthenor clapped Thomas on the shoulder and smiled. "I shall make a Dronon of you yet, Mr. Flynn!

"Now, Thomas, I want you to sing for me, and for the boy here," Karthenor ordered, getting up, removing the lute strap from a peg. He handed the instrument to Thomas—an admirable piece with a front of fir and a sound box of rosewood. It had been tuned by someone with a fine ear. Somehow, Thomas could not imagine the shepherd having so fine a touch with an instrument. It had to have been the wife, with her delicate bones and her long, sensitive fingers.

And all the clear arguments that he'd just heard issue from Karthenor's lips suddenly collapsed in on themselves. This woman they had murdered played the lute. This woman had played the lute, and for all Thomas knew, she might have been the greatest composer who had ever lived.

Karthenor had abused her, treating her worse than Thomas had ever treated any whore who might give it to him cheap, standing against the wall in some waterfront fishing village.

If Karthenor had really believed what he said about understanding the proper use of mankind, he would have found better use for this woman. The truth was that he took from her only what he wanted.

Thomas felt surprised at himself. For one moment, he had almost been deceived into believing that he and Karthenor shared an insight, belonged to some great fraternity of "Those who matter." It was an alluring lie.

As Thomas tested the instrument, plucking the lute strings so the clear notes reverberated over the room, Karthenor amended his commandment, "Sing for me tonight, Thomas. Sing songs that are sweet, so the child will sleep well. Sing the most beautiful tune you know, and sing it better than you ever have before."

So Thomas sang the ballad of Tara Gwynn, a love song for the first girl he'd ever loved, the one he loved the best. She'd died giving birth to his child. It was a piece he'd been working on in secret for many years, and he'd hoped that when he'd honed its rough edges, it would gain him some notoriety. It was to be his masterwork.

But as he sang, he did not sing for his lost love. Instead, he sang for the woman who lay dead at his feet. He sang of his loss for her, so that tears filled his eyes.

Perhaps it was not the most beautiful piece in Thomas's repertoire, though it was close, but it was the one he felt most deeply now. It shamed him to the core of his soul that on this night, of all nights, as the colored moons of Tremonthin crept out over the pine trees, shining through the windows of the cabin like ornamental lanterns, and the owls hooted in the spring woods, and Thomas had just killed a woman—it shamed him that the Guide made Thomas obey Karthenor's order.

He sang the sweetest song he knew, and he sang it more hauntingly than he ever had sung it before, better even than he believed he could have sung it.

Then he vowed never to sing it again. So what if his masterwork went unappreciated? This shall be my sacrifice, he told himself, to atone for my conceit.

For his part, Karthenor seemed to enjoy the ballad. It was hard to tell. The Lord of Aberlains wore his golden mask of Fale that glowed dimly, somehow baffling the eye in this darkness. Still, his face seemed unlined by care. The child in his arms slept peacefully. He and his men sat on couches or on the floor, and as the fire crackled in the fireplace, the firelight twisting among the logs, they stared away, enrapt by the power of Thomas's voice.

When Thomas finished his song, Karthenor ordered another, and another, until Thomas found himself singing long into the night.

When Karthenor was ready for sleep, he bent near Thomas's ear and whispered, "Well done, my friend. For this night's work, I give you a gift. I promise that when this work is done, when the accounts are settled and your niece has paid her dues, that one thing will I grant you: though my Dronon masters slaughter a whole world, one man will be left standing. I grant you your life."

Thomas did not answer. His Guide would not let him respond.

*T*hat night, as Orick slept with one arm resting over Tallea's neck, his paw planted firmly on her snout, he dreamed a dream that would change his life.

He dreamed that he was riding a florafeem, sitting under a yellow silk pavilion as bright as the sun. The florafeem's whole body thundered as it hurtled through the air. It soared through dark skies like blue velvet. Stars and worlds swung through the wide heavens.

Orick stared at the passing worlds in awe, then looked around in the bright starlight at the back of the florafeem.

Earlier in the day, he'd been surprised at the creature. Just as a whale will have multitudes of barnacles making their home on its back, the florafeem served as home to many small creatures—grasping gray plants that looked like anemones, black wriggling beasts that at first appeared to be some dark running liquid but which were more like worms. Another form of life might have been some purple fuzzy hairs that sprouted from the florafeem's back, or it might have been a grassy covering. Alien insects, like the halves of walnut shells with a dozen tiny legs peeking out, scuttled about, feeding on the fuzzy hairs.

All of this was as it had been earlier in the day, but Orick heard a breeze, blowing through some leaves, and looked to his right. Where Maggie should have been sitting was a currant bush, and in it sat a dove made of twisting flames of green fire. As Orick became aware of the bird, he realized just how searing hot the dove might be. Instead of feathers, its plumage was made of light, the palest of emerald in color. Its eyes glowed red like live coals, and it wore a spirit mask on its face.

"Are you hungry, Orick, me lad?" the bird asked.

"Aye, I'm starving," Orick said. "Show me to the table, then get out of my way."

"Well, if you're really hungry, have at it, then," the dove told him.

Orick looked about on the florafeem, hoping to find something to his tastes, but there were no platters of food sitting about. Instead, Orick studied the florafeem's back, and all about him, in the dark grassy fuzz, he saw strange shapes: graceful birds on wide tan-and-green wings whipped past him, and Orick realized that these must be Qualeewoohs, though he'd never seen a live one before. Tiny people were also making their way through this furry jungle, slicing at hairs with machetes. Tallea was there, a tiny bear wandering over a wilderness of alien skin, between a herd of crablike creatures. Then there were Dronon, Orick saw. Thousands of Dronon in the distance, crawling over the furze like black mantises, their mouthfingers clicking over voice drums as they spoke.

Orick saw nothing to eat, yet his stomach was in knots. "Where did you put the food?" Orick asked the dove.

"Why it's right in front of your nose, you doltish bear," the dove said. "Just kill something furry and swallow it down quick. It's just like eating squirrels. They might wiggle on the way down, but they taste *fine.*"

Orick stared at the tiny people, at the ratlike aliens, at the cruel Dronon, at Qualeewoohs and other things that wriggled like worms through the jungle of hair. Orick could tell these were sentient creatures all—there was too much wisdom in their eyes. But it wasn't their sentience that made the thought of eating them turn Orick's stomach. It was their repulsiveness. There was something dark and evil here. "Well, I'm not so hungry as all that," he grumbled. "I—uh—it wouldn't be proper to eat those dirty beggars."

"Why—'dirty beggars'?" the dove cried. "Look, you—I washed them myself just last week. You're not so much cleaner than them. You eat worms, don't you? And slugs and snails and dead things you find by the roadside? These are no more dirty than that. Be a good bear. Go ahead, eat one of 'em!"

Orick peered forward into the hairs of the florafeem. A little crablike thing scuttled away with knowing glances, but a languid girl Orick had known back on Tihrglas stood at the edge of a small clearing in the fuzz. She held a bottle of ale in one hand, and was staggering about drunkenly. "Eat me, Orick!" she called with a giggle. "What 'arm can a little soot do ya? Wheeeeee!" She tumbled drunk on her butt into a puddle of mud.

Indeed, as Orick took a closer look, he saw that all the creatures wandering the florafeem's back were sooty, stained, ruined. There were lewd women caked with rotting food. Smelly old men with greasy hair. And the Dronon. Orick could smell the biting tang of their stomach acids. Chewing one would be like eating a nest of ants in one bite.

Orick felt his stomach turn at the sight. The smell alone made him want to retch.

"Clean them, did you?" Orick complained to the dove. "I've never seen such a stinking conglomeration of ambulatory refuse. You could boil them in rainwater, and never get the first layer of muck off. I've seen hog's snot cleaner than that!"

"Come, my friend," the dove cajoled. Orick looked up. The dove blazed like a green sun. "No matter if they're filthy. Pick up one of the slimy things and swallow. You can even hold your nose as you do! Chase it down with whiskey afterward, and you'll hardly rue the bad taste!"

At the dove's words, some little people came from the woods at Orick's feet. One dirty little man turned ass-backwards and farted at the poor bear while others laughed and made rude noises. Qualeewoohs stuck out their foul purple tongues and rolled their orange eyes.

Orick's stomach was in knots, he felt so famished. He felt light-headed. Still, he couldn't abide the thought of eating one of those stinking aliens. "Look, you," Orick said, "it's not me that will be eating one of those malodorous pieces of animated offal. If you think I'm that hungry, you've got another think coming!"

"Ah, Orick," the fiery dove whispered, "what a thick head you've got. How can you say these poor brutes are dirty? What God has cleansed, how can you call it unclean?"

Orick looked back up to the dove, and suddenly the whole currant bush burst into flames. The flames were more than warm, they were a comfort, a blessing. They burned Orick to the core.

He woke gasping and looked about. Tallea slept beside him, and the hoverlamps above glowed dimly, still drifting up near the roof, so much like moons.

Orick lay wondering at his dream, filled with awe. The warmth he'd felt in his heart remained, the burning.

Always before when Orick had imagined entering the priesthood, he'd thought he would perhaps live in a quiet monastery, devoting his days to quiet contemplation of God's word. Now, though, he suddenly understood how mistaken he had been, understood why he'd never felt that his personal desire to enter God's service was quite the right thing to do. For months now he'd waited for God's spirit to confirm to him that his offering was acceptable.

But now a thrill ran through Orick, and he gazed up at the arching window, staring out at the stars. All of those worlds, all filled with heathens both human and alien.

Orick's eyes filled with tears of gratitude for the sudden realization that flowed into him. God had a glorious calling for Orick, more glorious than Orick could have ever conceived. It was a calling that would require all the labors of his heart, all the days of his life: Missionary to the Cosmos.

A ll the past night, the bright star guttered, like a white flame in the sky, outshining the moon and all other stars. Cooharah stared from his roost through the night, measuring the diameter of Brightstar against the width of Ruin's single small moon with its three bulges. It would have been difficult to roost on such a bright night. The stars themselves seemed dim under the dome of heaven. But Cooharah was not awake without cause. His was a quest that night, an attempt to discover direction from the stars.

Late in the night, near dawn, the path of the moon finally crossed the path of the distant bright star, and Cooharah saw the blazing white corona around the moon where light from the star leaked beyond the horizon of the moon. Cooharah let out a trill of triumph that split the air and reverberated off the rocks below his aerie, blasted over the tangled jungles below. Then he sang softly an ancient Qualeewooh teachsong,

> *"Bright star flies larger than the moon*
> *hurry the day, the hot drenching day.*
> *The bone years lie broken,*
> *forgotten, like fragments of shell*
> *amid our nests."*

Cooharah leapt from the circle of stones where he roosted, and for a while he floated out over the valleys below. A rich tangle of purplish bush lay far below him, and in the half-light he saw steam seeping up through the vegetation from the warm waters beneath.

A mistwife broke through the tangle, raising her long white tentacles a hundred meters into the air. From high above, the tentacles were beautiful, almost luminous things, waving in the breeze, tenderly probing the upper limbs of trees. But down in the tangle they would be deadly to anything that slept. The mistwife's strangling grip would pluck razor-fanged skogs from the trees as easily as Cooharah plucked boring weevils from his feathers when preening.

Indeed, as Cooharah wheeled lower over the tangle, he could hear the whistling cries of a hive of sfuz as they scurried over their webs from tree to tree, seeking escape. Their cries chilled Cooharah, for their whistles of terror were no different from their whistles of hunting, and all Qualeewoohs feared the sfuz. Crafty creatures, deadly hunters with their webs and snares and their quiet stalking.

In a few moments, once Cooharah had circled his aerie a few times and was certain that no sfuz were climbing the treacherous cliffs, Cooharah winged his way to his *cloo*, then dived, flapping his wings twice as he neared the opening, then dropping down to grasp the stone lip of his home with his heavy claws.

The cave was dark inside, but Cooharah could smell the warm spicy scent of decaying trammitroon leaves. Beneath it he detected the rich scent of his mate, Aaw, asleep in her nest. Her soft breathing resonated from the stone walls.

Cooharah tenderly went to his love and tapped her forehead, between her eyes, three times with his lower jaw.

It was a gesture of love that he'd never permitted himself to perform before, in all his long life.

Aaw's eyes snapped open, and Cooharah could see them, large in the darkness, a pale salmon in color. She stared at him in surprise.

He tapped her forehead again. "Open, open," he trilled the ancient words of ritual. "Two become one."

If Aaw had not been so surprised, she might have lowered her head and nipped the spirit mask on both Cooharah's cheeks, playing her part in the ancient ritual.

"Are you certain to the fourth degree?" she trilled instead. "The land lies wasted. The dew trees are drying, and we have only rocks to eat."

It was true. Both Qualeewoohs were starving. The ancient lake where their ancestors had hunted above the tangle was now dry, and the Qualeewoohs' prey, the skogs, were dying. There might be food aplenty in the tangles out over Ruin's shallow seas, but such food was impossible to reach—for the skogs that fed in the tangle above the ocean were so far from safe roosting sites that Cooharah and Aaw dared not hunt them.

"The bone years come to an end," Cooharah said. "Brightstar flies large. Soon, storms will wash all hunger from the heavens."

Aaw stared at him in disbelief, then looked out the oval opening of their *cloo*. She could see Brightstar flying large, as large as the moon—something her people had waited generations to see.

Aaw admitted, "The star is large, but do we dare bring a chick into the world?"

"We are old," Cooharah warbled. "Our feathers grow brittle. If we do not choose now to become one, we must choose to become empty, like the wind."

Aaw did not fear her extinction. Such was the curse of being born in the driest of the bone years. For ten generations her people had chosen to decrease their numbers. Aaw had never dared hope she would lay a fertilized egg of her own. But oh, how she yearned for it. With the drying of Stone Lake, and with her increased age, it had seemed that the chance would never come.

But now Cooharah solemnly stepped forward and tapped her forehead with his jaw again, three times. "Open, open. Two become one."

Tenderly she reached up and nipped the feathers at his cheek, just beneath his spirit mask, in ritual preening. Cooharah danced forward, snaking his long neck up beside hers.

She shook her tail feathers, pretending to lay an egg, and together the two Qualeewoohs began the long dance of life, enacting their hatchings, their years of learning, their hunts in the sky, their choosing of one another as eternal companions.

As the dance continued through the long night, unfamiliar hormones flowed into Aaw, making her dizzy, and she felt as if she floated through the room, until at last, just before dawn, she reached up and tapped Cooharah between the eyes with her own chin, saying, "Open, open, I am open."

Thirty years ago, Cooharah and Aaw had chosen one another for mates. Now, in the failing years of their lives, after decades of starvation and struggle, for the first time they consummated their love.

Later, her mate would carve the pictographs that commemorated this day into her spirit mask, then they would fly to the north, to far lands she'd only heard of in story, to look for a safe nesting ground beyond the drylands. But for now, she collapsed in easy joy.

E l e v e n

$\boxed{\it O}$ n the morning of his first full day of freedom, Zeus sat naked atop the east citadel of Felph's palace, watching Herm swoop and dive out over the east nature preserve.

Zeus sat naked because he was free to do so, his butt resting somewhat uncomfortably on the cold stone of a crenel, his elbows propped on the merlons at either side. His feet hung dangerously out over the citadel wall, a sloping drop of some three hundred meters.

The morning wind had a bite to it, but the dawn sun shining full on the matted hairs of his chest ameliorated the cold somewhat. Still, the only part of his body that felt truly warm was his head beneath his dark wavy hair.

Zeus could not stop laughing. He knew he sounded maniacal. Perhaps it was the glory of the day, or the lightness he felt with his Guide removed. Though the slim silver Guide had weighed only 180 grams, he now wondered how he had survived all these years, bowing beneath that onerous burden. So he laughed, and considered leaping from the palace walls to his death.

Why not? He was free. He could do anything, think anything.

Out over the garden preserve, Herm gave a whoop of delight, and hovered at the apex of his flight, a slender white spear in his right hand. His pinions flashed in the morning light, the undersides of his wings showing silver, then Herm dived, his wing tips back almost vertical, the spear thrusting down in both hands.

Zeus followed the line of attack to see why Herm rejoiced: a flock of skogs rose from the tangle below, a wedge of dark, compact creatures, flying so fast on their short wings they almost looked like cannonballs rather than something alive. Their vicious curling tusks seemed only to be smears of white.

It was a dangerous game Herm played. If he dived too soon, he would be hurled into their midst, and the skogs would flay him with their tusks. If he dived too slowly, he would end up behind the skogs, missing his prey. Only a perfectly timed thrust would win him a skog, and even then he would have to adjust to the added weight on his spear, try to avoid crashing headlong into the tangled limbs below.

Zeus howled in delight.

Herm flashed down toward the dark purple trees, intent on his prey. The skogs saw him, wheeled right.

With twitch of a wing tip, Herm corrected his course. Distances were deceiving. At first, Zeus imagined these were small skogs; but as Herm neared, Zeus realized they were full-sized—each large enough to make a fine meal for three days. Only now did Zeus see how swift was Herm's dive.

The skogs adjusted again at the last second, veering away. If Herm had been a diving raptor that relied on its talons, he'd have missed his prey. Instead, he thrust the white spear left, impaling a skog through the back.

Immediately, Herm tried to twist his wings, pull out of his dive, but the weight of the skog impaled on his spear threw him down, so he went crashing into the tangle.

Herm shrieked for help as he hit, and Zeus leapt up, whooping and clapping, "Wahooo, wahooo! You got one!"

But he celebrated too soon. Herm was two hundred meters out, three hundred down. Zeus had difficulty spotting him. Herm landed in the top branches of a whipparoong tree, with its platelike leaves. They cushioned his fall, and halfway hid the winged man, but suddenly Zeus heard a vicious bark, almost a hacking cough.

Herm scrambled to get out of the tree. The broad leaves swayed, alternately concealing Herm and revealing him.

The skog Herm had impaled thundered into the air, still trailing the spear, covered with gore—its own violet blood. The skog shrieked, then winged toward Herm, slashing with its razor-sharp tusks.

Herm dropped back in terror, ducking beneath it, struggling to stay aloft in the upper branches of the tree by bracing his wings against the foliage. He lost his footing, dropped between some branches. He covered his face with an arm, just as the skog slashed him.

Zeus bellowed and shook from a belly laugh. In a moment, the skog turned away. Herm had the presence of mind to grab the end of the spear, rip it free, and jab as the skog made a second charge. Quite by accident, Zeus felt sure, Herm impaled the beast under the right eye.

It seemed the skog was dead, but Herm cried in dismay. To the south, the flock had wheeled, and now the skogs flew swiftly toward Herm, barking in anger. Apparently the coughing and grunting sounds of battle made by one skog called the whole flock to its defense.

The settlers on Ruin had named the creatures skogs—a contraction of *sky* and *hogs*—because their tusks so resembled those of a pig. The skogs used their tusks to pierce the upper limbs of dew trees to get at the nectar beneath. Skogs tasted marvelous; like young pork marinated in fruity sweet sauce. On Ruin-they were considered a delicacy, but hunting them like this was foolhardy.

Zeus's throat grew tight as the skogs approached. The flock held at least twenty beasts. Herm had no way to protect himself from so many. If he lived through the attack, he'd be covered with scars. Almost, Zeus ran to get the medi-droid, but he decided to stay, to watch.

As the flock drew down, Herm struggled in the canopy of the trees, then folded his wings and dropped from sight.

The skogs slowed, as if considering whether to risk flying under the canopy to kill the winged man, then thought better of it. The skogs could fly well under the dark canopy of the tangle, but could also get trapped in the nets of a sfuz or find themselves struggling in the jaws of a grumpin. Besides, they could not save their comrade.

The skogs circled once, then veered, whining in grief.

Zeus waited for Herm to reappear, but the winged man did not come up. A soft gust of wind played over the trees, making their upper branches wave and bob. No sounds rose from the tangle.

Zeus called a dozen times, but got no answer. Zeus wondered if his brother had taken a worse wound from the skog than he'd imagined—a mortal wound? Perhaps he'd fallen through the first level of the canopy and broken a wing. Or maybe a sfuz had him. Heaven knew the devils could run along those tree limbs faster than any creature had a right to.

That was the problem on Ruin. Speed. Every predator on the planet moved faster than it had a right to.

At any rate, if Herm had fallen into a sfuz's web, he'd probably already be dead.

Zeus laughed. For years Herm had wanted to try spearing a skog from a full dive, but his Guide had always held him in check, making sure he didn't try anything too dangerous.

So of course Herm tried it this morning. It was a stupid way to die, but Zeus admired Herm's courage.

Zeus turned to go tell Felph that Herm had killed himself, when he heard a halloo.

Herm poked his head from the purple canopy, raised his spear, skog impaled. "Had to go down to fetch dinner!"

Herm struggled onto a limb, then jumped up, flapped his wings, and laboriously climbed into the air, carrying the skog. When he landed on the merlon beside Zeus, Herm's brow was covered in sweat. Purple leaves and bits of candy moss clung to him. His right arm bled profusely from a wicked gash that ran from wrist to elbow.

He tossed the spear to the stone roof, the bloody skog still twitching. The creature had a thick body, almost neckless, and a pudgy face with a jutting lower jaw that held two vicious tusks, each as long as a man's hand. The purple-black feathers on its back were thin as hair. Unlike many avians that lived in the tangle's canopy, skogs did not have hands at the apex of their wings—only a single vestigial claw, which the skog used for clinging to a tree while the creature burrowed for nectar. This particular specimen might have weighed fifteen kilos.

"Ah, that will make a fine dinner," Zeus said, stepping over to look into the creature's huge black eyes. He moved its head with his toe.

Herm laughed. He plopped down on a merlon and held his bleeding arm. "A real gentleman would rip off a piece of his clothing to make me a bandage— but then a real gentleman would be dressed in some sort of clothes in the first place."

Zeus leaned his head back and laughed. "If it's a bandage you want, I'll be happy to get you one."

He lurched forward and ripped off a swath of Herm's dirty tunic, so the winged man was now naked from the waist down. For a moment Zeus looked at his brother's organ, then jested, "If one of us must hang, then let us both hang together."

Herm laughed, looked at Zeus's organ, and said, "You call that hanging, oh shriveled one?"

"It's cold out here."

"Not that cold."

"Here now, let's fix you up. The loss of blood must be making you delirious if you think you're hanging any farther than me." Zeus wrapped the rag around Herm's wound, then tied both ends in a square knot—cinching it down harder than he needed, just to see Herm wince at the pain.

"There, that should save your life," Zeus grinned.

"A fine knot," Herm chuckled, wiping sweat from his brow with the back of his arm. "I didn't know you knew how to tie a knot."

"I am better at untying them." Zeus chuckled, rubbing his fingers together. "It builds dexterity—a trait one needs if one is to ever gain any degree of finesse at unfastening a woman's . . . uh, fastenings."

Herm climbed down from the merlon, leaned with his folded wings against the back of it, and shook his head. "Whew, I really am dizzy."

"Do you need a blood infusion?" Zeus asked.

"No, ah, I think I'm dizzy from love."

"Love?" Zeus asked. "You never speak of love. What, was one of those skogs more voluptuous than the others?"

"It's no skog that has my eye—it's the red-haired woman."

"Maggot?" Zeus asked in mock surprise. "You have your heart set on a woman? On a Lord Protector's wife?"

"Ah, yes," Herm laughed, his green eyes flashing. "Don't tell me you didn't notice her, too."

"Perhaps," Zeus admitted, "but mine is a professional interest. As a sampler of women, I'd like a taste of the fair Maggot. She does have a nice face."

"Hah," Herm laughed. "She has a face? I hadn't noticed. But those legs—I did not know the gods could make them so long. Do you think she has red hair all over?"

"Aye, she's a fine-looking woman," Zeus conceded.

Herm was eyeing Zeus's crotch. To his consternation, Zeus realized that the memory of Maggie—or perhaps Herm's description—was more arousing than he'd thought it would be.

Herm laughed, "So, the little wrinkled fellow has some life in him after all. And here I feared it had died."

"Not dead. It was merely resting. After last night, it deserved a good rest," Zeus groused.

"So you do want Maggie?" Herm asked. "I knew you would. Dangerous quarry, that one."

"No more dangerous than your skogs," Zeus said, and he saw from the veiled look in Herm's eyes that the winged man really hadn't been interested in Maggie. Indeed, Herm had only discussed the matter so he could arouse Zeus, forcing him to embarrass himself.

Herm had a devious mind, the trickster. Perhaps that is why Zeus liked him so much. Herm was better at the Great and Dreadful Game than Zeus. Herm resorted to craftiness when he wanted something, while Zeus tended to charge recklessly toward his goals, landing in more trouble than he'd like.

"Perhaps she is no more dangerous than my skogs, or perhaps she is. If you bed her, Gallen will kill you."

"If he finds out. Besides, it would be worth it, wouldn't it, to die between her legs?"

"You plan to bed her then?" Herm said.

Something in the tone of Herm's voice hinted at more than minor curiosity. It hinted at a proposal in the shaping, an offer to play the Game. "I'll poke her with *my* spear before you poke another skog with yours, oh mighty raptor."

Herm lifted his arm, looked at the bandage. The tan strip of tunic had soaked through with blood, and the wound was deep. It would be weeks in healing. "I'll be hunting skogs again before you know it, perfecting my technique."

"Technique? What part do you want to perfect, the part where you crash into trees, or the part where you defend yourself by throwing your arm into a skog's mouth?"

"Both." Herm laughed.

Just then, a service droid rolled up the entrance ramp to the top of the citadel and swerved toward them. "Zeus!" it called. "Your father requests your presence. He and Gallen are going on a minor expedition into the tangle, and would like you to accompany them."

Herm's green eyes flickered with interest. "Will Maggie be coming?"

"No," the droid answered.

"How long will they be away?" Herm asked.

"Three days," the droid said, rolling toward them.

"Ah, the poor woman," Herm whispered under his breath low enough so the droid's sensors wouldn't hear. "Who shall warm her bed while Gallen is gone."

"The Game is on?" Zeus mouthed.

"Three days, only," Herm whispered. "Three points if you bed the Lord Protector's wife—" he hesitated, then considered, "so long as you get her willingly."

Three points. At the moment, Herm was ahead in The Game by two points. If Zeus could bed Maggie willingly, he'd take the lead, and as a reward, he'd get to hold the bottle that held the Wind of Dreams. "How many points if I take her by force?" Zeus hissed.

The whole purpose of The Game was to entertain. Zeus would prefer to seduce the woman, thus getting the full value from the bet. But if he raped Maggie, he would have to suffer the consequences—death at Gallen's hands, perhaps; the entertainment value of *that* spectacle ought to be worth something to Herm.

"One point," Herm whispered.

Zeus smiled. Not enough to take the lead in The Game. Still, it was a free point, no matter what the outcome of his seduction attempt. Zeus whirled as the droid rolled near. "Tell Father I won't go with him. I'm staying home."

"I do not believe that he requested your presence. I perceived it as an order, though I may be mistaken in this," the droid apologized.

"Tell Father I am not his slave anymore," Zeus bellowed. "I don't take orders!" He turned his back. The droid simply stood, perplexed. "Wait," Zeus said. "I know a better way to get the message to him. Come here."

Zeus walked to the edge of the citadel, till he stood in the crenel, looking down hundreds of meters. The droid rolled to him; Zeus grabbed its metal frame and shoved it over the edge. The droid flipped end over end, bouncing against stone as it dropped; bits of its golden frame broke off. The droid crashed heavily into the canopy of the tangle. Woodland creatures hooted and squawked.

Zeus stared after it. Each droid had an emergency transmitter to notify the palace's central AI if the droid became incapacitated. The droid would have sent a message telling how it was destroyed. The AI would notify Felph.

Zeus imagined the look on Felph's face when he learned how he had refused to go on this expedition. If I'd merely said "no," he thought, Father would have forced the issue. By destroying the droid, I've sent the message forcefully.

Felph would be afraid to bring him on the expedition. Better to leave Zeus home. With Maggie.

Herm stood on the lip of the citadel, laughed, and said, "One point if you bed her in three days. Two more if you get her willingly!"

From inside his tunic, he brought out a small vial of blue glass, held it outward and up, in ritual. He remained very quiet, almost respectful, as he pulled the stopper. The Wind of Dreams.

The scent that issued from the tiny bottle was overwhelming. It filled the air, sweet as gardenias, gentle.

Yet immediately, the heady scent took effect: the wine was a concoction made by Hera's perfumery, a very sophisticated machine. By combining a devil's brew of proteins that stimulated one's emotions, then putting it into a scent, the perfumery was able to concoct a most intoxicating brew. The Wind of Dreams made one feel—effulgent, euphoric, invulnerable.

It made Zeus feel the way that he imagined he would feel at some distant time, when he took his rightful place as Lord of the Universe. Zeus inhaled deeply.

The scent had a singular, unusual effect on him. It made his organ hard. He stared at it through veiled eyes. Ah how he craved this little bottle. As one who has lived his life in servitude, as one born to crave power, yet who had always been denied the most basic rights, Zeus craved it more than he could speak. The scent brought water to his eyes.

Herm held up the Wind of Dreams. As the current high-scorer in the Great and Dreadful Game, it was Herm's right to keep the bottle. Herm chanted,

> *"Through darkest deeds this prize is won—*
> *by murder, theft, and dreams undone."*

Zeus intoned his portion of the chant.

> *"If I succeed, I'll hold the Wind:*
> *Let the Great and Dreadful Game begin!"*

A cold gust blew over the tower, filling the air with the bottle's marvelous scent. For once Zeus felt that the draft refreshed rather than chilled him.

Herm put the stopper back on the bottle. He broke into a deep, booming laugh.

Twelve

Y ou feel all right about this?" Gallen asked Maggie that morning. "You don't mind if I leave for a couple days?"

Maggie lay in bed beside him, her dark red hair in her eyes. She shook her head. "Just get your cloning done before you leave."

Gallen studied her face. Maggie looked pale, though her morning sickness had passed. He did not want to broach this topic, but he had to. "I'm not going for Felph, you know."

"I know. You want to beat the Dronon. So you're hunting for a magic potion? I have to tell you, Gallen, I wouldn't hope for too much. I don't understand how such a potion could do what Felph claims."

"Why not? We have that vial of Hope we got . . . where? I don't even remember the name of the world."

"Cyannesse," Maggie said. "And it wasn't a magic potion, just a spray containing the same chemicals that arouse hope in anyone."

"It felt magic to me, coming as we did from Tihrglas, never having seen such a thing. It felt magic. Who knows what the Qualeewoohs might have done. Try on the spirit mask, if you don't believe me."

Maggie glanced to the mask, lying beside the bed, shook her head thoughtfully. "For your sake," Maggie whispered, "I hope they've found magic."

Gallen took her hand, clung to it. He felt guilty. He whispered, "I don't like the idea of leaving you alone."

Maggie patted her tummy. "I have our son to keep me company. Believe me, if he'd kicked you as much last night as he did me, you'd know you weren't alone. Besides, you're the one who needs to run off into the tangle. I'm in no shape to follow. I'm just going to stay here and work on getting fat for a couple of days. Hera is here, and Arachne. This will give me a chance to get to know them."

Gallen could not put a name to his concerns. Maggie smiled, then took his left hand, pulled it under the covers, placed it on her womb. Gallen felt her warm belly stretch as his son kicked.

Maggie's eyes blazed with a light of their own. That is how I want her to be, always, Gallen considered. Shining with joy. He leaned forward, kissed her softly and with passion. Her breath tasted sweet, even this early in the morning.

In a few moments she climbed atop him, and they became tangled together for a long hour.

When their passion was spent, Maggie whispered heavily into Gallen's ear, "Don't take any chances out there."

"Ah, you're a madwoman, Maggie. First you nearly kill me with lovemaking, *then* you tell me to take care. You'll make me old before my time."

"I just wanted to remind you that you have something to live for. I—I don't want to make love to your clone."

"Too late, I already am a clone. You're making love to Belorian."

Maggie shook her head. "No, he died centuries ago. You're *my* Gallen O'Day."

Gallen kissed her eyelids and said seriously, "I know."

Moments later, a service droid announced itself at their door, requesting them to follow it to meet Lord Felph. Gallen dressed quickly in the black robes of a Lord Protector, put on his mantle, gathered his weapons, and packed his clothes.

The droid led them deep into the palace, along yellow corridors where holoimages gave radiation warnings. The doors were unmarked, but the droid told them that this was Felph's technical center, the birthing chambers where he made his children.

At a green door, the droid bid them enter a large darkly lit oval-shaped room perhaps fifty meters in diameter. Storage tubes for clones lined each wall, gray round lids smattering the white room with giant polka dots. In the center of the room lay a vivification table, a plain white table with various pumps around it that would allow Felph to infuse nutrients into a clone as he downloaded it with memories. The table's AI was built into a hood that spanned the ceiling, along with various lights and instruments, so that the AI looked like some menacing giant spider in its vast neural webbing, squatting over them all.

Lord Felph waited beside the vivification table, along with all his children, and Orick and Tallea. Gallen felt surprised, having believed that donating a sample of his genome would be a private act.

But he recognized immediately a level of tension in the room that was almost electric. Perhaps it came from the strained expression of Lord Felph, who wore a shabby brown robe and stood gazing at Zeus, his eyes flickering with anger. Perhaps it came from his children, who stared resolutely at the floor.

"Well then, there you are, finally," Felph said to Gallen and Maggie, hardly turning away from Zeus. "Here is the DNA sampler. Just set your hand here."

Felph pointed to a white pad near the table, and Gallen set his palm on the spot. A small device came up under his hand, whirred momentarily as it peeled away a tiny scrap of skin, then retracted, taking it into storage.

The central gem in Gallen's mantle glowed as the artificial intelligence overhead recorded his memories.

Felph turned, addressed his children. "I requested your presence because this is a big day. A very big day. It is the first day of freedom for my children." He clipped his words off, biting them back. "Already this day, some of you have used your freedom badly. I found Zeus running around naked on the roof, and he threw one of my droids from the citadel, after recording a little message for me."

Felph sighed, and he spoke in a tone of grief. "So, I must consider, 'What shall I do? What shall I do?'

"Herm, what shall I do? How can I hope for a civil response to a civil request from you children?" Felph gazed up into Herm's green eyes, stepped close, and breathed into his face. "What would you do?"

"Punish us, I guess," Herm said, hardly mumbling as he gazed at the floor.

Gallen nearly laughed. Felph's "children," though adults in form, were acting like five-year-olds. Felph took the role of aggrieved parent.

"Punish you. Hmmm . . . a good idea! A fine idea," Felph agreed. "And tell me, Arachne. You're the smart one here. How would you go about that? Shall I have you stand in corners? Should I take away privileges?"

Arachne did not move. Instead, she kept her face down and pretended not to hear. She shook slightly.

"Hera, then? How would you punish them?"

"I would do what you plan to do now," Hera answered with a smirk. Her blues eyes flashed beneath her auburn hair. She stood up straight, squared her shoulders.

"Which is?"

"You'll kill our clones and erase our memory crystals."

Felph folded his hands in front of his belly, tried to hold back his surprise at her answer. "You would do *that*, really?"

"Of course," Hera said. "You have no choice in the matter. You can't continue to spoil us."

At that moment, her words seemed to galvanize Felph into motion. Gallen sensed that what had, until a moment before, been only a threat, now became the chosen course of action. "Of course, of course. You're so right, my precious."

He turned back to the others. "Do you understand why I must do this? Why you've forced me to do this?

"You wanted freedom—all very well and good. I've given it to you. But from whom little is required, little is expected. In the past I've allowed you to make mistakes without facing their consequences. I've coddled you. . . ."

Felph stood for a second, eyes flashing, then rushed to Zeus's side and screamed. "And this is how you repay me, you insolent shit! This is how! I gave you life!" Zeus raised his hands, as if to block a blow if Felph tried to strike. "I give you food on the table and clothes on your back! I . . . I—Damn you! Damn you all!"

Felph turned and rushed to a gray tube, pulled the handle, and slid the tube out from the wall, opening it as if it were a giant drawer. Zeus's clone lay naked on a white bed. It looked as if it were sleeping, eyes closed sweetly. Its hair was long, and unlike Zeus, who was clean-shaven, the clone had a wispy beard that needed trimming.

Otherwise, the clone looked perfect, without blemish.

Lord Felph reached into a pocket of his drab robe, fumbled, and pulled out a gun. He put it to the clone's ear and pulled the trigger. A loud pop sounded. Blood spattered the room. The clone's head wobbled, then Felph pushed, rolled it over so it fell from its bed to the floor. The clone lay bleeding from a horrible wound that split its skull.

Felph reached up to the next shelf, pulled it open, drew out a second clone: another copy of Zeus.

Felph stuck the gun in its mouth, pulled the trigger three times, then dragged the ruined thing to the floor so it landed atop the first.

Gallen stood, stunned. As a Lord Protector, he wondered if he should save the clones, but his mantle told him the clones were mere flesh. They had no memories, no experience or personality. Indeed, they'd been grown in flesh vats and moved directly into cold storage. Electrodes kept their muscles toned. They were no more conscious than growths of skin or fingernails. They were Felph's property.

That is what his mantle told him, but Gallen knew better. The clones that Felph murdered might not have consciousness, but if Felph were to wake them, to simply feed and care for them, they would become normal people.

They were babies, fresh from the womb. Sleeping, merely sleeping.

Gallen didn't know how to handle this. He could stop Felph, but his conscience whispered no: it is better this way. Felph was right. No one should have the *right* to immortality. Life should not be squandered or abused.

Lord Felph pulled open a third drawer, another copy of Zeus, but younger—Zeus as he might look at twelve, instead of twenty-five. A boy with gorgeous dark eyes, the first growths of hair darkening his chest.

Gallen became aware of Maggie clutching his shoulder with both hands. Her teeth chattered, and she had such a look of horror in her face, Gallen could hardly bear it.

"Stop him, Gallen! Stop this!" Maggie pleaded.

Too late. At that moment, Felph shoved his gun into the clone's chest and pulled the trigger five times, snapping off shots so fast it was remarkable.

Unlike the others, this clone reacted to the attack. It raised its hands into the air, and it gasped, its muscles convulsing—by reflex rather than design. It coughed blood, and Felph stopped, looked at the thing in horror. Then shoved the gun back into his pocket and grabbed an arm, pulling the clone to the floor, so three bodies lay naked, one atop the other.

Two of the clones twitched and jerked. Felph, his face and trim white beard now spattered with droplets of blood, stood panting over his kills. His face had drained white, as if in shock at what he'd done.

"Enough!" Gallen said. "You don't have to do it like that."

Felph's eyes blazed with anger at Gallen's command, but he said, "Of course, you're right."

He turned to Zeus. "One life, that's all you have left. With freedom comes responsibility. I give you one life, and if you do not spend it wisely, the loss will be yours more than it is mine."

Felph looked up to the great roof above him, at the AI with its neural webbing. Silver-blue conducting cords twisted among the brownish masses of neurons, and the great central processor of the AI crouched in the middle. "Mem, erase all data on Zeus—all his memories, all his aspirations. Then lock all such data out of your system in the future. I want his memories gone."

The AI's soft voice whispered through the room, neither male nor female. "Done."

Zeus frowned up at the dome above him.

Felph continued, "Now wipe the memories for the rest of my children, and terminate their clones."

"Done," the voice came again, and it seemed to reverberate through Gallen's mind, the voice of doom.

Now Lord Felph frowned at Zeus. "You want to stay here and play instead of escorting us to the tangle? Fine. Gallen was to have been your instructor. You stay here, and ponder your future. If you ever want to be reborn, you will *earn* that privilege. We're going to our ship."

With that, Lord Felph stalked off, his brown robes billowing out behind him.

Young Athena looked up nervously to the AI, then scurried behind Felph, heading for the ship.

Gallen took one last look at the white corpses twitching on the floor, pools of dark blood spreading beneath them.

Then he and Maggie followed Felph, along with Orick and Tallea, while the rest of Felph's children—Zeus, Hera, Arachne, and Herm all stood motionless, apparently too frightened to move.

Once Lord Felph left the room, Zeus went to the revivification table at the room's center, leaned his palms against it, and stood for a moment, legs shaking so badly he could hardly stand. He exhaled a ragged breath, then glanced back at the others.

None of them took it so hard, mortality. Perhaps it was bred into him, but Zeus craved more.

When he could stop trembling enough to stand under his own power, he ambled to his clones, piled in a bloody heap. He squatted and held the chin of the young man he'd once been.

Vengeance for you, Zeus spoke without words. I shall have vengeance. He bent, kissed the clone's lips, tasted its foul breath.

"Well, what a misfortune," Herm said to Zeus. "Now it looks as if you will have to try to win all *three* points with Maggie, take her voluntarily. I can't imagine you raping her now."

The Great and Dreadful Game. Zeus hadn't thought of the repercussions the death of his clones would have on the Game.

As Zeus's eyes grew wide, Hera began laughing, a high sweet sound, full of joy. Zeus turned and gazed up at his wife, astonished by that tone.

"Five points I've won in the Great and Dreadful Game today," she said, "for killing Zeus's clones."

Zeus gasped, looked up at Hera in astonishment. She'd seldom been a player of the Game. And of course, Zeus hadn't been warned of her plan to get his clones murdered. That was part of the game: only the bettors and the score-keeper were ever notified of the bets in place.

It kept life interesting, wondering what those around you might be scheming.

"Points won," Arachne said. Arachne was the official scorekeeper. She never played herself, but it amused her to know the ins and outs of everyone else's schemes.

"You arranged for the murder of my clones?" Zeus shouted at his wife. "You! Hera? How did you do it?"

"I didn't do anything. *You* did. I knew you wouldn't want to go on the expedition, so you would have to do something to annoy Father. I just made certain I happened to be near him when you did, then I suggested that he needed to find a way to rein you in."

He did not ask Hera *why* she'd killed his clones. He suspected he knew. Maggie. Perhaps she had heard about his bet concerning Maggie. Hera knew she could stop Zeus from raping Maggie, at least, by providing such a horrendous penalty that he wouldn't dare take Maggie quickly.

But then another thought occurred to Zeus. Hera could not have known about his bet with Herm unless Herm had told her. Yet Herm had not left Zeus's sight all morning.

So it may have been that Hera had asked Herm to tempt Zeus into this bet.

Zeus had thought it exceedingly generous of Herm to offer so many points for a simple seduction. Now he saw why. Hera had bet against him. She would interfere.

Hera smiled, a mischievous grin. "Three points if you bed Maggie," she said. "Three for me if you don't. That was my bet with Herm."

This astonished Zeus—the depth of his wife's jealousy, the scope of her cunning. She could make a formidable opponent in the Great and Dreadful Game. Surely Zeus would have been more circumspect in betting this morning if he'd suspected how jealous Hera was.

She'd taken him off his guard last night with her talk of truces and feigned interest in Gallen.

It annoyed Zeus to be so easily handled; and it humbled him. He went to his dear wife, found himself aroused. He kissed her full lips, pressed himself against her. "You haven't stopped me," he teased. "I *will* have my pleasure with Maggie, though she could never give me as much pleasure as do you."

"Three points if you get her." Hera laughed sweetly; she sauntered from the room.

The ruthless woman, Zeus considered. How could Hera so casually have maneuvered Felph into killing their clones? She'd lost as much as he in this debacle. Now all Felph's children lay under the threat of extinction. It only showed Zeus how serious an opponent Hera would be in the Game. Still, he admired her.

Arachne was watching them both with an uncustomary frown. Zeus wondered what she knew that he didn't. "Why the furrowed brow, dear sister?"

The witch seldom gave him a straight answer; he expected none now. Still he could hope. She had, after all, been created to be his counselor. For heaven's sake, he needed the counsel now.

"I think," Arachne said, "that your game goes too far. We would all be better off, if no one played such games anymore."

"Goes too far? In what way?"

Arachne's dark eyes flashed. "You hurt others merely to gain status, without concern for those who've done us only good."

"So you would have me walk away from this?" Zeus asked. "Simply lose three points?"

"If you were half as noble as you were crafty, you would run from this game," Arachne said.

"Hah! Hera told you to say this, didn't she?"

"I mean it," Arachne said. "You're a fool. Gallen O'Day is a dangerous man. You know almost nothing about him. He will protect what is his!"

"Indeed!" Zeus laughed. "I shall have my points, whether you or Hera like it or no." He gave a hearty roar for no reason he could understand. It was a laugh of pain, as much as of pleasure.

When Orick reached the *Nightswift* in its docking bay, Felph had dozens of droids ready with clothing, weapons, temporary shelters. Gallen and Felph stood considering which items to take on the expedition, which to leave. As the men spoke, Tallea went to Maggie, licked her hand.

"Are you certain you'll be all right, here?" Tallea asked. "I'm worried."

Maggie knelt, hugged Tallea. "I'll be fine. The droids will be here to care for me, new people to meet."

"I wish I could take care of you," Tallea said. "But I keep finding I'm not of much use—without hands and thumbs."

"I'll feel better if you keep Gallen and Orick safe," Maggie answered. She was being generous of course. Tallea had been a fine swordswoman in her time, but as a bear she was clumsy and small. In a fight, Orick would have to care for her. Orick suspected Tallea knew that, and it rankled her.

Orick knew how miserable Tallea was. He felt guilty. She loved him, had given up everything to be at his side, and he'd decided to give his life into the service of God.

After his dream last night, he felt more decided than ever. Orick had always believed that he would be the monastic sort, living in some forest hideaway, devoting his life to study and good works.

But now he knew he couldn't spend his days cloistered in a monastery, leading an easy life of study. Last night he'd had a vision, a wondrous vision, in which God had called him to service. Missionary to the Cosmos.

Orick felt afire with the urge to go out and convert. He remembered the prophecies of John the Revelator, who saw all manner of beasts worshiping and crying praises to God.

I am among those in John's vision, Orick realized. Who better than me, a lowly bear, to carry God's message to the rest of his creatures?

I can't give myself to Tallea, Orick thought, but I can give her the gospel. She was in my dream last night, too. God has commanded me to speak to her. Yet how can I talk to her?

Tallea knew that Orick prayed. She'd joined him on a few occasions. Her attitude toward Christianity was respectful, though she seemed to think it quaint.

Where do I begin? Orick considered. How do I convince Tallea? Without realizing it, he'd decided to preach to her first—his closest friend. Yet the thought frightened him. He feared that Tallea would reject him.

Orick considered the words of the prophet Nephi from the Tome: "I will go and do what the Lord has commanded, for I know that he giveth no commandment unto the children of men, save he shall first prepare a way for them to do that which he has commanded." The verse filled him with resolve.

Well then, Orick decided. That's it then. I saw everyone in my vision last night, so I'll convert them all—Tallea, these folks on Ruin, even the Dronon.

But at the thought of the Dronon, even Orick's stout heart faltered. Right now, Tallea seemed daunting enough.

Orick and Tallea watched as Gallen had the droids pack supplies. Felph's young daughter, Athena, watched Gallen, quietly offering suggestions now and then. "Use the bigger, more powerful glow globes," she said.

Felph challenged, "But won't they draw predators?"

"Down as far in the tangle as we'll be, most predators hunt by smell; anything that can see our light would sniff out our trail anyway. But the brighter lights might blind them."

Felph grunted his assent, and they took the larger globes. Athena seemed to understand the dangers of the tangle better than any other.

Orick followed Tallea into the *Nightswift*.

Tallea watched Maggie through a shaded window. As a Caldurian, Tallea had spent a lifetime protecting the helpless. That is what drew her to Maggie now.

Orick said, "I know you want to stay with Maggie, I'm glad you chose to come with me."

"Why?" Tallea asked, her voice hopeful. She turned her full attention to him, eyes sparkling.

Now it was Orick's turn to pace. The big black bear hung his head, half closed his eyes. "I wanted to speak to you about something."

He let the silence drag out, and Tallea seemed to take it for a bad sign. She sighed, shook her shaggy head. "Please, Orick—you don't need to say it."

"What?" Orick asked.

"You want me to go away," Tallea answered. "I've felt it coming. We Caldurians are used to it. We bond with those we serve, and sometimes we . . . crave too much affection from our masters. I didn't mean to do that to you. I— I'll leave."

Orick could hear in the hollowness of her voice how much those words cost her. She turned, trying to hide the tears that welled in her eyes, and Orick wanted to comfort her. Yet he held back. To offer affection now might only hurt her more in the long run.

"I'll find a way to be happy," Tallea said. "Even Caldurians can forget in time."

"Wait!" Orick said, "That's not what I wanted to say. It's—another matter entirely. I know it's a hard thing to ask, but I wanted—I mean I've wondered—"

"Yes?" Tallea said, heaving a sigh of relief.

"How you feel about God?" Orick blurted.

Tallea sat, stunned. It was a simple question, yet it took her off guard. At length she said, "Some people say there are gods, and some say not. I know you believe in one God, though you say he has a son—who is also God—and a spirit, who sounds to me like a third god. To tell the truth, you sound confused, Orick. At the very least, I'm not sure how well you count."

Orick almost laughed. He was surprised at how much she'd understood, given how little he'd told her. "I worship one God," Orick admitted, "just as His son worshiped Him. I worship one God, just as the Holy Spirit serves Him. So you see, the other two hold a place of honor, they are subservient to one supreme deity."

"That makes sense now," Tallea admitted.

"The thing is, uh," Orick said, unsure how to proceed, "if there were a God who had created this universe, and if He could hear and understand your innermost thoughts and needs, doesn't it make sense that He could talk to you?"

Tallea considered. "I don't know. If you think he could create the universe and hear our thoughts, then, if he has such power, he ought to be able to talk."

Orick stared into her eyes. They held a desperation he had never seen before. He said, "And if such a being existed, how could I prove His existence to you?"

Tallea said, "I doubt that you could."

"What if He spoke to you?"

Tallea considered. "That wouldn't prove anything. It would only mean that some*thing* was speaking to me. It doesn't necessarily mean that that something is your god. It could be a liar."

"But it might prove there are greater powers in the universe than ourselves," Orick said. "Right?"

Tallea considered. "It stands to reason that there are."

"Then, I want you to talk to God, and listen to what He has to say," Orick concluded.

"Why—what would I want to talk to him for?"

"Because He created us," Orick said. "Because He is the father of our spirits, and He wants us to be happy."

"But I already am happy," Tallea said, and almost as soon as she said it, she scrunched her nose, as if recognizing the depth of the lie. She was miserable, Orick knew. She loved Orick. She loved him so much, she had given up her life, her humanity, to be with him, and now she feared that he would never love her in return. As a bear who was genetically enhanced to be something more than other female bears, Tallea was unique in the universe. If Orick did not return her love, she would end up alone. How could she say she was happy? It wasn't true, but the lie had come swiftly to her lips simply because she *was* so miserable. She couldn't admit it even to herself.

Of course, she had lied because she knew what Orick was asking. He wanted her to embark on a dangerous journey, to discover God. She said angrily, "The truth is, I don't want anything to do with your god. If he tells you that you can't love me, that you can't marry me no matter how much you love me, then I don't give a damn whether he created me or not. You say he wants me to be happy: well, I know what I need to be happy!"

Orick frowned. He tried to speak, but only a grunt came out. Of course she would be angry with God. Lots of people were. But Orick also knew she was lying still. The truth was that if she discovered that God lived, she'd have to make some difficult changes in her life, and Orick knew that for many, it was easier to deny God's existence than to change.

Orick didn't know how to proceed, what to say next. Should he lie, say that if she discovered God, her life would be easy? The truth was it might be harder. God requires hard things of His disciples. Should he ask her not to be angry at God? What good would that do?

He half turned to leave, then stopped. "You say you don't want to know Him, but you know me, and you love me. You had better figure out why you love me, because I tell you this: He shaped my heart and soul, as well as my body."

He turned to leave, and though his words were as honest and as humble as any Orick could muster, he knew he'd left volumes unsaid. Perhaps he'd been wrong to come to Tallea without any thought or preparation.

"Ah, forgive me," Orick said, not quite able to turn his back on her. "I don't know how to say this. I'm making a mess of it." He would have left then, but as he turned, Tallea must have recognized his frustration.

"I love your kindness," Tallea said, filling the silent void. "Is your god kind?"

Orick stopped in mid-stride. He gazed, realizing that she was apologizing. She wanted to speak to him. "He watches the sparrows and knows their thoughts. He weeps when one dies. He says He cares far more for us, than for them."

"If your god is so powerful," Tallea said, "why does he let them die?"

"He doesn't," Orick said. "He's prepared a way so our spirits can return to Him. With Him, we will live forever. The sparrows go to Him."

"If they go to him when they die, then why should *he* weep?"

"Because," Orick said, "He doesn't weep because they're dead, He weeps because of the pain they must pass through to reach Him."

Tallea asked, "Then we must wait for death, in order to be happy?"

"No," Orick said. "Our spirits can go to Him now. Our spirits can mingle with His."

"If this would make us happy, and if he loves us, then he should just do it."

Tallea could not hide the desolation she felt. Her voice cracked. She wanted happiness. She wanted it so much, she was willing to do just about anything to get it. Orick could tell.

"You wouldn't break into the house of a friend, would you?" Orick asked. When Tallea shook her head, he said. "God will not force Himself on you. When He sends His spirit, he does so only by your invitation, and only when you are prepared to receive Him."

So it began. Tallea seemed eager to hear his words. Orick had always loved her, he freely admitted, but he also loved God. Perhaps her desire to learn of God came only from jealousy, her desire to check out her competition. Perhaps she was curious because she did crave happiness; Orick could honestly claim to have found a measure of it.

So it was that Orick, Missionary to the Cosmos, began teaching the woman he hoped would become his first convert.

Zeus did not wait an hour to contact Maggie once Gallen departed. He felt pressed for time to carry out the seduction.

As he strode down the corridors to Maggie's room, he wondered, What kind of woman would marry a Lord Protector?

Someone who cares for others? Someone who has been hurt? Someone who feels the need for protection? Someone who values faithfulness in a relationship? Or maybe Maggie valued law in and of itself, needed structure in her life. All these, perhaps.

Zeus snickered at the possibility that Maggie needed structure in her life. Order . . . wearied him. He could imagine nothing more tedious than an ordered existence. Inwardly he shivered. If Maggie was one of those, it would be damned hard to pry her legs open.

There were other possibilities. Maggie might be attracted to strong men for their own sake. She might even adore violence. Perhaps she found it exciting to be married to a Lord Protector—someone who hunts and kills others who are just as predatory in nature. Perhaps Maggie had a wicked streak. If that were the case . . . Zeus grinned at the possibilities.

Then, of course, the fact Maggie had married a Lord Protector could be an accident. Gallen and Maggie were hardly more than children. Gallen couldn't have been a Lord Protector long.

But it was no accident, Zeus knew. Even if Maggie had chosen Gallen before he became a Lord Protector, he'd at least had the *potential* to become a Lord Protector. His personality was set, his nature formed. No, Maggie chose to marry a Lord Protector, regardless of whether or not he'd won his mantle.

Yet the fact that Maggie was young gave Zeus hope. Young women were more easily seduced. Newlyweds tended to still be in the habit of looking for mates, of fantasizing about others. Sometimes they felt concerned for their own adequacy as lovers, and would be open to experimentation.

Zeus's hopes ran high as he reached the door to Maggie's room, pressed the chimes to announce his presence.

Maggie appeared at the door, somewhat disheveled, her hair flattened on the right. She'd been lying down.

"Oh, it's you?" she asked, surprised.

"Yes, me," Zeus said, looking deep into Maggie's eyes. He could see no wickedness there—not the kind of flashing excitement of one who enjoys another's misery. Nor did he see sensual curiosity. She did not open the door wider in invitation, or look furtively down the hall to be certain they were alone. He dared only look into her eyes, though he longed to let his gaze slide down her body. The air was thick with her clean scent, a sweet perfume.

"Can I help you?" Maggie asked. Zeus imagined he could feel a certain weight behind those words, a hint of promise. If you need help, and I can assist, I will help you. Zeus almost smiled. No wonder she had wed a Lord Protector.

"Yes, please, I think you can. I . . . I mean I hope you can," Zeus said. He glanced back over his shoulder, as if afraid others might be watching.

"Is something wrong?"

"I need help," Zeus answered solemnly. "I want to escape from here, from Lord Felph. Will you meet me, tonight, at sundown?"

"You need my help?" Maggie asked, incredulous.

Zeus glanced back nervously. "You're a technician, right? I hope you can help. Will you meet me, in the North Garden, beside the peacock fountain? I— I'll give you dinner. I have no other way to repay you."

"Why not talk now?" Maggie opened the door wider, so Zeus could enter.

"No, Hera saw me walking down here," Zeus said, feeling inspired. "She's in league with Felph. I don't want her to know we're talking. Tonight. Meet me tonight." Of all his brothers and sisters, only Hera would dare interfere with Zeus's plans. She'd bet against this seduction. Zeus prepared to drive a wedge between the women.

"All right. Where is the North Garden?"

"Down this corridor, five doors to your right, then follow your nose. You'll smell roses," Zeus said. He turned on his heels and left.

It is better to leave now, he thought. Leave her with questions, nagging worries. Let her fears fester.

L ord Felph, I cannot condone another display like the one I saw this morning," Gallen said as he stood on the bridge of the *Nightswift*. They skimmed Ruin, crossing pewter-colored mountains that wrinkled the planet's surface. At this altitude, the thick air left a blue haze over most of the ground, baffling the eye.

Felph watched out the window, Athena by his side. He started at Gallen's words. "Cannot condone it, eh?" Felph grunted. "Hmmmph. What will you do next time?"

"Stop you," Gallen said.

"Fair enough," Felph replied. "Since I don't have any more clones to kill, it's all academic." He chuckled softly to himself. "Ghastly business, wasn't it?"

Gallen said, "Such things are best done in private."

"You think so?" Felph said, raising an eyebrow. "You don't know Zeus."

"No one should have to look upon his own murder."

Felph glanced back at Athena, and Gallen followed his eyes. The girl sat quietly in one corner, her back to the wall. She was the most beautiful child Gallen had ever seen, both stronger than a Tharrin, and more sensual. Felph asked, "Athena, my child, has Zeus ever discussed his desire to murder me in front of you?"

She looked at her father and scrunched back toward the door a bit, unwilling to answer. Felph told Gallen, "She listens far more than she speaks."

He waited; finally she said, "Yes."

"Do you think it prudent of me to strike first?"

Felph's withering gaze drew the next word from her. "Yes!"

Felph smiled victoriously, said to Gallen, "You see? I did only what I had to. Zeus is dangerous. I've bred him to dominate. He resents those who hold authority over him, and he thought himself immortal. I wanted to disabuse him of that notion. Now he will feel the pains of mortality."

"But it wasn't fair!" Athena shouted. "It wasn't fair to kill me, too! I didn't do anything!"

Felph looked back to the sweet, strong girl, smiled in apology. "I couldn't very well kill the others and leave your clones alive. How would that look?"

"You're always wasting my clones," Athena said. "You make me camp out in the tangle, where I get killed."

"No more," Felph said. "I won't make you go anymore. Now that your Guide is gone, I can't take chances with you. You're too precious."

"What about today? You're making me go with him—" she pointed to Gallen.

"You don't have to leave the ship," Gallen told her. "I'm a Lord Protector. I can handle myself."

She studied him with a calculation, as if measuring the thickness of his biceps, the girth of his legs. "You don't know what you're getting into."

Athena's skintight pullover, a camouflage suit in shades of black and purple, revealed her every muscular curve. Though Athena's face said she was thirteen or fourteen, her figure was that of a mature woman. Shapely, strong, graceful. Gallen said, "It does not matter if you think I'll live or die. If you're afraid of going into the tangle, I won't force you."

But Felph interrupted. "Of course she'll come. Athena has lived in the tangle longer than anyone. I've been acclimatizing her to it for years. You'll need her cunning."

"Six times this year—I got killed in the tangle six times this year," Athena said. "You call that cunning?"

Felph said, "Who else has ever lived more than a week alone in the tangle? You've survived for weeks at a time."

Athena lowered her head. "Teeawah isn't just *any* tangle. You can't just walk in."

Felph nodded to the viewscreen that covered the front wall of the cabin. "Ah, here it is."

In the past fifteen minutes they had traveled well over two thousand kilometers. Ahead, something strange showed on the viewscreen: all over the face of Ruin, the skies had been clear. When clouds appeared at all, they were high cirrus clouds, thin bands of white strewn like cobwebs over the blue sky. But ahead of the ship a storm raged, a storm unlike any Gallen had ever seen. Thunderheads loomed thousands of kilometers in the air, billowing in hues of darkest slate. At cloud top, lightning forked and darted like the tendrils of anemones as they feed from their rocks. In their lower regions, the clouds lost form, became a nebulous haze as torrential rains poured from the storm.

As for the tangle—Gallen could see the dark purples of Ruin's vegetation, but the trees and vines themselves were hidden in the shadow.

As quickly as Gallen saw the storm, the ship hurtled into it, smashing against clouds as if they were a wall. The ship shuddered in response, slowing, then everything outside the viewscreen darkened.

Felph motioned to the pilot seat. "This is your expedition, Gallen. You should take us down."

"Ship, stop forward progress, then begin gradual descent," Gallen commanded the AI, walking up to the controls.

Brilliant flashes of actinic light struck the ship, and static crackled inside. Gallen felt the ship list, buffeted by strong winds.

The ship lowered. The storm pelted the exterior with huge liquid droplets. Icy crystals broke apart on contact with the hull, sliding down the viewscreen windows. For long moments this was all Gallen could see, then the tangle appeared.

Gallen had imagined a leafy canopy, like that of some deciduous forest, but the tangle of Ruin was bizarre. Enormous grasslike plants spiraled above the canopy hundreds of meters, like twisted fronds of ribbon, while other trees sent out feelers, like enormous stamens that clutched the air—grasping, grasping. Gallen knew enough to stay away from them. One towering vine wrapped around itself, looking as if it were made of giant bells, welded side by side.

Lower in the tangle, huge growths had formed on the sides of plants, enormous lips of fungus in shades of orange or brown. Gallen could barely distinguish the shapes, the rain pelted the viewscreen so hard.

On one lip of fungus, a creature squatted. It had enormous black eyes that stared up at him menacingly. The creature had antlerlike growths on its head, a short trunk like an elephant's, a long dark neck with greenish splotches that might have been some froglike parasite gripping fiercely to it, and on its leaf-shaped body, it had enormous wings like those of a bat, filled with ragged holes, as if the creature had been blasted by lightning many times.

For a moment the creature gazed at Gallen's ship, as if trying to decide whether it was predator or prey. In that moment, the beast seemed old and powerful.

It backed up on its perch, opened its wings. Enormous claws extended from the apex of each wing. With these, the beast raked the air, warning the ship away.

Then it leapt from its perch and dived into the tangle, a wriggling horror, an escapee from the regions of darkness.

Gallen had never seen a creature so odd, had never even faintly imagined such a thing might exist.

Gallen looked at icy tangle. Climbing down would be nearly impossible. He asked Felph, "How do we get in?"

"Easy enough," Lord Felph said. "We drop the ship into the canopy, then pound the brush with phased gravity waves, breaking through the upper foliage. When we've gone as far as the ship can go, we have to get out and make our way down. Any ruins will be down on the ground."

"Upper foliage?" Gallen asked, concerned by the tone of Felph's voice. He'd imagined this wall of purple vines was the upper layer, and the ground would be a hundred meters beneath it.

"The tangle is at least two thousand meters deep here," Felph said. "The upper plants you see are mostly parasites, growing on the old-growth dew trees. But it's the ground we need to reach. Down deeper, the dew trees have grown for thousands of years, so that now their trunks are petrified by constant seepage. Storms rage almost perpetually over this tangle—they're caused by some rather odd geography, cold winds sweeping down from the arctic, clashing with wet air from the seas under the great tangle. Twenty thousand years ago, this area would have been warmer, dryer. A perfect Qualeewooh nesting site.

"But it's a mess, now."

Gallen considered. "There has to be a way to get some view of the ground. We need a topographical map, something that shows the features under the tangle. If the Qualeewoohs built here, they would have built above ground."

"Of course," Felph said. "I've done some echolocation, but the results are confusing. As I've said, the lower trunks of the dew trees tend to become petrified, so they show as stone. What on the map looks like a tower is usually just the trunk of a dew tree."

Gallen asked, "But people have found towers here?"

"One or two," Felph replied. "But no one has found Teeawah, the city itself."

"Do your maps show where ruins have been discovered?"

"Indeed," Felph replied. "But it's not the ones that have been discovered that we want. No one has reached the ruins of Teeawah. I'll get the map, and let you tell me where to look."

Gallen agreed. Felph ordered the ship's AI to radio the palace, download copies of the maps, then display them on the ship's holo.

The lights lowered; one viewscreen displayed an image in grays and reds. The map showed an area roughly four hundred kilometers wide and six hundred long, a wriggling, serpentine valley between the hills. Thrusting upward from it, like myriad hairs, were thousands of petrified trunks from dew trees. The five successful treks into the tangle had all been in the same general area, a great central plain where a few steep bluffs jutted from the foothills.

Yet as Gallen studied the map, he did not think the area looked promising. The bluffs weren't large enough to support a city like the one he imagined.

"Why do you think the Qualeewoohs built here?" Gallen asked Felph, not because he needed an answer, but because he wanted the old man to confirm his own ideas.

"A rookery," Felph said. "Aside from holy places—which are more historic sites than anything else, I don't see that the Qualeewoohs ever built anything except as a rookery."

Gallen considered what little he knew of Qualeewoohs' habits. At Felph's palace the Qualeewoohs had built rookeries into the face of the cliffs—and this whole valley was ringed with such cliff faces.

"The Qualeewoohs like to set their rookeries high," Gallen said.

"And far from water, to avoid predators," Felph agreed.

Gallen imagined himself winging through the cliffs that ringed the valley. As he did, he whispered, "They want shelter from wind. It keeps their *clooes* warmer, and it makes it easier for the chicks to learn to fly—fewer drafts and crosscurrents."

Gallen traced his finger along the cliffs. Felph began pacing beside him.

"They need some running water." Gallen considered. "It's too heavy to carry easily." He reached the very mouth of the canyon at the far north. Two arms of the mesa jutted out, each running a northeast, northwest angle. At the very lip where the mountains met, lay a deep defile. A river would be there.

"Between the arms of these mountains," Gallen whispered. "This is where I would look for Teeawah." Gallen felt almost certain he was right.

"Congratulations," Felph said. "Your very first try, and you have found it. Do you know how many hundreds of men have lost their lives in expeditions to this region? In all the Great Tangle, there is not a more treacherous pit than the one you pointed out. The place is crawling with sfuz who have tunneled their warrens around there for kilometers. I've tried to make the bottom of those cliffs many times."

"What are sfuz?" Gallen asked.

"Hunters, like giant . . . monkeys," Athena answered. "Or maybe more like spiders. They hunt—in so many ways."

Gallen could see that to describe them would be pointless. What was the winged creature he had just seen? A dragon? That name perhaps best described the beast, yet it seemed woefully inadequate. What name would describe a florafeem? A giant flying . . . half a clam?

No words sufficed.

"The sfuz set snares for unwary animals." Felph tried to be more helpful. "And they're just as likely to track you down while you're sleeping. But they can be far more canny: they train other animals to do their bidding. The word *sfuz* is a Qualeewooh word. Though we often translate it as *hunter,* it also means *relentless.*

"How do they kill?" Gallen asked.

"Nothing elaborate," Felph said. "With tooth and claw, which may be painted with poisons extracted from other animals. But the sfuz are very strong. They're adapted to an environment where they must climb up and down as easily as we move across the earth. And like other animals on Ruin, they're fast—much faster than most. In the tangle, quick reflexes seem to be the preferred adaptation. The sfuz walk more quickly than we run. In close quarters, in short bursts, they run almost faster than the eye can see.

"If I am right, the ancient ruins are home to the largest single nest of sfuz on Ruin."

Gallen said, "You mentioned that they train other animals, use snares—are these creatures sentient?"

Felph seemed to consider. "I don't know," he admitted. "The sfuz never talk to you, never seem to reason, but they know a hundred ways to kill you. Are such creatures sentient?"

"He is not telling you everything," Athena said. "The sfuz here in the tangle of Teeawah are fearsome. I have fought sfuz in other areas—but none like this! They regenerate. They can't be killed!"

Felph laughed. "Don't get the man excited. That can't be proved. They may regenerate, but we don't know that they're immortal."

"It's true," Athena said. "I killed one near my campsite. A few hours later, it roused and slew me!"

"There was a glitch in the transmission your Guide sent," Felph argued. "I've explained it before: when that version of you died, the Guide it wore sent the downloaded memories. The Guide must have been damaged in the attack. That's all. A simple transmission error."

Gallen felt skeptical. Immortal predators? Felph had said that no one had ever reached Teeawah, that the predators here were unusually nasty. Yet this seemed too much to believe. Still, he knew it would be dangerous. A question lodged at the back of Gallen's mind, something he feared to ask. "Is there a reason why so many sfuz nest here? Does this jungle provide more prey?"

Felph shook his head. "We are talking about a region deep within the tangle, without light, where few animals can survive. I don't think the tangle here could provide enough food for the population. The sfuz must be transporting food for hundreds of kilometers."

"That would take a great deal of effort," Gallen said. "Such effort doesn't make sense for predators."

"Agreed," Felph said.

"So what if these aren't just warrens under there?"

"What do you mean by that?" Felph asked.

Gallen stared at the topographic map. Everything suddenly seemed to make sense. "Imagine man has made a great discovery, the Waters of Strength, something that—I don't know—transforms him into something more than human. It lets him conquer self, nature, time, space. So he drinks the Waters, and all the men on earth leave.

"But then baboons come, and they too drink of the Waters. Only the Waters weren't made for them. Maybe they're not bright enough to understand what they're for. When they drink the Waters, they find themselves able to regenerate.

"How important would those Waters become? Would you want your enemies, or your prey, to find them? Would you simply nest in that region, or would you fortify it?"

Lord Felph's eyes grew wide at the implications.

"A fortress?" Athena asked. "You think they've built a fortress?"

Felph stroked his jaw in contemplation. "Interesting," he said. "I must admit, I've never considered *that* possibility. Obviously, you have a military mind. A fortress, to protect something of value. . . ."

Gallen stared down at the map, pointed to an abutment on the side of the mountain. "This is where we'll go in."

Sixteen

Maggie spent much of the day in her room, lost in thought. She could see why Zeus would be terrified after Lord Felph's maniacal display this morning. The murder of Zeus's clones, the sight of his brains spattering against the floor, had shocked Maggie to the core. Certainly it must have dismayed Zeus even more.

If Maggie were Zeus, she'd leave, too. Indeed, this whole morning, Maggie had been thinking: whatever her promise to Lord Felph the night before, she saw now he was mad. She'd come to Ruin searching for a place to bear her child in peace. She'd hoped Felph's palace might afford security.

Now she had to wonder. Felph frightened her; but what had he really done?

Destroyed clones—lumps of unaware flesh. Violence against clones, however terrifying, was not the same as violence against a person.

Still, Felph seemed threatening.

Or was he simply trying to teach a lesson? Felph claimed he wanted to teach his children responsibility. They'd never had to learn the consequences of their actions.

Silently, Maggie damned Felph for what he'd done to his own children. Never mind that he claimed to love them. He was as manipulative as anyone she'd ever met.

Yet she didn't entirely trust Zeus, either. She'd been warned that he was more than he seemed. She knew she couldn't trust appearances.

Maggie lay on her bed most of the afternoon, unable to rest. She wished Gallen were here, or that she'd gone with him. She craved the security of his presence.

At the same time, she recognized that this would give her an opportunity to get to know Felph's children. It might be necessary to rescue them from their father. Such an operation would be messy, if Felph refused to let them go.

Maggie imagined various confrontations with the old man. He was moody, unpredictable. He kept a gun in his pocket.

Gallen might have to kill him. But what would that accomplish? The Controller in Felph's head kept contact with the artificial intelligence in Felph's revivification chamber. If Gallen killed Felph, the AI would download his memories into a clone, resurrecting the man. Security droids could secrete Felph in hidden wings of his palace, where Gallen wouldn't be able to strike.

Maggie might have to dismantle the AI in the revivification chamber. If Gallen had to kill Felph, it would be better to leave the man dead.

But killing Felph would not be enough. Certainly, Felph had formidable resources. As they'd flown the florafeems, she'd seen silver torsos of security droids roving the perimeter of Felph's grounds. While Felph might reasonably claim that these droids kept predators off his grounds, those droids could also keep his children *on* his property. So if Felph's children were to escape, those droids would have to be neutralized.

Maggie knew her thoughts were traveling down dangerous paths. Sabotaging the ground's droids, murdering Felph. The ideas seemed paranoid. Yet defeating the killer droids, murdering Felph—both were jobs that would require certain technical knowledge only Maggie could access. The mantle she wore held the key to freedom.

So much for searching for a safe place to have her baby. Felph's palace, as luxurious as it seemed, might be nothing more than a glorified prison. Certainly, Felph's children were virtual slaves. The stone walls suddenly seemed suffocating.

Yet even now, Maggie couldn't be certain Felph was the monster she imagined.

Was Zeus merely trying to play on Maggie's sympathies for his own reasons?

Maggie found herself in a quandary. She wanted to question Felph's children, yet Zeus's hints made her feel insecure talking to anyone. Zeus had said that Hera was certainly Felph's spy. Then there was Herm; Maggie did not trust the winged man. He always wore a slight smile which said, "I know more than you. I have secrets."

So, Maggie was in a turbulent frame of mind as she made her way to the North Garden.

The evening came peacefully, Darksun dipping over the west hills in a blaze of gold that painted high clouds in shades of saffron. Almost immediately, even before the sun fell, Brightstar began to blaze, gaping like a hole in the night.

Maggie walked down the stone paths, along hedges that carried rose blooms in a hundred shades of blue. The scent of freshly tilled earth, of grass trampled under the wheels of gardener droids, all mixed with the scent of myriad roses.

Felph's roses were exotic. Some had been genetically altered to exude a bouquet of natural scents, like lemon, ginger, or tangerine. Other blooms had odd-shaped petals. Maggie had seen frilled roses on Tangor, roses that looked more like carnations. But Felph's collection included tufted roses with cottony petals. Others had enlarged stamens and small silky petals, like orchids.

The climbing roses scaled elaborate arbors carved from white marble, which arched over her head, forming extravagant walls around her, until she came to the center of the garden, secreted deep within the hedges. There, on a small hillock, an onyx statue of a huge peacock, his tail in full display, stood regally near a rocky pool while statues of peahens seemed to delicately feed in the grass around the pool.

The waters of the pool did not have a fountain, as she'd expected. Instead, the water merely burbled up from below ground, adding small liquid sounds to the scene. A few sparrows winged over the pool, dipping into the water. As Maggie watched, a nereid splashed, swimming on her back, her breasts bobbing in the water as her tail flapped lazily. Maggie stood watching the thing, unsure if it were some genetically altered creature or merely a viviform. Whatever she was, the nereid was lovely. She had a creamy complexion, sweet face, hair of a sea green, blue eyes filled with delight. The nereid splashed about, as if unaware of Maggie's presence, and Maggie decided that the creature must be a viviform, a work of art that only mimicked life.

Maggie waited on a stone bench for twenty minutes, till Darksun set. Then Zeus appeared with a basket. Maggie could smell sweet scents within—fresh bread and fruits. Zeus hardly said hello before he opened the basket, brought out a bottle of wine and two cups, filled them. He set the plates, then began opening silver containers of food.

"Grilled skog in raspberry sauce with fresh mint," he said, not at all enthusiastically. The next plate contained rye bread, covered with cheese and poppy seeds, followed by vegetable dishes and a compote of mixed tropical fruits, cooked in brandy.

All these Zeus served with a singular lack of energy, a self-absorbed air, so Maggie wondered what sort of inner storm might be brewing in him.

After he'd set the last bowl on the stone bench and became so brooding he forgot to remove the lid, Maggie took his hand. "What's troubling you?" she asked. "What are you thinking?"

Zeus hung his head. Here in the dark, with only moon and starlight shining on him, she could not see his eyes. They were lost beneath lanky hair. But when he startled, glanced up, starlight gleamed in his dark eyes. It surprised her. She had not been prepared for the intensity, the passion in his eyes. "I . . . I feel guilty," he whispered. "My problems aren't yours. I should not have tried to involve you in this. Forgive me. It was . . . so thoughtless."

Zeus uncovered two platters. The only sound to pierce the night was the ringing of silver.

"It wasn't thoughtless," Maggie said. "I know you wouldn't do it lightly. Are you frightened?"

Zeus gave a laugh. "Frightened, of my father? No. The man loves me—he says. He loves me so much, he will never let me go. But I am not frightened of him. . . .

"Forgive me, Maggie—this is none of your affair. You should not become . . . embroiled."

He fell silent again. She said softly, "Let me judge that. I understand your pain. I was imprisoned by a Guide once. I know what it is to be a slave."

Zeus looked up at her; hope kindled in his dark eyes. "Then you know how it feels, year after year, longing for release! I think, I think this morning some mad fit took me. I swear, I ran naked out into the sunlight for the first time, and I wanted to throw myself from the citadel in joy, to feel *perfect* liberty, to be unencumbered."

Zeus got up, stalked to the edge of the fountain, and looked out over the gardens to a line of stars that lay heavy on the hills. "What a fool I must appear. I thought that because Felph removed my Guide, he would let me go free."

He stood, hands clasped behind his back, staring up.

"I could help you," Maggie said. Thinking furiously. She had determined earlier to reserve judgment, to let him reveal himself slowly. But now, here in his presence, hearing the intensity behind his words, she didn't doubt that he fervently wanted to be free. She'd been imprisoned by a Guide for only a few days. What would it be like to remain imprisoned for years, craving freedom, in the way that Zeus had been genetically engineered to crave?

Zeus shook his head, then wandered back to the bench. From his basket, he silently brought out a single candle, lit it, and set it between their plates. Once again he became lost in contemplation.

"Please," he said after a moment, "let us not mar a fair dinner with foul conversation." He raised his glass of wine in salute. "To my fair Maggie, who through her kindness has already won for me all the freedom I've ever known."

Zeus drained his cup, and Maggie followed suit. The wine was stronger than any Maggie could remember having tasted, with a fruity bouquet, mildly sweet.

They ate quietly. The food was superb. Despite her dark thoughts, Maggie found that the wine and surroundings lightened her mood. The stars shimmered, the aroma of roses washed the air. A slight warm wind breathed through the gardens, while burbling pools made their own music. Maggie felt light-headed.

Zeus refilled her wine. "No, no more for me," Maggie apologized. "I'm feeling foggy."

"Ah, I'm sorry," Zeus said, breathing deeply. "You're right. I've had too much, too." He stood. "Will you walk with me?"

Maggie tried to stand; the ground seemed to wobble under her. Zeus caught her elbow before she fell, steadied her.

He laughed. "Take off your shoes. The grass here feels good under your feet."

He pulled off his own shoes. Maggie did the same. He led her down a trail to the north, through the thick carpet of grass, along a dark border of roses.

The sky blazed with stars, for Brightstar was now setting. Maggie heard a faint whooshing noise and looked up. Under the starlight, dozens of creatures, like small florafeems the size of plates, hurtled through the night sky in a bouncing gait, like stones skipping through heaven.

Zeus led Maggie to a palace wall. They looked over darkened wheatfields. "There are the meadows of freedom," Zeus said, "where I want to run."

"How far do you think you need to get?" Maggie asked. She had thought Zeus would want to leave the planet. Now she wondered if he might only want to get away from the palace, live in the desert, as unpleasant as that sounded.

"I must get off-world, get lost in the wider universe. If I do, Felph might not follow. I hope he'd let me go."

"He has your genome in stock," Maggie said. "If you fled off-world, it would be easier to build a replica of you than hunt for you."

"I've been thinking of the Milky Way," Zeus said absently. "So far away. It sounds exotic. Do you ever consider returning?"

"Yes, I'll return," Maggie said.

"Where to?" Zeus asked. "Tell me about the world you long for."

The question troubled Maggie. She could not return to Tihrglas, not legally. Higher technologies were outlawed there thousands of years before she was born. The wights enforced that ban, artificial beings she'd been raised to believe were malevolent spirits. On Tihrglas she'd been ignorant of the larger universe—of space travel and genetic enhancements, of telecommunications and nanotechnology. In a coastal village she'd worked in an inn from sunrise to sundown, wearing out her hands and her joints. Nearly everywhere in the universe, life was easier than it had been on Tihrglas. Droids did the dirty work. AIs handled tasks that were too tedious for mankind. Genetic engineering and medications removed most afflictions from life.

Yet Maggie was beginning to suspect that technology really failed to make her life much richer. It did not give life a purpose, a sense of fulfillment.

As Maggie considered what kind of world she dreamed of, she considered her memories of life on Tremonthin—where the Inhuman had downloaded the images from a hundred lifetimes filled with struggle and toil, craving and desire. People had access to life-enhancing technologies on Tremonthin, yet it had brought mostly sadness in the lives she recalled. It merely gave men a goal, perhaps a false goal, to struggle for. No, if it was contentment she wanted, her thoughts returned to Tihrglas, to the serenity she'd sometimes felt at the end of a rugged day when she finished cleaning the kitchens at Mahoney's Inn, or the enjoyment she'd had just listening to old Dan'l Sullivan play his fiddle by the stove on a winter's night, while the old folks reminisced.

I know too much, she realized. Six months earlier, when she'd been on Dronon with Gallen trying to fight the invaders on their home world, her mantle had filled her with elation at discovering the secrets of Dronon technology. She'd imagined that the heart-pounding wonder would never end. Learning the secrets of Dronon technology would help give her life focus, the purpose she'd always sought.

She'd been so naive. Now she knew better: true, the Dronon built powerful gravity drives, better than those mankind had developed. The plasma cannons on Dronon warships shot farther than those mankind used. Their walking hive cities were marvels of technology by any standard.

All of it was worthless.

Maggie had dropped her brogue accent months before. Now for Zeus's sake, she affected it. "On my home world, it's like this we'd be talking, and it's not the kind of place you'd brag to your mother after."

Zeus laughed at her accent, thoroughly charmed.

"The streets get all full of mud after a rain, and when I was a lass, I liked to look in the puddles, to see how they mirrored the sky, and to see how the dark pine trees glowered above me. It's a smart man who knows how to keep to the margin of the road when he's riding a horse, for many a horse will slip and fall in the muck.

"The rain was dear to me—the smell of it. Not the tang of a thunderstorm on the horizon, but the smell afterward, when the air is all washed-out, and it's only pine trees you're smelling.

"And the colors: in spring, the rain cleans the trees and fields and makes the whole world a brighter green—or at least that's how me ma told me. She didn't have a true notion why grass gets greener after a rain, or why crocuses looked brighter. She'd never heard of nitrogen in the air, and how rainwater fertilizes the ground. She just knew it happened, so she said the rain 'washed' things.

"That was the way of folks on Tihrglas. We found easy answers to questions, and we were happy with them.

"After a rain, Ma, she would flutter about the house, her hands busy stitching clothes or setting a new fire or kneading bread or washing a dress, and she'd sing, happy as a sot with a new bottle. I'd ask her why she sang, and she'd say, 'Frogs sing after the rain. Birds sing. So should we.' Then she'd dance round the house." Maggie smiled.

"It sounds a happy place," Zeus said.

It had been, it had been, Maggie realized, before everything went wrong, before her parents died. Tihrglas was a good world. It had just gone bad for her. Maybe that's the way of it, she told herself. Maybe most worlds are fine, till the weight of misfortune crashes down on us. She looked up at Zeus, who stood dark against the stars, staring over the countryside, and offered, "I'll help you get away."

He shook his head thoughtfully. "I don't know, Maggie. I've been thinking. Even if I can get away, should I?"

Maggie did not follow his logic. After a moment, he explained, "Consider this. Imagine I escape, with your help, and Father decides to build another like me. What would be my point? I'd have my freedom, but my clone wouldn't have his. Father would only tighten his grip, hold this one more fiercely. He'd never let it go.

"I . . . don't know if I could live with the guilt of knowing I had purchased my freedom at the price of another's. Hera and Arachne are on Felph's side, yet I'm afraid if I leave, he will treat them harsher for it. I can't tolerate the thought of leaving them behind. . . ."

Maggie frankly felt surprised by the nobility inherent in Zeus's convictions.

"What other choices do I have?" Zeus agonized.

"Perhaps you should stop Felph," Maggie said.

"Stop him, yes, but how? Nothing short of murder would stop him—and even then, assuming that I could be rid of the man, how free could I be with such a thing on my conscience?"

So, he spoke of killing. Maggie suspected it might be necessary. Usurpers were the same across worlds, whether human or Dronon. Good men like Zeus could not tolerate their deeds, yet found the idea of eliminating such men repugnant.

"There are laws to protect you," Maggie said.

"On other worlds, not on this."

"You could fight to change those laws. A world cannot subsist under tyranny unless its people capitulate."

"What could we do? Father needs nothing. We have no economic clout to force him into submission—his workers are nearly all droids, under his control. Nor do we have any military might. He controls the arsenals.

"Even if we could rouse a dozen people, marshal them against Felph, he could buy the sympathies of the majority. He treats them well enough now. What do they care if he is a tyrant only within the walls of his own palace?"

Of course, Zeus was right. Felph was, for all practical purposes, unassailable.

"I've pondered how to win my freedom for years, and I can see no way, though Felph has loosed my bonds," Zeus said. His voice sounded strained; Maggie yearned to comfort him. He turned away. Maggie reached to massage the tension from his back. His muscles felt astonishingly tight. She had not guessed at the strength under his silk shirt.

Maggie recalled her own imprisonment at the hands of Lord Karthenor. Of all the ugly and wretched incidents in her short, dark life—of all the abuses she had suffered—that outweighed them all. She'd watched her mother die, had felt the weight of grief when a father and three brothers drowned. She'd watched Veriasse die in single combat, his face burned with Dronon stomach acids, his bones shattered. She'd seen Orick nearly sliced in two, and recalled the look in Gallen's eye when the Inhuman's agent burrowed into his brain. Yet when Karthenor had imprisoned Maggie, the agony felt greater than the sum of all her other torments. She'd nearly perished. To salvage her, Karthenor had forced her Guide to suffuse her with endorphins. Even that would not have kept her alive. She'd have perished at Karthenor's hands, had Gallen not rescued her.

"I'll help you get free," Maggie said vehemently. She knew it was insane. She'd planned to be more careful. "I can get you free." Immediately she regretted the words. She might have to eliminate Lord Felph. Maggie could not easily stomach the idea of murder. Yet Felph's actions will bring ruin on his own head, Maggie justified her thoughts. If he dies, it will be a deserving death.

Zeus turned, his face now in shadow. Maggie could see only a gleam of his eye. "You would do that for me?"

"Not just for you," Maggie said. "For Hera and Herm, Arachne and Athena. All of you, whether your brother and sisters value their freedom or not."

"Thank you," he choked, awe in his voice.

Zeus reached up his right hand, stroked her jaw. Maggie felt surprised. One did not notice it until standing next to Zeus, but he was huge. Muscular. Maggie had thought him rugged before, but somehow the starlight softened his features. Perhaps it was because she knew him better, felt his suffering, but she found him attractive.

Perhaps that is why when he leaned down to kiss her forehead, she did not startle backward.

When he kissed her lips, she did not retreat. What am I doing? she wondered. This isn't like me.

This is innocent, she told herself. This is innocent. This is only a kiss of gratitude.

Zeus wrapped his left arm around her shoulder, held her head. His lips tasted so sweet.

Maggie knew this was wrong. She wanted to back away, yet she felt curious and surprised at this turn of events. Zeus was handsome. She felt flattered he found her attractive. His kisses tasted so sweet. She felt—so drawn to him.

It must be the wine, she thought. It's clouding my judgment. Zeus held her tighter, and Maggie tasted those lips, and remembered. . . . Two thousand years back, in a lifetime she remembered from Tremonthin, she'd been Kweetsah, a slave girl to a race called the Yamak'hai. On her first night as a slave, her masters had dressed her in red linen and placed bells on her wrists, then escorted her to Overseer T'nok, a huge man with long arms, covered in red hair.

T'nok was not of the Yamak'hai. His subspecies was unknown. Yet his masters valued T'nok, for his kisses drove women mad with lust.

So the overseer kissed Kweetsah for a long sweet hour, fondled her until she felt giddy and overcome with desire. Then T'nok delivered her to her new husband, an old man who was quite plain. Yet she felt so overcome by lust, felt such a need for lechery, she'd slept with the new husband willingly. T'nok's kisses could do that to any woman.

Pheromones, Maggie realized, heart pounding. Zeus's kisses were laced with the same pheromones T'nok's had been. She stepped back from Zeus, dizzy. She was quivering with anticipation, almost blind with desire. It took all her strength to back away.

Zeus stepped forward, kissed her once more, and stroked her left breast with his free hand. She nearly melted into his arms.

Maggie knew that if she did not leave now, she would not be able to. She shoved Zeus in the chest. He backed off.

"Forgive me!" he cried. "Oh, Maggie, forgive me!"

"No, it's all right," Maggie shook her head, trying to clear her thoughts. *He's nothing but an innocent child,* she thought, still dazed. *He feels gratitude for his freedom and confuses it with something more. I should know better. I must be drunk.*

"I did not mean to take advantage," Zeus whispered hurriedly. "It's just that . . . I think I love you."

"What?" Maggie said, still shaking her head. Zeus's kiss had done something to her, nearly blinded her. She tried to make out his form, but little flashes of light seemed to baffle her vision.

"I know it sounds crazy . . . premature," Zeus hurried, "It even sounds strange to me. You're one of the few women I've ever met, aside from my sisters. At first I thought it was only the, because you are so exotic and beautiful that I felt this way.

"Yet, when I look in your eyes, I can see goodness in you. When I smell your hair, I smell your strength. How can I deny what I feel now? You've made me crazy!"

"Stop!" Maggie shouted. She knew she should not have let herself get into this predicament, yet she wanted this man now in a way she'd seldom wanted Gallen. "I'm married."

This was all happening too fast. She'd planned to be more careful, to weigh Zeus, evaluate him over days. Yet in only a couple of hours, she'd found herself bending to his every whim. She'd promised to free him. She'd even thought of killing his father. She'd nearly bedded him.

This was all happening too fast. The pheromones had undone her.

"But—what does your marriage have to do with anything?" Zeus asked. "You could love two dogs, and no one would think ill of you. You could love two flowers or two colors. Just because you love Gallen, does not mean you can't love me, too, the way that I love you."

Zeus gazed at her imploringly. Maggie wanted to go to him, but she remembered how Gallen had hurt her, on a night much like this, with a woman as beautiful in her way as Zeus appeared now, a woman whose kisses had also been laced with pheromones. Maggie could not betray a trust so deep.

"No," Maggie said as Zeus advanced, reaching for her. "No!"

"Maggie—" he began to say, and suddenly a change seemed to come over him. He seemed angry with her. He straightened his back, clenched his jaw. He towered menacingly, and Maggie feared he would strike.

He stopped, hands shaking.

Dave Wolverton

"Zeus? Maggie? Is that you?" a woman's voice came from uphill. A woman rounded a corner of the road between two towering walls of roses. She bore a candle in her hand.

"Ah, it is you," Hera called. "In the garden I found your candle burning. I hoped you wouldn't be far."

"You were walking?" Zeus asked, incredulous. "Here in the North Garden?"

"As I've often wanted to at night," Hera said with a slight nod, "before our lord freed us."

Zeus held his tongue, subdued for the moment. Maggie felt sure Hera had followed them, had perhaps been watching them all along.

"Oh," Hera said in surprise, looking at their faces, at the way they stood too near one another. "I'm not disturbing anything?"

Zeus touched Maggie's elbow from behind, a gentle warning, though she needed none. "No," Maggie said. "We were just about to come in."

"Indeed, my pet," Zeus told Hera, "I'm glad you found us. I'd enjoy your company on the walk home. I fear it is getting cold out here."

"Cold? I don't think so," Hera said.

"Believe me, it has been cooler than I like," Zeus answered, gently putting his hand on Maggie's shoulder. He squeezed it as if to say, "We'll talk tomorrow."

As Zeus left with Hera, Maggie nearly collapsed. A sudden release of adrenaline accompanied Zeus's departure. Maggie's hands and legs shook so badly she could hardly walk.

She dropped to the grass and sat, taking great wracking breaths, almost sobbing.

Gallen, Gallen forgive me for what I almost did, she told herself. On Cyannesse Gallen had made love to a Tharrin, had given himself to a child who was forced too soon to become a woman. He'd done it because the girl was sweet, because she needed comfort. Mostly, Maggie now realized, he'd done it because of pheromones. If the Tharrin's release of amorous chemicals had been anything like Zeus's, it would have required the steadfastness of a saint to walk away.

Gallen was no saint. Neither am I, Maggie realized.

Tomorrow. Zeus wanted to meet her tomorrow. Maggie felt dizzy with desire. It so frightened her, she ran back to her room, leaving her shoes in the garden.

As Zeus went to Hera, he took her arm in his, and decided to leave his dirty plates and picnic basket by the fountains till morning.

They strolled along up through the flowers, until they'd left Maggie far behind, and Hera said, "I hope I spoiled your evening."

"Never fear, my dove," Zeus answered. "I had the quarry cornered, but was about to let her go anyway. Some women appreciate a man who struggles for self-control in the face of her overwhelming charms. I want her to think well of me."

Hera laughed lightly. "I rather doubt she'll think of anything but you, tonight."

Zeus chuckled. He'd halfway seduced Maggie. He imagined she would sleep uneasy, fantasizing about him.

Let her suffer the night, and let Hera think she's scored some minor victory. The night had turned out better than Zeus had hoped. Even if he did not get Maggie to lift her skirt, he suspected he had gone his siblings one better.

He hoped he could trick Maggie into helping him murder Lord Felph.

*O*rick sniffed as he stepped from the ship. The ground under him felt spongy. His paw sank deep on the first step. Though they'd waited hours before disembarking, the air was still filled with pulverized limbs and leaves, detritus pounded into atoms by the shuttle's phased gravity waves.

Upon entering the tangle, the ship had burrowed a thousand meters, until the atomized foliage and hapless animals beneath the ship got so deep that the ship could burrow no farther.

Orick looked up. The sky above was perfectly black, as if in a mine shaft. No light could reach him, the sky was up so far, the clouds had been so thick.

"I smell smoke," Tallea said. It came faintly, masked by the moist scent of alien trees.

"It's nothing to worry about," Felph said. "The gravity waves we used to pulverize the trees create some heat. The powder beneath our feet will stay hot for weeks, but won't catch fire. There isn't enough oxygen in the mix."

"Shhhh . . ." Athena warned. She held a brilliant glow globe in one hand, a pistol in the other. "Follow me."

The young woman walked down a mild slope, bouncing with each step. The powder at her feet drifted up like blowing smoke. Orick followed at Athena's heel.

Drops of water splashed down from time to time, and the going was slow. Massive tree trunks, wide enough so a house could fit inside, thrust everywhere through the tangle. Fallen trees provided roofs and pathways, and detritus had collected in crooks of branches or on ribbon trees, creating something of a false floor, paths for them to tread.

Along many trunks were ledges—outcroppings, formed by enormous growths, like giant colonies of mold. Epiphytes and parasitic plants had lived here but then rotted away as the canopy of the tangle climbed higher, robbing the plants of light, so that even though the area showed signs of plant life everywhere—hanging vines and rotted trees—little survived. Only dew trees, massive as houses, still lived.

Everything seemed familiar, nothing was familiar. Giant worm vine twisted in broad ribbons, forming roads that Athena eagerly sought. Yet the branches and deadfalls combined to form strange caverns. In places, the immense weight of the foliage above caused plants to collapse, so that frequently the trail led down at a precarious angle.

Though the air was humid, Orick felt surprised at how little water seeped in from the canopy above. Often, water ran down a winding tree trunk in rivulets, but surprisingly, just as often Orick was able to find dry footing.

Still, the journey became treacherous.

Little lived here. The tangle was strangely silent, save for an occasional creaking of limbs, the thud of heavy branches snapping far above.

Yet Orick felt as if the tangle were alive in spite of its silence. Watching, writhing. Everywhere was movement, distant creakings, water cascading, soggy footfalls.

A march of several hours along various fallen limbs brought them far enough down and away from the havoc wrought by their ship that Orick could finally breathe easier, and they dropped to a false floor, with real dirt.

Here was life in abundance. Huge pale worms, perhaps five meters in length, each as thick around as a good-sized rattlesnake, fed among the humus, while small armadillo-like creatures scampered about, growling when one of the party approached. Here were sounds hard to identify—buzzing insects, strange hooting. As they moved into this region, Orick felt frightened.

Athena dimmed her light. To Orick's surprise, along the ground were huge clods he'd thought were turds, but these glowed pink, with their own dim light. Athena kicked one over. Orick saw that it had a dozen small legs at its base, so thin they could hardly move such a massive body.

Athena grabbed several of them, placed them in a net at her hip. She gave one to Gallen. "Darkfriends," she explained. "They give light to attract mates, but they are very much in tune with other creatures of the tangle. They dim if they smell enemies."

"So if the lights go out, we'll know that something wants to eat us?" Orick asked.

"It's better than no warning at all," Athena admitted. "I'll flip on my torch, if that should happen. But beware. We're down at least fifteen hundred meters. Here, we are not far above the first lairs of the sfuz. If we find a good path, the sfuz will know of it. Watch for traps."

Orick wondered, "What kind of traps?"

"Snares and webs. The webs of sfuz glisten like water. It takes a keen eye to tell the difference." Athena stopped a moment. "If the sfuz attack, they usually drop from above. Watch for them."

Athena took the lead, followed by Gallen, who kept his vibro-blade in one hand. His mantle of black rings jangled on his head; Gallen seemed little more than a shadow, sometimes tinkling as he walked. Behind Gallen, Felph sauntered along easily, carrying only a walking stick. He wore an amused expression. Orick wondered at his aloofness, until he realized that Felph did not care if he lived or died down here. If he died beneath the tangle, he would be reborn.

Behind Felph came Orick, followed by Tallea, who remained watchful, sniffing at the ground as she prowled.

Orick breathed deeply, testing musty air. The pungent odor of dew trees, like rotting oranges, somehow made him hungry. The worm vines smelled rich with turpines, like cut and polished ash. The air was thick with their scent, so heavy Orick felt almost as if he were traveling through liquid. Beneath these aromas lay the heavier odor of molding detritus. All sound was muffled, deadened. Orick had never experienced such total quietness outside a cave.

Some huge insects fluttered up, seeking escape. Others skittered away to the far side of a tree, defying gravity.

Twice the group slowed and climbed down holes, dropping to some deeper level beneath this wretched tangle.

The dullness of sound, closeness of vegetation, the smell of decay—all became suffocating, till Orick wanted to run. Their scent could lead him back to the shuttle. Orick knew he only had to follow it. Yet he suspected that even in the shuttle, he would feel closed-in, trapped. He kept his nose down, followed Gallen.

After many hours, Athena located a wide branch in the crook of a tree, then called a halt. "It's dark out," she whispered. "I think the sun set an hour ago."

"That doesn't matter," Felph whispered. "Let us all press on."

"It matters," Athena warned. "We're getting tired. The farther we march, the more certain it becomes that the sfuz will cross our trail. If we are tired when they find us, we will be less alert, less able to fight them."

Felph grunted in disgust. "Fine then, sleep if you must!" He squatted against the tree, leaning back, and Orick saw it—a misty white vine hanging behind Felph, so thin and watery, it seemed almost invisible.

"Stop!" he shouted. Felph stood bolt upright.

Orick ran to the vine, sniffed it. It had an odd odor, somewhat like shellac, or some material he'd once smelled boatmen use as glue. The vine came to rest a handspan from Felph's back, where it ended in a glob of goo that was hidden with crushed dust. The line was tight as a lute string.

"Good eyes," Athena praised Orick, patted his head. She scrounged till she found a long limb, then touched the gooey end of the web. It snapped, ripping the limb from her hand, pulling it up far into the darkness above. "Had one of us touched the trigger, we'd have been carried as easily as that stick," Athena warned. "The pull is enough to snap your neck. Let this be a warning. There is no rescue from the snare of a sfuz. We might manage to retrieve your corpse."

She gave Lord Felph a hard look, as if ordering him to thank Orick for his very life. Felph merely grunted, leaned back where the snare had been.

"Not here," Athena hissed. "We can't rest here. The sfuz will check its snare. We don't want it to find us."

"Of course we do," Felph replied. "I brought Gallen here to become acquainted with the vermin. What better way than to rest here, till the maker of that trap comes?"

Athena looked into Gallen's eyes. He merely shrugged. "I'll keep first watch," Athena whispered.

They set a glum camp. Gallen unpacked a bit of cold food, some fine ham from Felph's larder, along with fresh fruits and bread. The food lightened Orick's mood, made the darkness here seem more bearable.

Gallen took a canister of explosive foam, sprayed it on the trail behind them, then set wards that would light up and emit sound if something large approached.

Felph lay on a thermal blanket.

And Gallen stood, ready. "I will keep vigil with you," he told Athena.

"Get some sleep," she said. "The sfuz live far below us by day, but in an hour, they'll make their journey up for their nightly hunt in the canopy of the tangle. We shouldn't have any problems until then."

"My mantle can watch with you," Gallen said. "It can waken me at the first sign of trouble."

Athena shook her head. "The sfuz don't give warning." She stood, went around camp, setting out darkfriends at equal distances, as if Gallen's wards and precautions were worthless. When the darkfriends were separated by a few yards, they began glowing fiercely, then ponderously began making an hours-long journey back to one another. The night glowed around them as they struggled in the dirt. Almost, Orick could imagine he was in a deep forest back on Tihrglas, with merry campfires guttering about. But the light of these creatures was too dim, and the trees beside them too desiccated, too twisted and alien to remind him of home.

Lord Felph lay back, resting comfortably in his little nook, watching the frightened faces of the others with amusement. Athena took watch in the deepest shadows she could find amid this pool of light. Surprisingly, though the darkfriends seemed to gleam brightly, their light didn't shine far; the twisted branches around Athena threw enough shadows so she remained concealed. Gallen lay beside Felph and soon fell asleep.

Orick could not rest. He could see better in the darkness than a human, and decided to keep watch a bit. Meanwhile, Tallea opened Orick's Bible and began reading from the book of Genesis, but found it rough going. She could not understand the archaic language of the book, the symbolic references, figures of speech. So Orick expounded the Bible's teachings, beginning with the creation of the Earth, the fall of Adam, and the promises God made to Noah, Abraham, Moses, and other prophets. He told how David slew Goliath, how Elijah healed a pagan of leprosy—until he got to the life of Jesus, whose birth in Bethlehem was announced by a new star shining in heaven and by the voices of angels.

Orick felt glad of Tallea's interest. The she-bear often asked pointed questions. And as Orick taught, he began to see patterns he had never considered. He saw how the stories he knew so well each added to a great theme which told how God spoke to man, giving him promises if he should act well, then helped man reach his highest potential. At times, Orick found himself relating ideas he had never considered. He felt sure God was inspiring him, that he was expounding beyond his natural wisdom.

Even more gratifying, he found that his words were taking root in more than one heart. As he spoke, his voice filled the little hollow. Athena had been keeping guard, but by the tilt of her head, Orick could tell she was not listening for sounds of predators, she listened to him, and after a bit she did not even keep up a pretense of disinterest, but came and crouched quietly beside Tallea, her pulp gun resting casually on one knee.

Athena watched Orick intently, absorbing each word, saying nothing. Orick was reminded of the words of Christ, "The gospel is likened unto a fisherman who cast his net into the sea, and gathered fishes of every kind." Orick had cast his net for Tallea, and was pulling in a decidedly odd fish.

But as sure as God walked in the Garden of Eden, so did Satan, and it seemed to Orick that he was just getting to the best parts of the New Testament when Lord Felph roused from his nap and sauntered over.

Orick had been expounding upon the Beatitudes, and he quoted, " 'Blessed are the poor in spirit who come unto me, for theirs is the kingdom of heaven.' " Then Orick added, "This is God's promise that He will strengthen us, regardless of our weaknesses, so that we can withstand His presence.'

" 'Blessed are the meek, for they shall inherit the earth.' This is God's promise that all things shall be given to those who submit to His teachings.

" 'Blessed are those who hunger and thirst after righteousness, for they shall be filled with the Holy Ghost.' This is God's promise that He will not leave you comfortless, in moments of trial, but shall grant His spirit to meet your needs."

Felph groused, "Speaking of tribulation, how is a man to sleep, Orick, with your incessant babbling?"

"I was just telling Tallea and Athena here about the life of Jesus," Orick said.

Felph sat next to Orick, wrapped his arms around his legs. Felph's eyes were a bit puffy, swollen, and his face looked drained, tired. Yet he stroked his short beard thoughtfully and studied Orick from under heavy lids. "Ah, yes, a venerable enough chap, I gather. But I find other gods more intriguing."

"Other gods?" Tallea asked. "You mean there are stories of other gods?"

Orick got an uneasy feeling. The Bible mentioned such gods—Baalim and Asteroth, Moloch and Diana. To worship them was forbidden. On Orick's world, nothing was known of their ways. Orick believed God wanted to keep it this way.

"I always found Asteroth fascinating," Felph said, watching Orick's reaction. "I loved the way her worshipers used fetishes, and all the delightful sacred orgies they threw. Devotion toward the divine mother—with all her creative forces, and her concern for hearth and home—those make so much more sense to me than worship of a war god. Don't you think, Orick?"

"God is not a god of war," Orick said, "but of peace."

"Yes, well, tell that to the Canaanites, and the Hittites and Jebusites and the Perizites and the Ammonites and the Philistines. I'm sure I'm forgetting a few, but those were just some of the nations the Israelites slaughtered under inspiration of your God of Peace."

"I'm sure He had a good reason," Orick countered. "God could not simply allow His people to die at the hands of their enemies. He must protect them."

"Protect them, of course," Felph said. "Now if I recall correctly, with the Hittites, Joshua slaughtered their men, their women, their children, all their flocks and herds, then burned their cities, melted their idols, and ground the gold into dust and threw it into the rivers. Isn't that right?"

"Yes," Orick admitted glumly.

"I can understand discarding the gold, and I suppose cities were dirty enough back then that burning might have been in order. Personally, I'd even back that God of yours on his decision to kill the children in the cities. But for the life of me, Orick, I can't figure out what the poor sheep did so wrong! Really, was it their fault if those shepherds had unwholesome amorous preferences? Oh, and let's not even mention the babes—Sock it to those mewling infants, Jehovah!" Lord Felph cackled horribly at his own jests.

Well, whatever presence of the Holy Spirit Orick had felt, it had about all fled by now. It wasn't as if Orick didn't have answers to Felph—he believed that God ordered the flocks destroyed so the Israelites would not be tempted to fight over the spoils of war. As for the babes, who knew what had really been done? The Bible was so old, it was probably filled with some inaccuracies. An uninspired scribe might have thrown in the thing about the babes. But Felph was throwing out questions of such moral complexity they were difficult to answer, especially for someone like Tallea, who needed to receive the milk of the gospel before she could tolerate the meat.

"There are answers to the questions you pose," Orick said.

"Ah, those who have ears, let them hear!" Lord Felph joked.

Athena saw how Felph annoyed Orick. She said, "You were telling us about the Sermon on the Mount. . . ."

"Yes," Orick tried to remember where he'd left off.

"Are you certain your Jesus wasn't an impostor, Orick?" Felph asked. "None of his 'miracles' seem very miraculous to me. Their effects would be very easy to accomplish with modern technology."

"But they didn't have modern technology back then," Orick countered.

"Perhaps, but imagine this, Orick: imagine that a modern man went back in time, with the idea of posing as the Son of God. Using modern equipment, he could have easily performed the 'miracles' you describe."

"What of turning water into wine?" Orick asked.

"Nanotechnology," Felph said. "A small tablet filled with nutrients and the proper nanoware, and in moments your water turns to wine."

"What about healing the sick or raising the dead?"

"Who knows how sick those people really were?" Felph argued. "Nano-docs can work wonders."

"What of walking on the water?"

"An antigrav sled, floating just below the surface. I've accomplished the same effect myself."

"What of calming the troubled seas?"

Lord Felph fell silent, considering. "Weather satellites. Jesus knew when the storm would end."

"I don't accept that answer," Orick said. "Even after a storm calms, the seas stay rough. So what about it, how about calming the seas?"

"I don't know—*yet*," Felph admitted. "Such technology doesn't exist at the moment."

"And here is another question for you," Orick said. "Can a man travel back in time that far?"

"Time travel is possible, though the technology is strictly controlled," Felph said. "One can go back in time a few days—even a week."

"But we're talking twenty thousand years."

"If we had an energy source large enough, one that he could carry with him, so that he could duplicate the effort over and—" Felph began.

"It's not possible, is it?"

"No," Felph admitted. "It's not, by modern standards. But you're missing my point entirely, Orick."

"Which is?"

"I'm getting to that. I'm not saying that a man went back in time—either from our present day, or from some future. I simply wanted to say this: that as a species, we are evolving into something equal to your god."

Orick found the statement befuddling. "Look at me," Felph continued. "I've been alive for four thousand years. I've worn out thirty clones, and lost another fifty by accident. I've been 'raised from the dead' some eighty times. I won't live forever, but who knows how long your 'God' lived. And though I'm not omniscient, as your god supposedly is, I could gain something near that. I could collect all the knowledge of mankind into one huge Omni-mind, as the Tharrin do, and use it to help me rule the stars."

"But that isn't the same as what I'm talking about."

"Yet it is very near," Felph said. "One might argue that, as god's children, we are naturally struggling toward godhood ourselves—seeking the same rights and powers you ascribe to your god. So, my question is this, Orick. Who is to say that this isn't all your god wants of us? Perhaps he created us, knowing that just as a salmon will swim upstream, or that a gosling will take to the air—perhaps in the same way, he knew in time we would evolve into gods. Perhaps that is all he wants."

Orick considered the idea, rejected it as pure fantasy. Too often, he'd felt God's spirit, promptings that told him his life, his actions, mattered deeply. He didn't buy for a moment the notion that virtually without any struggle on his part, his children would someday become coequal to God. "I find your philosophy to be a bit . . . implausible."

Felph laughed. "How so?"

"Because it requires no moral effort," Orick said. "Attaining perfect love, perfect hope, perfect faith, perfect harmony among mankind—won't *just happen.* Your four thousand years of life hasn't shaped you into a godling."

"Touché, Orick. Yet there are special cases. Some men struggle to become gods. In time don't you think one of them will succeed?"

Orick said, "Someday, one of your descendants might gain all knowledge, all power, and all goodness. But that does not free me from the responsibility to do all I can with *my* life to achieve those same ends."

Lord Felph considered Orick's words, his brow wrinkling. "For a young bear, you have learned much. I'll think about your arguments, but I am not certain I care for your god. Other gods were worshiped in his time, gods who were more personable, more earthy, more human—and therefore perhaps more approachable."

Does the man hear nothing I say? Orick wondered. "We don't invent gods to suit our needs. We follow God to attain our potential."

Felph laughed. "Well, perhaps *you* don't invent gods, but that happens to be my life's work." He glanced slyly at Athena, who still squatted beside Tallea. She arched her back and yawned. In that moment Orick could see her full figure, the graceful curve of her breasts, the dazzling auburn hair curling down nearly to her waist.

"I'm afraid you're asking too much from your children," Orick told Felph. "If you hope that they'll be gods, you'll be disappointed."

"Of course, of course—" Felph said excitedly. "In this generation. But eons from now, in the twentieth and thirtieth generations . . ."

Felph turned to Athena. "What do you think? I bred you for wisdom, child. Who is right, me or Orick?"

Athena stared up at her father, and said shyly. "I think . . . a foolish man loves the sound of his own voice. A wise man listens to the words of others."

Felph frowned. "Confucius. Are you quoting Confucius at me?"

"No," she said. "I'm quoting myself."

"So you're calling me a fool? For not listening to a bear."

"His words aren't his own, but come from those who sent him," Athena said softly. Orick almost laughed, for he had just quoted that line from the Scriptures a moment ago, only it was Jesus speaking about his doctrine.

"I've read his Scriptures," Felph said. "I'm sure I recall the words as well as he does. And I've read other ancient texts, too—the *Koran*, the *Egyptian Book of the Dead*, the *Popolvuh*—"

"A wise man does not merely hear words, he listens." Athena grinned.

"You believe my children will fail?" Felph cried in dismay.

Athena gazed into Felph's eyes, bit her lower lip. "You think that because you made us to crave, to crave power and life and love—we will seize those things, and that will drive us toward greater heights. If you imagine that this is progress, Father, then, yes, we will progress. But I fear that we will only become supreme consumers.

"You say you admire 'more human' gods," Athena continued. "But I fear you admire yourself too much. Perhaps you cannot imagine anything more noble than man, but Orick here has just revealed it to me."

"So you will become a Christ worshiper?" Felph said. "You'll let this bear turn you against me!"

In answer, Athena stood, turned her back, and walked to Gallen, prepared to wake him so he could take his watch. Orick stared in wonder, his heart swelling with joy.

He glanced from the corner of his eye to see Tallea's reaction.

Something huge and black, like a giant spider, landed atop Tallea with a whump, and Orick cried out, startled. It was only there for a moment, moving rapidly. Yet for a fraction of a second he saw it: the creature had six enormous long hairy legs all spreading out from a compact, round body. Its face was something from a nightmare. The face was generally doglike in shape, but it had no ears that Orick could see, and it had no hair. Instead, the slate gray skin looked as if it had burned away. Its dark eyes were horribly large.

The creature bit Tallea's neck, and Orick shouted, "Here now!" and leapt to his paws, thinking to kill the creature.

But at that moment, something heavy landed on Orick's back, knocking the breath from him. The big bear dropped with a groan. Everything went black.

For a moment, Orick did not know if he'd been knocked unconscious, or if the lights had simply gone out. Then he remembered that the darkfriends would quit shining when they sensed enemies. And for some reason, Gallen's warning devices hadn't worked.

Lord Felph shouted, "Sfuz!" Orick was vaguely aware of screaming—Athena shrieking for help, mingled with a sudden whistling, a sound like dozens of birds twittering loudly. He heard scuffling feet as Felph scrambled away. He felt something pierce his back, a sharp talon. Something was tearing him open, yet Orick seemed paralyzed, unable to react. In this darkness, if he bit and clawed blindly, he might accidentally kill Felph.

He had to be cautious.

A terrible light exploded, a blinding white. The creature attacking Orick shrieked and rolled away.

Orick swatted in the direction the creature had rolled. He felt a thud as he raked his claws through flesh, snapped bones.

Tallea roared. In a moment Orick was beside her. The brilliant light had blinded him, but now another dim light shone. Athena must have got out a glow globe. His sight began to clear. The huge spiderlike being that had attacked Tallea shrieked in pain and rolled on the ground, kicking its legs in the air. The light devastated the sfuz. All around, Orick could hear the nasty creatures shrieking.

Orick pounced on it, bit its throat; gooey blood spurted into his mouth. He leapt on the thing once, twice. It did not die all the way—merely slowed in its movements.

Orick was growling at the top of his voice, and thus did not hear Gallen and Athena shout. Instead, he heard the concussions of Gallen's pulp gun as he fired twelve shots, heard the hum of Gallen's vibro-blade.

All around was whistling, and Orick found that his right shoulder was suddenly covered with a sticky web. He couldn't get his front paw off the ground—it felt as if it were glued. Tallea shouted for help, and Orick suddenly realized that dozens of sfuz were dropping from above on sticky webs. He blinked fiercely, trying to get the tears from his eyes, trying to see well enough to defend himself. As Orick's vision began to clear, another web landed across his face, gluing him more firmly to the ground.

He drew his head back, trying to break free. As enormous as Orick was, he could not budge the web. He uttered a hopeless prayer, wishing for the strength of Samson. "God help us."

A second brilliant strobe went off. Everywhere, sfuz shrieked in pain. Gallen was tossing photon grenades—small weapons intended to blind an enemy at night. The grenades were small enough so Gallen could easily hold a dozen in his pack. Perhaps more than anything else at hand, the grenades affected the sfuz, for they were born to the magnificent blackness that reigned here beneath the tangle.

As suddenly as the fight had begun, sfuz leapt away, whistling frantically. Orick's eyes adjusted. He pulled at the web that pinned his head. He bit its strands, chewing free. Tallea grunted, doing the same.

Lord Felph seemed miraculously unaffected by this whole thing. He'd somehow rushed from Orick, over to Gallen and Athena. No sfuz had leapt on his back or captured him in its web. It seemed oddly miraculous. The old man chuckled merrily. "Well-done, Gallen! Well-done! My, what one can accomplish with a Lord Protector. Why, if it weren't for you, we'd be stuffed in their guts like sausages in casings!"

Orick stopped chewing, yanked himself free. Felph stood in his robes, grinning. All around them were signs of a massacre. Gallen stood, a dozen dead sfuz sprawled at his feet. In the fray, Athena had taken his vibro-blade. Now she crouched, at his feet, poised, the silver-blue blade shimmering in the darkness, humming like some living thing.

Yet it was not the others who held Orick's attention. It was Gallen. Orick had never seen the boy look so pale, so panicked.

"They came out of thin air!" Gallen said, shuddering. "Just out of the air. I've never seen anything move so fast!"

"Let's get back to the ship," Athena said. "This isn't over. Some got away. They'll be back with reinforcements."

"There were no scouts. . . ." Gallen said. "None came looking for us. My mantle would have seen them."

Orick's hair stood on end. He hadn't seen the sfuz till they dropped from above. He looked up. The air above them stood open for at least sixty meters.

"Well, Gallen, you reacted admirably," Felph said, grunting in satisfaction.

Gallen still crouched, trying to look all directions at once. "You said they trained other animals. Could they have used one against us?"

"How do you mean?" Tallea asked.

"The sfuz must have had help setting the ambush," Gallen said. He looked all about. "Insects?" he asked, shaking his head. "Something larger— like a crow—flew overhead an hour ago, but I thought it was just hunting insects."

"Maybe," Athena agreed. "They train such creatures to hunt, the way our ancestors trained dogs."

"Let's get out of here," Gallen said.

Athena grabbed the darkfriends, stuffed them into the net on her hip.

Orick stared at the corpse of a sfuz. Its face, he saw now, was more purplish than gray; its teeth were unnaturally long and sharp. He'd thought it had large eyes before, but now he saw that each large dark eye was actually two eyeballs, separated by a thin membrane. One eye aimed up, while the other aimed down. It made sense that such a creature would always seek to attack from above or below.

Its fur, which started just behind the ears, was shorter and thicker than a bear's, bristling. He saw now that each sfuz had four legs and two arms. The creature's legs had four or five claws, or hooks on them, all in a row along the length of the leg, so the sfuz could crawl upside down or sideways among the trees simply by hugging the limbs. The foreclaws were more like hands, each with a thumb and two fingers, all of which had saberlike claws.

Orick moved his shoulder experimentally. He'd been clawed on the back, and he could smell blood. Yet he felt little pain. Months before, in order to save Orick's life, Gallen had fed the bear some nanodocs, tiny machines that went about repairing injuries to Orick's body. They worked so quickly that even now, Orick could feel some heat in his back where the machines hurriedly mended his torn shoulder.

"Are you all right, Tallea?" Orick asked. He smelled blood on her.

"A scratch," the she-bear said. Orick looked into the wound on the back of her neck, saw dark blood pooling. He licked the wound, then licked her muzzle affectionately.

Gallen and Felph had readied their packs. They hurried ahead. Orick did not want to be left behind.

The journey back up was arduous. Orick hadn't realized how rapidly they'd descended—walking down limbs, climbing from one drop to the next. It had seemed a fairly level journey as they came down, but where possible, when the path had taken a downward turn, Athena had led them lower.

They ran for an hour, then Gallen suddenly raised his pulp gun and fired into the air.

Something large and black dropped. Gallen went to the thing. It was a bird, a hairy red bird, with a ratlike face filled with rows of sharp teeth. Gallen's weapon had ripped away most of its innards.

Gallen bent to study the creature. "It's the same one that flew over us earlier. My mantle says it has the same infrared register. It came flying ahead of us, and was just turning back."

"It's called a *blood rat*," Athena said. She turned the creature on its side. Just behind its head, she found a thinning in its hair. "This one has been wearing a collar."

Lord Felph grunted.

"They didn't just train this one," Gallen said. "They had to have communicated to it, somehow."

Athena shook her head. "I can't see how. It's just a dumb animal." Indeed, it looked like a rat with wings. Its head was no larger than a cat's; Orick thought it odd that such a creature could communicate with the sfuz. The sfuz were as large as humans, though not as massive.

The group began hiking, almost running up the trail. Orick watched Tallea. The she-bear had been more sorely wounded than she wanted to tell, and she lagged behind, dragging her right front paw. Orick kept urging her to hurry, to keep up.

They were still a good hour's march from the ship when Orick detected a distant whistling. In the deep foliage of the tangle, with a thousand branches crowding around, it was impossible to tell where the sound came from. That it was the whistle of a sfuz, Orick had no doubt. Once having heard that high, keening, almost hysterical pitch, he would never forget it. The sound reminded him of laughter, of whistling laughter, yet more frantic, more intense.

Gallen stopped. "They're behind us," he said with certainty. He leapt away.

Orick and the others followed with renewed strength, though Orick was sweating from exertion.

A moment later, Gallen stopped. Ahead, perhaps not a hundred meters, they heard whistling. Yet at this moment, they were running along the track of a worm vine that wound a precarious way among the immense boles of dew trees, each many meters in diameter. Orick could not see around that path, but the sfuz announced itself.

The ululating noise stopped. Almost simultaneously, another whistling seemed to come far above and behind them.

"That's the same sfuz," Gallen whispered in awe. "My mantle says it has the exact same voiceprint."

"It's teasing us," Felph guessed. "It must know where we are, so it's running along limbs above us, whistling. Because it went into a different chamber, it sounds as if it is moving around us."

"No," Athena whispered, "that is a hunter's whistle. That sfuz is hunting us. I think . . . I've heard that sound when a pair of sfuz attack, and I manage to kill one's mate. That sfuz is furious."

The fur at the base of Orick's neck rose again.

"Quietly, then," Gallen whispered. They ran. They climbed a wide tree, up through some thick spongy fungus, till they found the trail they'd come down. Then they hurried through a narrow defile where ancient withered roots, like long gray fingers, hung from above.

As they passed this, Orick heard heavy whistling behind him. He brought up the rear of the group, so he pivoted instantly, lashed with one claw.

The sfuz was charging, but as quickly as it had appeared, it turned aside, scurried around the trunk of a tree. Orick's claw raked empty air. He stood befuddled, unable to find his quarry.

"They've found us!" Tallea shouted. "Run."

Gallen burst ahead at full speed.

They ran for twenty minutes, Orick expecting an attack at any second.

The sfuz went for reinforcements, Orick realized. Or it hoped to organize an ambush ahead.

Lord Felph kept lagging behind, stumbling from exertion. Orick heard whistling again, far below it seemed, so far he thought he might be imagining it. Yet it was not one voice that resounded through the tangle now, it was a thousand voices, united.

Felph fell to the ground, panting for breath, forcing everyone to stop.

Gallen reached to pull him to his feet. "Hurry!"

Felph shook his head. "It's no use. We're too far from the ship. We'll never make it!"

"You can't know that!" Gallen said. "You have to try."

Felph laughed. "No, no I don't. *You* have to try!"

Orick understood. Felph was giving up. He didn't need to make a grand dash for escape. He would be reborn. Felph was right. He merely slowed the others down. Leaving him was their only hope for escape.

"I can do you a small service," Felph grunted. "Give me the darkfriends. Gallen, give me a weapon. When the sfuz attack, I'll hold them off a few moments, buy you some time."

"You certain?" Gallen asked.

Felph chuckled. "Really, boy, one way or another, this body will get eaten today. I might as well."

"Fine," Gallen said, unceremoniously. He tossed a pulp gun on the ground beside Felph. Athena unsnapped the webbing that held the darkfriends. The grubs tumbled out.

As one, Athena and Gallen turned and ran, with Tallea close behind, but Orick could not leave Felph so easily. "Are you sure you won't come with us?"

"I'll follow as I can," Felph said, then laughed. " 'No greater love hath a man than this: that he lay down his life for his friends!' You see Orick, I'm just like your Christ. I'll be your messiah today."

Orick did not laugh. It seemed sacrilegious to do so. Still Felph continued. "I lay my life down, but I shall take it up again!" He staggered to his feet, grabbed a darkfriend in one hand to use as a light, and said, "Hide not your light under a bushel, Orick. Let your light so shine, that others will see your good works and glorify your father in heaven!"

Four thousand years old, Orick realized, and in all that time, all Felph had learned from the Scriptures was to mock them.

Orick turned and ran, following the fading light that Athena carried. Felph cackled and shouted epithets as he ran. Once he looked back, saw Felph struggling up the trail.

Orick was a fast bear, and strong. He caught up to his friends shortly. In a moment, the sound of Felph's cackling died away. A moment later, he heard a dull thud that might have been a distant explosion.

Had Felph fired his weapon?

Orick held his breath, but did not stop. His blood so pounded in his veins he could not be certain, but he fancied that another shot followed, then a wailing scream.

Perhaps. Perhaps he imagined it. Orick ran for his life.

Eighteen

*T*homas Flynn regarded himself as pragmatic. He wanted little from life—a woman to keep him warm at night, decent food in his belly, a fine instrument to play. And he wanted to live forever.

But now, as a slave with Lord Karthenor's Guide directing his every action, Thomas's hopes grew cold.

The morning after he'd killed the shepherd's wife for Lord Karthenor, Thomas Flynn conjured an escape plan. He did not know how to remove the Guide Karthenor had affixed to his skull. He could not run or fight.

But he could plot. Karthenor himself had given Thomas the key, the night he'd ordered Thomas to play and sing.

In the morning, Thomas found that his Guide would not let him speak, but as Thomas set the fire and began frying up fresh eggs and ham for Karthenor's men and the shepherd's toddler, a tune came to mind. Thomas found himself humming.

It took him several moments to realize that though his Guide would not let him speak, it would let him sing. Thomas had long known that with a song he could melt the heart of most young maidens, and lighten the heart of the sourest codger.

So all morning he pondered the message he would send, then, when his plan felt complete, he composed a song. It was not a perfect song—in fact, Thomas found it damned bad by any standard, but Karthenor had ordered him to sing a sweet tune, and Thomas composed a sweet tune for the words. They let him say what he needed to say. So as Karthenor sat spooning eggs to the orphaned child, Thomas got down the lute and sang,

> *"You say our lives have meaning.*
> *Like you, I want to live in the sky.*
> *But I am bound,*
> *By you I'm bound.*
> *In these chains I slowly die."*

Karthenor stopped feeding the boy, who immediately began grabbing for the spoon. Karthenor glanced up at Thomas in surprise. "You have something to say? Speak, Thomas."

Thomas tried to infuse his words with charm and sincerity. "This Guide is a damned nuisance, man! I'm an artist. Even if you think me only a drudge, thumping my lute strings as if I were beating a rug, I'll be needing use of my fingers to practice."

Karthenor laughed. "Fine, you may practice your instrument and sing— so long as you don't grow tedious. Anything else?"

"Yes," Thomas said, and found his heart thumping, voice tight. He wasn't sure if the lie would come off. "You told me last night something of your philosophy, and I've been thinking. I agree with you. I came from a backward world, and when I saw the chance to get out, I jumped. And as for recognizing the worth of man, well, a man's only worth comes from what he makes of himself, sure. So I want to know, how do I join you?"

Karthenor smiled, a clever, intimidating smile. His gold mask gleamed brightly, half-reflecting the sun that shone in through the window by the rocking chair, where Karthenor sat.

"I've seen potential in you," Karthenor said. "When I questioned you, I saw that you could be one of us, perhaps.

"But I must ask: do you expect me to believe you would help us hunt and destroy your niece, your only kin? On your world, family bonds are important."

Thomas dared not lie, but his Guide allowed him some freedom in answering. He skirted the truth, choosing his words carefully, "Maggie *is* my only kin. But that didn't stop me from leaving her to grow up alone. Facing trials in life builds strength, and I'd rather have a strong niece than some weepy cow. I tracked her down when I heard she had an inheritance coming. I wouldn't have stolen it. I planned only to use it as seed money, to make a little profit for myself, then leave her with what she owned."

"But would you fight her?" Karthenor asked.

"For the right cause," Thomas said, recognizing that he could hide behind half-truths, evade answering all night. "Yes, I'd fight her."

Karthenor grinned slyly. "Is the Dronon cause the right cause? Is my cause the right cause? Tell me fully."

The Guide would not let him lie to so direct a question. "No, it's not.

There's nothing wrong with using people, that is the basis of the capitalistic system. Folks hire themselves out like oxen, trading their lives cheap. But I don't believe you use them well, Karthenor. I don't believe you understand how to manipulate others subtly, and I don't think you have to make a person's life miserable, even if you do take him slave. There's no justification for being plain vile."

Karthenor nodded thoughtfully. "You're right. I tend to be crude in my attempts at manipulation. To expand on your metaphor, I sometimes yoke racing stallions to the plow.

"And it may just be," Karthenor said, "I'm not as idealistic as I like to pretend. To be blunt, it amuses me to use people. I like the thrill, the power."

Karthenor looked at his men to see their reactions. Neither seemed surprised. Karthenor continued, "If I did not like your singing voice, Thomas, I'd dispose of you. But . . . in my mercy, I spare you. This also makes me feel powerful. Maybe that's all I'm really about—power.

"Those with the least power tend to crave it most. Perhaps when you have been a slave long enough, you too will crave power. You might yet become Dronon.

"But I suspect it will take time. A very long time. . . ."

Karthenor's words dashed Thomas's hopes for a quick release. Shortly after, they departed the shepherd's shack, the toddler riding the front of an airbike, tucked under Karthenor's arm.

By midday they reached a gate, left Tremonthin for a heavily populated world with high technology. There, Karthenor abandoned the toddler, leaving him on a deserted road at the edge of a city.

In rapid succession they drove through several gates, till they reached a gray alien planet with tortured, pitted plains. Strange animals seemed almost to agonize under a dim red sun.

Karthenor stopped to make a radio transmission, then waited. By evening, a huge walking vehicle approached, a black city that stalked across the ruined land like a giant tick, the metal of its legs crashing and grinding as if each step were agony. At its front, three red lights blazed like fire, showing Thomas his first Dronon—creatures that in the distance he thought looked like giant flying ants. They manned the city's gun emplacements.

The Dronon city marched to them, halted. Karthenor and his men ascended, climbing handholds along one huge leg.

Thomas had never thought himself afraid of heights, but when he'd reached sixty meters in the air, he looked below at the rocky plain, gray in the twilight, and his hands began shaking.

"Do not be afraid," Karthenor ordered from below. Thomas's Guide stilled his shaking hands; he climbed with confidence.

The dark interior of the hive city smelled acrid, a biting scent that burned Thomas's sinuses. White powder dusted the metal floors. Karthenor warned Thomas to avoid the dust. He bid Thomas follow through dark halls, dimly lit with red globes, passing Dronon sentries who lined the tunnels, sometimes clinging with all six limbs to a ceiling so they hung like gaudy fixtures.

Deeper within, the air became hotter, stifling. Bangs and groans issued from deep recesses of the hive. As the city turned and walked, the floor pitched like a ship at sea. The jostling did not bother the Dronon, who scurried about on six legs, but it was hell for a human to walk in here.

Sometimes the group would stop, then climb rungs on the wall to reach a higher level. Thomas studied everything—the black-carapaced warriors so large and cruel; the elegant, almost gaunt, scholars with their tan bodies and green facial markings. Small white workers rushed everywhere, like immature roaches, prodding and carrying items. As for the machinery—the alien angles to the tubing, the strange faceted lights—for Thomas it provided only a bizarre and incomprehensible backdrop to the Dronon activities. He was, after all, nothing but an old man from a world where his people shunned anything more complex than a rake.

At last Karthenor reached a great room with a gently curving floor, where a bloated Dronon queen sat, gorging herself on huge chunks of meat. Small workers frantically scurried about, attending her needs. The queen Dronon had ruddy golden-colored chitin, with faint bronze tints beneath her legs.

When Karthenor reached this chamber, he and his men each fell to one knee, bowed their heads, and held their arms forward, palms raised above the floor.

Karthenor said, "I have come, My Queen, as you bid."

The queen spoke, her mouthfingers tapping her voicedrum. A translator pinned to Karthenor's lapel spoke. "You are just in time. The great work is accomplished. A few hours past, an ansible transmission pinpointed the location of the human's Golden Queen in a far galaxy. We will fly to her. The Tharrin will not have time to warn her. She will not escape."

"Excellent," Karthenor said. "It will be an honor to accompany you, as it is an honor to serve you."

The Dronon queen dismissed him. Thomas followed Karthenor and his men to a small chamber within the city.

In a dim room, several levels down from the queen's chamber, Karthenor and his men rested. Fresh air blew into this room through open vents, and the Dronon had placed six cots in three tiers along the walls. Nothing about the room seemed quite right. The Dronon had made the beds too long and too narrow, as if expecting men who were nine feet tall and thin as rails. Some beds were on the floor, others smashed right up against the ceiling. These Dronon, Thomas felt sure, had never seen a human.

Once in the room, Karthenor unpacked a bit of food for his men and gave Thomas a bar of some kind of grain with fruit and nuts mixed in. Karthenor was an odd man. Sometimes he'd forget to feed Thomas all day. Other times he overfed him. Whatever his mood called for. Thomas felt grateful to eat.

Karthenor said, "I have good news for you, news I dared not speak until now—not on any human world.

"You've traveled through the world gates, Thomas, something almost no one ever does. The Tharrin jealously guard gate technology, fearing the gates could be ill used.

"But when the Dronon got control of the Tharrin's Omni-mind, they pried some secrets from it, and learned that gate technology is far more powerful than the Tharrin ever let on.

"As you've seen them, the gates lead from world to world, each taking you to only one destination. But there is no reason a gate cannot be programmed to take you to any destination you desire. Nor is there any reason a gate cannot be built large enough to send a ship across space.

"Of course the Tharrin would never use them this way. They wouldn't like the idea of warships winking across the galaxy in the time it takes you to drink a shot of whiskey. It would make mankind too powerful, lead to easy confrontations.

"Fortunately, the Dronon don't have the Tharrin's compunctions against the use of gate technology.

"The Lords of the Seventh Swarm have built a gate that leads to all worlds, and they've built it large. Large enough for warships to fly through.

"Tonight, we fly through it, and you will see your niece for the last time. Tomorrow, the galaxy will be ours."

When Zeus woke, Hera had already left the room. Her side of their huge bed was empty. Zeus sprawled on his back, naked, luxuriating in the extra space. Hera is a clinging vine, he thought. She clung to him in her sleep, chasing him across the sheets all night in an effort to cuddle. She clung to him around other women. It annoyed him when she stepped between him and Maggie, just when Maggie felt ready to succumb to his persuasions.

Zeus did not eat when he rose. His stomach seldom woke before midday. He got up, decided to stroll around the palace naked. He'd enjoyed the sensation of the morning air on his skin yesterday, had reveled in his newfound freedom. Today he would celebrate Felph's absence by going out naked for the whole day, if the mood took him.

He went first to the garden where he'd rendezvoused with Maggie. If the wench had enjoyed his presence last night, he hoped she would come this morning. Besides, she'd left her shoes by the fountain. Perhaps she'd return for them. She might even use them as an excuse in her own mind to justify a walk in the garden, hoping for his return.

Zeus reached the north halls, found the sun high. He usually woke near dawn, but it must be nearly nine o'clock. No wonder Hera had slunk off before he awoke.

Zeus whistled as he made his way between the rose hedges, hoping it might attract Maggie, if she couldn't see him.

When he reached the peacock fountain, resplendent in the morning sun, he found Herm sitting on the stone bench, tinkering with a gun, cleaning it.

Herm looked up at him, saw he was naked. "My, you look elegant this morning."

"I just couldn't find a thing to wear," Zeus laughed, walking up to the fountain. The nereid viviform swam about, just under the clear waters, rolling to her back, then to her stomach. Her generous breasts were so inviting, Zeus found it bothersome. Unfortunately, her maker had not given her all the female parts Zeus would have wished.

Zeus looked in the grass for Maggie's shoes. They were gone, along with the dishes from last night.

"Too bad you slept late," Herm said. "The object of your desires came by earlier and retrieved her footwear. You must have made a great impression on her. I suspect that if she saw you now," Herm looked pointedly at Zeus's crotch and his green eyes flashed, "she wouldn't be merely impressed, she'd be astonished."

"Ah, I've nothing she hasn't seen," Zeus chuckled.

"Really?" Herm said, raising a brow. "I thought Hera caught you last night *before* you began waving it around."

"Nice timing, that," Zeus said, unable to hide his annoyance. "Did you spy for her? Did you fly about, keeping watch?"

Herm grinned. "And interfere in your affairs? No."

Zeus eyed Herm, growing angry with the winged man. Herm affected his slightly superior smile, and his lidded eyes concealed more than they revealed. Certainly Herm hid something.

"I think you're lying," Zeus said. "You're plotting against me. I could kill you for that." Zeus raised his right hand threateningly, palm out. He stood but ten feet from Herm, a bit far to throw an electric shock, took a step closer.

Herm stiffened in fear, watched the hand. He held his gun loosely, dared not move.

"I'm sorry you think so ill of me," Herm said, "me, your oldest and dearest ally. Why would you believe I'm against you?"

"I can tell, you're hiding something!"

"Dear brother," Herm whispered, his voice smooth and oily, "what has got into you? You threaten *me*? How many times have I acted as your messenger when you wanted to make a tryst? How many times have I lied to Hera on your behalf? Do you believe I'd side with her now?"

Zeus held his arm steady, studying Herm's eyes, waiting for him to say more.

"If you want to know," Herm said at last, "I spent the evening abed, recuperating from this rather severe wound—gotten, I might add, in your service." He held up his arm, displaying the bandage, reminding Zeus of the skog he'd killed, part of which Zeus had fed to Maggie last night on his amorous escapade.

"You're still hiding something." Zeus could seldom read Herm's face, yet the winged man frequently held secrets.

"A surprise," Herm said. "I haven't told you everything about this morning: I got up early, to hunt skogs," he held up his pistol, "and I spotted Maggie here in the fountain, as naked as you are now! She said she'd come to retrieve her shoes, but I think she came for more."

Zeus wanted to leap for joy, but still didn't trust Herm. "You're just saying that."

Herm grinned at his expression. "I assure you, it's true."

"Odd," Zeus considered. "She seemed tame last night."

"Perhaps she needed to warm to the idea," Herm said. "But she's interested in you, now. She asked me to bear a message."

"Which is?"

"She says she has work to do today, preparing for Felph's return. But she wants to meet you tonight, here. She said she will be naked, and wants to see you similarly attired!"

"Hah!" Zeus laughed, unsure whether to believe such good fortune. It seemed too much, yet Herm had borne similar messages for Zeus to women here on Ruin. Never had he lied before. He would not do so now. "Hah! A wild one, eh?"

"It seems so. Will you do it?" Herm smiled.

"Meet her here, naked? I . . . I don't know. Have you told anyone else—Hera?"

Herm shook his head. "Only you. Maggie left not half an hour before you got here. She asked me to stay."

"So no one else knows of this?"

"No one," Herm said.

Zeus decided to trust the winged man. "Tell no one. In fact: tell Hera you spoke to me and you discovered I have a tryst with Maggie tonight—in her rooms. That should drive her mad, trying to discover how to interrupt us in the lady's private chamber."

Herm smiled wickedly at the ruse. "Very good, my brother."

When Maggie woke shortly after dawn, she lay abed for a long time, missing Gallen, staring at the spirit mask he'd left propped in a corner.

Such an odd thing, with its vacant eyeholes, watching her: the surface of the mask seemed to be of leather, lacquered and painted. A base of dark browns and blacks lay under silver, filigreed in fascinating curlicues. Tiny pictographs were filigreed above the silver lines. Over all this lay splotches of dark blue and purple paint, weaving about in confusing jumbles.

Other bits of silver had been engraved into "teeth" on the mask, where it fit over a Qualeewooh's own teeth, lending them strength. These little metal teeth were carefully notched, forming serrated edges, and were then filed to incredible sharpness. Maggie thought the teeth cruel, frightening.

On inspecting the mask, Maggie could not decide what color she thought it to be—blue, purple, silver. The odd mix of colors made it so that the hues seemed to meld and flow, rivers of color, blending together. The mask seemed alive with movement.

As she stared at the mask, perhaps she slept. Perhaps it was only the gradual sinking of her tired eyes, but suddenly she thought the mask did move, that it wrenched aside. She imagined dark eyes, staring from the holes.

Maggie found herself suddenly alert, heart pumping madly, terrified of the mask.

This is silly, she told herself. I shouldn't be lying here, frightened of some piece of leather.

But it was more than leather. It was a receiver. Gallen had put it on, seen . . . something.

I should investigate, Maggie thought. What kind of technologist would I be, if I didn't investigate?

Strengthening her resolve, she grabbed her mantle from beside the bed, put it on, then grabbed the mask, examined it.

The sensors on her mantle could detect no emanations of heat or light coming from the mask. Maggie studied it under magnification. She could discern wood and pulp mixed into a heavy black resin. The base of the mask was leather, with tiny dimples in it, the remains of small feathers.

With a jarring sense of revulsion, Maggie realized the leather was not just a piece of some dead animal—the leather was Qualeewooh skin. This poor bird's face had been plucked, then the mask painted on in the form of a black resin. Once the mask hardened, the silver had been inlaid over the resin, and the whole thing painted again.

Maggie detected no electronic components, no nanoware. She had her mantle test the air around the mask, listening for electronic signals on every frequency. She picked up radio traffic from AIs sending bursts of binary language, music and holovision signals from Devil's Bunghole. She listened desperately for some message from Gallen, though she knew he was far to the north, out of her range.

Nothing more.

Maggie picked up the mask, looked inside.

Skin. Nothing in the mask but dried skin that smelled faintly oily. Maggie held her breath, put on the mask.

Think nothing, expect nothing, she told herself, clearing her mind. She didn't want to imagine she'd received a message. She inspected the mask's interior, saw the wrinkled gray leather within the mask, smelled its oily scent, like the dried skin of a snake. Nothing should happen, she thought. This isn't real technology.

Yet as she drew the mask on, time seemed to slow. The act of pulling it over her face seemed almost impossible, as if she moved through honey. She could breathe easily enough, found her heart beating at the same pace. Her muscles moved normally.

But her thought quickened. That seemed the answer. Her mind seemed to race far faster than it ever had before, as if she suddenly had all the time in the universe to ponder.

The mask felt too narrow to fit her face—but the leather stretched wide enough when she pushed. She heard an odd buzzing, or, more precisely, she imagined she felt movement in her head, felt motors turning or gears tumbling through the slow muck of her consciousness.

She sat on the bed, gazing through the mask's eyeholes, which were not quite aligned for human eyes. She could not see things just in front of her.

Her heart pounded. I shouldn't do this, she thought. I shouldn't wear this. It's too much like the Inhuman. I'm leaving myself open to alien ideas. Felph had said this was dangerous, wearing a mask too much drove one mad.

Yet she wore it now precisely because she had been invaded by the Inhuman. She'd lived over a hundred lifetimes in different bodies, none quite human. She did not fear the spirit mask.

She sat for a long moment. Nothing seemed to happen. She looked about the room, thinking, This is a waste.

She closed her eyes, wondered if she should take off the mask. Something drove her to leave it on one moment longer. The buzzing in her head grew louder, louder, insistent.

And the room disappeared.

Maggie looked about, found she wore no mask. She stood on a distant world where there was no sun, moon, or stars. Only a midnight sky without an apparent source of light. Yet Maggie could see. The ground beneath her provided light, like a pane of clouded glass. Pure white light welled from deep in the ground. The land around her was perfectly flat. No mountains or hills marred the skyline, no crevices. The ground felt too hard to hold so much as a footprint.

Maggie felt so fascinated by this, she knelt, gazed deep into the heart of the earth, struggling to see the source of light.

Her breath fogged the glassy surface, and she rubbed her arm over the condensation, wiping it away. She held her breath, staring deep into the ground, watching.

There, below the glass, she saw movement—small figures walking. She recognized herself, standing in a green field. Gallen held her, dressed all in the black of a Lord Protector, clinging to her for support, as if terribly ill. Both of them gazed up at the horizon expectantly, nervously, and something dark wriggled there, something black and horrible.

Suddenly a Dronon Vanquisher hurtled toward them. Its wings rumbled, and it held its battle arms high for attack. It felled Gallen in one deadly stroke, then hurtled past. Maggie shrieked and leapt, fearing the Vanquisher would burst from the earth.

Yet nothing came for her. Maggie stood on the plain of glass, backing from that horrible spot in the ground. Certainty filled her: it is coming. It is coming for me. Terror filled her.

She gazed into the ground, hoping to see more. Around her, light shifted from white to various colors. It was as if bubbles began rising from the ground, bubbles of color that burst against the air, then dissipated. Within each bubble she saw a scene, so that no scene remained for more than a split second—she saw herself as a child, her mother comforting her after a fall; in another place, she sat outside the circle of fire at Mahoney's Inn while old John Mahoney himself led the local fishermen in a rousing song; in another scene, she piled dung in a rich man's garden back in Clere, while Father Heany stood on, watching; in another she was an infant, and her father tossed her in the air.

It was as if moments of her life were surfacing, moments she'd forgotten, moments half-remembered, moments she had not yet seen—all foaming over, here for her to see.

In one bubble, she and Gallen lay dead while a Dronon Vanquisher tore at their corpses.

"Save me! Why doesn't someone save me?" Maggie shouted, her heart drumming. She knew this was no vain threat.

Then Maggie heard a dim whispering voice, "We are here."

As if on its own volition, her chin tilted up, and she saw a light, a green flame, hurtling through the midnight skies like a comet.

As it neared, the flame enlarged, till for a moment she thought she saw an X in the sky. As it drew close, she saw it was a bird, a great bird of light, flying on wings of green fire.

"I hear you," a voice whispered. "I come."

The bird of light was upon her, so close she could touch it. The Qualeewooh was a creature of flame, the darkest emerald. It wore a spirit mask, and Maggie recognized the whorls and pictographs engraved there.

A bird six thousand years dead. On the horizon behind it, flocks of Qualeewoohs, dazzling like stars, rushed toward her.

Maggie shoved the mask from her face so hard it clattered to the floor, and she leapt up on the bed, suddenly afraid the bird of her vision would come for her.

She stood a long ten minutes, scared witless. Everything she'd seen was clearly impossible. Yet she had felt the coolness of the smooth earth, had seen the lights and heard voices. She could no more deny it than deny her own existence.

It seemed impossible.

Magic. The Qualeewoohs' technology was so different from man's, she'd have thought it magic. Yet Maggie knew she'd seen the owner of that mask. He lived, beyond human understanding, in a place where past and present fused with future. And he is coming. He—she felt certain this Qualeewooh was male—had promised to come, and others were coming with it.

Maggie stood on the bed, trembling so badly she finally let herself collapse, fall to the bed, and curl in a ball to think.

She wasn't certain. She wasn't certain what she'd heard and seen. It all seemed too incredible, so far outside her experience she could not put faith in it. She realized she had not physically "spoken" to anyone in the vision. Her mouth had not moved, her tongue had not formed words.

Her plea for help had been the cry of her soul, of something so deep within her, her bones would have screamed though her mouth was struck silent.

And the bird of light had not spoken. It had not said, "I come." It had said both less and more, speaking mind to mind. It had said, "I come. We come. It comes."

What did that mean? We come to save you? The future comes? Was the creature counseling her to prepare for the inevitable?

All of this seemed right, she decided. And more.

Everything inside her cried out to put the mask back on, to commune with this creature till she gained complete understanding. But she recalled Felph's warnings. Those who wore the masks too much faced madness.

She'd met one of those unfortunate souls at Felph's party. Not only had he gained no understanding from the masks, he'd lost touch with reality.

So Maggie curled in a ball for two long hours till she calmed. I can't let this mask control me, she decided. I can't let it influence me. If the vision of the Vanquisher I saw lies in my future, who knows when it will come? I cannot spend my life running from it. And perhaps it means nothing. Perhaps it is but one possible future.

Once Maggie got up, she decided to throw herself into work, take her mind off the mask and its strange message. She spent the morning working in Felph's technological wing. The events of last night had unnerved her—the way Zeus had groped her, the way she'd found herself considering the extremes she might have to go to in order to free Felph's children. She'd even fantasized about killing Felph, and that notion seemed so . . . irrational.

This morning she needed to get away from Zeus, think about this in the clear light of day.

She entered the palace's technological wing under the guise of planning to download some of the memory crystals from her mantle into Felph's system, but she stayed long after she finished, studying Felph's files. His security systems were hopelessly inadequate to keep her off his terminals.

The information she found disturbed her.

Security in the palace was nonexistent. Last night Zeus talked longingly of his hope for escape. Before studying the files, Maggie had imagined that Felph must have killer droids circling the palace. Though Felph did have four security droids posted outside, he hadn't programmed them to keep his children in, nor to keep strangers off the grounds. They only destroyed stray predators.

On reflection, Maggie saw that Felph didn't need any high-security measures. His primary defense was simpler than killer droids: it was the vast seething desert, separating his oasis from any tangle within three hundred kilometers.

So Zeus's fears seemed unwarranted. Leaving the palace would be as simple as flying out. Felph's droids cared for dozens of florafeems; they would accept any human request for use of the beasts. A quick check of the beast handlers' memory showed that Zeus himself often took the florafeems to visit Devil's Bunghole.

Maggie thought, But Zeus intimated to me last night that he'd never left the palace, that Lord Felph held him prisoner. Maggie retrieved video images the droids had filed of Zeus's most recent trips. Maggie confirmed that the young man had been lying.

What she found left Maggie heartsick. She'd suspected that Felph was some kind of monster. Now she realized he was nothing more than an old man, an errant old man who had long ago fled society, and yet had not given up on mankind. She'd judged him harshly, more harshly than one person should ever judge another.

Yet Zeus had lied to her. Maggie recalled being the victim of hundreds of seduction attempts in past lives—many of which failed, some of which succeeded. Just as often, she'd made such attempts. But never had she run across someone like Zeus—handsome, clever, manipulative, rife with pheromones, and apparently lacking any moral compunctions whatsoever.

Zeus was dangerous. So dangerous, Felph had felt compelled to destroy his clones in order to keep the young man in line.

Yet Maggie had fallen for Zeus's smooth talk. He'd seemed so sincere. The thought made her boil.

Maggie wondered: she knew that a Guide could send audial or visual hallucinations. Perhaps Zeus's Guide had done this to him. Perhaps he hadn't known the truth about the lack of palace security—as difficult as Maggie found this notion to credit. Perhaps his memories had even been edited, so that he didn't remember his trips outside the palace.

She checked other records, questioned Felph's AI about the programming of Zeus's Guide. Zeus had complained he'd been held captive, made a slave, but the programming she found told a different story: Felph had programmed the Guide to forbid Zeus from murder. Beyond that, it kept Zeus from endangering himself, from lying when confronted by Lord Felph, and from rape.

That was it. Zeus had been free to leave the palace any time. He'd done so, often.

So Maggie studied much of the day, seething. Zeus had been playing games with her. From the moment she'd met Felph, she'd campaigned for him to free his children. Zeus knew how important she held her freedom.

So last night, she realized, as he spoke to me, it was not escape he wanted, it was a liaison. She remembered how he'd fondled her, how he'd pressed his kisses upon her.

Love me, free me, he'd pled. And I was fool enough to take him seriously.

In the early afternoon, Maggie felt tired, so she returned to her room to nap. The child in her womb seemed to be of a different mind. He did not kick so much as merely stretch, pressing his feet against her ribs, turning somersaults till she imagined he'd go mad from dizziness. Such internal gymnastics did not allow for decent sleep.

So Maggie was not in a good mood when her door chimes announced a visitor.

She opened the door. Zeus stood, one elbow casually resting against the doorframe. He wore an elegant silver-gray dinner jacket over midnight blue pants, and he carried a yellow rose in his teeth.

As mad as she'd been all afternoon, Maggie looked into his smoldering dark eyes and found—she wanted to laugh in his face.

She could not look in those eyes and see a hint of deception, only of passion. She restrained herself from laughing, and only smiled.

"For you," Zeus said between clenched teeth. He leaned at the waist till he planted a kiss on her lips. Opening his own lips, he nudged the rose into her mouth.

He knows how his kiss affects me, she realized. Maggie grinned, holding the rose in her mouth, thinking, I'll get even with you, you ass.

"Did you miss me?" he asked.

Maggie decided to play his game. "I planned to ask you that question myself."

"Does the hummingbird miss its morning nectar?" Zeus asked. "Would the moon miss the sun if it refused to shine? No less than I missed you."

"You're so sweet," Maggie said. "Where did you ever learn to say such sweet things?"

"You inspire me. I find myself rising to the occasion."

Maggie smiled thoughtfully. Zeus stood close to the door, as if begging entrance, but she didn't want to let him in.

Maggie hadn't seen the genetic records yet, but she suspected Felph had twisted his son's genome. Felph was rich enough to create any kind of child he wanted: why a sociopath like Zeus? Felph said he wanted leaders, people strong enough to defeat the Dronon. But what kind of man would that take?

In that moment, it came clear to her: a violent man, a man who abhorred authority and would rebel against any who sought to rule him. A controller who desperately needed to be in charge. A passionate man, one who craved to create, to leave a legacy. At the insight, Maggie drew a breath in surprise.

"Ah," Zeus said, "I take your breath away!"

"I suspect you have that effect on all the women." Maggie sought to recover.

"I wouldn't know. Outside my sisters, you're the only one I've ever met."

"I find that hard to believe," Maggie said. "You handle yourself so well."

Zeus hesitated slightly, wondering at hidden meanings. "I understand you had a long talk with Herm this morning?"

Maggie didn't know what he was talking about, but if Herm wanted to pretend they'd talked, she decided to play along. "Yes, it was a fascinating conversation."

"You talked about me?"

"Nothing could be more fascinating." Maggie laughed.

Zeus smiled, waiting for her to go on, but Maggie didn't give him the pleasure.

"So, you will be meeting me tonight, in the garden?"

"No," Maggie said.

"But, Herm told me you would?" Zeus countered.

"I . . . I wanted to," Maggie said, "but I have a lot of work, more than I'd first imagined. I may have to work late."

"Shame on my father," Zeus said, "working a woman in your condition so. We should punish him." He smiled pleasantly.

"Seriously," Zeus said, "you must eat, and the garden is pleasant. If my father complains about your lack of performance, I'll assure him you performed quite satisfactorily." At this, he gazed longingly into Maggie's eyes, licked his lips.

"All right, I'll meet you," Maggie said, wondering what game Herm had been playing at. It seemed everyone here played games. Zeus played Maggie, Herm played Zeus. Where did it end?

"I admired the dress you wore last night," Zeus whispered passionately.

"Thank you," Maggie said.

"Leave it home tonight. Our skin will be warm enough." Zeus leaned forward, kissed her. "Until tonight, then."

Maggie stood in the doorway, watching him leave, heart pounding.

When he'd passed down the hall, she returned to the technical wing, to the computers in Felph's revivification chamber. For three hours she studied Zeus's genome, found it to be all she'd feared. On the Rand scale, his violent tendencies measured a perfect 8.2 on a scale of ten. Any higher, and he'd be a threat to society. Any lower and he wouldn't be capable of the cold-blooded murder required of a dictator.

His Parcher indicators put him at four thousand in creative impulse—levels one would expect to find in a great composer. But Felph had also raised Zeus's testosterone levels unnaturally high, and had boosted the number of nerve endings in his genitals, accompanied by a hypothalamus design that craved stimulation. Zeus could not help but crave sex, enjoy it more than others.

Manipulation was Zeus's art. He could play a woman's emotions the way a great violinist played the violin.

Of course the genetic manipulations went far beyond this—Felph left virtually nothing to chance with Zeus. But the most arcane changes had to do with Zeus's nervous system. There were some distinctly odd modifications, including seven genes on the twelfth chromosome that totaled some fifty-three thousand pairs of amino acids in total length.

This change in particular baffled her. It suggested Zeus's nervous system had been hijacked to fulfill some secondary purpose, yet the information in Maggie's mantle was insufficient to name that purpose. Could these modifications be nonhuman in origin? she wondered.

"Affirmative," her mantle whispered.

"Can you check with Felph's AI and find out what these modifications are for?" she asked her mantle.

A moment later, the mantle whispered, "The information is classified. Felph's AI cannot release that information. However, by cross-referencing these genes with information found in Felph's library, the genes seem to be a modification of those found in an extinct earth life-form, the *electrophorus electricus*—a breed of carp which emits a powerful electric shock."

"Zeus is a chimera?" Maggie wondered. A creature part human, part animal. A dangerous one.

"Yes," her mantle whispered.

A loud hissing erupted from the far side of the revivification chamber. A gray polka dot on the wall popped free. For half a second, Maggie wondered if she'd inadvertently tripped a switch that would animate a clone, but realized she had done nothing. A tube slid out, displaying the sleeping form of a man in his twenties, with deep brown hair and a hawkish nose. It took her a moment to recognize Felph, but she could see it in the contours of his face. At each leg, sinuous tubes were inserted into Felph's ankles. One pumped blood from some hidden recess in the cryochamber into Felph's body. The other tube drew away a clear liquid, the artificial blood used in cryosleep.

The lights on the clone's Guide blazed a pure white as the artificial intelligence downloaded Felph's memories into the younger body. Maggie's heart began thumping.

Felph has died, she realized, and now he is being revived. But what of Gallen?

Gallen had gone into danger, but he couldn't get hurt, could he? He was the one who slew the Lords of the Swarm. He was the Lord Protector who had brought down the Inhuman on Tremonthin.

Yet in her mind, she recalled the sight of Veriasse, his face half-burned away, flailing about wildly as the Dronon Vanquishers sliced him to ribbons. Even Lord Protectors die.

Gallen believed so much in his own invulnerability that Maggie wanted to believe it, too.

And this was just the kind of place where Gallen would die, blindly charging into some situation hotter than he was prepared to handle.

Felph had been killed out in the tangle, fighting who knows what. He'd been with Gallen, and Gallen hadn't been able to protect him.

Maggie's heart pounded. But if Gallen were dead, it did not matter much. In a few weeks, his clone could be raised, its memories restored. But something important *could* be lost. Orick and Tallea weren't cloned.

Don't worry, don't worry, she told herself. Maybe nothing bad happened. Maybe Felph slipped and fell. It could have been as easy as that. But Felph had been a spry codger, Maggie knew. She doubted it would have happened so easily.

To learn what had happened, all she needed to do was ask the clone. Maggie held her breath as the download continued.

Gallen wasn't the type to let his charges die. He'd never lost someone entrusted to his care. So he must have fallen into some heavy combat, and hadn't been able to save Felph. That was all Maggie could think. It could take hours for the clone to revive fully. Maggie sent Gallen a message, calling him with her mantle, hoping for the best.

*C*ooharah and Aaw flapped their wings, struggling desperately in the thin air to climb a ridge of angry red mountains, the evening sun just touching the peaks, painting them shades of crimson and rose.

"Oasis to the east," Aaw whistled. Cooharah looked down at a cliff beneath him. An ancient diagram painted dark green showed the way.

"Can we trust it?" Cooharah asked, weary of chasing promises.

"What choice do we have?" Aaw asked, chuckling low tones of despair.

In three days, he and Aaw had eaten little food. A few insects, a rodent. In these wastes, nothing could be found. The barrenness of the land surprised even Cooharah. All along this route, their ancestors had left ancient glyphs painted on the rocks, signs for their children to follow. The signs read, "Fly east forty kilometers for food," or "Oasis past mountain to west."

But the land had changed over centuries. The oases where Cooharah's ancestors watered so long ago had long since dried. The promises of food were all empty.

Cooharah had begun to lead Aaw north in hopes of finding a nesting site, an oasis where they might raise their chick. Now Cooharah feared they would die.

It was not just the lack of food. True, they'd eaten little in three days, but if they were safe in an aerie, where they could rest, a few days of hunger would not have been so bad. But this ceaseless flying, the almost frantic zigzagging over the desert, had worn them, was affecting their senses.

After winging so far over the desert, Cooharah felt dizzy. The hot wind ruffling his feathers seemed to suck the breath from him, and his body felt disjointed. It was as if his wings flew of their own accord, without conscious thought.

They veered east, circling a mountain, and hope filled Cooharah. Before them a ragged pink mountain soared, fluted in strange and magnificent shapes.

Cooharah had never seen aeries like this: his people had no names for minarets and citadels, crenellations and vast gardens. His people had never imagined fluted columns, or strangely arched windows that made such odd entryways.

Yet the sight before them was magnificent: waters cascading over palace walls in splendid silver threads.

"Oomas, oomas!" Cooharah whistled, using the Qualeewooh word for humans. Neither Cooharah nor Aaw had ever seen the aliens—odd, stubby creatures, with hair like rodents. It was said that they built machines to fly between worlds, and that they were far wiser than even the wisest of ancestors.

Yet they wore no spirit masks, and therefore had no souls.

It was widely known that oomas stole the spirit masks of ancestors, and some of the stubby creatures even killed living Qualeewoohs, tearing off the precious masks. Cooharah could not condone such madness, even though he understood it. If the humans did not have spirits, what extremes might they go to to gain one? Killing a Qualeewooh, robbing it of its spirit mask, could not give a spirit to the humans, but despite all their learning, humans did not know this.

"Shall we go? Shall we drink?" Aaw whistled.

Water. The oomas had water flowing from their aerie. At the least, Cooharah and his mate would drink. In this desert, water might keep them alive for another day or two.

"We drink," Cooharah replied. "Watch for food."

As they dipped over the ridge, Cooharah let himself glide down the hillsides into the shadows of the coming night, buoyed by the brisk updrafts from the valleys.

The fields below were green in the evening. Often, the plants had strange, colorful growths.

Silver things wandered along the ground on tedious legs. Cooharah suspected these were not living beings, yet he wondered. Could they be the stubby-legged oomas his mother had taught him of? Certainly their bodies were silver-like-reflected-water, not tan-like-the-hair-of-desert-diggers. Cooharah did not approach the silver creatures, fearing they might be dangerous.

And how should we treat oomas, if we find them? Cooharah wondered. Should we flock with them, or flee from them? Some Qualeewoohs would flock with oomas, gaining profit thereby, while other Qualeewoohs found death at the aliens' hands.

The oomas' reaction to Qualeewoohs seemed to arise from the proximity of other oomas. If many oomas flocked together, they would not kill a Qualeewooh. But lone oomas were dangerous.

Cooharah found it odd that the actions of an individual depended on whether others of its kind hovered near. Cooharah found this so incredible, he dared not believe it. Better to avoid the oomas altogether, to flee from them.

"If we see oomas, flee," Cooharah whistled.

"Agreed to the second level of fervency," Aaw whistled back.

They flew to a stream flowing through the green fields, then dived headlong into the shallows, washing themselves. The water stunned them, for it was icy so high in the mountains. For a long moment, both Qualeewoohs waded, dipping their mouths into the water, then raising their heads high so the sweet, clear water flowed down their gullets.

The foot of the mountain before them was bathed in sunlight, and Cooharah spotted the natural purple of wild plants from the tangle. Though the humans raised their own strange herbs, an oasis of sorts still survived here.

Above the tangle, a flock of skogs rose, wheeling over the twisted vines like black bullets, dodging between the uppermost branches of trees. It was a strange sight, for skogs seldom flew so high above the tangle. These skogs had not been hunted in a very long time.

"The chase begins!" Cooharah whistled, leaping into the air. He chose a path low to the ground, in the shadows, barely skirting the odd alien vines. Aaw flew at his tail.

They swept into the tangle, winging up through shadows, veering through the branches. Down here, they kept hidden from the skogs above them.

Both Qualeewoohs prepared for the hunt while on the wing.

The silver teeth inlaid into Cooharah's spirit mask had been filed to perfect sharpness earlier in the morning, and he'd not had a chance to make a kill since then.

With a flick, Cooharah used the small hands at the apex of his wings to retrieve a long, thin blade from his weapon belt, then dropped it and caught it in his talons. The blade—the chosen weapon of his flock—was designed for midair decapitations.

In a moment, Cooharah spotted dark skogs pinwheeling above. His belly grumbled; the sight of prey made Cooharah see red. He was so famished, almost the sight of food drove him into *acrahas*—the frenzy.

But Cooharah reigned his passions. To let himself fall into the hunting frenzy would be dangerous. One did not mindlessly attack a flock of skogs, with their sharp tusks.

So Cooharah fought the hunger madness, yet doubled his speed, till his body became a blurred shadow beneath the creepers and branches of the tangle.

The best angle to attack a skog was from behind and beneath, rising unseen to slice at a soft belly or to slash a throat. Cooharah had practiced his techniques since he was a chick.

But behind him, Cooharah heard a rattling, a throaty chuckle that spoke of desperate need. Aaw's hunger had become too terrible to face. She'd fallen into the *acrahas.*

Though Cooharah flew fast, Aaw burst past him, winging up through the trees, the need in her rising from her throat in the closest sound to a growl a Qualeewooh could approximate.

Cooharah thought fast. With Aaw mindless from hunger, she'd need his protection in case the skogs circled back to attack.

With the sound of Aaw's need rising from the tangle, the skogs broke ranks, flying distractedly in every direction, wings flapping loudly.

Aaw burst up from the foliage and caught one young hen skog in her mouth, ripped off its left haunch in mid-flight and gulped the bloody meat, tossing the body up and away.

Half a second later, Cooharah caught the carcass as it dropped, tore off flesh with his own teeth. He shot up above Aaw in that moment, preparing to toss the bloody remains back to her, when something huge swooped past him.

Cooharah realized that just as he and Aaw had risen from the tangle to attack the skogs, some larger predator had dropped from above for the same purpose.

Cooharah dropped the body of the skog in surprise and twisted, wheeling sideways, then flapped his wings hard to slow, and gazed down. He wheeled in a semicircle, watching. He had never seen a creature like this one: the beast was part mammal, part bird. It had vast, speckled wings that rose from the shoulder, and in this respect it reminded Cooharah of a whipparoong—but in no other respect. Instead of antlers on its head, it had long wavy hair, but that seemed to be the only part of its body that had hair. Its face, long arms, and legs were all hairless. It hid its body beneath some cloth much softer than the leather harness that adorned Cooharah's own torso.

The winged beast flapped hard and soared just above the tangle, looking up at Cooharah and Aaw in frustration. It screamed some loud war cry and shook its fist in the air, angered that they had wrested away its prey.

For her part, Aaw still chuckled her blood hunger, securely under the sway of *acrahas.* All the skogs had fled, dispersed in several directions, too shocked from the triple assault to form a counterattack. Cooharah watched several of them dive into the tangle, where in moments he knew they would be so far beneath the sunlight he would never catch them again before nightfall.

With nothing left in sight to eat, Aaw shrieked with need, and dived at the strange creature.

The beast rose to the challenge and flew straight up at her, beating its wings furiously. It held something in one long hand, a weapon that discharged with the sound of thunder.

Something flew from the creature's hand, hitting Aaw's wing, so that several pinion feathers blew off. Aaw cried out in rage, dived, twisting just to keep aloft.

With fear pumping his heart, Cooharah whistled for Aaw to be patient, so together they could face this beast from the realms of the oomas worlds.

With a blinding dive, Aaw hurtled at the strange beast. Their foe pointed its weapon at her, discharged, but at the last second she twisted away. Their foe moved too slowly, and his missiles sailed harmlessly past Aaw's tail feathers.

Cooharah knew of flocks who used missiles to hunt prey, but he'd never heard of any alien creature that did so, except for oomas.

Aaw managed to spin on her back as she passed, raking the beast's soft underbelly with her talons. The surgically inserted nails of metal in her talons flayed the beast from chest to groin, so that one second it was roaring and waving its weapon menacingly, and the next it faltered, trying to hold its own guts in with one long arm.

Distracted by the sight of its own blood, the creature glanced down. Cooharah struck.

Cooharah dived from above and behind, aiming between the beast's wings, slashing forward with all his might. When his blade struck the beast's neck, Cooharah was unprepared for the thickness of its bones. He'd never met a foe so strong. The blade nearly ripped from his talons, and Cooharah flapped his wings frantically for half a second, trying to draw it out.

Fortunately, just when Cooharah feared the blade would tumble into the tangle and become lost, the beast's head severed from its body and tumbled.

The beast itself rolled over through the air, dropping slowly, till it landed with a thud on a worm vine.

Aaw dived to feed. Cooharah followed.

They tore flesh from the creature and gobbled it as the last rays of sunlight illuminated the upper brush of the tangle. They did not speak as they ate. Their hunger was too great; besides, Cooharah feared that predators from the lower reaches of the tangle would be making their journey up for the nightly hunt. He wanted to be away, winging over the plains in the starlight, before they arrived.

In a few moments, they finished feeding on the strange beast. Cooharah and Aaw flew off, heavy from their meal.

They did not speak for a while, but eventually Aaw's sanity returned enough so she managed to trill, "That was a beast from the world of oomas. Will the oomas be angry with us for killing their beast?"

Cooharah did not know. It was said the oomas kept some animals for food. Cooharah suspected they had just stolen food from the oomas, but he did not know. If he had stolen food, he owed the oomas a debt; that would be a bad thing. Still, Cooharah could not be certain. The Qualeewoohs did not keep flocks and herds in this way, so there was no correlation between the two species, no way for Cooharah to categorize such a debt.

On the other hand, he and Aaw were not responsible. Aaw had been suffering from *acrahas*. In ancient times, his people had eaten chicks from one another's nests when driven by such need. Such things were understandable, though disappointing. All things must be forgiven one who suffers *acrahas*.

"Perhaps the oomas will be angry," Cooharah said, "but we must be forgiven if we have killed their beast. Still, it would not be wise to tell them what we have done. We do not know these oomas. They have no souls. Perhaps they would use this as an excuse to try to steal ours. We must leave."

"Agreement to the third level," Aaw trilled.

The Qualeewoohs winged their way beyond the palace, heading south, back toward the great desert.

Twenty-two

Z eus decided he couldn't meet Maggie for dinner in the nude. He had to wear something.

So he colored himself with golden pigments, and had his service droids paint two vivid blue lightning bolts across his broad chest, meeting just below his navel.

Then he had his droids braid his long hair in tight knots, weaving metallic blue beads into it.

When he finished, he put on his eye shadow and mascara, painted his lips, sprayed his hair with lightly scented pheromones, and put on his only article of clothing—a bracelet for his right thigh, which emitted a soft pink, pulsating light. In the darkness, it would draw Maggie's eyes downward, focusing them in regions of delight.

At last he checked himself in the mirror, just as the serving droids arrived with dinner.

For the evening's repast, he'd chosen a number of dishes that could be eaten lukewarm—one pudding to be eaten on the chest, one saucy meat dish to be eaten on the navel, and a sticky compote of fruit to be eaten . . . elsewhere.

Zeus selected three potent wines from Felph's own vineyards, began spiking each with a capsule of Delight, a drug to lift the mood, alleviate fears, leave one giddy and euphoric. It was simply a concoction of natural amino acids found in the human body—a distillation guaranteed to make a woman feel as if she were living the best and brightest moment of her life.

Yet Zeus frowned as he dropped two capsules into the first bottle of wine. Maggie hadn't reacted as strongly to the drugs last night as other women did. Perhaps it had to do with her pregnancy. The hormones in a woman's body at such times might dilute the natural effects of the Delight. Zeus was not sure. He doubled the dose, putting it in a delicious pink wine. If Maggie didn't react to one of the weaker wines, he'd bring out this bottle as a last resort.

For music, he ordered the players—a set of twelve portable droids that each had speakers mounted inside—to set the mood for the evening by playing Asplund's Symphony to Erotica in D-minor, a magnificent arrangement composed around the different stages of foreplay, leading to a musical climax most women found enormously arousing, whether they were with a sex partner or not.

Once the feast, the drinks, and the music were chosen, he sent the service droids ahead to arrange things. He ordered them to hide in various parts of the garden, so the music would float ethereally from the distance, while food droids appeared one by one, wheeling in from different directions.

Last of all, he sent a droid out with a simple mat, something to let him and Maggie make love in a warm, dry environment, should she want it that way. If not, there was always the pond.

Zeus checked himself in the mirror one last time, then strode through the corridors of the palace out to the North Garden.

The pebbles on the garden path crunched softly beneath his bare feet. Air perfumed by a million roses stroked the hairs of his bare chest, hardening his nipples, playing between his legs.

Already, the strains of Symphony Erotique began rising from the garden— a stirring serenade of violins and violas over bassoons, a sound of flowers opening, of release.

As usual with Zeus, when a passionate mood took him, his focus narrowed. He'd been daydreaming about this tryst all afternoon. As he strode along in the starlight he did not notice the towering columns of roses along his path, the magnificent draping flowers, larger than plates, nodding from perfect vines.

He did not even hear the symphony, or the sound of the gravel crackling under his feet. Instead, his mind filled with images of Maggie in the starlight, her tender lips, his hands stroking her red hair, the full mounds of her breasts.

Only barely did he keep from breaking into a run. Eagerly he rounded a corner among the high hedgerows, following the scent of spiced meats, came in full view of the peacock fountains.

Things were not as he'd expected.

A table sat beside the pool, a circular table large enough for ten. Above it stood a wooden gazebo, with soft dark netting. In the netting hung tiny lights, like dozens of fireflies.

Maggie sat at the table—along with Gallen, a young stranger, Hera, Arachne, Athena, and the bears. Only Herm was not at the table. They all spoke softly, enjoying a sumptuous meal. None of them seemed to have noticed him.

Zeus turned, creeping to run back for some clothes, when Hera called, "Oh, My Sweet, we've been waiting for you!"

Zeus was trapped under the gaze of them all, naked. He could not hide his arousal, dared not put his hand in front of him to cover himself, lest it draw more attention to his state.

"I . . . uh," Zeus stammered.

"Come back here. I know, you thought we would dine alone," Hera called, her voice muted from under the gazebo. "But Father arrived early, so I invited everyone."

Zeus found that his arousal had ceased, so he turned slowly. Zeus was more embarrassed by the presence of Gallen than of the young stranger. Then Zeus understood. All this was planned to humiliate him. The cloth over the gazebo was a sound-muting net, so he would not have heard their voices on approach. The tiny lights, no brighter than starlight glimmering off the dim pools, worked as camouflage.

From the exultant grin on Hera's face, from the cruel smile Arachne bore, he knew Hera had contrived this. She'd lured him here, naked and aroused, before the others. Herm, Arachne, Maggie, Hera—all of them played the Game against him.

Arachne flashed two fingers. Two points, then. They'd played the Game. Hera won.

Zeus smiled, even as he fumed. Well-done, my love. You played me like a puppet, and I danced to your tune. In spite of his chagrin, Zeus could not help but be proud of his wife.

"I love your new look," Arachne called to Zeus. "So . . . manly."

There was nothing to do now but try to seem nonchalant. Perhaps most embarrassing was Gallen's reaction. His jaw had dropped in such a way Zeus knew it went against all his principles to appear naked in public. Ah well, thank the heavens for a bit of body paint. At least he hadn't come totally nude.

The stranger beside Gallen said, "Well, I must say I don't care for it at all. Zeus, you're taking this nudity entirely too far." Only then did Zeus recognize his father's clone.

"If you looked as fine as I do," Zeus told him, "you'd run naked, too. I must say, Father, a young body has not strengthened your appeal."

"Oh, don't say that," Arachne grinned. "He looks very handsome. I've thought of nothing but incest all evening."

Lord Felph smiled appreciatively, and Zeus saw that Arachne was trying to appease the old man. She wanted to head off any arguments before they began.

Felph must have recognized it, too, for he made certain to get in the last word. "At the very least, consider wearing a breechcloth. If you look in the historical archives, you'll find that they reached the height of fashion under the Beeorso Dominion. You'll see some tremendous examples of what can be done with a simple piece of cloth."

"Well, Father," Zeus said to change the subject, "I see that you had a successful expedition." He decided then and there that if his father didn't want him naked, he'd damned well run around naked for the next three hundred years.

"If you call getting eaten by sfuz successful, then, yes, I suppose this was an astonishing triumph. I don't doubt that at least a hundred of them are sucking the marrow from my bones at this very moment."

"Successful, I mean, in that Gallen and Athena at least made it home alive, and you did find some sfuz."

"Oh, yes," Felph laughed. "Gallen fought gloriously. I do believe that he might actually be capable of making his way down to the bottom."

"Not likely," Gallen said, "with so many."

"Ah, but you see their limitations," Felph said. "They are not very bright."

Zeus took a seat next to Hera, and she smiled at him, a sweet, confident smile. Perfectly lovely. She reached down and grasped his knee, then massaged his leg.

"Perhaps they are stupid, but we shouldn't be overconfident," Gallen considered. "Athena said that, considering how long it took a hunting party to find us, she thinks we were at least a dozen kilometers from their nesting site. Who knows how many of them there are? Or what they're capable of."

Lord Felph frowned a bit, an old-man's gesture that seemed out of place on his fresh young clone. "Time, space, nature, self. I wonder what the Qualeewoohs discovered that would make them believe they conquered those?"

"Who knows?" Gallen asked. "Certainly, the Waters don't give the sfuz such power."

"Perhaps that is only because the sfuz aren't wise," Athena cut in. "Whatever transformation the Waters work upon them, it may not change the way the creatures think, nor affect their basic natures. The sfuz are hunters of the deep tangle. They live down in the shadows, and hunt the upper boughs by night. That is their nature. It may be that they could do more—conquer space, leap through time, but just do not desire it."

"Perhaps they do things we never imagine," Arachne put in, and every head turned to her. "Imagine that if a sfuz looked up from the tangle on a clear night, and saw the light of a star, and longed to be there. If it had drunk from the Waters and conquered space, it might find itself there in an instant—and in that instant, it would be consumed in fires it had never imagined. Thus ends the sfuz." Arachne looked pointedly at Zeus. Don't get burned, she was telling him. No one else seemed to notice.

"So travel between space may be practiced among the sfuz—" Gallen put in, "to their own detriment."

"It is always a danger to those who do not recognize their limits," Arachne said.

At that moment, Orick chose to ask a question, one that had always bothered Zeus. "I don't understand all of this. If the Qualeewoohs are immortal, and if they've conquered space, then why don't they show themselves?"

Felph leaned both elbows on the table, folded his hands, and stared deeply into them. "I believe that the ancient Qualeewoohs live, but not in physical bodies. They've abandoned those.

"Some on this planet understand the folklore better than I, but Qualeewooh belief goes something like this: Qualeewoohs say life is something one 'flies through.' That is all that they do, they fly through life toward some distant destination. Their journey, they say, began long before birth, and will continue long after this life. They move toward 'the Enlightenment,' a moment in one's life where light, where pure intelligence and its attendant powers, become infused into them, in that moment when the image of what we desire to become is engraved into our flesh.

"When that moment comes, an exchange will be made, the new body for the old."

Orick said, "It sounds to me like they're talking about the resurrection."

"Perhaps it *sounds* to you as if their doctrine is the same as yours, Orick," Felph countered, "but only because we are filtering their doctrine first into human terms, then comparing it to something we understand. However, the Qualeewoohs see a thousand shades of differentiation between your concepts and theirs.

"The Qualeewooh see this life as a time of preparation, a time during which they must 'soften their bones,' so when Enlightenment strikes, they will gain the full effect of it.

"Now, this is the most interesting part of their beliefs, as far as I'm concerned: they say 'The Waters of Strength' are 'The Strong Blow' toward Enlightenment. The Waters were designed to 'Shape Bone' toward Enlightenment."

Felph drew silent for a moment, then sighed. "I do not know if I can explain this any better, but the Waters of Strength quite literally are meant to transform one into Qualeewooh gods.

"And, Orick, while you may take comfort in the thought of resurrection, the Qualeewoohs have no similar concept. For them, the Enlightenment is not a comfort. The act of attaining godhood is destructive. Just as you must destroy a block of wood to carve it into a work of art, even so, the elders of the Qualeewooh believe our hopes, our desires—all will be pared away, until we each become equal with the divine image. But what that divine image is, even the Qualeewoohs don't know.

"But I do know that the Qualeewooh gods aren't physical beings in the sense that you and I are familiar with."

"If they are not physical beings, what else could they be?" Orick asked.

Lord Felph shrugged. "A good question. I don't believe in beings of pure energy—not in the sense that the Qualeewooh gods are spoken of. Energy beings—if they do evolve or exist at all—are too ephemeral. Born on lightning, they would die on lightning, and none of us would be the wiser.

"But there are types of matter that we cannot detect, or that we can detect only dimly. Some theorists believe that as much as ninety percent of all matter is undetectable to mankind through our instruments. The Qualeewooh seem to have a word for it. They call it 'dim matter,' and it is in this invisible matter that they say their ancestors yet live."

"You're talking about interdimensional travel again," Maggie said.

"Precisely," Felph said.

"Wait a minute," Gallen said. "I don't see how this is possible, to transmit a body from this dimension to another. I mean, I'm not a technologist, but . . ."

"Think of it this way," Maggie said. "Suppose you take a person's memories, his personality, and you download that into an AI. Even though that person may die, his or her personality, experiences, and ambitions live on, right?"

"Right," Gallen said.

"Then imagine that we download those memories into a clone. In our parlance, we say that the person is revivified, right? The person is still alive, still the same in all important ways."

"Right," Gallen said, obviously not certain where Maggie was going.

"But imagine for a second that those same memories are downloaded into an android, a machine that thinks and feels in every way as if it were human. Is it still the same person?"

"No," Gallen said. "An android is still just an ambulatory storage facility."

"But the android doesn't know that. Many people have been downloaded into machine bodies, and they seem to like it. They aren't troubled by disturbing dreams, they don't have to deal with the emotional side of life. In short, to them life seems better without dealing with emotional issues."

"Yes, but such people lose their humanity," Gallen said. "In time they forget *how* to feel, how to relate to other humans."

"So they end up going to Bothor," Orick said, "where they don't have to deal with regular folks. We've been there."

"Well," Maggie said, "some theorists say we *can't* travel to other dimensions in our physical bodies, but we *could* create artificial bodies in another dimension, then download our personalities into those new bodies. It wouldn't be much different from being an android."

"No," Felph said. "You've got the analogy right, but you've just missed it. If I understand the Qualeewoohs, they consider *this* life to be the experiment. They say they existed as dim matter before this world, and they've come here to gain experience in our dimension. Their goal is to take that experience back to the dim worlds. There are lessons they can learn here in mortality they can't learn elsewhere."

"Such as?" Orick asked.

Felph shrugged. "I don't really care. It has to do with self-testing, preparation for greater knowledge. Qualeewooh mumbo jumbo."

"If the Qualeewoohs are telling the truth," Maggie said, "have you considered the possibility that they really are creatures who've somehow traveled to this dimension? That the 'Waters of Strength' might just be the ticket home?"

"Odd as it sounds, I've considered that," Felph said, "but it appears to me that they evolved here. I can't credit that theory."

"But you're convinced the Qualeewoohs have learned to transport their consciousness between dimensions?" Maggie asked.

"I . . . am persuaded that they've done something," Felph said. "What that is, I can't guess. But when I wear a Qualeewooh spirit mask to bed at night . . . You know, the Qualeewoohs have never revealed the secrets to making those masks. The masks seem to be made of nothing special—skin, metals, a few plant fibers and paints. . . ." Felph's voice grew silent, and he bit back his words as if afraid to speak them. Still, he spoke, and his voice was both frightened and respectful, "but even using the same materials, I cannot duplicate the effect. There is something about a Qualeewooh having worn the mask that makes it viable, that makes it receptive to messages. It's almost as if . . . by communicating from one Qualeewooh to another, the mask itself becomes a living thing, an ear that still hears, though its master has passed on."

Zeus had been watching this whole exchange, but as Felph fell into his reverie, Zeus got a chill down his back. He knew people who used the masks. Several local hermits would not sleep at night without the masks on their faces, for they said the voices of the Qualeewooh Masters soothed them, even though they did not always understand the words spoken.

Yet in the past, Lord Felph had refused to let Zeus wear a mask. Like many other things, he considered it to be dangerous. The masks often had mind-altering effects on people. Zeus considered. I should wear one tonight.

Lord Felph suddenly looked up, just as a fireball crossed the sky, lighting the heavens. "You know," Felph said, "it's damnably late. Why isn't Herm here?"

Hera, who had kept her hand on Zeus's knee for the past few minutes, suddenly moved it higher up Zeus's thigh. "I asked some of the droids to find him and invite him here for dinner," Hera said. "But that was hours ago."

Felph glanced at the servant Dooring, who'd just come to bring dessert. "Dooring, what did Herm say when you invited him to dinner?"

"The droids couldn't find him," Dooring answered. "As far as I can tell, he isn't in the palace."

Felph raised a brow. "Has he left the grounds?"

"The perimeter droids didn't record it," Dooring answered. "We are searching the palace grounds."

Lord Felph looked about at the group, and Zeus could tell by his mannerisms, by the minor trembling in his jaw, that Felph was worried. He looked pointedly to Zeus. "You don't have anything to do with this, do you? Did you have a fight with him?"

"No!" Zeus said too loudly, surprised at the accusation in Felph's voice. "No!"

Felph half leapt from his chair. "Look me in the eye and tell me. If you killed him by accident, in a fit of passion, that is one thing. But if you murdered him in cold blood—"

"I swear," Zeus said. "I had nothing to do with this!"

"He's telling the truth," Arachne told Felph. "He had nothing to do with this." Felph took her defense of Zeus at face value, making no more accusations.

"Last I saw him," Zeus said, "he had a gun, for hunting skogs."

Felph tensed. Hunting skogs was dangerous. He ordered the droids, "Use fliers. Search the tangle."

Twenty-three

I t didn't take Felph's droids long to find Herm. In an hour, the droids retrieved the corpse from the canopy of the tangle, where it lay in plain view.

A droid bore it to the garden. Athena took a glow globe from her pack to inspect the remains.

Maggie wasn't prepared for the horror. Herm's head was lopped off. Gone the handsome green eyes, the aquiline nose, the perpetual, secretive smile. Gone the glorious mane of dark hair. Gone, too, his left wing and lower leg. They'd been eaten—along with certain organs. Blood smeared everywhere. The corpse smelled no better than it looked.

If Maggie felt unprepared for Herm's demise, she felt equally unprepared for others' reactions. Athena remained stoic, stared at the body as if imagining every detail of how he had died.

Hera sobbed, falling to the ground, seeming unable to move, muttering Herm's name. Zeus raged, shaking fists, crying for vengeance. Yet rather than running into the wild, searching for Herm's killer, he held Hera tenderly. Zeus seemed in shock, on the verge of collapse, yet he helped Hera back to their room.

Maggie wondered if she should help Zeus and Hera. They had never faced death before. Born with the promise of immortality, they faced death with all the profound comprehension of adults, coupled with the complete emotional naïveté of toddlers. Maggie felt astonished at the debilitating combination.

But the most astonishing reaction came not from Felph's children, but from Felph himself. He went to the headless corpse, sprawled on the lawn, and lifted the remains, cradling them as if Herm were a child.

The image of Felph, face pale in horror, eyes wide in shock, on his knees, cradling Herm's corpse in the ethereal light of the glow globe would stay with Maggie the rest of her life.

"Herm!" Felph sobbed. "Herm! My beloved! What's happened? What?" He spoke to the corpse as if it might answer. Felph's shock, more than his children's, surprised Maggie. You killed him, Maggie wanted to say. You wiped his memories from your AI, destroyed his clones. If not for you, he'd be alive.

Maggie dared not speak such hard truths. Nor did she reprimand Felph when his shock turned to rage, and he shouted at Gallen. "You're the Lord Protector! How could you let this happen? What . . . what . . . I demand an answer!"

Gallen said, "I was gone. Remember, we were in the tangle."

Lord Felph looked away, struggling, as if he could not recall. "But, but my son!" he said with supreme tenderness. However harsh Felph might seem, Maggie heard love in his voice.

Felph gazed down at the corpse, as if for the first time. "Oh," he said, like a little boy in surprise. "Did you see this?" He reached into Herm's chest cavity and pulled out a feather, short and gray at the base, dark green at its tips.

"What is it?" Gallen asked.

"A Qualeewooh feather," Felph said.

Felph lifted the neck of the corpse, looked at the stump. "*Loolooahooke*," he whispered, "the ancient art of decapitation. See how clean the cut is? A southern Qualeewooh did this. A wild one, out of the great wastes."

Felph suddenly looked up, focusing on Gallen. "A murder has been committed. My son is dead. I demand vengeance. You will hunt this Qualeewooh, and bring him for punishment."

Gallen bit his lip. "There must be thousands of Qualeewoohs," Gallen said. "How will we find it?"

"It should be easy," Felph said. "We are in a vast waste—no water or food for hundreds of kilometers. The killing took place today. Unless the Qualeewooh is hiding in the fields, it must be flying over the wastes. Finding it should not be hard."

Gallen said softly. "You say this is the work of a wild Qualeewooh. Does it understand our law?"

"What does that matter?" Felph asked. "Herm is dead!"

"It matters," Gallen said, leaning close. "I enforce the law, but you want vengeance. I won't deliver this Qualeewooh simply so you can slaughter it."

"I *am* the law on Ruin!" Felph shouted, tossing Herm's corpse to the ground. He strode to Gallen, saffron robes stained with dark blood. "I make the laws here. I'll have vengeance, with or without you! There are plenty of Qualeewooh poachers on this rock! I could hire a dozen of them. They'd be glad of the pay!"

Gallen stared into Felph's face. Gallen's eyes became hard, impassive. Maggie thought he would argue, that he'd turn away and quit this job forever. Instead he simply nodded. "Okay, I'm your man. I'll find them. But I demand pay."

"Pay?" Felph said. "I've already offered you half of all I own!"

"To find the Waters of Strength. You've offered me nothing for the Qualeewooh. If you're willing to pay poachers, you should be willing to pay me."

"All right," Felph said. "Ten thousand credits, if you bring me the Qualeewooh."

Gallen shook his head. "Too low."

"It's a generous offer," Felph argued. "I could hire five men for the price."

"It's not money I want," Gallen said.

"What then?"

"A fair trial," Gallen offered. "I want a fair trial for the Qualeewooh."

Felph's eyes blazed, and he thrust his jaw forward. He was beside himself with rage at Herm's death, and Maggie could see that he was in no mood to be generous. Yet he reconsidered. "Define fair."

"A download. We will download the Qualeewooh's memories into both you and me, then we can judge the creature based upon its thoughts and intents. No sentence will be handed down unless we both concur that the sentence is fair."

Felph shook with anger. He could hardly refuse such an offer, not without seeming churlish. Indeed, perhaps he sensed that if he did not concede, if he merely took vengeance, he would damage his own soul. Yet by the hardness in his eyes, Maggie could tell that he did not trust Gallen. He feared Gallen would not agree to a sentence, regardless of the crime.

"You will agree to death?" Felph said. "If you find it justified?"

Gallen whispered coldly, "I've killed men before, dozens of them. A Qualeewooh is the same."

Felph sighed deeply, as if his anger suddenly abated. "Very well, then."

Gallen turned to Maggie. "I want to be certain we get the right Qualeewooh. I won't slaughter innocents. Maggie, can you rig up a scent detector on an antigrav sled—like the Seekers the Dronon send after us? It should be able to match the scent on that feather, tell us if we find the right Qualeewooh."

Maggie hesitated, thinking. "I'd need some sophisticated olfactory sensors."

Felph said, "The perfumery in Hera's sleeping chamber. It has a scent detector subtle enough to do what you require. I can provide everything." Felph turned to address the droids, commanding them to bring the provisions.

"What else will we need?" Maggie asked.

"Nothing," Gallen said. "It shouldn't take more than a day. I've still got food and weapons on ship."

"And Zeus," Felph added, addressing Gallen. "Take Zeus with you. He should be there to help avenge his brother. Otherwise, he'll always regret this." The hesitation in Felph's voice said more than words. He still didn't trust Gallen. He wanted to make certain Gallen returned with his prize. So Felph would send his son to ensure that Gallen returned.

"Do you think it wise?" Gallen asked. "He's pretty torn up?"

"All the more reason for him to go," Felph said. "The deeper the pain, the greater the need for action. I insist on this."

Gallen nodded, none too quickly. "All right. Zeus comes, too. Is it likely the Qualeewooh will be flying at night?"

"Not hardly," Felph said. "It will sleep after such a heavy meal."

Gallen stood, thoughtful. "Maggie will need some time to put together a Seeker." He addressed her, "Can I leave at dawn?"

Maggie considered. Even she wasn't certain of Gallen's intent. Perhaps he wanted them all on the ship together, the easier to leave this world once and for all. "I can throw a Seeker together, but I think I should come—in case it needs adjusting or if it falls apart."

Twenty-four

*C*ooharah could not sleep, though his full belly weighed on him, making his thoughts sluggish. He and Aaw slept in the open, on a small pile of rocks. It was not dangerous to sleep so, this far from the tangle. His only fear in the desert was that thin, translucent glass snakes might crawl from their sandy burrows and slip quietly up to drink some blood as Cooharah slept. The snakes drank little, but Cooharah and Aaw might be days from water. They couldn't afford the blood loss.

Yet fear of glass snakes is not what kept Cooharah awake, gazing at stars that burned so steadily tonight, blazing in the heavens. No, not glass snakes. It was voices whispering in his head, the reproach of his ancestors. "Blood debt," they whispered. "You owe the oomas a blood debt."

Cooharah envisioned a Qualeewooh composed of light, beating its wings among the stars. It stared at Cooharah accusingly.

The voice of his ancestor came clear tonight, of all nights, when it bore a message Cooharah didn't want to hear. The onus of a blood debt was heavy. If Cooharah had stolen food from another Qualeewooh, he owed food. Twice the amount taken.

With a creature as large as the one they'd killed, Cooharah could not pay the debt with less than six skogs. Probably eight. Of course the skogs could not be killed on the oomas' territory. They must come from land near Cooharah's own aerie.

But Cooharah and Aaw had no aerie, no territory to hunt. Their oasis had gone dry. The Qualeewoohs lived only on hope, thin as it was. Rain would come soon. The oases would be watered anew. Rivers would flow—a few months from now. But presently Cooharah and Aaw had no hunting territory.

"Even if we owe the oomas," Cooharah said to his ancestor, "we cannot pay now. Their oasis is far from others. If I kill a skog, I won't be able to take it to them. I will die."

"Blood debt. You owe a blood debt," the ancestor whispered. "Double payment. Food for food, chick for chick. Turn back."

"Negative to the third degree," Cooharah trilled. "I owe no blood debt. I—how do I know it was an animal the oomas owned? It could have been a predator the humans are well rid of!"

The green ancestor flapped its wings. Its eyes blazed like twin suns. "Blood debt," it whispered. "You owe a debt."

Cooharah knew he owed a blood debt. He'd never heard of any predators brought by the humans that used projectile weapons. This beast must have been a pet, perhaps a guardian. The humans had given it a weapon.

Cooharah could not bear the accusation in the ancestor's voice. If he could have removed his spirit mask, he would have. He would have clawed it from his face with his tiny paws, pried it, tearing flesh from bone. Yet to do so was suicide. Cooharah could not deprive Aaw of a mate, someone to hunt for her and her chick in the new land. No, the spirit mask was part of him. His parents had painted it to his face at adulthood, and it would remain a part of him till he died and his own chicks used it to line the walls of some aerie.

Cooharah closed his eyes, trying to clear his mind, trying to deny the voice commanding him to return to human lands. "Not now," he screamed silently, prying at his mask with the thin fingers at the apex of his wings, clawing till blood ran down his jaws, soaking his feathers. "Not now. Someday. Someday I will pay!"

Twenty-five

L ate into the night, Maggie built her Seeker. With her mantle of technology, it did not seem an onerous chore. Her first task was to disconnect the olfactory sensors from Lord Felph's perfumery, a gaudy piece of equipment that took up a quarter of Hera and Zeus's bedroom. The tremendously complex machine had olfactory sensors coupled to an artificial intelligence, along with synthesizers for creating scents. It could offer thousands of base perfumes, alter them at request.

She removed the faceplate from the perfumery and studied the machine, considering which tools she needed to remove the olfactors. She wondered how sensitive the equipment might be. She'd seen Dronon olfactors used on Seekers, but they might be more sensitive than this. She didn't know if this would work.

"Perfumer," she asked, "can you smell me?"

"Yes," the perfumer answered.

"Can you differentiate my smell from that of other humans?"

"Each human scent is unique, though it varies from day to day depending on the amounts of oil secreted by the skin; the colony types and growth rates of microbes growing on the skin; secretion of hormones; and the presence of chemical modifiers—such as perfumes or soap residues."

Maggie wondered. The Dronon had only begun sending Seekers after her a few weeks earlier. She'd been forced to run so fast, so far, she hadn't considered options other than running. She suspected the Dronon had only *her* scent.

The nanoscrubbers in Gallen's robe would make him difficult to track. On Manogian II, while Gallen, Orick, and Tallea were busy in a market a kilometer distant, a Seeker had found her. But the Seeker found only her, Maggie recalled. So perhaps the machines targeted only her. She was the Golden Queen. She was the one the Dronon wanted.

"Perfumer," Maggie asked. "Can I change my body scent, to make it unrecognizable?"

"Yes," the perfumer answered.

"How?" Maggie felt hopeful.

"First, chemical and radiation therapies may kill exterior microbe colonies on your skin, and you could be seeded with new colonies of different varieties." Maggie understood this. Every person has microscopic mites living in their eyes, lips, and skin. Funguses, viruses, and bacterial colonies are also common—so common in fact, most people have strains of microbe evolve to exist specifically on their own bodies.

The perfumer suggested that these could all be removed, thus altering the scent caused by microbial infestations.

"Second," the perfumer added, "natural body odors can be masked. I can develop temporary scents for your use, or I can develop a permanent scent, to be continually administered."

"How?" Maggie asked.

"Scent-generating cells can be inserted into the oil follicles of your skin. This technology is beyond my capabilities, but I can refer you to clinics that perform such services.

"Beyond this," the perfumer offered, "your skin and body oils contain a unique aroma that can be altered through gene therapy by introducing retroviruses tailored specifically for your genome. In most planetary systems, such a radical treatment is not legal for use in scent therapy. This procedure is considered too dangerous for pregnant women."

"You know I'm pregnant?" Maggie asked, surprised the perfumer could tell just from her scent.

"Yes."

Another thought occurred to Maggie. This perfumer could duplicate scents. "One last question: can you copy my scent?"

"Yes," the perfumer said.

"Do so," Maggie said. "Make twenty grams of it."

She pocketed the small bottle the perfumer filled. Maggie considered her options. So she could change her scent—change it completely—given time and resources. She hadn't needed to come here at all. She could return to a civilized world. With a new scent, the Dronon would never find her. Maggie almost wept from relief. I must tell Gallen, she thought.

She pulled off the perfumer's olfactory sensors and artificial intelligence, connected them to a hoversled. She didn't need to hook up a second AI to pilot the vehicle. A radio could let the sled talk to their ship, so flight instructions could be continuously relayed to the Seeker.

Though the Seeker was easily built, Maggie could not rest. I know how to hunt this Qualeewooh, because I have been so hunted, she told herself. She wondered how it would appear to the Qualeewooh—humans coming after it in superior numbers, bristling with weapons. The Qualeewooh could not escape her, Maggie felt certain. It might fly far and wide, but her Seeker would track it. It might come at Gallen with knives, but the Qualeewooh could not withstand a Lord Protector. Though Maggie knew Gallen hoped not to hurt the creature, Maggie felt for it. The Qualeewooh's predicament and her own were too similar.

I am not like the Dronon, Maggie told herself. I'm coming to save this Qualeewooh, not to destroy it. Yet she wasn't certain. Gallen would track the bird, hoping to learn what had happened, then dispense justice. Perhaps the Qualeewooh *had* murdered Herm. Perhaps Gallen would kill it. Gallen would do what was right—as best he could determine. But in dealing with nonhumans, human minds failed at the task of judgment. So she fretted.

Gallen spent his evening checking his ship before departure. He had enough supplies to last a week on thin rations—long enough to jump to another world. Felph had outfitted the ship with weapons—heavy incendiary rifles, assorted pistols, repulsor shields, grenades—enough for a small war.

As Maggie finished cobbling her Seeker together, she went to the ship, found Gallen on his bed, servicing his old incendiary rifle. She stood in the door, leaning against the frame for support. She could hear the bears snoring in their stateroom.

Gallen's face appeared thoughtful, pensive. He frowned at his weapon, apparently so involved he did not notice her presence. She thought that odd. "What are you thinking, my love?" she said.

Gallen looked up. "Thinking about tomorrow."

"What are you planning?" Maggie said. "You want to save the Qualeewooh. That much I'm certain of. But what beyond that?"

Gallen shook his head absently. "I don't know. Something bothers me about Felph. I feel . . . that he is not as reasonable as he wants to appear. He's furious at the Qualeewooh who killed Herm. I don't trust him. I can't let Felph murder the creature, simply because it isn't human."

Maggie understood. Her experience with the Inhuman, the memories of a hundred lives remembered and wasted, left her keenly sympathetic for the Qualeewoohs. Yet Maggie had to wonder. Felph seemed genuinely fascinated by the birds, by their history and heritage. Perhaps he would not be totally unfair to the creature.

"What of Zeus?" Maggie asked. "Do you think he'll give us trouble?"

"I can't imagine that he'd be much trouble."

Maggie sighed. "I checked his genome today. He can throw an electric charge. He's dangerous, even when not armed. That's why Felph wants him with us."

Gallen glanced at her. "My boots and gloves won't carry a charge. If he tries anything with me, he'll be surprised."

"But you can't guess what he might do," Maggie said. "I don't trust him. If we leave here, I wouldn't feel comfortable bringing him along."

Gallen gave her a long stare, as if trying to divine why she'd just said such a thing. Maggie knew it was out of character to sound so cold, but she definitely didn't want Zeus following.

Please Gallen, she thought, just accept this.

He shrugged. "Whatever you say." Gallen set the rifle he'd been servicing on the bed, apparently satisfied. "We could drop him in town before we leave. Would that be all right with you?"

So the matter of Zeus seemed settled. Gallen knew what danger he presented. Maggie's mind felt at ease. A few days ago, when running from the Dronon, she'd felt desperate to find a safe place to deliver her child. She'd been so frightened, she'd wanted everything—food, shelter, medical facilities. Now that she'd rested, now that she'd put some distance between her and the Dronon, she felt more prepared to meet circumstances as they came. Maggie's mother had delivered her with the barest medical facilities; and on Tremonthin, through memories granted her by the Inhuman, Maggie recalled giving birth dozens of times—everything from dropping a child in the bush, to delivering twins as Princess Loa of the Davai, with all her maids and nurses attending.

After bearing that many children, delivering one more should not be hard. But to Maggie, this child would be special. All the memories the Inhuman had foisted upon her, all the propaganda and pain—all came from people long dead, the reminiscences of ghosts. The children she'd sired and nurtured, that she'd cried and prayed over—all had grown old centuries ago. Some died ignominiously; some gained notoriety on Tremonthin. Ghosts still, all of them.

In the past few months, Maggie had begun to come to terms with the Inhuman. When it had first downloaded its memories into her, her grip on reality had seemed tenuous. She'd become so lost in the past, to some degree she'd lost herself. But time healed much. Maggie no longer found it difficult to differentiate her own past from the lives of others. She took comfort in asserting her individuality.

So even though she recalled mothering hundreds of children, of nurturing them to adulthood, she knew that for the first time, she and Gallen would bring their own child into the universe. Flesh of their flesh, bone of their bones. A new beginning.

Maggie yearned for this child. Inadvertently, the Dronon had given her a great gift: the memories of rearing hundreds of children. Because she'd been infected by the Inhuman, she'd be a better mother than someone who came to the task as a novice.

Maggie said, "All right. I'd drop the babe under a bush if you wanted. But after it's born, we go back to civilization. I just spoke to the perfumer. On most worlds, scent therapists could change my aroma completely. We can have a new life. Four months, till the baby is born—that's all we need."

Gallen beamed at the news. "Great. I'll look forward to it. But I don't think you'll bear our son while squatting under a bush. Wherever we land, this ship will serve as a better home than a lean-to."

Maggie studied the ship's ivory walls. Clean, smooth. Her home in Tihrglas had been more cramped. The couches and beds served well. If a world were nearly terraformed—with birds and beasts intact—Gallen could forage for food. It seemed an ideal dream—a cozy place without anyone to bother them.

*Z*eus had Hera to comfort, and to offer comfort in return. They talked long into the night about Herm's death, about the brevity of life, about how there were no longer any guarantees.

He expressed his anger at how she'd humiliated him, and Hera told him in turn how she felt humiliated by his infidelities. In an odd way, he felt relieved that she had deceived him, had lured him to stand naked before Lord Felph, Gallen, and Maggie. It was a powerful reminder of how much she loved him, how jealous she felt when he squandered his affection on lesser women. Hera was a great woman—cunning, crafty, devoted.

The cruel joke she'd played made him love her all the more deeply, yet he felt equally touched by her tenderness. The blow of seeing Herm's corpse devastated Hera, as it did Zeus.

Even now, as he considered his loss, waves of grief washed through Zeus, battering him. Herm had been his constant companion, his support. Herm understood Zeus's moods, laughed when he joked, arranged liaisons when he wanted a woman. He never judged, as Lord Felph and Arachne did.

So after Hera fell into an uneasy sleep, when Lord Felph came to Zeus's room and beckoned him into the hall, then asked him to accompany Gallen on the hunting party, Zeus accepted.

Felph clapped Zeus on both shoulders, stared into his eyes, and said. "I send you on a man's errand. Don't fail me."

"I won't fail you—or Herm," Zeus replied. The lights in the hallway shone dimly so late. Everything was perfectly quiet.

"I know," Felph said. He looked down the corridor, to the darkened atrium just off the north wing, as if afraid someone might overhear. "Bring this Qualeewooh back, understand? I don't trust Gallen O'Day. You've seen him. He may be efficient in his way, but he's soft. I'll not have him freeing the Qualeewooh that killed your brother. You remember that."

"I'm not likely to forget," Zeus had answered.

"Good. And remember," Felph said, "Gallen works for us. You don't work for him. I expect him to follow your orders."

The coldness in Felph's voice surprised Zeus. "If he doesn't?"

"Take command of this expedition," Felph said. "See that he does his job."

"You expect trouble?" Zeus asked. "If I kill him, Maggie and the others will make trouble."

"Kill him?" Felph said, shocked, as if the thought had never occurred to him. "Why would you even *think* of killing him? I need Gallen to get the Waters of Strength." Zeus's thoughts had been traveling dangerous paths, and he'd imagined Felph's had followed the same. Yet obviously his father had never considered the implications of what he asked.

"You expect me to force Gallen to concede to your wishes," Zeus said. "I doubt he can be pushed so far."

Felph shook his head, as if saddened by Zeus. "I only meant for you to take charge. I—I never thought of harming anyone. But you—you think killing him will gain anything?"

"You want this Qualeewooh, and you want the Waters of Strength," Zeus said. "You want me to go with Gallen, because you're afraid he'll leave Ruin, depriving you of both. So you want me to force him to stay, to get the job done, but I know of no way to force him. The only path I can see clear is to replace him."

Felph shook his head, dismayed. "Replace him? You can do that!"

"You don't need Gallen," Zeus said. "It's his mantle you're after. If I took it, you could be assured that the Qualeewooh would be caught, and then *I* could go into Teeawah!"

Felph nodded, speechless for a moment, studied Zeus's eyes. "I should have known," he said sadly. "It's my fault, not yours. I made you to hunger after power. I crafted you to be strong. I should have known you'd try to grasp for glory the easy way."

Felph turned, shaking his head. "I . . . I'm sorry. I'll send Arachne or Hera with Gallen, convince him to return with the Qualeewooh, as agreed. If we can't . . ." Felph shrugged, signifying he would do no more. "Then Gallen will leave." After a long silence, "If he does, perhaps you should go with him."

That final turning of the back, the tone of abandonment, spoke volumes. Felph wanted someone to convince Gallen peaceably, and if he could not, then nothing mattered.

Nothing mattered. Zeus could go his own way, wander the galaxy. Like a broken toy, unwanted, a thing formed for the delight of its creator, now deemed worthless. Felph's most cutting words were unspoken. I'll let you die. You're not worthy of more life. You matter not.

"All right." Zeus spoke before Felph could walk away. "Of course you're right. I'll convince Gallen to do as you ask."

Felph turned, querulous. "How? Speak up. You had better be persuasive, or I'll send Arachne!"

"Please, Father," Zeus said, "send me! Give me this honor. The problem is . . . you give me nothing to barter with. You want Gallen to concede to your wishes, but he only wants assurance you'll be fair. He doesn't know you as I do. I'll convince him you are just."

Felph watched Zeus. Zeus had been able to speak with an urgency, a compelling tone, that demanded Felph's attention. "How will you do this?"

"I . . . don't know, yet," Zeus said. "But I have Maggie's ear, and she has Gallen's. She was willing to serve you to win our freedom. In spite of our Guides, you required little of us. I'll let her know. As for Gallen, I'll tell him you were angry last night, that you could think of little more than vengeance—but your wrath fades quickly."

Felph eyed him a long moment. "Whatever you do, don't whine and wheedle." Zeus had to stifle the urge to sigh in relief at the acceptance of his offer. "I want you to be a statesman, a diplomat—not a beggar, nor a thug. Go convince Gallen to keep his bargain. If you do, you'll make me proud."

Felph left, his still-bloody robes flowing behind him as he strode down the corridor. Zeus let out his breath. Almost his father had abandoned him. Almost he'd doomed Zeus to mortality.

As Zeus went back into his room, to Hera's arms, he lay the night, unable to sleep, thinking. He considered ways he might convince Gallen to bring the Qualeewooh back to the palace, but in his mind's eye, he could not envision any plan working. Gallen did not trust Felph. Gallen must have recognized a certain lack of character in the man, and all Zeus's impassioned pleas might not change Gallen's mind.

Zeus wondered. If he had Arachne's insight into the human mind, he might be able to persuade Gallen that Felph's intentions were honorable. But the truth was, even Zeus doubted Felph.

Zeus thought, Or if I had Herm's cunning tongue, I could have lied so sweetly, Gallen would never know the truth. Or even if I had Hera's basic decency and cunning, or Athena's quiet wisdom, I might have found a way to twist Gallen to my will.

But Zeus lacked all such gifts. The truth was, that in the Great and Dreadful Game, Zeus was the worst player in the family. His bullishness left him ill disposed to intrigue and diplomacy.

The real problem, Zeus decided, was that Felph did not recognize a more viable plan, even when revealed to him.

Zeus considered the possibilities. If he murdered Gallen for his mantle, then killed Orick and Tallea—he'd still have Maggie. He liked the fiery redhead. Zeus had bet Herm he would sleep with her. Three points if he took her willingly, one if against her will.

It would be ironic, he thought, if I won that last point after all. A pity Herm couldn't have lived to witness it.

He imagined how it would be, wearing the mantle of a Lord Protector, hunting down the Qualeewooh. Certainly, if Zeus returned home with the quarry, Gallen and the others all dead, then Lord Felph could not complain. No one outside the palace would ever know what had happened to Gallen and Maggie. Felph would not tell, Zeus felt sure, not so long as Zeus followed his wishes. In fact, after the deed was done, Zeus decided he could make up a lie, tell Felph some reason why he *had* to kill Gallen in order to get the Qualeewooh.

Felph would have his Qualeewooh, and Zeus would get . . . what? The mantle? Then Zeus could get the Waters of Strength.

Yet as Zeus pondered the possibilities, he realized that giving the Waters of Strength to Lord Felph would be impossible—not until he had tasted them first.

What better way to drink from them, Zeus wondered, than to discover them myself? I could drink, and if they do me no good, Felph would get them in turn.

But if they give me the kind of power Felph believes . . .

So Zeus spent a sleepless night, plotting, wondering. It seemed so callous to consider murder so casually. Yet Zeus needed that mantle—and the Waters of Strength. Without them he would die. Felph would let him die.

With them, he would never be under Felph's thumb again.

Hera woke several times during the night, and Zeus rocked her to sleep. When he finally rose next morning, his eyes were gritty, his mind clouded from too much thought.

As Zeus dressed, he felt surprised Hera continued to sleep so soundly. She'd spent so much time weeping during the night, he did not want to disturb her. After kissing her gently on each eyelid, he slipped out the door just as a droid wheeled the breakfast buffet to his room. He grabbed a sticky Votifrian wafer and mango juice, then headed for the ship.

Arachne met him in a hall near the landing bay.

She sat, back to the wall. She looked calm. Of all Zeus's children, she alone seemed unsurprised by death. Her dark eyes looked up with familiar intensity. Her silver hair was unbraided. She'd merely combed it behind her ears. This style so radically departed from the norm, she seemed undressed, incomplete.

"So," Zeus said softly as walked toward her. "Did you anticipate this? You knew of Herm's death?"

"I hadn't imagined it. His death was so . . . random. But I smell death in the air, more deaths coming. I spoke to Father. I know what he wants from you. And I know what you plan to do."

"You know what I plan?" he asked in mock surprise. The truth was, even

Zeus had not yet decided what he would do. He kept thinking yes, I'll kill Gallen, then again no. Right now, he leaned toward no. He feigned ignorance. "So why are you here? Do you have some words of warning?"

"Don't go on this expedition."

Zeus laughed. He had imagined that she would give him some faint hints about how best to handle Gallen, or warn him not to kill the Lord Protector. "Surely you can be more direct. Exactly why don't you want me to go?"

She studied his eyes. He could hardly bear her scrutiny, the careful way she studied his lips, his face. "You plan to kill Gallen. Even you aren't certain that you'll do it now, but the temptation will come, and when it does, you will succumb to it. I fear that nothing I say can change your mind. But what if I could tell you something you don't know? What if I told you that if you kill Gallen, you will die? Would you stay here then? If I asked you to, would you walk away from this fine palace, from Lord Felph and his plots, from your dreams of glory?"

Zeus considered. Leave Lord Felph and the palace. "What would I gain from it?"

"Nothing," Arachne said. "But I'm asking you to walk away, to leave now and wander the desert. You could become a hermit. You will gain no glory. You will die old and alone, unloved. You would be miserable all of your days. But in doing so, you would let others live. This is what is best."

"Best for whom? Best for me?" Zeus asked.

"Best for everyone but you," Arachne said. "Father doesn't see it completely yet, but he has begun to have misgivings. He'll discover that you are a mistake. He wanted to create a new race of leaders. He thinks the Tharrin are too weak to control the world. He imagines that humans would be more amenable to someone like you, a powerful leader with human frailties. But our father is a fool. He thinks force must always be met with greater force. He doesn't recognize the futility of his dream. Even if you could become a leader, others more cunning and ruthless would simply rise up to take your place, and we would find ourselves governed by men no better than Dronon. Creating you was a mistake. Don't let Father's shortsightedness lead you down this path."

"I don't plan to kill Gallen," Zeus said, surprised at the vehemence in Arachne's tone, surprised at her conviction. "*His* actions dictate what will happen today, not mine."

Arachne shook her head slightly. "You've decided to kill him, whether you know it or not. The temptation is too strong."

Zeus stood, considering. He did not like Arachne's half-truths and innuendos. So she knew he'd been considering murder? Certainly she couldn't expect him just to walk away from this opportunity, just to run into the desert for a reason only hinted at. "So why have you come? To ask me to walk away from home? Or will you help me? You hint that if I kill Gallen, it will lead to my demise. Certainly my wise sister has some advice for me."

"I've already given it," Arachne said wearily. "But you will not follow it, no matter how sane my counsel, no matter how faultless my reasoning. So I am left with only one hope."

"Which is . . . ?"

"That you die today. Better that you die, than that you live on in misery."

Zeus instantly became suspicious. He studied her hands, the folds of her yellow robe, searching for weapons. He wondered if she planned to shoot him in the back. But he could not imagine Arachne doing such a thing.

"Do you plan to kill me?" Zeus asked.

Arachne nodded. "I'll do my part."

"How?"

"With deadly knowledge." Arachne waited for a moment for those words to sink in, waited for Zeus fully to realize she planned to tell him something that would lead to his death. She said softly. "Beware of Gallen. He is more than he seems."

Arachne fell silent, and Zeus waited for her to continue, yet she did not speak. He stood over her, lingering. Her vague warning troubled him.

Gallen was a Lord Protector, a supreme fighter, but could he have hidden abilities, abilities like Zeus's? Or was Arachne lying in an attempt to keep Zeus from attacking Gallen. If she wanted Gallen to live, perhaps she hoped Zeus would be frightened of him, would keep his distance. Or perhaps she spoke truly, and she planned to create some indecisiveness in Zeus, keep him from attacking quickly. Perhaps Arachne believed that if Zeus was indecisive, the Lord Protector could counter Zeus's attack.

In half a moment, Zeus realized he needed to know more. Arachne would be reluctant to tell him. Yet he didn't have time to wheedle information from her. So he came to a decision. He was standing over her, and with a swift but soft kick, he smashed Arachne's nose and her head slammed into the wall with a thwack.

She half slumped to the floor, but her eyes were open. She stared around, dazed, and Zeus bent low and grasped a handful of her hair.

"Now, you prescient little bitch," Zeus breathed into her ear. "You're going to tell me *exactly* what you know about Gallen O'Day. What is he that I should fear him?"

For half a moment she did not speak, and Zeus looked around quickly. He did not want to be overheard, and he suspected that at any moment, Gallen or Maggie might come down this hall to the ship. He didn't want Arachne warning them of his intent.

He took her by the hair and began pulling, dragging her toward the nearest door, an entry to the droids' service chambers. Arachne recovered from being stunned and grabbed his wrists so he wouldn't pull her hair out. She kicked, screamed. He considered killing her, but decided against it for now.

Instead he commanded the door to open, then commanded it to close as he passed, and he led her down the service tunnel, an entry broader than it was high, with minimal lighting. A hundred meters down the tunnel, he tossed Arachne to the ground.

"Now, bitch, tell me everything," Zeus whispered. He placed the heel of his boot on her throat, ready to crush her esophagus if she didn't answer.

"No!" she said.

Zeus was forced to punish her, but he dared not give a killing blow. Blood gushed from her nose, and both her eyes were beginning to blacken. Kicking her face again would gain him nothing. So he slammed her in the chest with his heel, driving her breast into her ribs.

She gasped in pain and began coughing. Whether she coughed blood, whether he'd punctured a lung, he did not care. He'd begun to lose patience.

"Tell me, big sister," he growled. "I don't want to be hard on you. Were you lying? Who is Gallen O'Day?"

Arachne gasped, struggled to answer, and Zeus picked her up, by the material of her robe, pressed her against the wall.

"He's . . . he's Lord of the Sixth Swarm, you fool!"

The news astonished Zeus so much he stood up straight, let Arachne slide down the wall. He knew that if he were ever to gain position in this universe, he would have to fight the Dronon. He'd imagined this would happen decades or centuries from now. Yet here sat Gallen, Lord of the Sixth Swarm, all unaware of Zeus's intentions. Zeus only had to kill Gallen in order to take his place. It seemed . . . so fortuitous.

"You aren't lying, are you?" Zeus asked.

Arachne coughed, spit blood. She shook her head.

Zeus considered what to do next. As if reading his thoughts, Arachne said, "You don't have to kill me. I won't tell anyone."

This annoyed him, the fact she knew his thoughts before he did. "Why not? Why wouldn't you tell?"

"Because, I've already killed you," she whispered. "I've told you the thing that will kill you. Nothing I do now will change that."

Zeus feared she still withheld something, that she knew more about Gallen than she dared tell. She knew the Lord Protector could kill him, and she wasn't saying how. He reached for her throat, and Arachne spit, "It's not Gallen you should be afraid of, you fool! It's power. It's power!"

Zeus shook his head, not understanding.

"Imagine that today, even if you beat Gallen, even if you live out the day— why do you think he is here? He's running from the Dronon! The Lords of the Seventh Swarm are chasing him across the universe. Eventually they will find him.

"But what if they found you, instead? Could you beat them in single combat, could you best the Dronon? Gallen *knows* he can't. Death lies that way. Yet you run toward it. You seek his position.

"And what if you *do* happen to beat the Dronon? What if you do gain a place of respect and power in this universe? What if ten thousand worlds elect you as their ruler, and you even manage to unseat the Tharrin? What then?

"I have already told you," Arachne gasped, coughing. "Someone more ruthless and cunning than you will cut you down. If not in a hundred years, then in a thousand.

"And you will know, you will know all your life, that I told you it would happen. You will be forced to watch for it, to prepare. You will die the thousand deaths of cowardice before that one last one takes you by surprise."

Zeus sat back and folded his arms. He'd always believed Arachne had more prescience than this, that she somehow saw what would happen an hour from now. In his heart he knew she really only understood people. Her knowledge was frightening, but more general than specific. She didn't *really* know he would die by violence. Her theories were based only on some general beliefs about human nature and her own vain hopes for his demise.

But I won't walk that path, Zeus told himself. When I am a leader, I will be kind. People will love me and protect me. They'll keep my memories on file, my genome available on a hundred planets. They'll build replicas of me for a hundred thousand years, until I am wearied by mortality, and even then, my consciousness will be stored in the Omni-mind, so I'll live as long as I desire.

He stepped back, wondering once again what to do about Arachne. He couldn't let her go tell everyone he'd been beating information out of her.

"You said I don't have to kill you?" Zeus asked.

"Yes, please, let me go!" she whispered. "I won't tell what happened here. I'll say I fell—down the stairwell outside my room. You know how steep it is. No one will doubt me."

Zeus nodded thoughtfully. "All right," he said, as if the matter were settled. He turned away.

Abruptly he spun back, kicking with all his might at where her head had been. Surprisingly, she had moved, just a bit, so her chin was lifted to connect precisely with his heel. She'd relaxed her neck enough so it snapped cleanly.

She pitched sideways onto the floor, her neck twisted at an exotic angle, blood pooling on the stone floor by her nose.

Zeus stood, astonished, confused. She'd known at that last moment he would spin, deliver the death blow. She hadn't tried to run from it. She'd embraced it.

Indeed, she knew Zeus so well, she must have come to meet him this morning, knowing she would die.

If that were true, she'd sacrificed her life. But why? To deliver a message? To tell him that Gallen was Lord of the Sixth Swarm? No, she hadn't wanted to tell him that.

No, her message had been simple: walk away. Walk away from power. You are too imperfect to hold it. It will lead you to destruction, and will bring misery to others. Felph created you by mistake. You are a mistake.

It was a hard message to hear. Obviously, Arachne held Zeus in low regard. Certainly, it had been a hard message for her to deliver, considering what it cost her.

If she bore the message knowing the consequences, then should I not listen? Zeus asked himself.

Too late. Too late to ask that question. I've killed my sister. I am committed to a course of action. I must move forward.

Yet Zeus knew that he wasn't committed. Arachne had given him the answer. Live in the desert. Hide. You don't have to kill Gallen, you can try to hide from what you are.

Am I so ugly, Zeus wondered, I must remain hidden, covered?

Zeus looked for a place to hide Arachne. He couldn't let her corpse be found. The solution turned out to be obvious. Down the corridor from him were recycling chutes where droids disposed of excess food, which was ground into compost.

Arachne always liked the gardens, Zeus thought. Now she would feed the flowers. He pulled her down the hall and slid her into a chute. She would stay in the gardens forever.

Zeus used a strip of cloth from Arachne's dress to wipe her blood from the floor, tossed it after the body, then went to begin the hunt.

Twenty-seven

G allen looked through one of the *Nightswift*'s viewers for signs of a Qualeewooh flying over the red desert. He was searching the sky, one square kilometer at a time, scanning images of the rim rock, and the yellow-and-orange sands below. The ship's long-range sensors could give good visuals on any Qualeewooh within fifty kilometers.

The ship hovered twenty kilometers in the air, and as Gallen conducted a visual search, the Seeker Maggie had made circled Felph's palace on a wide trajectory.

They had been hunting for two hours. Gallen had asked the ship's AI to display anything with a wingspan of more than four feet. So far the AI had shown nothing, but suddenly Maggie's Seeker picked up a scent and rocketed north on a zigzag course.

Gallen could see nothing in that direction; he ordered the ship to watch for him while he rested his eyes.

Gallen let the sensors on his mantle show him the scene behind his back. Orick, Maggie, Tallea, and Zeus all sat on the bridge behind him.

Orick had been teaching Tallea. He said, "Then the disciples went to Jesus, and asked, 'Lord, if a man sins, then repenteth afterward, and sins again, how many times shall we forgive him? 'Til seven times?'

"Jesus answered, 'I say unto you, not seven times, but 'til seventy times seven.' "

Tallea asked, "Four hundred and ninety times? Why that number?"

Orick sighed in exasperation. His lesson on repentance and forgiveness seemed taxing for the bear. Orick's Christian concepts seemed almost beyond Tallea's grasp, but Orick had understood these concepts since he was a cub. The knowledge of such things was in the air back on Tihrglas.

"It's not the number of times you forgive that's important," Orick answered Tallea. "It's just a metaphor. What Jesus really meant was that we should continue to forgive offenses, even when we've tired of it."

Zeus asked Orick, "This god of yours, Orick, why does he care what we do?"

"He is the father of our spirits," Orick answered. "If you had a child, and I harmed it, you would rightfully take offense. In the same way, if you harm God's child, He takes offense."

Zeus said, "You say your god is forgiving. But who will he forgive? And what?"

"He will forgive you," Orick said boldly. "He has said 'Though your sins be as scarlet, yet shall they be white as snow.' "

Zeus looked away. His long black hair was mussed, his dark brown eyes intense, brooding. His jaw quivered, as if in anger or fear. This talk of sin seemed to aggravate him.

Zeus suddenly whirled back toward Orick. "Quit staring at me, bear! I don't need your repentance!"

"I . . . I'm sorry," Orick said. "But you look—agitated. I thought maybe I could help."

"I don't need your help," Zeus said.

"Perhaps you need God's help," Orick answered.

Zeus stood abruptly, turned his back to Orick, and gazed into the monitors above Maggie's chair. He said, "There's our quarry!"

Maggie had aimed her monitor well north of the Seeker, where two lonely Qualeewoohs flapped their wings slowly in the morning light. The picture was grainy, but Gallen could clearly make out the dark feathers.

Gallen said, "Ship, send the Seeker north at six hundred kilometers per hour until it intersects those Qualeewoohs. I want to see how they smell before we go in."

"Affirmative," the AI said.

Gallen's mantle whispered a warning, flashed an image of Zeus standing behind him, slightly crouched, as if ready to spring. Zeus's hand strayed to the pistol holstered on his right hip.

The bears crowded near to look at the screen, unaware of Zeus. Gallen could see from Zeus's shaking hand, from the quivering jaw, he wanted to draw his weapon and fire. Yet he was afraid—for good reason. Gallen realized, Zeus doesn't know the powers of a Lord Protector.

Go ahead, draw, Gallen silently urged. Gallen would spin and shoot before Zeus knew what hit him.

Zeus hesitated, eased his stance. He'd decided to wait.

So we wait, Gallen thought. Yet he wondered at the reason behind Zeus's show of aggression. He doesn't trust me to bring in the Qualeewoohs, Gallen knew. But something more seemed to be going on.

Gallen took the helm, brought the ship down, keeping the Qualeewoohs in sight. The ship bounced as it pounded through air currents, shaking the cameras.

In moments the Seeker screamed up behind the prey.

When the Qualeewoohs sensed the pill-shaped Seeker on their tails, the birds split—one right, one left—and hurtled to a small hillock crested by standing stones.

"Quarry identification is positive," the ship's AI whispered, its deep voice filling the helm.

The Seeker followed the Qualeewooh that had split right. Winging toward a cleft in the rocks, the Qualeewooh spun in the air, folding its wings to make the narrow escape.

The Seeker, traveling at just under ninety kilometers an hour, could not match the bird's deft maneuver. It slammed into a stone abutment and exploded into a fireball.

In seconds Gallen's ship reached the site. The Qualeewoohs dived into the rocks, seeking shelter in a crevice. On the barren plain beyond this rock pile, Gallen didn't see so much as a bush or gully for a kilometer. He'd cornered the Qualeewoohs.

Gallen reached into his pack, pulled out the Qualeewooh translator Felph had given him, and hooked it to the voice mike he'd been carrying ever since he'd confronted the Lords of the Sixth Swarm on Dronon.

That done, Gallen opened the ship's hatch and called, "You two in the rocks, come out." His voice rang as if with a shout, echoing back from the stone walls below.

Gallen waited, but the Qualeewoohs didn't emerge from hiding. He repeated the order.

After a full minute, he looked over at Orick and Maggie. "I guess I'll have to go get them. Anyone want to follow?"

He didn't want Maggie to come, felt relieved when she declined. Orick said, "They won't be so afraid if you meet them alone. Maybe it should just be you who is talking to them."

"Good point," Gallen said.

Zeus immediately grumbled, "I'm coming, too."

Maggie lowered the ship a meter from the ground, and Gallen climbed down, followed by Zeus. The hillock stood no more than sixty meters high, yet Gallen found it a rough climb up the huge stone slabs, leaping from foothold to foothold. He stretched his senses, let his mantle magnify incoming sounds. Everything was still. He ordered the mantle's motion detectors to kick in.

He wasn't afraid. Instead he felt coiled, ready. He'd hunted more dangerous prey. Yet the Qualeewoohs couldn't be ignored as a threat. One had mastered the art of aerial decapitation.

Together, Zeus and Gallen reached the top of the hillock, stood on a huge flat rock. Gallen looked down on all sides. To the east, he heard a scratching sound, something scraping rock as it tried to dig deeper for cover.

"Come out," Gallen said. "We must talk."

Almost instantly he was aware of a form to his right, swerving up to meet him. It came so fast, only his mantle let him react. He drew an incendiary rifle, leveled it at the bird.

A Qualeewooh whipped up the ravine toward them, batted the air with its wings so it hovered nearby, staring at them. Gallen hadn't been prepared for the awesome sight.

The bird was huge, at least thirteen feet at the wingspan. Forever after, he'd hold the image of that encounter, the Qualeewooh beating its wings, the wind coming off them like a storm, the dark purple brooding of its feathers, the strange black mask over its long face, filigreed with swirls of silver, the dark eyes, like black quartz with a tinge of violet, staring at him.

Gallen wasn't prepared for the intelligence in those eyes, the intensity, the crazed gleam. The Qualeewooh opened its mouth and whistled, a strange sound that somehow reminded Gallen of ropes twisting in the air. Gallen saw rows of teeth in that deep, beaklike face.

"Even if you take my mask, you will have no soul," the Qualeewooh whistled.

Gallen pointed his rifle at the Qualeewooh's breastbone. "If I wanted to wear your mask, you'd be dead. I came to talk."

"Speak," the Qualeewooh whistled. Only then did Gallen notice that the creature bore a thin blade, a scimitar, in its left hand. The small hand protruded from the apex of the wings, and the Qualeewooh had expertly concealed the blade in its pinion feathers.

"You killed our friend," Gallen said. "Yesterday. You ate him."

The Qualeewooh swooped forward, landed on the rock beside Gallen. Standing up, it was nearly as tall as a man. It held its head back on a snakelike neck and stood for a moment gazing at Gallen, just blinking.

"We killed an animal," the Qualeewooh said. "Not human. It had wings."

"It was a human with wings," Gallen said.

"He was my brother!" Zeus shouted.

The Qualeewooh made a high, keening whistle, and bobbed its head up and down rapidly while blinking. The translator on Gallen's lapel interpreted the keening wail. "Noooooo!"

The Qualeewooh waddled forward, extending its neck, and laid its head on the ground, twisted up slightly to the side. "Blood debt we owe. Blood debt. Two lives for one."

With the sound of that wail a second Qualeewooh, a small and beautiful female, scrabbled from the rocks, winged its way up the slope, and lit nearby, bobbing its head, calling, "Two lives! Two lives!"

The Qualeewoohs looked at one another, a mournful glance, and the female waddled forward. "An egg is in my pouch. We are two. Slay us. Cooharah shall live."

"No, I plead to the fourth degree," the male said. "Aaw shall live. Slay me and her chick."

Gallen studied the Qualeewoohs. Both birds appeared to be hot. The blue gathers of skin at their throats jiggled, cooling them. With them sitting on the rock, wings folded, they did not look so noble or marvelous. He could see spots on the male where feathers were missing or broken, could see the wear on their lone blade, the thin nap on the bag the female wore. The bag Aaw wore strapped across her chest was decorated with feathers and beads, held closed by a circular pin. It looked to be made of some thin strands of woven reed.

Gallen noticed blood at the edge of Cooharah's mask. These Qualeewoohs were poor, tired. They had nothing to offer but their useless lives, and they begged to throw them away, pleading loudly, squawking. Honorable and pathetic.

Gallen decided to put Zeus to the test. "Here are your murderers. They don't want a trial. You want to kill them?"

Zeus stared at the Qualeewoohs in disgust, his hands bunched into fists, his face pale. He seemed to struggle, to seek control. Back in the ship's cabin, fifteen minutes earlier, Orick had been preaching about understanding and forgiveness.

"No." Zeus looked away, shook his head. "Let the damned things go."

Gallen said softly, so the translator would not pick up his words. "Felph will be angry."

Zeus shook his head. "I don't care."

Gallen stared into Zeus's dark eyes. "Maggie believes you want to leave Lord Felph, leave this world. Is that true?"

Zeus took a deep breath, nostrils flaring, looked up at the clear sky, the distant sun beating mercilessly. "Leave this happy place? The family fortune? I don't know." Gallen understood. It's hard to leave comfort for the unknown.

Gallen remembered when he'd left his home. He'd not had it so soft as Zeus. A life of poverty and work, but with the comfort of good friends and family as recompense.

"Where were you going?" Gallen asked the Qualeewoohs.

Cooharah, answered. "We look for an oasis, a place to nest."

Gallen debated in his mind whether to warn the Qualeewoohs that Felph wanted them dead. Judging from how they acted, the fool birds would probably demand to return to the palace for execution. So Gallen said, "You'll find an oasis two hundred kilometers to the northeast, but you won't be safe there. Men may hunt you. Continue on till you get to the great tangle."

"Negative to the fourth degree," Aaw said. "We owe blood debt. We must pay. The ancestors tell us so."

"We can't take your lives," Gallen said. "Human law won't allow it. You are forgiven the blood debt." Gallen unsnapped the canteen from his belt and poured water into an indentation in the rock so the birds could drink. "Go in peace."

Gallen turned and climbed down from the rock, heading for the ship, acutely aware that behind him, Zeus had not yet moved.

Zeus eyed Gallen's back, tense, as if considering Gallen's rationale. If Zeus did not attack now, if he did not slay the Qualeewoohs here, he'd lose the opportunity. Gallen used the sensors in his mantle to study the big man.

At last, Zeus followed, leaping down from rock to rock. "Stinking, ignorant savages," he murmured.

The Qualeewoohs flapped their wings, glided downhill, then circled the ship, gawking, and flew off to the north.

Gallen stood watching them leave, when his mantle sent a warning that rang in his head. "Warning—imminent attack!"

Gallen ducked and spun to block, imagining Zeus was attacking, but Zeus only startled backward in surprise. Gallen's mantle continued. "Fifteen heavy battle cruisers have exited hyperspace at one hundred kilometers. Neutron mines have fired into orbit."

From the *Nightswift*, Maggie shouted through the hatch. "Gallen, get in here!" Apparently she was getting the same news.

"Neutron mines?" Gallen asked his mantle as he ran for the ship. The heavy mass of densely packed neutrons made it almost impossible to navigate a jump into hyperspace—the gravitational distortions caused by the mines could send a ship slamming into a star or crashing into a planet. If Gallen left Ruin now and hit a mine, his ship might even tear apart in the upper atmosphere. Yet there was a secondary danger: if the mines were set too close to Ruin's gravity well, they'd get pulled in like meteors—meteors heavy enough to shoot through the planet's crust like bullets, creating a global catastrophe. Enough neutron mines placed in low orbit could decimate a world.

Gallen reached the ship, jumped into the hold, ran to the bridge. Their little cruiser was fast, very fast for a civilian vessel, but it lacked weaponry and didn't have enough armor for combat. Maggie stood at the console, looking about, obviously upset.

"Identify those ships!" Gallen ordered the ship's AI, hoping against all odds that for some reason he couldn't fathom, human boats would be in the sky.

The ship's AI answered in its damned neutral voice, "Six Dronon Golden-Class vessels, and nine Dronon War Hives. Sensor jammers have just been initiated. All radio contact is now impossible. I cannot confirm new arrivals of ships, nor can I verify the locations of mines."

Gallen looked at Maggie. "Six Golden-Class vessels!" she breathed.

"What does that mean?" Zeus asked.

"The Dronon Lords of the Swarms are here—all of them," Gallen said.

Maggie asked, "Ship, with the jammers on, can the Dronon read our position?"

"So it's true, what Arachne said?" Zeus asked Gallen. "You and Maggie really are the Lords of the Sixth Swarm?"

"Negative," the ship answered Maggie. "The Dronon cannot read our position unless they make visual contact."

Maggie glanced back to Gallen. "We need to get under cover. The palace?"

Gallen shook his head, thinking furiously. "No, your scent is everywhere there." The Dronon would obviously send Seekers. And in his mind, he saw a vision of clouds, of the towering storms above Teeawah. Felph said they raged there almost constantly.

"Ship," Gallen nearly shouted, "take us to Teeawah. Get us under the clouds, top speed."

With a lurch, the ship hurtled forward. Gallen feared the moving ship would show easily on Dronon scanners, but he only hoped that now, having just reached Ruin, the Dronon wouldn't have had time to begin extensive planetary surveillance. Besides, even if they had, he imagined, the tangle was huge. He could hide in that mess for weeks.

For twelve long minutes his ship hurtled through the sky at mach fifteen, fast enough so the heat shielding on the ship's hull began to flame. Gallen's heart raced; his breathing came uneasy.

Almost as soon as he saw thunderheads looming, lightning at their crowns, they slowed, bursting into their envelope. Under sullen skies, the tangle gleamed wet. Dark purple trees thrust up in exotic corkscrews or folded on themselves like nautilus shells; others towered like giant hairs.

As the ship maneuvered through this growth, the wind drove rain against the viewscreens in steady sheets.

The storm here had worsened over the past two days. Gallen had never seen a deluge like it, as if the heavens poured out all the waters in the world.

Gallen changed course, let the rains cool the burning hull. He imagined how the ship must look from outside—this behemoth oozing steam. If the Dronon used infrared sensors, even these clouds might not hide the ship. Gallen only hoped that the rain would cool the hull soon.

The ship soared over something huge and pale, slightly pink, like a blind snake void of pigment, worming its way through the trees. The creature must have been two hundred meters long, and eight meters in diameter.

Zeus studied the viewscreen. "Mistwife," he said. "It must be hungry to hunt in daylight. It comes up from the ocean."

"At the bottom of the tangle?" Gallen asked.

"Yes," Zeus said. "They live in deep water and hunt on nights when rain slicks the trees."

Perhaps they are amphibious, Gallen decided, or perhaps like large worms. In any case, it sounded as if they needed moisture. As the ship soared past the creature, Gallen suddenly saw dozens of others like it, worming their way out of the tangle.

"It's excited," Zeus said. "It senses our movement."

Then Gallen understood. There were not dozens of mistwives. This was a single organism. He suddenly envisioned it, like an enormous anemone, sending up tentacles to fetch food. Yet Gallen found that almost impossible to imagine. The ship was two thousand meters above sea level, yet this creature sent dozens of tentacles up through the tangle, questing, searching for food. How large was a mistwife? How powerful?

Gallen didn't want to find out.

He soared under the storm, counting on the steady throb of lightning, the ionization of the atmosphere, to shield him from the Dronon's electronic detection. The ship began to pick up urgent broadcasts from Lord Felph.

That could only mean that the Dronon had turned off their signal jammers, so that they could begin their hunt. Gallen dared not answer Felph's calls.

And he dared not stay airborne. The Dronon would search the planet via conventional radar and with imaging detectors. The constant lightning that speared through the clouds should make it difficult for the Dronon to search with infrared, but Gallen couldn't be certain. If the clouds thinned, if the lightning slowed even for a few moments, he might be found.

The wisest course would be to land immediately, but not near this mistwife. It might crush the ship. Gallen wondered if he could find a region that would be safer, more secure.

But it wasn't a hiding place that he wanted. They could hide in the tangle, maybe for weeks, but they'd run out of food, if the Dronon didn't find them first.

Now that the Dronon had set a picket around the planet, he wouldn't be able to blast off.

We cannot hide, and we cannot run, Gallen realized. Which meant that he would have to fight. On a sudden impulse, he commanded the ship to return to the coordinates where he'd gone on his brief expedition with Lord Felph.

"Where are you going?" Maggie asked. "You don't plan to look for the city?"

"The Dronon will find us eventually," Gallen said softly. "I won't just hide. We have to *do* something."

Twenty-eight

L ord Felph had long tried to keep a low profile on Ruin. It seemed inevitable that the Dronon would come to the Carina Galaxy, and he'd made certain that the coordinates of Ruin were kept quiet. The Carina Interplanetary Federation had removed the planet's name from star charts. Conventional radio chatter on Ruin was kept minimal, and then broadcast only at low intensities on tight beams. Felph didn't want the planet showing up under scrutiny.

As for ansibles, he didn't own one. He knew it made him look reclusive to outsiders. Most planetary governments would have considered instantaneous communications a necessity. Not Felph. Billions of people had lived fine lives without the damned things, thank you. That's what shuttles were for, carrying messages out to civilization.

But when the Dronon appeared in the skies over Ruin, Felph knew that some seventy years of painstaking precautions had been wasted. His world was the first in the galaxy to come under attack. The whole planet fell hostage in the blink of an eye.

Felph puttered about his palace, fretting all morning. Why this day, of all days? With Herm dead—Zeus and Gallen gone.

Felph tried, but after the Dronon appeared, he couldn't raise Gallen over the radio. The Dronon's jammers might have interrupted communications in any case, but Felph suspected that Gallen kept silent for other reasons. Even if Gallen couldn't hear the transmissions, Felph reasoned he would hightail it back to the palace as soon as he saw the Dronon. But apparently the Lord Protector knew enough to crawl under a rock when Dronon invaded. Felph had to appreciate that.

At the same time, he wished he'd hired a more intrepid man. A *real* Lord Protector would have done something about the Dronon.

Once Felph failed to contact Gallen, he decided to ask Arachne for counsel. That's what he had created her for, but the woman was not at her loom, and a search by the droids proved she wasn't in the palace.

As for Hera and Athena, neither of them had any idea why the Dronon ships had arrived. Hera's advice was, "Sit quietly, and see what happens."

Athena was more practical. She set out to find Arachne, and by considering the places where the woman might have gone, she chanced upon several loose hairs and a couple of drops of blood in the lower corridors, by the launching bay.

She followed a trail of blood droplets into a droid access corridor, found hairs by a recycling shoot.

Moments later, she retrieved Arachne's corpse, carried it up, laid it before Felph in his upper offices, and described how she'd found the body.

He stared at it in dismay, shaken, unwilling to believe his eyes, hardly hearing a word. Arachne, his best counselor, murdered. Her face was covered in blood and bruises. Her silver hair mussed. Her dark eyes looked up blankly, like those of a stupid cow.

All that wisdom, all that beauty, all that insight—lost. There was nothing for it but to clone her, start again. Yet Felph wondered. Even if I clone her, will she be as wise? She'd accumulated so much knowledge in her short life; Felph despaired of ever recreating a creature quite as lovely, quite as prescient.

Felph's heart hammered, and for a long while he simply stared at the corpse in shock. She'd been killed in the corridors, near Gallen's ship. Beaten to death.

Who could have done it? Gallen? The bear? And why?

Surely Zeus would not have done it, Felph told himself, even as a cold dread filled his breast.

Felph did not have long to wonder. Two hours after he'd first discovered the Dronon presence and scant minutes after Athena located Arachne's corpse, his perimeter security droids suddenly wailed a priority-one intruder alert.

The exterior security cameras showed a dozen craft approach from the southeast. Vanquishers, with black carapaces gleaming in the dull sunlight, skimmed through the grainfield on airbikes.

They halted at the front gate of the palace. Felph, flanked by his two remaining daughters, drove a house transport down to the main gate—a structure of rose quartz that stood some forty meters in the air, supported by twin pillars of red sandstone.

At the gate, Felph commanded the palace AI to open the doors; silently they swung outward.

Felph studied the Vanquishers. Each Dronon rode a bike like nothing ever built by humans. The sleek silver machines reflected the dull red morning sun. The Vanquishers straddling them were more repulsive than Felph imagined they would be. Their black carapaces and amber wings appeared regal, but the clusters of eyes, along with the sensor whips protruding above the strikingly cruel mandibles, made them look too much like insects.

For all that, their appearance did not shake Felph so much as the casual way they held their weapons. The huge battle arms of each Vanquisher, with their serrated lower edges, looked crablike. Each arm cradled a Dronon pulp pistol or incendiary rifle. The Vanquishers held the weapons as if they intended to use them.

One Dronon pulled within a few meters of Felph; dozens of mouthfingers under its mandibles began clicking. A small device that seemed to be mounted to the exterior of the Dronon's skull, just above the mandibles, translated, "We seek the Lords of the Sixth Swarm, Gallen O'Day, and his Golden Queen, Maggie. Our Seekers detect her scent on your premises."

Felph suddenly became aware of how fiercely his heart pounded. "Maggie, the Golden Queen?"

It suddenly made sense—a Lord Protector and his wife, here on the far edge of nowhere. Arachne must have known. Perhaps she'd said as much to Gallen, and in order to keep his secret, he'd murdered her.

As Felph recognized who Gallen was and why he'd come, a fierce hope began to burn within him.

I created Zeus to beat the Lords of the Swarms, Felph wanted to tell the Dronon. He should be here now, to challenge your lords to Right of Charn.

But Zeus was with Gallen.

Zeus looked to Hera, who stared at the Vanquishers, wonder and fear warring in her eyes. She was so beautiful, so flawless. She would make a fine Golden Queen. If only Zeus were here to fight beside her.

"Gallen and Maggie left, this morning, to work in the desert. They disappeared when you showed up."

"They are hiding," the Dronon's voice drummed out. "It is madness to hide from us. They dishonor their species. They will be destroyed."

Not madness to hide, Felph wanted to say. Wisdom.

A plan began to blossom, taking solid form in his head. If the Dronon found Gallen, they'd find Zeus, too.

"I think I know where they will hide. I'll help you find them," Felph whispered, "in exchange for a promise."

"What do you require?" the Dronon Vanquisher clicked.

Dave Wolverton

"When the Lords of the Swarms challenge Gallen and Maggie to battle, I want to be there."

In answer, the Dronon Vanquisher did an unexpected thing. He put his head forward, crossing his battle arms in front of him, and bowed to Lord Felph.

"It is agreed."

Twenty-nine

*T*wo days earlier, when Lord Felph had piloted Gallen down into the tangle, he'd simply plummeted, letting the ship use phased gravity pulses to pound the tangle beneath into pulp.

The technique had a certain brutish simplicity to it, but Gallen opted now to pilot his ship down by skill, diving into crevasses, following side tunnels as far as possible before battering through the deepest layers of growth, using his antigrav only as a last resort before skirting sideways into some new pocket. By doing this, he hoped that he would not leave a visible trace as to the path he took into the tangle.

Certainly, a ship flying overhead would not be able to see where he'd landed. But the tactic also allowed him to delve far deeper into the tangle than he had on his first little excursion, taking him closer to the city, with its legendary Waters of Strength.

And by penetrating farther into the tangle, he hoped the vegetation might permanently shield his ship from Dronon sensors.

He hoped it would be safe to travel in the morning. The sfuz should be sleeping, and Gallen suspected that his ship could descend into their territory faster than he could ever go on foot.

When he got five hundred meters beneath the tangle's canopy, Gallen felt confident that his exhaust would no longer show up on infrared scanners. He stopped the craft, let it hover a moment.

He addressed the others. "I think before I go any farther, I should let you know: I won't force anyone to come with me. It's Maggie and me the Dronon want. I'm going into the tangle, but I'm willing to go alone. The rest of you can stay on the ship."

"Och, what are you saying, Gallen?" Orick asked. "Don't try to get noble on me, you'll just muck it up. I'm coming with you."

"I'll follow Orick, wherever he goes," Tallea said.

Gallen said, "Zeus, there's no reason for you to come. . . ."

Zeus said nothing, merely watched the bears, brow furrowed. Gallen expected Zeus to leave, despite Orick's bold facade. If he wanted to return to Felph's luxuries, he had only to ask. Gallen was fully prepared to give him control of the ship.

Zeus smiled wanly. "I couldn't leave you out there alone. I don't know much about the tangle, aside from what Athena has told me, but I should be of some help."

Gallen hadn't anticipated this. Half an hour earlier, Zeus had seemed ready to attack them almost without reason. Now, he wanted to help? "You really don't need to come," Gallen said.

Zeus laughed nervously. "My friend, if anyone else were going into this tangle intent on reaching the bottom, I'd part company in a most decisive manner. But you're a Lord Protector, seeking the Waters of Strength. You believe if you don't find them, you'll die. While others have sought the Waters from greed or fascination, your motives are purer. I think . . . you could make it. I want to be there if you do."

Gallen said, "You're taking a great risk."

"Smaller than you take," Zeus said. "The life of your wife, your child, your friends—all hang in the balance." Zeus's eyes went unfocused, though his lips held a smile.

Gallen was forced to wonder. He went back to the pilot's seat, began talking with the ship's AI, letting it help pilot them down into the weave of bizarre trees, cluttered with odd growths—vines and parasitic flowers that would soon fail so far from light. Still, here in the upper branches of the tangle, life flourished—strange batlike creatures fluttered about the ship's lights on translucent wings, eating insects, while other creatures danced away, racing along vines, leaping from one branch to another. They feared the ship.

And everywhere was water. Up above there had been rain, but the water from it ran down narrow leaves or along vines till it collected in streams or pooled in strange scallop-shaped bowls—some type of parasitic plant—that grew along some of the larger tree trunks. With so much water streaming down, waterfalls cascaded through the tangle, punching holes to the realms below.

Though in places the detritus collected, creating false floors in the tangle, Gallen found that if he followed some larger rivers, he did not need to use his gravity drives to puncture holes through the ground. Nature had done the job for him.

Gallen piloted the ship for hours, picking a path deeper into the tangle, till the living plants and vines faded. The ship's lights began to display creatures of darkness—blind animals clinging to trees, living off debris that fell from above. In spots, when Gallen's lights brushed the path ahead, hordes of dark insects shaped like the halves of a walnut shell would die, dropping from tree limbs as if torn away; apparently they were so sensitive to light, his lanterns shocked their nervous systems.

Gallen took a torturous path down, and at five hundred meters, discovered the detritus had become so thick, he couldn't find any more holes the size of his ship. He would either have to break through, or they would walk.

He asked Maggie's opinion on how to proceed, and was surprised when Zeus answered, "Don't try to take the ship any farther. The mistwives sleep down here. They might feel the struggles of the ship."

Gallen considered. Zeus knew more than he spoke. If the giant mistwives, with their long pale bodies, were as blind as other creatures down here, they probably would have a strong sense for motion. The ship's pulsing gravity waves would vibrate the trees. The ship would be like a fly in a web, its death throes calling the spiders.

"All right then, we land," Gallen said. He picked a spot among the branches where humus was thick, docked the ship.

He got out to check the landing site. He didn't see any of the long, two-toed tracks of the sfuz, yet the ground here was soft and thick. It had not been disturbed in years. On their initial voyage, he'd spotted sfuz spoor early.

But this time Gallen had landed far away from the ridges where he imagined Teeawah would have been, farther out toward the center of the valley. With all this rain, Gallen imagined that beneath them the tangle would give way to lakes and rivers. Certainly the roots of the great dew trees would block the streams, choking them like beaver dams. The mistwives would be in those waters. The thought gave him a chill.

The ship's lights showed vapor hanging in the air like tattered cobwebs, air so still Gallen could hear his heart thump. In the distance, a strange noise echoed through the tangle—the crashing of falling detritus, then a thundering boom. Gallen didn't know if it was a natural cataclysm—a log breaking—or if the gravity waves his ship emitted had dislodged something. More frightening was the concern that a living creature had made that noise—a mistwife, moving aside whole trees?

Gallen returned up the gangplank into the ship. "This is a good place to camp," he told the others. "I think we should get some rest, do some packing."

"Camp? In the middle of the day?" Orick asked. "What are you after thinking, lad?"

"If I'm right, the Dronon don't know we're here yet," Gallen said. "But eventually they'll find us. Our ship will detect any sensors they use to search for us. Once they find us, they won't give us much rest. I think we should take what we can get."

"What about the sfuz?" Zeus asked. "Won't they discover the ship."

"Not likely. I've parked us out over the water, about even with the tops of the cliffs where the sfuz live. I didn't exactly plan this, but there's no sign of sfuz here—no sign that they ever come here. So now I'm thinking that maybe the fox doesn't hunt where the wolf is on the prowl."

"Meaning?" Orick asked.

"The sfuz won't come searching for us—not with the mistwives about. No sfuz has been through here in months, I'd wager."

"But, it's still early morning. The sfuz are sleeping," Orick said. "Shouldn't we make tracks while the sun shines?"

"I didn't say we'd sleep all day," Gallen said. "You've got two hours to rest, then we leave."

Thirty

A s the doors to his stateroom closed, Orick felt pensive. He had to decide about Tallea. He'd taken her into danger before, but never into anything as foolhardy as this. He owed her a decision.

So he wondered: do I continue teaching her as a missionary, as if she were some young cub first learning its catechism, or do I tell her of the love that's in my heart?

Tallea had clambered into the room before him, her lumbering form oddly mesmerizing. For a black bear, she was rather small. Attractive, but not a classic beauty. His feelings for her ran deeper than they should. Orick had been drawn to her all along, even when she was still human. And it wasn't right. No one who wanted to devote himself to God should feel this deeply in love with a she-bear.

Tallea hopped on the bed and closed her eyes, resting. When Orick didn't move to join her, she said, "Gallen is right, we should get a moment's rest while we can."

Orick considered climbing next to her, but didn't. He just stood, forlorn, trying to make up his mind about her.

Tallea opened her eyes to slits. "Did you want to tell me more of your stories about God?"

The idea hadn't occurred to him. "They're more than stories. At least they feel like that to me."

Tallea didn't speak for a moment. "You can if you want. I don't mind."

But Orick felt uncomfortable. "I'm sorry," Orick said. "I shouldn't have been making you listen to them all this time—"

"Oh no, you're not making me," Tallea said. "I like hearing them. They make me feel—"

Orick didn't believe her apology. "Really, I didn't mean to cram it down your throat. I should be . . ."

"What?"

Orick made a little noise, half growl and half bark, a sound of consternation among bears. "I just wanted to say, thank you for listening. I didn't mean to preach at you like this. I keep doing all the talking, and you do all the listening. It's good of you, but *your* problems are so much . . . bigger, or more important, or something. . . ."

"What do you mean?" Tallea asked, all innocence. Orick suspected she knew what he wanted to say. "Well, I keep babbling on about things, and for the last couple of days, I haven't talked to you at all about—you know, other things. I talk about only what I want to talk about, not what's important to you."

"I see," Tallea said, all coyness. She wriggled on the bed, putting her muzzle under her paws, staring at him. By giving him her complete attention, she begged him to go on.

"I mean," Orick said, "well, what about you? I know you aren't happy as a she-bear, but I don't dare so much as ask you how you're feeling?"

"I feel fine," Tallea said.

"But, you told me you missed your hands. Don't you miss having human hands?"

"You can do a lot without hands," Tallea said. "I have a nose that works better than my old one ever did. I never get cold. I don't miss my hands."

Orick's mind did a little flip. He couldn't quite believe what he was hearing. Tallea seemed suddenly—well, changed. She seemed so at peace. Orick argued, "Yes, but you've got all kinds of other problems!"

"Nothing larger than the giant David slew," Tallea said. "The angel of death has passed me by. What should I fear? My friends have not betrayed me or sold me for silver. I see no crosses on my horizon."

Orick considered her words. She wasn't just telling him she felt peaceful, she was speaking in symbols, the symbols he'd taught her over the past two days, and the sincerity in her eyes told him that not only had she been listening, but his stories were important to her. He wondered if the spirit had touched her. "I . . . I don't get it."

"I was in a bad mood when I complained," Tallea said. "I see that now. You let me think about other things. My problems aren't as big as David's Goliath. It might be true I was human once, and I've lost that. But you must also remember that I was a Caldurian—restless, protective, never able to sleep. So I've been thinking, what did I really lose? I lost my hands and my appearance, but as a bear I feel so much more . . . at peace than I ever could as a

Caldurian. I think maybe I should quit thinking about what I lost, and consider what I've gained."

"And the angel of death?"

"That's easy," Tallea said. "If nothing else, I still have life. The angel of death passed over me, and I'm reborn. If I don't like this life as a bear, then when I die, I can always hope to be something else. All I have to do is live worthily, so the Lords of Tremonthin will resurrect me. How could I be sad?"

"Yes." Orick could feel a hollowness in his chest, a deep sense of guilt. True, at this moment she made light of her problems, but he'd wronged her. "But, you came back to be with me, and I—"

"—You aren't responsible for my decisions. I made them without consulting you. You're as much a victim of my shortsightedness as I am."

Orick felt astonished. "I don't understand. A few days ago, you were so mad at me?"

"You took my mind off my own problems," Tallea said. "Seen in a different light, they aren't so bad."

"But . . ." Orick had more to say. Indeed, he had something tremendously important to say but didn't quite know how to put it. "Tallea, I have something to confess to you. Something I should have said: when you decided to be reborn—I—when you died, I'd never felt hurt like that before. I'd never felt so desolate."

Tallea's eyes widened.

"I didn't want to tell you," Orick admitted. "I was afraid it might sound like a commitment, a commitment I'm not ready to make. But even when you were human—with hairless skin and those gangly legs, I still . . . uh, cared for you."

"What are you trying to say?" Tallea asked. Orick felt that she knew what he wanted to say, but she was going to make him confess.

"Uh, Tallea, I think I have strong feelings for you."

Tallea perked up her ears, just as some dogs do, and stared at him. "I know," she said. "You love me. Why don't you admit it? You want to marry me."

"I'm not saying that!" Orick stammered. "Just because I like you, doesn't mean we have to do anything rash."

Tallea laughed. "Still, I know you love me. You show it in everything you do—in the way you look at me when you think I don't see. I felt it as a human, when you licked my ankles or warmed me at nights with your fur. You love me. You've always loved me. That's part of your nature."

"Yes, but I'm not making a commitment," Orick blurted.

"You're committed to the things you love," Tallea said. "It's a part of you. You can't separate commitment from love. Right now, Gallen might well be walking to his death, and you're going to tag along. Why? Because you love him. You say you want to be a priest and serve God. Why? Because you love Him. You can't just walk away from God, any more than you can walk away from Gallen O'Day. And you can't walk away from me. Why?"

"Because I love you," Orick said.

Tallea grinned, a gesture that looked foolish on humans and more so on bears. "Yes," she said. "You want to marry me. You want to commit, but you can't. Not until you figure out how to serve all of us at once."

"Yes," Orick said, "but I've already made a commitment to God. I made promises to Him."

"To serve Him?" Tallea said. "But how do we serve Him? You told me just this morning. 'When ye are in the service of your fellow beings, ye are only in the service of God.' So I ask you, Orick, isn't marrying me the same as marrying God?"

Orick stood there, flabbergasted. "That's a pretty loose interpretation of that Scripture."

"Is it?" Tallea said. "You take the Scriptures literally most of the time. Why not this one? Is it just inconvenient?"

"Well," Orick said, "you're stretching it. Besides, that's just a line from the Tome. Not everyone accepts it as Scripture."

"You told me if I prayed, God would answer my prayers," Tallea said. "So here is my prayer: 'God, you know I love Orick and Orick loves me. If You think his devotion to You is more important than his devotion to me, I pray that You will strike me dead by sundown. I'd rather die than live without him.' "

Orick gulped, fearing Tallea had blasphemed. It wasn't right to say an insincere prayer. The problem was, he feared just as much that it was sincere. He looked about the room, wondering if God would strike her with a lightning bolt or if He would choose some other weapon. To tell the truth, if she was going to follow Gallen O'Day into the tangle, God might not need anything more than a cold-hearted sfuz.

"Don't talk like that," Orick said, taking a sudden chill. "I wouldn't want God to answer that prayer."

"It's too late," Tallea said. "The prayer has been said. But I'm not afraid. You said God loves me, and I know you love me. God won't deny me your companionship."

"We seldom appreciate what God has in store for us," Orick said. "We all seek comfort in our lives, but God just gives us problems, to make us grow."

"You forget how many difficulties I've already had to contend with," Tallea said. "God can only stretch a person so far before He begins ripping them apart." She sounded angry.

"Don't go getting all riled at God," Orick said. "He'll never let you be tempted beyond that which you are able to bear."

"Of course not, you and I both can *bear* more than the next man."

Orick wrinkled his nose at the pun. "Back on Tihrglas, there always seemed to be a few folks who'd make such puns at a bear's expense. I grew tired of hearing such jokes as a cub—everything from tales of bear-breasted women to those old stories of a bear named Repeating who always repeats everything you say. I get so mad when I hear those jokes, I can *bearly* stand it."

"I'll try to remem*bear* that," Tallea said, "next time I *bear* my soul to you."

"If you're going to *bear* your *sole* to me, at least put a little fish sauce on it, please," Orick said.

Tallea said, "Ah, no fish jokes. I had a pet sole, once. His name was Full."

"Soulful?" Orick said. "Was he your sole possession?"

Tallea winced. "Okay, I won't play that game with you anymore. I'm beat."

"*Bear* me no malice," Orick said.

With a growl, Tallea leapt from the bed and landed on Orick's back. She nipped his ear, and Orick backed away, put one paw on her chest to hold her down. He planned to chew her for a minute, but suddenly she had her paws around his head, and Tallea began licking his eyes and muzzle, kissing him passionately, and Orick's heart pounded with excitement.

He kissed her in return, more lustily than he first intended, and in moments she held his face and began alternately nipping his lips and licking him. Tallea was on her back, and Orick straddled her, his nostrils filled with the scent of her. Knowing how much she wanted him, Orick found himself enticed beyond measure.

But to give in to her, to give her control of his passion would lead to only one conclusion. *Am I a beast, that I must be so controlled?* Orick wondered. It seemed so base, so corrupt. How could Orick aspire to godliness, if God gave him such lusts. *God help me,* Orick considered. *God save me from her.*

It was not until hours later, when they were marching through the tangle, that Orick considered the prayers that he and Tallea had both uttered, and realized that God could only answer both their prayers by taking Tallea's life.

Thirty-one

*Z*eus could not sleep. Though he had a couch in the common room of the ship, and though the lights were turned down to simulate darkness, his eyes stayed wide-open as he wondered if he should kill Gallen and the others.

Zeus did not count himself brave. He couldn't make light of danger. Some people could ignore danger, just as they ignored pain. Not Zeus. His sense of self-preservation was too powerful, too encompassing. *Maybe ignoring danger isn't really brave,* Zeus considered. *Maybe it's just a form of stupidity, and I'm too smart to fall into that trap.*

When Gallen had found the Qualeewoohs, Zeus had been tempted to slay the Lord Protector then. But something stayed his hand. At first he told himself it was curiosity—the simple desire to find out what Gallen would do with the Qualeewoohs.

But his reasoning went beyond that. Killing Gallen for his mantle would have been easy. Zeus had no feelings for the man. But Orick's sermon had shamed Zeus.

Killing Gallen was one thing. Zeus had been framed to crave power, to take it at any price. He'd killed Arachne without much thought. But killing an innocent like Maggie or the bears was beneath him.

This realization struck Zeus to the core. Zeus had not often made such self-discoveries.

Dave Wolverton

And when Gallen asked Zeus whether to kill the Qualeewoohs, Zeus had declined. Once he'd seen Herm's killers, Zeus couldn't sustain his rage. The birds were so regal, so worn, so repentant.

He couldn't kill them, not when their deaths gained him nothing.

But Zeus told himself that it was more than compassion that caused him to spare Gallen and the Qualeewoohs: it was knowledge.

He felt that some deep, subconscious sense guided him.

Despite his lightning bolts, Zeus did not believe he could make it into the depths of the tangle alone—not fighting the sfuz. The creatures were too numerous. No, to make it to the cisterns, Zeus needed Gallen's help. Perhaps that's why I left him alive. In my heart, I knew I'd need him. His help could be worth more than the mantle. And looking back, Zeus realized that he could not have held Gallen's trust if he'd killed the Qualeewoohs. The deed would have lessened Zeus in Gallen's eyes.

Zeus realized, if Gallen takes me to the Waters, fighting beside me, all I have to do is drink. Then I will gain such power that I won't need his mantle any longer.

But Zeus recognized that if the Waters of Strength flowed in some cistern deep inside the cliffs of Teeawah, Zeus could not afford to let the others drink. The Waters would make Zeus a power without equal.

Then Gallen's mantle would mean nothing, and Zeus could kill them all. Indeed, he would be forced to kill them all.

Thirty-two

A/fter all his dealings with the Dronon, Gallen was surprised that the Dronon hadn't begun searching the tangle before he left his ship.

He'd turned off the engines when he first landed, ceased all radio transmissions, and manually dismantled the ship's transponder. Gallen feared the Dronon would commandeer the starport facilities at Felph's palace and use the computers there to demand that each ship send its code. The ship's AI couldn't ignore such a request; it violated the ship's programming, and once a ship sent its code, it automatically broadcast its exact latitude, longitude, and altitude.

After Gallen had verified that his ship wasn't emitting any gravity, radio, or heat waves he felt somewhat secure. The Dronon wouldn't be able to find him using the passive sensors that detected such emissions.

This meant that they would have to begin using active sensors—directing energy and particle streams in an effort to search the planet for large metallic objects. It would take time to scour the surface of an entire planet, but the Dronon had plenty of ships capable of helping in the search. It wouldn't take *much* time.

Gallen's greatest hope was that the Dronon's sensors wouldn't penetrate here, so far beneath the tangle.

Yet he still felt afraid. The Dronon had a tool he couldn't defeat so easily. The Seekers. The Dronon could still track by scent. But he hadn't left any scent within two thousand kilometers, and here in the tangle, air currents moved sluggishly. Their scent might not reach the surface for days—maybe weeks.

But if by chance the Dronon found that scent, they would be able to follow it easily.

While the others rested, Gallen packed enough food for five days, wondered if it was too much. He hoped to find Teeawah sooner, but in all honesty, it could take months. He had no idea how to reach his destination except through an interlaced network of caves that might be impassable. Quite possibly, he might find that he was in a section of the tangle that didn't connect to the caves.

And if he didn't find the city soon, he'd die. He was a lone Lord Protector, leading his friends into an enemy fortress. Part of him wanted to deny that anything bad would happen, but he'd seen some of the prowess of the sfuz. They were so fast. He wouldn't be able to protect his friends in a pitched battle. Gallen wouldn't even be able to protect himself against so many enemies.

In all probability he was leading them all to their deaths.

Gallen clenched his fists and cursed his fate. If only he hadn't beaten the Lords of the Sixth Swarm. Only an odd combination of determination, skill, and luck had put him here. Yet if he'd walked away, if he'd simply refused to fight that first battle so many months ago . . . the Dronon would still rule the worlds of man in tyranny.

No, Gallen could not truthfully regret his fate. The Dronon war had cost millions of lives each day. Gallen had won a temporary peace for mankind. A few months of reprieve, a few months of joy on ten thousand worlds. Some fifty quadrillion people lived on the Unified Worlds. Gallen had won something for them, and even if he and his friends died in these lightless depths, their lives would not have been wasted.

But in spite of the facade he tried to erect for his friends, Gallen didn't believe that he would survive this trip. The tangle seemed too thick, too dangerous. His destination too uncertain. The Dronon too likely to attack.

Even if he did find the Waters of Strength, who knew if they would have any effect on him?

Gallen had too many foes to combat, too little to hope for.

He felt overwhelmed. I am but one man, Gallen thought. Too much depended on him. Not just Maggie and Orick and the few friends around him— it was Arachne and Athena and the gray people that Felph held in such low esteem. And beyond that was the wider universe—Everynne fretting somewhere back on her Omni-mind, his mother living in her quaint home on Tihrglas, Ceravanne trying desperately to find her own peace under the tutelage of the peaceful treelike Bock.

Gallen wanted to collapse, to turn aside and run. He'd never faced a task so daunting. The prospect of failure terrified him. If I die, he thought, Lord Felph could resurrect me. But Maggie, Orick, and Tallea would be dead. He couldn't face that. To live on without them would be damnable. He'd never forgive himself.

So he had to beat the Dronon. He had to go on fighting, drag himself forward no matter what the consequence.

Regardless of the outcome, he had to go on, keep fighting, because . . . because he loved them all, loved them so profoundly that for a moment he stood in awe of the simple power of his emotions, just considering, remembering the faces of friends that were beginning to be lost in the haze of time.

He closed his eyes, tried to recall the woods outside his home on Tihrglas, the call of the kiss-me-quicks hopping in the bushes, the towering green pines, the way the maples on the hillside north of town reflected the reds of the sunset in the autumn till they shone like coals.

Gallen's mantle recognized his desire, sent him recorded images of home—sights, sounds, smells—so that suddenly Gallen found himself standing inside the common room at Mahoney's Inn, the first night he'd met Everynne.

There were John Mahoney and Father Heany smoking by the fireplace, just after teasing Gallen about how he fancied young Maggie Flynn. And over in the corner sat Sean Mullen, a terribly thin man who'd once given Gallen's mother a cow. Gallen hadn't thought about him in months. Beside him sat Ian O'Bannon, an old fisherman who'd taught Maggie to dance—another friend Gallen had forgotten. The fellow had once told Maggie that she should stay away from Gallen, saying, "You'll have naught but misery from that one— always out playing the hero, trying to impress folks." Gallen could smell the beer in the air, the sweet tobacco smoke, the scent of wool and sweat. He could feel the heat of the fire warming his hands.

Yet this memory belonged to Veriasse, not to Gallen, so that he saw himself and Maggie as they had been that night, two shy teenagers sitting off in a dark corner, trying to hide their affection for one another from everyone in the room.

Gallen laughed at the image. Both he and Maggie had looked so skinny, so young, so innocent—just six months before.

Is that how I was? Gallen wondered to himself. A child. A barbarian. A wild animal. Despite all the dark times since, despite his loss of innocence, Gallen looked at the young man he'd been a few short months before, and decided he would not trade places.

Not even if he died today because of it. He thought about the warning Ian O'Bannon had given Maggie. He'd believed Gallen wanted to impress folks. He'd never understood, never understood what Gallen dared tell no one—that he did what he did because he loved people, loved them so deeply that something inside him just had to give and give until he had nothing left to give.

Even his dear friend Orick didn't understand it. Orick thought that Gallen fought because of some innate need to struggle. But Gallen realized at this moment that he fought, even when he'd run out of strength and out of hope, because that was all he could do. Someone had to fight, and he would fight on, yet wish desperately for the fighting to come to an end.

Gallen sighed, withdrew from his reverie, went back to work. Felph had loaded an odd assortment of weapons for the earlier expedition. Felph's arsenal held weapons one normally only found in military hands—class II small arms. Most of it was offensive weaponry; Felph had little defensive armor. That wasn't odd. Getting military body armor was nearly impossible.

Gallen replenished his supply of photon grenades. An explosive foam would work as land mines. An intelligent pistol with smart missiles would help him quietly neutralize individual sfuz. He did find one automated defense system—a class IV defensive weapon, that might save their lives with its powerful shields, but Gallen felt compelled to leave it behind. The power unit on it was low, and the thing weighed so much that even having Orick haul it around could prove impossible.

Once he'd sorted the weapons, he stared at the piles—light grenades, concussion grenades, heat grenades; small arms; assault pistols; explosive foams; Black Fog. Enough weaponry to kill five thousand men. It wasn't enough.

Not against creatures like the sfuz, who Athena believed would rise from the dead. Who knew what powers the sfuz might have? The thought made him feel jittery.

More disconcerting, Gallen had an odd feeling of discomfort, the feeling he was being watched. It seemed unreasonable to imagine he was being watched in his own ship. Yet the feeling had grown as he brought the ship into the tangle—an enigmatic sensation, an itching at the base of the brain.

If he didn't know better, he'd have sworn the sfuz were watching him not from without, but from within. He imagined another consciousness wandering through his mind, turning over his thoughts and fears and ambitions, trying to discover what lay beneath. Sometimes he'd find his eyes wandering about the ship, and it seemed almost as if another entity commanded them, was searching through Gallen's eyes.

It *seemed* an odd sensation, an almost paranoid fear. But the Qualeewooh's spirit mask had shown him he was dealing with powers he couldn't comprehend.

And if the sfuz were drinking from the Waters of Strength, did the sfuz's ancestors speak to them? Could they be warning their descendants of Gallen's plans? Did the sfuz wear their own spirit masks, deep in their chambers, dreaming disturbing visions of Gallen's descent.

And if they did, how could Gallen fight such creatures? He looked through his arsenal again and again, the creepy sensation hounding him.

He wondered. If I drink from the Waters of Strength, what becomes of me? The Qualeewoohs say they defeated space and time, self and nature. What does that mean? Will I speak to my ancestors, whispering my child's name as I walk between the stars?

At twelve hundred hours, Gallen went to Maggie's room, kissed her awake, roused the others. He felt he should give them some warning before they departed, but there was little to say.

He, Zeus, Orick, and Tallea bore the heaviest packs, while Gallen gave Maggie an intelligent pistol and a glow globe. Let her be the lightbearer here in the darkness.

Gallen said, "I want to avoid the sfuz at all costs. We can't let them know we're here. So we'll travel in silence. No talking until we strike camp, and I can put up some buffers. If we're discovered by even one sfuz, kill it before it can warn others. Use an intelligent pistol. They're quiet and accurate.

"If we do find ourselves in a pitched battle, we'll need to win swiftly, then retreat from the sfuz, circle into their lair.

"Right now, the sfuz should be asleep. We're out over a valley, about four hundred meters above it. I suspect there's water beneath us, so the sfuz won't come out here.

"The cliffs are to the north of us, about five kilometers. I don't know how far we'll have to go to find Teeawah itself, or how well guarded it might be."

Zeus's face was pale, and Maggie stood holding her belly, her expression thoughtful.

"Now, here is the hard part," Gallen said. "When we near the city, we should find sfuz tracks. That's how we'll know we're close. We should be able to follow some kind of trail. But first, we have to wait for the sfuz to leave for the night. I . . . don't know how we can manage that. We need to wait for them to leave, and at the same time, we can't let them see us or catch our scent. We'll have to go in while they're on the hunt."

"Gallen," Maggie said as if he'd forgotten something, "they won't *all* leave."

"No," Gallen said, "their young will be in the city, I guess. Maybe the old and the weak." He didn't want to mention the guards he suspected might be there.

Maggie frowned in shame. "We'll be slaughtering families."

"We have no choice!" Gallen told Maggie. He knew what she was feeling. She didn't want to slaughter the sfuz. They'd both been infected by the Inhuman; they both knew how passionate, how beautiful a life could be, even if it was not a human life.

Despite Felph's protests to the contrary, Gallen recognized that the sfuz were smarter than mere animals: they used tools. They created fortresses. They domesticated other animals. They were self-aware, and valued their own lives— as much as Gallen valued his own.

What right do I have to kill them? Gallen asked himself. What right do any of us have? The Waters of Strength, if they exist, are not mine, any more than they belong to the sfuz.

The Dronon, Gallen saw, recognized but two classes of human—those that opposed them, and those who could be used as tools. Am I to the sfuz what the Dronon are to man?

He wondered if he should tell the others about the itching that filled his head, warn them. He didn't want to frighten them. Sfuz that revived after death were bad enough. He didn't want to tell of creatures invading his mind.

"Maybe we can sneak into Teeawah," Gallen said at last. "We'll find a way. Let's go." He hit the switch to open the ship's doors. The others filed into darkness by the light thrown from the interior of the ship. Gallen closed the doors. Darkness folded round them.

Maggie held the glow globes up, squeezed so that a spark breathed into flame in her hand.

Gallen led. The sensors in his mantle could read magnetic north, tell his elevation, and store an image of the sonar maps of this region. Gallen knew exactly where he was headed.

He took off through the thick humus.

The ground beneath his feet had built up from rotted limbs and detritus. Only the ancient boles of fallen trees held the soil, so all around were sinkholes. But the trees, hundreds of meters long, created paths of a sort, roads they could travel. So long as they kept finding such paths that led toward their destination, they would be fine.

It was a strange journey. Above them were false roofs at various levels where trees had collapsed, so that always they were in odd chambers where a roof might drop low or block the path altogether, while in other places a roof would rise a hundred meters in the air, and Gallen would find himself in a huge cavern.

Bits of fallen leaves and trees had filled nooks all around them. Gallen led the way through strange and twisted tunnels, creeping along beneath huge fallen beams.

Sometimes, back home, Gallen had traveled up to the headwaters of the Morgan River. In the winter, floods would wash trees and bracken downstream, and these would gather at the river bends, sticks and dirt forming huge piles. In summer, his father's hounds would chase mice or squirrels through those piles of drift for hours. Now, Gallen was discovering how the mice must have felt, groping through such a mess.

Once, Gallen passed a huge circle just on the right side of the path, a place where the ground seemed to have been dug away. The circle was too round, too perfectly symmetrical to have formed naturally. It looked like a mine shaft. Maggie held up her light. The hole dropped far into the darkness. Gallen looked up. It continued above as far as the eye could see.

Not a mine shaft, he decided. A tunnel. Something a mistwife could climb up through.

Suddenly Gallen feared to breathe, to move. He wondered if the vibrations caused by their walking would call a mistwife.

Orick stepped to the edge of the pit and looked down. Gallen dared not speak, dared not warn him. The bear nosed around, then turned, knocking a clod of dirt into the pit.

From far down below, Gallen heard the echo of a splash, followed by a wondrous thrashing sound, waves beating against one another as something enormous moved in the water.

Orick opened his mouth wide in terror, backed from the pit as if bitten. Gallen gave a curt gesture, urging everyone to flee. He didn't know if the light would attract the mistwife, what the beast might be capable of.

Maggie and Tallea rushed past Gallen.

A horrible groaning escaped the pit, a sound like a tree makes in the deep forest as it collapses under the weight of snow. Then Gallen heard rushing water.

The ground beneath his feet trembled, and Orick scrambled past. A hissing erupted from the pit. Something was rising, rushing through the hole.

Gallen reached for his weapons belt, unsure what to grab. None of his weapons would defend him against something this big.

An enormous form gushed up through the hole, water tumbling from it, propelled by no means Gallen could distinguish. Enormous worms, pinkish gray in color, dozens of meters long, shot up above him, writhing to find purchase in the next layer of the tangle. Suddenly the worms each broadened, and Gallen saw fluke-shaped webbing holding them all together at the base, followed at last by a broad head that sported an enormous white eye.

When the mistwife's eye passed Gallen's level, the creature jerked to a halt.

It gazed at the glow globe Maggie held.

Gallen ran. He couldn't force the others to retreat without light, yet the mistwife had seen them. He needed a barrier of some kind between them and the creature. He pulled out a small canister of Black Fog—the only one he had—and tossed it behind. It hissed and spurted darkness, spinning under the pressure of escaping gas.

Darkness wouldn't stop the creature. The ground rumbled as a tentacle snaked toward Gallen.

Gallen retreated as the tentacle burst through the rising Black Fog. Gallen ripped a heat grenade from his hip pouch and tossed it into the humus, knowing it would be far too small to kill the mistwife, hoping it might sting the beast.

Gallen spun, ran after the others as fast as he could. The grenade exploded into light and thunder, its searing blast filling the cave with smoke. For a moment the ground quit rumbling. Gallen had gone a hundred meters or more before he heard a terrible shriek that caused the earth to tremble. It was a high, thin sound, a squeal of consummate power and wrath.

Then the mistwife advanced. The ground beneath Gallen shook, as if the mistwife were trying to tear the world apart. Behind Gallen, Black Fog filled the tunnel so much that he could not make out the flames thrown by the heat grenade.

The sudden movement of the creature made a wall of Black Fog billow toward him. Gallen sprinted to keep ahead of it.

Maggie and the others had been running on a trail made by a fallen tree. Now they'd reached the end of this particular tree. The passage ahead was blocked. But above them was an opening to another passage.

Tallea scampered up the sheer, muddy cliff, but Orick couldn't follow. He clawed at the mud, but it wouldn't hold his weight. Maggie stood at the bottom of the cliff, helpless to advance farther, Zeus at her side.

Behind Gallen, a second tentacle whipped into the light. It bore no scars or burn marks from the grenade.

Gallen spun and hurled a second heat grenade as far back as he could. It blazed like the sun; the smell of smoke filled the narrow chamber, overwhelming.

Again the mistwife shrieked; the ground shook furiously. The mistwife was grappling with the bole of the tree that they stood on, twisting it.

Gallen grabbed Maggie to keep her from falling. The tentacle withdrew from them, but the smoke that filled the passage was choking them all.

Suddenly, the end of the log Gallen stood on pulled away; a pit opened beneath them, perhaps six meters down, and Zeus tumbled in. It led to a small tunnel. Gallen and Maggie couldn't go up to Tallea. They could only go down to Zeus.

"Come down with us!" Gallen shouted to the she-bear; he grabbed Maggie, helped her slide down into the tunnel.

In moments the bears scampered behind him, and Gallen ran. He didn't want to wait and see if the mistwife would try for them again.

Here a path led down an ancient highway of worm vine. The road was broad and smooth, the roof above them higher than before.

Behind, Gallen could hear the mistwife thrashing. The crash of giant trees being ripped apart, the creature's horrible shrieking cries.

Gallen wondered if the mistwife's cries of pain would attract sfuz.

No, he decided. If I were a sfuz, I wouldn't go to investigate something that caused a mistwife to shriek.

Yet as they passed one wide chamber, Gallen could clearly hear the mistwife above him, shrieking in rage. And he realized that the mistwife was eeling ahead of them, going north and climbing upward.

Gallen got a cold feeling in his stomach. "I think the mistwife is heading toward the cliffs," he whispered.

Zeus said, "She's angry. Maybe she thinks the sfuz are to blame."

Of course—of course, Gallen realized. She is the huntress here, and the sfuz are her prey. She knows where to find them.

He'd imagined hunting for days or weeks to find Teeawah, but now he saw that he would only have to follow the mistwife through her hunting passage. It would lead to the sfuz.

"We have to go up higher, and go north," Gallen whispered, gazing ahead. Nearby, a jumble of trees had collapsed into a pile, and the cave forked.

One route appeared to head in the direction he desired. "That way!"

Thirty-three

A board the Dronon starship *Acquiescence*, Thomas stood thoughtfully gazing down onto the bridge.

The Dronon starship seemed unthinkable by human standards: the deck, though clean, was much like the birthing chamber on one of the great walking hive ships. A bevy of Dronon technicians clung to the sides of the dome-shaped walls like insects.

The technicians, with their twisted vestigial wings, their tan bodies and strange green facial tatoos, reminded Thomas of mantises, waiting to strike. Yet the technicians had no prey but the monitors and various switches they guarded.

Higher on the walls, in a great circle, were viewscreens that displayed images from on planet. Dronon hunting teams showed their Lords images captured as warships swept through a strange alien jungle, beneath a terrible storm.

The ships were diving into the woods, lights blazing through a nearly impenetrable gloom of foliage and mist, flying thousands of meters down into this vast and bizarre wood.

From here aboard the *Acquiescence*, the Dronon would coordinate the work of the thirty-six hunting teams. Thomas watched the spectacle of the pursuit in horrid fascination.

Lord Karthenor had retrieved several people from the surface of Ruin— the dictator Felph and his two beautiful daughters. Karthenor spoke to Felph as if he were a "guest," enjoying Dronon hospitality, but Thomas knew Felph and his daughters were hostages. If they lied about Maggie's whereabouts, if they tried to deceive the Dronon, they'd pay dearly.

But Felph, a young man with glittering eyes that said he knew far more than a young man should, aided the Dronon to the best of his abilities.

Thomas didn't know whether to pity Felph, or to hate him. With his Guide on, Thomas could only stare, bearing silent witness to his treachery.

Karthenor said to Felph, in discussing the Dronon invasion, "This is a rather unprecedented move of solidarity, to fly all the hive ships of the Golden Queens here in unison. But the Dronon see the wisdom of combining their strength. Once they conquer mankind, they'll share human technology equally. With both our species working together, we will begin a new era of prosperity."

Felph looked out through the central viewport near the ceiling, where Ruin seemed to float above their heads, a ball of red sand blotched with hazy purple seas. Hundreds of brilliant objects floated around the planet, but Thomas could see they weren't stars—they were Dronon warships, along with technical support crews.

Nearby, several technical support crews had already begun creating a massive ring of black metal in space, a new gate that would let the Dronon fly their ships back to their own home worlds, once they'd found Gallen and Maggie.

"Marvelous, marvelous." Felph mouthed the words without enthusiasm as he studied the construction of this massive Gate to All Worlds. "But I have to wonder, Lord Karthenor. Wouldn't the golden age you speak of be just as grand if humans stood at the helm? What if *we* took control, discovered the secrets of *Dronon* technology?"

Karthenor studied Felph with an appreciative smile. "The Tharrin would never do that," Karthenor said. "The notion of dominating another species would offend their principles."

Felph shrugged. "Well, the Tharrin aren't human, are they? I ask you again, what if humans took control?"

Karthenor stared down at Cintkin and Kintiniklintit, Lords of the Seventh Swarm. In the center of the dome, the Golden Queen lay in a huge pit, her bloated body filling a remarkable portion of the room. Hundreds of small, white worker Dronon scurried around her, constantly feeding her some obnoxious milk, or grooming her body by cleansing it with their mandibles, or hauling off the sickly yellow eggs that dropped from her egg sac every two minutes.

The sheer number of Dronon in the room invited a sense of claustrophobia. Yet more intimidating than all this was Kintiniklintit himself, the Lord Escort who stood at the queen's side, receiving his own ministrations from fawning attendants. Dozens of Vanquishers surrounded him, enormous, deadly creatures with their black carapaces. Beelzebub, Lord of the Flies.

Lord Kintiniklintit dwarfed all his counterparts.

Karthenor nodded toward Kintiniklintit, considering Felph's treasonous attitude. "Marvelous specimen, isn't he? He's one of the first Dronon Lords who has been modified through genetic manipulation. He outweighs his rivals by sixty percent. Most of his exoskeleton has been reinforced, so he can withstand greater damage in the arena. I believe if he wanted to, he could seize control of the whole Dronon empire. But he's biding his time, wisely I might add. He's a young Vanquisher, and is studying the battle techniques of his enemies."

That was all Karthenor said, but the implied message was this: we can't conquer the Dronon unless a human can survive in the arena with this monster. I'm backing Kintiniklintit.

Felph did not answer. He just eyed Kintiniklintit with an amused twinkle in his eye. "We share an unhealthy fondness for eugenics, I see." Felph glanced at Karthenor. "You've met my beautiful daughters. When you find Gallen and Maggie, you'll meet my son, Zeus. I hope you find him admirable. Sometimes, there is more to a man than meets the eye."

Thomas heard the threat under those words: don't back Kintiniklintit until you know the competition.

Lord Karthenor smiled affably. "A son? You have a son?" he waved expansively at Kintiniklintit. "Then we both have sons, for though he was born to the Lords of the Sixth Swarm, Kintiniklintit is as much *my* son as his father's." Thomas was stunned by the admission. "So, our sons will do battle. How amusing."

"Fortuitous," Felph said, "I hope."

"Amusing, whatever the outcome," Karthenor said. As if to change to a safer topic, he added, "It's odd, don't you think, that a species as advanced as the Dronon never considered the benefits of genetics till they met man? You'd think any self-aware species would instantly recognize the benefits of genetic manipulation—to cure disease, improve intelligence. But the Dronon never saw it as anything more than a curiosity.

"You see, they knew what to do with those who were deformed or sickly. They killed them. Threw them away.

"The result is that for millions of years, the Dronon have been almost free from genetically transmitted ailments. So they never considered the possibility of *improving* themselves. . . ."

Karthenor waited for Felph to respond. Clearly he wanted to know what "improvements" Lord Felph had made to Zeus. There was a dangerous glimmer in Karthenor's eyes, a stern tightness about his mouth. If Thomas weren't wearing a Guide, he'd have warned Felph of the dangers of revealing too much.

Perhaps Lord Felph was smarter than Thomas credited. With a grin, he simply said, "Hmmm . . . interesting."

Around the room, a rhythmic, pounding hum reverberated as Dronon technicians kept up constant chatter. But suddenly Kintiniklintit began loudly clacking his mouthfingers over his voicedrum; the other Dronon quieted.

Karthenor seemed to have no difficulty understanding the Dronon's words. "Ah, it looks as if you have steered us correctly, Felph. For that, I thank you. The Dronon located the ship precisely where you said it would be."

The central screen, which took up nearly a third of one wall, displayed a three-dimensional image of a glowing blue spaceship buried deep beneath the tangle.

"I suspected he'd be there," Felph said. "I had some work for Gallen in this region."

"Work?" Karthenor asked.

"Searching for ancient ruins. The natives on this world once stood on the verge of creating technology. It's rumored that an ancient city lies there somewhere, but it's the devil to get to—local predators, you know."

"Hmmm." Karthenor shrugged, uninterested in the matter.

Dronon technicians in one sector of the dome suddenly began humming loudly, and Karthenor spun on his heels, watching the monitors they tended. The Dronon cleared away from several screens. Klaxons began screaming a warning in the distance, while brilliant blue lights flashed along the floor of the dome.

In space, all around the planet, Dronon battleships suddenly began to dive landward. Felph wrung his hands nervously and shouted, "What's happening? Where are they all going?"

Karthenor studied the ships, his dark eyes darting from monitor to monitor. "The other Swarm Lords know we've found Maggie's ship, and they're trying to get to her first. They're sending in Vanquishers—their own search parties."

Thomas almost grinned. So his niece was a treasure, and all the Dronon were going to fight for her, fight for the chance to challenge Gallen O'Day.

Karthenor waved to a screen at the far right. "See, the Lords of the Fourth Swarm are sending down six full Flights—over forty-six thousand Vanquishers. I should have anticipated this!" he grumbled. "With thousands of worlds at stake, the opportunity to loot mankind's technology. I should have known!"

As the Lords of the Fourth Swarm launched six battleships toward the planet, the others were forced to deploy their own troops in ever-greater numbers. Sixty thousand Vanquishers from first swarm, ninety from second.

Within minutes, over half a million Vanquishers departed for Ruin. Thomas wished he could talk, at least enough to hurl a curse at the Dronon. He hoped the Vanquishers would do more than merely race toward Gallen and Maggie. He hoped they would fight over their prey. At least that way, if Gallen and Maggie died, some Dronon would be lost, too.

Thomas could think of nothing to do—no way to help his niece, but to pray silently. "Hide, Maggie. Hide!"

Thirty-four

M aggie hurried to keep up, terrified beyond her ability to tell. Distantly, the earth rumbled from the sound of the mistwife flailing in her anger.

Gallen ran ahead of Maggie, following crazy trails, trying to go upward when possible. Time and again as she climbed, Maggie found herself grabbing wildly at ancient roots in the ground, all of them cold as ice and hard as iron.

The landscape had no color. Everything was washed in shades of gray, covered with the same dark molds and slimes.

Dully, almost constantly, she heard wild thrashing, the terrible cries of the mistwife. They were getting closer to it as they climbed.

They came to a cavern filled with iron gray molds, standing like inverted trumpets, which felt like foam rubber beneath her feet. Nothing lived here except for the odd blind insect that skittered off when it felt the ground tremble at their steps. Beyond the occasional trickle of water, she could no longer hear any sounds. The air smelled fetid, full of rot and mold. The stillness, the heavy, oppressive air weighed her down, made her feel as if she would suffocate.

For nearly two kilometers, they found no sign of sfuz or any other animals, until at last Gallen crouched above a pair of prints in the humus, crossing their path. "A young sfuz," he said. Maggie was no expert tracker, but even she could see detritus filling the prints; the edges around the tracks had crumbled. The sfuz that made them could not have passed this way within weeks or months.

Still, it was a good sign. A juvenile had passed this way, exploring the tangle, hunting.

Gallen tried to follow the tracks back to a lair, but they led around the lip of a dangerous sinkhole, then climbed directly up a steep tree. Still, they were getting near the lair.

"Maggie," her mantle whispered. "I have just received a message from the ship. The Dronon are making a powerful sensor sweep of this area. They've discovered the ship's location." Gallen turned and frowned at Maggie. Apparently, his mantle had just relayed the message to him.

It had taken Gallen and Maggie two hours to fly their ship into this mess. They'd snaked through dozens of passages, gone up almost as much as they'd gone down. Even if the Dronon knew their ship was here, it could take them hours to find a path to it. Once they did, they'd follow Maggie's scent.

She imagined Dronon Vanquishers, thousands strong, hunting through this tangle. She wondered what would happen when they met the sfuz.

"Gallen," she hissed. "We have to stop!"

Gallen halted. The light from her glow globe cast enormous shadows, shadows that frightened her because for a moment she thought she saw something huge and black struggling toward her from a passage.

She went to Gallen's side. "The Dronon will be hunting here," she whispered. "And the sfuz. Maybe we shouldn't try to get so close to Teeawah."

Gallen looked up toward the passage that had frightened Maggie. "We don't know how close we are, yet."

"Close enough so their children play in these passages."

Gallen looked forward eagerly, then frowned as he glanced at the trail behind. "I don't know what else to do."

Maggie's heart pounded. Her mouth felt dry. She unstrapped the canteen from her back and took a swig. She didn't know what to do, either. The tension in the air was so thick, she could hardly swallow. She nodded, let Gallen lead them forward.

He can't do it all, Maggie thought. He can't lead us. He can't fight for us. He can't do it all. Think. Think. She didn't want to go forward, could barely force herself to keep up.

They hurried up the passage, came to a bend. Gallen halted. To their left, a great hole opened, perfectly round. This one was twice the diameter of the one they'd encountered earlier. Another mistwife. Huge. Huge.

Maggie's heart pounded. Gallen and the others tiptoed ahead.

Think, Maggie told herself. She reached into her pockets, shoving her fists in to get warm; her fingers closed around glass.

She pulled it out. The bottle of scent from the perfumery. She stopped, considered it for a moment.

The Dronon would follow her, chase her with their Seekers. She couldn't let them find her.

She motioned with her hand for Gallen to come back. He had already gone fifty meters ahead. He returned reluctantly.

Maggie didn't dare speak. Instead, she reached up, fumbled with his robe. Its nanoscrubbers could hide her scent, clean it from the air as she walked. If she wore his robe, she hoped, she'd be almost undetectable to the Seekers.

Gallen frowned at her, confused, tried to pull her forward. Apparently he thought she was only cold, and he considered this a poor place to give her the loan of a cloak, but Maggie refused to be led away till she had the cloak off him and over her own shoulders. She pulled the hood up over her head, then took the bottle of scent, carried it to the lip of the great hole in the ground, the mistwife's passage.

The dirt here was slippery, loose. If she got too near the edge, she'd fall in. But she had to do this, had to reach out over that dark hole and pour a few drops, a few precious drops of her scent down that hole.

When she finished, she put the stopper back on the empty bottle and dropped it into the thick humus at her feet, covered it with dirt, then fled.

Every second, she listened for the sound of something rushing up that shaft, something shrieking and tumbling. If this monster came after them, they might not escape.

When she'd gone a few hundred meters, she sighed in relief. Yet her relief was short-lived.

If I made it safely, won't the Dronon? she wondered. She'd hoped the mistwife would kill any Seekers that came after her. She'd imagined the machines hurtling over the lip of that pit, and the Dronon buzzing away, crashing into the jaws of the mistwife.

But what if no mistwife lived down that hole? The pit was vast, twenty meters in diameter. Perhaps its maker had died centuries ago.

Maggie couldn't know, might never know. She only knew she had to keep running. By now it was late afternoon. The sfuz would be waking, leaving their chambers. The group needed to find a place to hide.

Thirty-five

*G*allen glanced back down the trail behind him, watching for sign of pursuit, then looked ahead again. Before them was a small pond, water pooling from a rock cliff, that stretched up into the darkness. The pool appeared deep and still. Tiny blind fish and insects swam in it, yet Gallen dared not drink that water, for it had an unhealthy green tint to it. Besides, it was not the solemn pond, with the sound of dripping from above, that interested him. It was the cliff.

The weathered yellow stone had been swept smooth eons ago by wind and rain, yet here in the tangle, it looked as if wind would never touch it again.

Still, on the cliff before them faint pictographs could be seen in dim green characters. A bird, with both wings spread, looking up to its right. Lightning bolts seemed to be flying from its eyes. Zeus stared at it, mesmerized, mouth open in wonder.

"What is it?" Orick asked.

"A Qualeewooh," Zeus said, "who wears no spirit mask."

Gallen wanted to say something in response, but he, too, suddenly felt a sense of wonder. Even the most ancient depictions of Qualeewoohs he'd seen portrayed them with spirit masks. But if the masks were created to be receivers so the Qualeewoohs could hear the voices of their ancestors, then there would have been a time before the ancestors spoke, a time when no Qualeewooh yet wore a mask. A time before the Waters of Strength.

Gallen shook his head. This particular chamber in the tangle was fairly large, but had no openings to either side. It came to an abrupt stop at the cliff face. Here, the trail ended.

The last fork in the trail that Gallen had seen was hundreds of meters back. Even if he knew where an entrance to Teeawah was, he knew he wouldn't reach it easily. That in itself made him uneasy, but he faced another challenge. It had been three hours since the Dronon had pinpointed his ship.

The Dronon were now hunting them, deep in the tangle. His mantle picked up their radio chatter—the incessant clicking of Dronon mouthfingers over a background of static. It wasn't coming over just a few channels, but over hundreds or thousands.

The Dronon must be crawling through here en masse, he realized. More of them than he'd imagined possible were filtering through the tangle. It was only a matter of time before they found him. Gallen couldn't afford any more blind alleys or delays.

"Come on," he whispered, leading the party back the way they'd come.

Maggie turned and hobbled, neck bent, nearly stumbling with fatigue. For the past four hours they'd been climbing up and down, seeking routes through this maze. They'd found few signs of sfuz—excrement here, a hole dug there. Gallen realized that they'd come too low. The entrance to the city must be higher up the cliffs. Down here, where nothing lived, the sfuz did not bother to hunt. That's why he'd found so few tracks.

Gallen walked with Maggie, holding her hand, trying to give the comfort she needed. He watched her face in the bobbing, unsteady light; saw that more than the energy had drained from it. Her hope, too, was going.

"Don't worry, darling," Gallen whispered, emphasizing the brogue accent he'd all but completely discarded in the last months. "I'll not let nothing bad happen to the prettiest girl in Clere." He clenched her hand reassuringly.

Maggie smiled, but kept her mouth shut. None of them really should be talking, even though it looked certain that no sfuz were close by.

For another hour they hiked, backtracking from one cavern to the next, climbing up higher whenever possible. In one passage, they finally found a trail that had seen some use, and Gallen tried following it—climbing vertical trees as if he were a sfuz, squeezing through a tunnel so narrow Maggie feared she wouldn't be able to make it.

When they reached the end of the tunnel, they found they hadn't come to a sfuz lair, but had reached something—a vast yawning pit filled with the shells of some crablike animals, along with hundreds of skeletons. At first Gallen imagined that the sfuz had disposed of bones here, but movement in the pit caught his eye. It wasn't shells, but actual crablike insects, each with a dozen thin legs, climbing among corpses—sfuz corpses. In this graveyard, scavengers fed.

The fact that some sfuz died at all suggested that not all of them were allowed to drink from the Waters of Strength. Gallen wondered. Like any great treasure, some would horde it, deny it to others. Gallen guessed that these were the lowest of the sfuz, the wasted, those who did not merit immortality.

Gallen turned away in disgust, listening to the clacking jaws, the faint scrabbling of insects. Worse yet, among the corpses, some dead sfuz had burn marks. These were sfuz Gallen had killed only the day before.

Maggie sat at the edge of the stinking pit, put her head in her hands, trembling from weariness.

"Come," Gallen said. "We're not far from their lair. We have to keep moving."

He took them back the way they'd come, past their previous path. Not a dozen yards from where they'd first joined the sfuz trail, they turned a bend, found an opening to a tunnel with a road ten times as wide as the trail they'd been traveling.

The road was trampled hard as cement. The walls rose dozens of meters, and Gallen could see fresh wooden beams shoring the walls of this tunnel. This wasn't just some wild path through the tangle—it was a highway.

We must be near Teeawah, Gallen realized, looking northward along the subterranean highway. There was an odd reek in the air, the sour smell of sfuz hide, almost nauseating in its intensity. Thousands, perhaps hundreds of thousands of sfuz must live here.

As Gallen stumbled onto this thoroughfare, he stood a moment, unsure if he should go forward. How could he hope to reach the city undiscovered?

Yet even as he worried, his mantle picked up a strong, clear radio signal. Dronon were coming, and one of them was relaying a report to its masters. Down the bend, on the highway leading out of the city, lights shone.

Gallen raced back to the narrow trail off the highway, urging Maggie to hide her glow globes, and the small group scurried back down the corridor. In moments the highway tunnel filled with the echoing sounds of a Dronon march, the clicking of mouthfingers over voicedrums, the rattle of weapons against carapaces.

Zeus, Maggie, and the bears scurried farther down their narrow tunnel, squeezing round a corner. Gallen halted far back in the darkness, listening. In the shadows he knelt in the dirt, mouth pressed close to the moldy humus, and peeked out at the highway, letting his mantle capture and illuminate the image.

A Dronon Vanquisher suddenly filled the passage before them, flashed a light over Gallen's head, and fired a pulp gun blindly, just to make certain the passage was clear. Dirt sprinkled down on Gallen, and he dared not move. In half a second, the Dronon moved on, and Gallen saw the marching bodies of others come into view.

The Dronon had come in force. For ten minutes he watched Dronon, hundreds of them, marching in formation, scurrying through the cavern like roaches, weapons at ready. Twice more, scouts glanced down his long passage, each flashing a strong light into the crevice. Gallen drew back around the corner, out of sight. Sweat poured down his brow. Gallen seldom became frightened, yet his heart pounded.

When the echo of footsteps dimmed, when the Dronon had passed, Gallen sat, trying to calm himself. Twelve hundred. A contingent of twelve hundred Vanquishers, all armed with incendiary rifles and pulp guns.

Gallen waited, unsure what to do. He didn't want to follow the Dronon. It would be better, perhaps, to put as much distance between himself and the Dronon as possible. But his gut instinct told him that the highway out there led to Teeawah.

He looked back to Maggie for counsel. "What now?"

"Follow them," she whispered. "To the city."

Gallen nodded, uncertain. His arms and legs trembled, but not from fear— it was the ground trembling beneath him. Not the deep rumbling of an earthquake, not even the milder reverberations of a mistwife moving through its tunnel. Smaller.

Gallen stilled his breath. Distantly, he heard small-arms fire.

The Dronon firing pulp guns. The concussions caused the tremors. For two solid minutes, the rumbling continued, and Gallen finally recognized a crackling, too. The sharper retorts of incendiary rifles.

A battle raged, nearby. Here, underground, sound wouldn't carry far. Gallen smelled smoke, a smoke he realized might take weeks to clear from the tangle.

Suddenly, down the highway, just outside his little tunnel, the whistling cries of sfuz erupted, rapidly drawing close. Hundreds of them, perhaps thousands, were fleeing the city, Gallen thought.

But something was wrong. The pitch of their whistles wasn't the high, desperate whine he'd heard before from retreating sfuz, but rather the low cries of hunters.

The Dronon guns had gone silent.

"Damn," Gallen whispered, unprepared for the revelation.

The Dronon had reached Teeawah. And died.

How many sfuz were out there? Twelve hundred Vanquishers, gone just like that.

We're next, he thought.

He turned back, urging the others to flee down the narrow trail. Zeus took little encouragement, retreated the way they'd come. Gallen wondered how safe it would be. Their trail led to a dead end through one corridor and to the mistwives in another.

And the Dronon should be following us, Gallen realized. The Seekers should be on our trail. He couldn't retreat.

But sfuz and the city lay ahead. He couldn't go forward.

When they reached a small chamber where ancient limbs thrust up from the floor, Gallen called a halt. "Zeus, spread some of this down the corridor," he said, tossing Zeus the canister of exploding foam. Zeus took it, disappeared up the trail.

Gallen heard the hiss of foam as Zeus sprayed the floor and walls. In sixty seconds the foam would set; anything that touched it thereafter would explode in a fireball.

"Maggie, you and the bears take cover here between these branches, and break out some food. We need some rest." He indicated the two largest partially petrified tree branches, which thrust up. From behind them, they'd have some protection.

Maggie sat and drew her heavy pistol, a conventional weapon with high-explosive charges and a silencer. No sooner had she got down than the sfuz found them.

Several dozen charged down the narrow corridor, whistling in anticipation. The sfuz boiled through the cavern opening like ants, grasping the cavern wall with their strong fingers, apparently unmindful of gravity. Some were running along the ceiling, others erupting around walls, while yet others scampered along the floor. They seemed intent on finding their prey, mindless with rage.

Gallen turned, firing his intelligent pistol as rapidly as he could, targeting individual sfuz.

Maggie didn't have time for such niceties. She opened fire with her pistol, blasting as fast as she could squeeze the trigger, counting on the explosive force of her projectiles to rip apart anything in her path.

Maggie's weapon worked well in close quarters. As she fired, sfuz dropped from the ceiling, raining down in bloody gobbets on their kin, their hunting cries turning to death screams.

The black creatures seemed to seethe from the walls, their horrible, long, twisted limbs writhing. They curled up on themselves as they died, sometimes kicking out savagely with long limbs. Their dark eyes gleamed, their fangs flashed in the pale light thrown by the firefight, their claws raked the air.

These were not adults, Gallen suddenly realized. These are juveniles and children, smaller than adults, but no less deadly, apparently, for they had just slaughtered a thousand Dronon.

But at what cost? Gallen wondered. How many sfuz died.

Gallen took to targeting the sfuz that got past Maggie.

Maggie screamed, "Back me! My clip's empty!"

Gallen's own weapon was nearly out of missiles, and in his mind, he practiced drawing his vibro-blade, considered how he might best hold off the sfuz till Maggie could reload.

He needn't have worried.

Zeus came charging around the bend, firing his incendiary pistol. He got off three shots before Gallen shouted, "No!"

The plasma from the pistol burned like the sun, setting the ancient detritus along the walls afire. The fierce heat of the blasts was like a furnace burning Gallen's face. Gallen raised his arm to shield himself, to cover his mouth. The smoke that erupted in the chamber was so overwhelming, Gallen feared they would all suffocate before they escaped.

The sfuz retreated. None dared enter this chamber.

Gallen looked back, wondering if he could retreat. Zeus had just mined the passage. Explosive foams were seldom used in real campaigns—they were too nondiscriminatory, and couldn't be easily disarmed. In fact, Gallen hadn't brought the solvents needed to disarm the foam.

They couldn't retreat past the foam, nor could they go forward through the blaze. Yet as smoke billowed into the chamber, Gallen knew if they stayed here, they'd suffocate.

He had to close off the passage ahead—conserve the oxygen here. He reached into his weapons pouch, found a heavy grenade, and tossed it toward the corpses of the sfuz.

The grenade exploded, dirt sprayed toward him in the hot wind. The cavern shook. Detritus rained from above, filling Gallen's eyes. He raised his hands to shield his face.

A second explosion rocked the cavern behind. Falling dirt had detonated the foam.

The ground gave way beneath him.

Maggie shrieked.

Gallen grabbed her arm, then they were tumbling, the earth opening to swallow them, an avalanche of dirt and rotted humus storming down upon them.

Thirty-six

F elph stood beside Lord Karthenor aboard the Dronon vessel *Acquiescence,* watching the viewscreens on the dome above them, the Dronon cameras displaying hellish nightmares.

In one region deep in the tangle, Dronon Seekers had captured Maggie's scent, only to find that it led down a huge shaft. A giant mistwife rose up to greet the Dronon, and now hundreds of Dronon engaged the monster, trying to fight their way past, with no assurance that Maggie had ever escaped the monster's grasp.

The presence of hundreds of thousands of Dronon in the tangle aroused every mistwife in the region, so that on nearly every screen, the monsters hunted through the tangle, shrieking in pain, madly swatting Dronon who did not fight so bravely as they did mindlessly.

Yet, for Felph, other screens displayed far more interesting battles. Dronon Vanquishers high in the tangle were blasting through sfuz hunting parties.

The sfuz had the element of surprise. In dozens of places, the creatures boiled out of secret holes by the thousands or dropped from above or clambered around trees.

The small sfuz were no match in single battle for Vanquishers, with their thick carapaces and heavy battle arms. The sfuz died easily enough. But there were so many, so many, and they were so fast, and they were learning.

The sfuz concentrated not on direct assaults, but upon ambushes and trickery.

Dronon warriors were marching down an apparently safe path, then suddenly dropped into a pit. Another Dronon stepped into a snare, went flying against a tree, his carapace cracking open like a melon. Elsewhere, a Dronon battalion came upon the bodies of scouts who'd been bludgeoned by sfuz who wielded clubs.

In many battles, when a dozen sfuz suddenly dropped from a ceiling, the Dronon instinctively fired their incendiary rifles—the Vanquishers' customary ready weapon. Yet a single shot fired in these close quarters raised choking smoke from the moldering tangle—smoke that strangled the Dronon in minutes. Dronon lungs were less efficient than those of a sfuz or a human.

Indeed, across every monitor, the caverns had begun boiling with dark smoke. In places, dry logs burned out of control. Everywhere on the screens, Dronon were choking, dying by the tens of thousands.

Felph was astonished at the carnage, dismayed to the core of his soul. Tens of thousands of troops died in sfuz attacks, yet Felph saw cameras that focused on only a sixth of the Dronon forces.

Elsewhere, others were also falling prey to the sfuz.

"My god, my god," Karthenor swore, shaking his head in dismay, the rings of his golden mantle tinkling. "Why didn't you warn us?"

Felph shook his head, "I suspected the sfuz had a stronghold, but I never imagined . . ." he answered truthfully. There were more sfuz than he'd believed possible, perhaps millions of them. He'd envisioned a battle for the city—but nothing like this.

Now he saw it had been folly to imagine that he, Gallen, or anyone, would ever reach Teeawah. Folly. Utter folly.

Yet on one monitor, he saw something intriguing. A Dronon contingent marched down a broad highway unlike any he'd ever seen in the tangle, and came to ancient cliffs of sculpted yellow sandstone. The Dronon cameras distorted the colors, giving everything a yellowish hue, but they could not hide the thing Felph hoped to see.

There in the cliffs were holes, thousands on thousands of *clooes* excavated by Qualeewoohs, each a perfect dark oval.

"There! There!" Felph shouted. "There it is!"

As soon as he had said these words, monstrous black forms began wriggling from the holes, hundreds upon thousands of sfuz, hurling themselves down on the Dronon, boiling from holes one after another, racing across the roof and walls of this vast cavern.

They reminded Felph of spiders, thousands of horrid black spiders seething from their lair.

The Dronon troops began shooting. A firestorm ensued, tracers of white-hot plasma erupting through the dark caverns. Everywhere the sfuz were falling, burning, dying. And for a minute it looked as if the Dronon would take the city. But the sfuz were too many, too many.

The camera caught images of Dronon, struggling beneath dozens of dark forms, thrashing with large battle arms, firing into their own ranks. The camera's holder had several sfuz leap on him from above, and the jumble of images that ensued showed fangs and purple blood flying, flashes of light.

Suddenly the cameraman was free again, and the Dronon continued firing in a desperate attempt to drive off the sfuz. The boiling plasma that issued from the rifles burned in a thousand hot spots, white lights shining, brightening the cavern through layers of dark smoke that crept along the ground, over the ceilings.

The vast chamber was clogged with smoke. Dronon Vanquishers began pumping their legs rapidly, trying to force oxygen into the intake holes on their massive rear legs so they could breathe. The Dronon cameraman tried to retreat from the killing ground, stumbled to the road, and left the camera going. Under the eerie glow of a thousand burning incendiary charges, Felph watched the fearless Vanquishers strangle beneath a roiling wall of smoke.

Felph shook his head in dismay. If the Dronon die, if the Dronon suffocate, the sfuz will, too, he considered.

"These holes?" Karthenor asked, pointing to the *clooes* on the monitor. "You're sure these are part of the ancient city Gallen is searching for?"

"Indeed!" Felph said. "That is the place."

Karthenor sighed heavily, gauging the damage done, the casualties of the battle, then turned and shouted over the hum of the room. "Lord Kintiniklintit, have your forces engage the city. Gallen and Maggie may already be secreted inside."

Lord Felph's jaw dropped in awe. Teeawah had eluded him for six hundred years. Now he saw that it would have eluded him forever.

At this very moment, a window of opportunity opened. The Dronon were liberating the city, but in a day the Dronon would be gone. They'd find Maggie and Gallen and kill them, then withdraw their troops.

In only a few hours, the sfuz who'd drunk from the Waters of Strength would begin rising from the dead, once again begin defending their lair.

The sfuz that infested the ruins would return, feeding off the carnage. Felph would never again be able to mount such an intensive invasion into this region.

But today the Dronon would take the city, probably never realizing what treasure they held.

Today, Felph could drink from the Waters of Strength.

"Lord Karthenor," Felph said, "I'd like to go down to the city, now, before your troops demolish the archaeological ruins."

Karthenor turned, studied Felph with an enigmatic smile. "You want to go there?"

"Indeed," Felph said. "I've searched for the site for ages. Now I see that once your troops leave, I dare not ever return."

"What are you searching for?" Karthenor asked. By his tone, Felph knew he suspected something. "Chances are you won't get in or out alive. What could be worth the risk?"

The great statesman Kenrand once said, "A politician's greatest asset is his ability to create a facile lie when confronted by constituents." Felph hoped he was up to the task.

"I have a dozen clones who await wakening back in my palace. This body is but the raiment I wear. If it dies, I'll put on another. But knowledge, knowledge of the philosophies of the ancient Qualeewoohs, now there is something of abiding worth!" He smiled, with just a bit of a gleam in his eye, as if he were mad. It was a role he played often, to good advantage.

Karthenor stared down at him, impassive behind his golden mask. The lord fingered his robe, nervously rubbing the fabric between two fingers.

"Send a Dronon escort with me, if you don't trust me," Felph said. "I have nothing to hide, and nothing to gain. I can be of no further help in this quest. I swear, you know as much about Gallen's whereabouts as I do."

Karthenor frowned. He wouldn't send a guard with Felph. He was a counselor to the Dronon, but apparently didn't have the authority to order Vanquishers about. Felph had counted on that. But Karthenor did have resources. He smiled, turned to an elderly slave in a dirty tunic who wore a silver Guide in his silvering hair. "Thomas Flynn, go with our friend here. Guard him with your life, then make certain he returns safely to me as soon as Maggie is captured."

Karthenor pulled a heavy pistol from his own holster, tossed it to Thomas Flynn. Karthenor nodded toward a Vanquisher, spoke rapidly into a translator, ordering a shuttle for Felph's and Thomas's use.

Thirty-seven

T he dirt shifted beneath Maggie's feet, and she felt herself sliding. She screamed. Gallen reached, grabbed her arm. Detritus rumbled down from the ceiling. As the ground opened to swallow her, Maggie had but one thought: *my baby!*

Gallen must have thought of the child, too. As he fell, he pulled her on top of him, to cushion her fall with his own body.

Maggie's breath left her, expecting they'd tumble dozens of meters, but instead the floor dropped only one. Dust filled the air in a cloud. Maggie squinted through the dust and smoke, spitting dirt out of her mouth.

Their path ran along the spine of an ancient dew tree. A section of it had given way, spilling only a meter. The tunnel to the sfuz was blocked by a cave-in, but the path back to the ship remained open. If anything, now that the floor had dropped, the passage was more open than before. Fresh air was rising from somewhere beneath them.

"This way. Quickly," Gallen said, grasping Maggie's hand, pulling her back down the trail toward the ship.

She looked around. Orick and Tallea seemed fine, indestructible as bears are. Zeus crawled about blindly. A chunk of dirt had struck his head.

Gallen stopped at his side. "Can you stand?"

"Uh, uh, fine." Zeus waved Gallen away with his pistol.

"Hurry," Gallen urged Maggie. "The sfuz might dig through."

Perhaps, Maggie considered, but they wouldn't dig soon. The plasma discharged from Zeus's pistol would stay at ten thousand degrees for several minutes, longer if buried beneath this dirt.

Still, she pressed forward. She stumbled over the trail, thick with fallen rubbish, following Gallen, checking to see that Zeus got up.

When they reached the fork in the trail, Gallen stopped. One path led to the sfuz graveyard and the cliffs beyond. The other led back toward the ship.

Distantly, Maggie heard the ground rumbling. Another cave-in? A mistwife? Another firefight? She couldn't be certain. She stopped, unwilling to run until she knew where the danger lay.

Gallen looked up. "Gunfire. Somewhere above."

Orick grumbled, "Gallen, we can't keep running. Between the Dronon, the mistwives, and the sfuz, one of them will get us."

Gallen stared at the dirt roof, held by cross-fallen bits of timber. He shook his head in frustration.

Maggie felt worn to the core. It wasn't just the physical work of dragging herself through this maze, it was the stress of worrying about her child. Gallen held her tenderly.

"All right. We'll hole up. I'll go down the trails and see if I can find a path to the city. There has to be one."

He led them past the sfuz burial pit, until they reached a small chamber near the cliffs, perhaps five meters wide and ten meters high. It looked fairly defendable, should it come to that, and any attack could come from only one direction. Maggie only hoped that she wouldn't get cornered in here.

Gallen opened his backpack and set out a blanket for Maggie to rest on. Then he drew food from his pack—a bottle of juice and fresh bread. Maggie bit into the bread, surprised at how good it tasted. It seemed she'd come down here ages ago, not hours.

Zeus just threw himself to the ground, lay dirty, exhausted, holding his head. The bears next to him panted. Maggie smelled smoke. She remembered she hadn't reloaded her pistol. She pulled out the clip, inserted a hundred caseless cartridges.

Gallen knelt at her ear and whispered. "Maggie, I'm going to search for a way into the city."

"No, stay here and rest with us," Maggie said, uneasy at the thought of Gallen leaving.

Gallen shook his head. "The Dronon are attacking up above us. I don't know how many there are, but my mantle is picking up thousands of signals— up above us, in the tangle. We need this diversion. We need the Dronon to draw the sfuz off, but I can't be asking you and the others to run constantly like this, not in the shape you're in.

"I'll try to find a way into Teeawah—sneak in if I can. Or if I can't, I'll come back for you. If I'm not back in six hours—"

"—Three hours, just let me rest for three hours," Maggie said.

"Four hours, then," Gallen said. "If I'm not back in four hours, I probably won't be back at all. Do you understand?"

Maggie's heart pounded. The stress was making her chest and arms ache. She nodded dumbly. "I love you."

Gallen brushed some fallen hair from her eyes. "I love you, too. Don't take my robe off. Maybe it can hide your scent. I'm going to cover your tracks up ahead, where the trails cross. But keep your eyes open. Don't take the safety off your weapon."

Maggie licked her dry lips. Gallen kissed her, long and slow. She savored the taste of his lips, the smell of his hair. She held him for a moment. When he pulled back, it felt as if he'd been wrenched from her.

She had an odd feeling. I'll never see him again, she thought. It was a fear she'd never faced before, one she'd never conceived. Not when Karthenor took her prisoner on Fale, not when the Inhuman took his mind on Tremonthin. She'd never believed she would lose him.

Yet now the fear came, as if the future held a black certainty.

When Gallen pulled away, she almost grabbed him and held. When he turned his back and hurried into the darkness, she almost followed. He carried no light, just jogged into the shadows, relying on his mantle to help him place his next step.

Maggie sat with her weapon across her knees and ate her bread, no longer noticing its taste. Everyone remained awake.

Zeus came up beside Maggie, stood watching her for a moment. "Will he come back if he finds a way into the city?"

Maggie shook her head, staring at the ground. The soil here was so thick, so rich, she imagined. She wished she'd found such soil elsewhere, in a place where she could have planted a garden. "I don't know. No, he won't come back. Not unless he has to."

"He'll go searching for the Waters alone?" Zeus asked.

"He will, if he thinks it's safest for us," Maggie answered.

Zeus said nothing, but after a moment she realized he was breathing hard, just staring off into the darkness, as if he could peer through the dirt and darkness of the tangle.

"He'll come back," Maggie said.

Zeus nodded, then asked, "Do you have an extra glow globe?"

"Check your pack," Maggie said. "I'm sure Gallen left each of us one."

Zeus went off, a little nearer toward the entrance to the tunnel and sat. It was a good place to take guard duty. He laid his pistol over his knee, then opened his pack, pulled out his light, some grenades, and a bit of food, began munching something that Maggie couldn't make out.

Nervously, he watched the opening to the tunnel.

Maggie felt the ground shake from time to time, evidence that fighting still continued above.

She measured time by the beating of her heart. No one spoke for many, many minutes. No one dared disturb the silence.

Orick and Tallea began whispering softly, Orick telling her of the saving ordinances of the gospel, and after a few moments, they headed farther back into the tunnel, back into the wider chamber, where the tunnel met the cliffs. Maggie imagined that they wanted to be alone.

Zeus held his light, letting it grow dimmer and dimmer, until it gave no light whatsoever.

Maggie busied herself by recalling songs she'd sung as a child, songs about green trees and young girls in love.

And death. Songs about death. Really, there seemed to be no theme to the songs that came to mind, just one senseless tune after another.

After a long time, her eyes grew gritty and tired. She closed them, and might have slept.

Thirty-eight

Orick whispered to Tallea, "Then one night a leader of the Pharisees, named Nicodemus, came to Jesus' room, and Jesus told him, 'Verily, verily, I say unto you, except a man be born of the water and of the spirit, he cannot enter into the Kingdom of God.' "

Tallea frowned. "Why not?"

Orick hesitated to discuss such dangerous things. If he spoke of her need for baptism before she was ready, he feared she would balk. So he wanted to lead her to the idea gradually, let her get used to it. But he had no idea how to proceed. "Well, it's a ritual . . . that shows our willingness to submit to God, keep His commandments. And in return, He forgives us our weaknesses and prepares us so we can live in His kingdom."

Tallea began to tremble slightly, as if afraid, and she raised her ears. "Are you baptized?"

"Och, of course," Orick said. "Everyone gets baptized—I mean, even Jesus got baptized."

"He did?" Tallea asked. "But you said he was sinless. Why would he need to be forgiven?"

"Och, I don't know!" Orick said, for he'd never considered the matter. On inspiration, he nosed into his pack, opened his Bible to the tale of Jesus' baptism. Orick put his paw on a glow globe, causing it to glow fiercely, so that he could read:

"Then cometh Jesus from Galilee to Jordan unto John, to be baptized of him,

"And John forbade him, saying, I have need to be baptized of thee, and comest thou to me?

"And Jesus answering said unto him, Suffer it to be so for now: for thus it becometh us to fulfill all righteousness."

Orick suddenly realized that John had asked Jesus the same question that Tallea was asking him now. "In here, Jesus had John baptize him, but notice he said, 'Suffer it to be so for now.' I think it means that in the future, Jesus planned to baptize John—or more accurately, he would redeem him from his sins, which is what baptism is all about."

"But what about the passage, 'for thus it becometh us to fulfill all right-eousness'?" Tallea said.

Orick considered the words 'fulfill all righteousness.' "Jesus was sinless, in both thought and deed," Orick said. "So even though he didn't need to be redeemed from his sins, he did need to keep his own commandment. He was setting an example, showing us that baptism is important." Orick began to recall that somewhere in the dim past, one of the monks at Obhiann Abbey had mentioned this concept.

"If baptism was necessary for Jesus, isn't it necessary for me?" Tallea asked.

Orick hedged, "Well, it's a symbol of willingness to keep God's com-mandments, and, uh—"

"But I need it, right?"

"Well . . . uh, officially—"

"Will you baptize me?" Tallea asked.

Orick hadn't considered. He wasn't a priest. He had no proper authority, didn't even know where to go to get it. He'd found Christian religions on some worlds. On Abbo, he went to the Orange Catholic Church for a service, but they had such a jumble of odd notions, all tied to the worship of some Saint Aesop-land, he couldn't make hide nor hair of it.

"What's wrong, don't you want to baptize me?" Tallea asked.

"Well, like I said, it's a sign of willingness to keep God's command-ments—"

"Which ones?" Tallea asked. "To love one another, even as we love our-selves? Or the Ten Commandments? I remember all ten. I don't lie or steal. I've killed a few folks, but I can give that up—"

"Well, uh—" Orick scrambled for an answer.

"Won't you baptize me?" Tallea asked. "Please? I'll do it—I'll do whatever you ask!"

Orick hadn't anticipated this. He'd sort of thought that he'd have to beg and wheedle and convince Tallea of her need for baptism. Then they'd maybe go back to Tihrglas and find a priest to do it proper. He'd imagined it would take weeks and months—maybe years—before Tallea would develop enough faith to concede to the need for baptism. He hadn't thought she'd convert in a matter of two days, then come demanding it from him like this. "It's not so easy. Only some folks have authority to baptize—priests and whatnot."

"But you wanted to be a priest!" Tallea said, hopefully. "Don't you have even a little bit of authority?"

"Well," he conceded, "the Tome teaches against it, but then the Tome teaches against a lot of things, and not everyone believes the Tome as much as I do.

"Back on Tihrglas, in some cases—like when infants are stillborn—an attendant will baptize, then have the act ratified by a priest, later. Some people teach that in an emergency, anyone can baptize—"

"Isn't this an emergency, Orick?" Tallea's eyes were so insistent, so full of hope. "There's a pond by the cliff. You could do it there."

Orick wondered. He felt that God had called him to this work, had made him Missionary to the Cosmos. And if God had called him, didn't that constitute some authority?

Certainly God wouldn't demand that he take every baptismal candidate back to Tihrglas for a dunking. He'd be so much afoot, he'd never get any work done. No, Tallea was right. She needed baptism, and he needed to do it. Like John the Baptist, crying repentance out in the wilderness.

The Great Tangle of Ruin would be Orick's wilderness, and the pond here in these lightless regions would be his River Jordan.

Why, if only I had some locusts and wild honey to eat, Orick thought, I'd be another John. Certainly, even John the Baptist had never envisioned anything like this.

"All right," Orick said, "for thus it becometh us, to fulfill all righteousness."

It seemed a very sacred and dignified moment, as Tallea carried her glow globe in her teeth, to the back of this tunnel, and set it beside the still waters, beneath a rock, so that the pressure would make the glow globe stay lit.

There, they watched the ripples on the pond's surface, the light reflecting off them, onto the stone cliff above. They listened to the perfect stillness around them, and Orick talked to Tallea about repentance, about her need to continue the struggle to become better with each day of her life. Indeed, he hardly felt she needed the talk. She'd already shown that she would give her life for others, had been adjudged worthy of a second life by the Lords of Tremonthin—a very special tribute to the life she'd lived.

Orick knew hundreds of baptized scoundrels back on Tihrglas who would never be her equal as a person. For her, the baptism seemed little more than a formality for her entrance into heaven, and Orick felt it a great honor to do this.

So when he finished speaking to her, he had her offer a brief but heartfelt prayer, then they both climbed into the water, swam about.

The pond was deep and cool—the clear water disappearing somewhere into the rocks far out of sight. For a moment, Orick feared that some huge creature might infest the pool. Little blind fishes swam in it, along with some of Ruin's water insects. The water was tinted by bluish green algae, a soft and vibrant color. It smelled of some strange, earthy minerals.

Orick had never considered how he might baptize someone. He'd seen priests do it—gripping the candidate's hands and having them lean backward into the water. But neither he nor Tallea had hands, and both of them floated higher in the water than did a human.

After floundering about for a minute, Orick decided there was nothing for it but to put his paws on Tallea's back and push her under, so he offered a brief prayer, "Having been commissioned of Jesus Christ, I baptize you in the name of the Father, and the Son, and the Holy Ghost. Amen."

Then he shoved her down with all his weight, until he felt certain she'd been submerged. He let her up, and she splashed about, gasping for air, spattering droplets of water all over him.

She kissed him, licking his wet muzzle, and Orick kissed her in return, so full of love and gratitude and hope, he could express it no other way.

Then, something strange and wonderful happened: Orick felt his lips begin to burn, as if they were on fire, and his heart pounded hard.

Tallea must have felt it too, for she got a panicked look in her eye, and she swam toward shore.

Then, everywhere, every cell in Orick's body felt as if it burst into flame at once. It was not an uncomfortable feeling. In fact, Orick felt oddly at peace.

Yet he was burning.

He wondered if the water had begun to heat and boil for some inexplicable reason, and he began dog-paddling. And the burning grew hotter, flaming.

The words of John the Baptist came to mind: "I indeed baptize you with water, but one comes after me, whose shoes latchet I am not worthy to unloose, and he shall baptize you with fire, and with the Holy Ghost."

Then Orick felt as if he were consumed in flame, and he heard Tallea cry out, as if in pain.

Never, never in all his years, had Orick had an experience like this. Never had he imagined it.

He felt his own spirit within him, like some dark force, twisting within his body, seeking escape. He opened his mouth, and cried, "Father, save me!"

He wondered if this was the judgment of God. He wondered if God would punish him for his temerity in baptizing Tallea without holding the priesthood. He felt—he felt as if he were under the judgment of God, and that any moment he might be burned to a crisp or ripped apart.

"Father, forgive me!" Orick groaned in fear.

He looked up above him.

In the darkness, at the top of the cave, a green light shone. A bird of emerald flames winged overhead in a swift pass. It had emerged from solid rock, and it disappeared into the ceiling. Then reappeared and wheeled, swooping lower.

And Orick recalled. The bird of light. The Holy Ghost descending upon Jesus in the form of a dove.

Orick realized that something divine and marvelous was happening. He'd never felt as he did now. He'd never heard of anyone back on Tihrglas having such an experience.

He was both terrified and grateful at the same time.

This is my judgment day, Orick realized. This is the end. Any moment, the spirit would either take him to greater heights, or it would destroy him completely.

There were those at Obhiann Abbey who claimed that one could not look God in the face and live. Yet others argued that it could only be done if one were transformed, made holy.

Orick gazed upward steadfastly, knowing that such a moment was at hand. "Forgive me, Father," he whispered. "Transform me. I seek no harm. I will do no evil, now and forever."

Then the spirit came, hovering over him on wings of green light, and Orick gazed steadfastly into its eyes for the space of half a heartbeat.

The fires within him raged, and he felt as if he would melt in the presence of this manifestation.

The bird of light whispered to Orick's mind, "So be it."

And as feverishly as the burning had begun a moment before, now the moment passed, and the bird of light dissipated, like a mist under the morning skies, and Orick felt a profound peace, like nothing he'd ever experienced in his life.

Tallea had paddled to the shore, and now she sat in the water, looking upward where the manifestation had been.

"Does this always happen?" she asked, panting hard, looking to the top of the cave where the bird had been.

Orick paddled beside her, marveling at the deep and abiding sense of peace he felt.

"Hardly ever," he answered, wondering.

God had forgiven him, he realized. God had allowed him to baptize Tallea, and had sent His messenger to let Orick know that the ordinance was accepted.

For a long time, neither he nor Tallea spoke. Instead, they rolled about in the pond for several long moments, kissing playfully, gazing into one another's dark eyes, then climbed back onto the ground and just sat, nuzzling. Orick licked the water from her face, and she did the same for him, until at last they sat, began talking low.

Tallea told Orick of her childhood, her dark past raised as a Caldurian warrior, trained in a crèche of stone with bars of steel by harsh swordsmen, enslaved by her love for her masters.

She spoke of sleeping in dark towers on nights when the wind whipped the ragged banners, snapping them in the blackness, and told of the cold rains that skittered against the stones of the guard towers where she stood watch, and said how she would gaze down on the village below and see the glow of firelight in some window, and wish desperately for a place inside, a place safe and warm, where people would accept a child who was not quite human as a beloved daughter, not just a tool to be wielded.

She felt that love now, that acceptance, and Orick did too, more profoundly than he had ever imagined possible.

Tallea talked of her hopes for the future, her love for Orick that felt so much deeper, so much easier to come by, than the compulsions that drove her to serve her masters, and she thanked him for freeing her.

So they rested, dripping and cold, speaking words of hope and comfort.

Yet something nagged at Orick's mind, something odd. He kept recalling the bird of light, and wondering. It had not looked much at all like a dove.

It had looked . . . he decided, like a Qualeewooh.

Thirty-nine

M aggie opened her eyes. She hadn't heard the ground shake for a while. She wondered how long it had been since Gallen left. She finally realized she could simply ask her mantle the time; silently she questioned the mantle's AI.

"It is 2:21 P.M.," her mantle answered.

When did Gallen leave? she asked.

"At 9:14 P.M.," the mantle said.

Five hours. He'd been gone more than five hours. He'd promised to be back in four, or he would never come back at all. Maggie's heart began racing. She shook slightly and began to sob.

She looked about. Off in the deep shadows, at the far end of the tunnel, Zeus appeared to have fallen asleep, head hunched over. His light had gone out. Orick and Tallea were nowhere in sight.

She got up, called "Zeus?" He didn't stir.

She stepped forward, held up her glow globe. What she'd thought was Zeus, leaning forward with head bent over his knees in the shadows, turned out to be only a crimped limb. Zeus had left.

"Zeus?" she called louder, toward the tunnel leading out.

An uneasy feeling assailed her. Zeus had gone, following Gallen. She should have known he would, by the way he'd watched longingly after Gallen.

Orick and Tallea were gone, too. She'd last seen them heading to the back of the tunnel. She followed their trail, found them beside the water, lying asleep, Tallea's glow globe wedged under a rock so that it maintained enough pressure to keep it lit.

"Orick, Tallea—Gallen isn't back yet. And Zeus has gone."

"What?" Orick asked, startling awake.

"Gallen isn't back, I said. He promised to be back in four hours. He's late."

"And Zeus went after him?" Tallea asked.

"I don't know. He crept out while we slept." Maggie didn't want to accuse him. She hoped he'd gone in search of Gallen. But she didn't trust the man. Despite his handsome features, his lordly air, she could not dismiss the way he'd tried to seduce her.

"He must have been worried," Orick whispered, as trusting as ever. The big bear lumbered over on all fours, looked up, and nuzzled Maggie's hand, trying to comfort her. "It will be all right. There's not a sfuz or a Dronon that can stop Gallen. Maybe he just got held up for a bit."

"Maybe," Maggie whispered, trying not to cry. Her voice broke, and she stifled a sob.

"Maybe we should go find him," Orick said. "Without his robe, I should be able to track him fine. Would that make you feel better?"

"Yes," Maggie said. "Please." She went back to her pack, fumbled about as she began putting away her food, getting out some weapons. Maggie was so nervous, she could hardly think. A cold chill seemed to dog her. Her thoughts came disjointed. Searching for Gallen would be dangerous. She'd always relied on him to protect her, Gallen with his knives and his swords and guns and mantle. The idea she might be able to help him seemed absurd.

But even if I can't help him, she thought, even if I go only to find his body, this is something I have to do.

She wished Zeus were here. Orick and Tallea had great hearts, and would fight beside her no matter what, but she'd been in one little firefight with the sfuz, and she knew how fast those things could move.

She wouldn't be able to pull her trigger fast enough in a concerted attack. Before, she'd had Gallen with his mantle and intelligent pistol and grenades, and she'd had Zeus backing her up when her clip emptied. This time, she'd have nothing to protect her.

All her defenders were being stripped away.

When everything was packed, Maggie took her glow globe and squeezed it tight so it would blaze as brightly as possible, then held it aloft in her left hand while gripping her pistol in her right.

Orick took the lead, and Tallea followed, both of them hurrying along. They went several hundred meters, found where Gallen, followed by Zeus, had departed from their old trail, then taken a new track up a steep incline.

It was tough climbing, along a narrow ledge of stone cliff, through a chasm where water had once tumbled down from above. Orick could barely squeeze through the opening. They'd seen this little cave before, but Gallen thought they could not get through. Obviously, on the trip in he'd taken the easier trails only out of concern for Maggie.

Now that need drove him, he'd taken a more precarious track.

As they hurried along, Maggie crawling on her hands and knees, she tried to still her breathing. After a long and treacherous climb up the narrow tube, it opened into a wider chamber, where the air seemed thick and close. Everywhere she could now smell the scent of smoke and burning detritus.

Something about this passage frightened her. Partly it was the strong smell of fire ahead. She detected more than the burning of humus—she could also smell cooked flesh. Up ahead, somewhere, there had been a battle, a fight with incendiary rifles unleashing their deadly plasma. Something had died.

But it was more than the knowledge of the carnage ahead that frightened her. No, the thing that frightened her was this: she had an overwhelming sense that this little passage, this sinkhole where water had once gouged a channel through the forest floor, led someplace she did not want to go.

It was the sense that as Gallen had kept searching for a passage into the Teeawah, hoping to enter the lair of the sfuz, he'd suddenly found a good tunnel, one that headed precisely where he wanted to go. And she did not want to follow.

The smell of smoke grew stronger, the charred flesh and burning hair.

The passage suddenly opened wide into a much larger chamber. At the mouth of this passage, Gallen's and Zeus's footprints lay deep in the dirt—a large beetle had fallen into one, and it struggled to climb out.

Maggie felt frigid, disjointed, as if a stranger were manipulating her own body like a marionette.

Gallen's path led through a narrow defile where the sloping timbers of an old tree gradually dropped lower and lower, again forcing them to crawl, until a side passage opened to a larger chamber.

Here the roiling smoke suddenly became overwhelming. Here the smell of bodies was strong. Orick and Tallea stopped at the mouth of this chamber, wary, but Maggie could not slow, could not stop—ahead, in the dim shadows, she saw lumps on the ground. Her light glinted off the carapaces of dead Dronon Vanquishers—dozens of them, sprawled on the floor.

Maggie's heart pounded. So Gallen had met the Dronon at last, down here in the tangle.

The bears held back, but Maggie had to enter, had to know how Gallen had fared.

Maggie held her light aloft. She could not see the roof of this chamber, it was so high, but ahead—encircled by dozens of dead Vanquishers, she could see a human figure lying facedown in the dirt. Even as she held the light up, the man raised up feebly, head lolling, and she saw a pale face, bruised and bloody, the golden hair.

"Gallen!" Orick shouted, and the bear bounded forward, leapt over the corpses of Vanquishers.

Gallen looked up, his long golden hair falling down around his face. With a start, Maggie saw that his mantle was missing. His eyes were black, his nose and chin covered with dried blood. He struggled to raise his head, to push himself off the ground. His mouth was swollen, teeth knocked out.

Unsteadily, he gasped, "Or—Or— Go back!"

Gallen collapsed, and Maggie rushed to him, choking back her horror. Tears streamed from her eyes. As she neared, she looked down at his right leg. It was mangled, covered in blood, and a stout chain held it pegged to the ground.

Suddenly light blared around her, and Maggie raised her pistol, tried to aim, but the lights blinded her. On the far side of the cavern, a Dronon voice clicked, a translator buzzed.

"Welcome, Maggie Flynn, O great and honored Golden Queen. We bring you greetings and a challenge from Cintkin and Kintiniklintit, Lords of the Seventh Swarm."

High up, all around, wings buzzed, and with the movement Maggie saw Dronon Vanquishers by the score, clinging to the ceiling, ready to drop. But where was Zeus?

Then she knew. Then she knew death had come. With her husband and protector broken at her feet, the Lords of Seventh Swarm threatening. She raised her gun, tempted to shoot the Dronon, but there were so many, so many, and she knew if she opened fire on them, she wouldn't just be committing suicide, she'd be killing her friends, Orick and Tallea.

Silently, she screamed, No!

Forty

*T*homas Flynn stalked behind Lord Felph, following a trail of corpses through the tangle. Between the boles of vast trees, smoke hung in the air in iridescent wisps, reflecting the light of Thomas's glow globe.

The air was remarkably cool despite the smoke. The fighting had died down two hours ago, yet Felph and Thomas often passed roving patrols of Vanquishers who still hunted for Maggie and Gallen.

Though Felph hurried, his journey through Teeawah took longer than anticipated. He'd pinpointed the course he wanted to follow, using a map provided by the Dronon, but following the precise route proved impossible. The Vanquishers simply flew when they wanted to travel up or down, so Felph ended up traveling twice the distance as the Vanquishers to reach the ancient city.

On the trail in, they passed the corpses of fantastic monsters—the purple-black sfuz with their thin legs, the long pale corpse of a mistwife, some previously undiscovered creature Thomas called a *troll*—for it had greenish skin and hair that looked like roots, all with a nose at least two feet long. Dronon dead littered the path in places, primarily asphyxiated by the flames thrown by their own incendiary rifles. Felph robbed their corpses of pulp guns, gave a spare to Thomas.

Only once did they spot a sfuz—a frantic creature so busy dragging a Vanquisher's corpse it did not notice Felph till he shot it. Thomas felt surprised at how the sfuz had not seen them, for they had not hidden their light. Perhaps in this battle, with its massive carnage on both sides, the mind of this poor wretched beast had snapped.

In its death throes, the sfuz protectively wrapped four legs around its head. Thomas gazed deep into its indigo eyes. Fires had burned here. Three spots in the turf still smoldered from incendiary fires, trailing thin white plumes of smoke.

Felph halted, watching the sfuz, his leg propped up on the thorax of a dead Vanquisher. He sniffed.

"How long have you been working for Karthenor?" Felph asked.

Thomas could not answer. Karthenor had ordered Thomas to be silent earlier in the morning. Thomas's Guide would not recognize Felph's request.

"Are you a slave, fresh captured?" Felph asked.

Thomas nodded.

Felph considered. "Do you think a man should work for what he gets, or just take it? Receive reward without sweat?"

Thomas shook his head no.

Felph watched Thomas thoughtfully. "Me neither." Thomas wondered if Felph planned to free him. Perhaps so, but if he did, he wasn't saying. Rather forcefully he said, "I don't think it should happen. In fact, I don't believe it ever does. Remember, Thomas, everything has its price. Everything. Even you. Karthenor believes he has captured a prize. But you will cost him. It is a law of nature, and nature will not be violated."

Aye, everything has a cost, Thomas silently agreed, but my ignorance cost me more than it's worth. Give me a hand, man. If you removed this Guide, I'd write a song to immortalize the deed!

Felph studied Thomas's eyes. Go on, man, save me! You can read everything I want to say from my eyes.

"Indeed," Felph said, "everything has a price. Even compassion. I would free you if I could. I have the tools in my palace. But I cannot do so now. Perhaps I will never be in a position to do so. But remember, my friend, you are free if you so desire to be. Karthenor may force you to do his will—his Guide might control your actions even past the moment when your brain ceases to function—but so long as you do not let his will supplant yours, you are always free."

Lord Felph stroked his thin beard, a gesture that somehow made him look much older, then he turned away and headed down the trail, as if he'd decided to let Thomas be.

Thomas despaired. Freedom of thought was not much at all. Freedom of thought was an itch, begging to be scratched. And Thomas wondered if the moment would come when Karthenor's will would supplant his own.

We two are too much alike, Thomas realized. With very little difficulty, he and I could be the same man.

Felph led the way deeper into the tangle. Their path led past several dozen dead sfuz, up a steep incline where rainwater washed down, making a thin stream that ran with green and purple blood.

The time of day or night did not matter, though Thomas felt weary. The interminable darkness told his body to rest despite the fact Thomas had been awake for only ten hours that day.

All around, the hoary shadows of the tangle assaulted him, the tatters of roots hanging from above, the musky mineral scent of mold and rot, the constant dripping. The scenery seemed appropriate for a nightmare, and every two hundred meters they chanced on some new horror, some new site of a slaughter, until at long last they trudged up a path and came to the golden cliffs of Teeawah.

There holes opened in the rock like giant eyes. Smoke curled out from them, and from the openings hung the bodies of sfuz, chopped in half by gunfire.

Lord Felph jogged up to the holes, raising his glow globe over his head, peering into the dark recesses of the lair. At one point, he held up the light, then pointed his gun into the shadows and fired—an almost nonchalant gesture. From inside the cave, a shrill whistle erupted, the death cry of a sfuz.

"Here is a passage!" Felph shouted. "Back behind these bodies." He jumped up into the oval opening, climbed in. For one second Thomas saw the opening lit from inside. Felph seemed to be the pupil of a great burning eye, then the image faded as Felph hurried inside.

Thomas came up, surveyed the inside of the fortress. The bodies of a dozen sfuz sprawled on the floor, wrapped in their own arms and legs. These did not ooze blood. They'd been asphyxiated.

The hollow chamber here was shaped something like an egg. Thomas had imagined there would be furnishings inside, as if it were a home back on Tihrglas with a butter churn in one corner and a sofa near the fireplace.

What he saw repulsed him. The floors lay bare of furnishings, but in every corner bones and dung lay in fetid heaps. All along the wall were odd trophies—dozens of flesh-covered heads from some large creatures, like ogres, each with a huge horn on its forehead; a collection of animal tails were tacked in another line; an assortment of dried turds and testicles were pinned into the stone with wooden thorns. It wasn't until Thomas whiffed the ungodly odor from these items that he realized they weren't to look at—these items were here to smell.

Maybe the sfuz relished these bouquets as humans would the scent of flowers. Or more likely, this room seemed to form a library of scents, where young hunters could learn to track prey.

"Here's what we're looking for," Felph said, holding his light to a large passage that opened near the wall. "A common area. The Qualeewoohs connect these from various points. They twist a lot, and can be tricky."

With that, he held his glow globe aloft, began searching along a wide passage with a low ceiling that led deep into the city. Everywhere, side passages led to small rooms. Felph ignored these as he clambered over asphyxiated sfuz.

"Let me tell you something," Felph huffed. "We have perhaps two hours before these dead sfuz begin to reanimate. By then, we'd best be well away." It was such an odd thing to say, and the young lord said it with such sincerity, the notion took Thomas's breath. Did he really believe these dead would rise again?

In the past weeks, Thomas had seen so many wonders, he couldn't question this. If you told me they'd all transform into hummingbirds, Thomas thought, it wouldn't faze me.

They found another large passage that merged with the one they were in, like streams meeting to form a river, becoming one enormous tunnel, heading downward.

Here, in the depths of the city, the numbers of dead diminished. It was as if all the sfuz had gone to do battle. Yet ahead, Thomas heard an odd whistling, and Felph immediately fell into a crouch, waving his weapon.

"Well," Felph whispered. "It seems we have company. The sfuz must be guarding their Waters. Get your weapon ready to fire."

Thomas did as ordered, though he'd never fired a pulp pistol. It was similar enough to Gallen's incendiary rifle, he thought he knew how to handle it.

He held it stiffly, at arm's length, afraid of its explosive power. Felph frowned at his stance.

They descended down the wide corridor to meet the sfuz.

|O| rick smelled the dead Dronon before he saw them, but he smelled Gallen, too, and bounded forward, calling Gallen's name.

Gallen raised up, like a heap of bloody rags coming to life, and Orick froze in horror.

"Or—Or— Go back!" Gallen choked.

From the far end of the chamber, as lights suddenly blazed, a Vanquisher stepped forward, a shadow among shadows, and knelt low, crossing its battle arms before it, pointing its head to the floor. Its mouthfingers pounded over its voicedrum and a translator said, "Welcome, Maggie Flynn, O great and honored Golden Queen. We bring you greetings and a challenge from Cintkin and Kintiniklintit, Lords of the Seventh Swarm."

"No!" Maggie screamed.

"This land is ours," the Vanquisher continued his ritual greeting. "All land is ours! A great Golden Queen comes among you. She is worthy! Prepare for battle!"

Behind Orick, Maggie screamed again, "No! No!" The sound of it nearly broke his heart. A dozen times in the last months he'd heard her wake in the night, screaming those words.

Now it comes, he realized, the sum of all her nightmares.

Above him, dozens of Dronon flapped their wings. By instinct Orick reared on his hind legs, prepared to battle. He sniffed the air, and immediately dropped to all fours. He was a bear, alone against Dronon with heavy weapons. He couldn't fight. To Tallea's credit, she too had reared on her hind legs, and now stood, roaring her rage, so the sound reverberated through the chamber. The nearest Dronon shrank back reflexively.

Give 'em hell, Orick thought. He ran to Gallen, found Gallen nearly unconscious.

"Gallen, Gallen?" Orick grumbled, and he licked Gallen's face, trying to shock his friend awake. He tasted blood and dirt.

Gallen struggled to look up. He seemed unaware of what was going on. He choked out the words, "Get out of here. The Dronon were here. Don't let them get Maggie!"

Orick tried to survey all the damage at once. Gallen's face was a swollen mass. Blood stained the robes of his arms and legs. His mantle was gone, lying in the dirt a dozen paces out of his reach. His right leg twisted at an unnatural angle, broken in more than one place, chained to a stake in the ground.

"Are you all right?" Orick asked in shock, knowing Gallen was an inch from death, not knowing what else to say.

Gallen just dropped his head and began to sob, his shoulders shuddering under the impact. "Found . . . city. Ahead. Beat me. They beat me . . . so bad."

Orick looked at the dead Dronon lying about—hacked with a vibro-blade, carapaces smashed from kicks. Gallen must have put up a terrible fight, an unholy fight. At least two dozen of the creatures lay dead. He'd never imagined anything like it.

Orick suddenly became aware that Maggie had rushed up beside him and had fallen to her knees. He'd been so focused on Gallen, hadn't registered her presence still standing behind him. She just knelt, hovering above Gallen, her hands out, wanting to touch him, afraid to touch him, lest she hurt him further.

"Gallen, lad, what can I do for you? What can I do?" I'll fight in his place, Orick thought. That's what I'll do. He can't fight, so I'll take his place.

Gallen shook his head. Nothing. You can do nothing, he was saying.

"I know, I know," Orick said. "I'll cut myself, let the nanodocs in my blood heal you, the way we did for Everynne that time."

Gallen's head wobbled back and forth, and Orick reached with one claw, pricked his right paw, then began smearing blood over Gallen's head on the top. He felt as if he were a bishop, anointing a priest with holy oil. He dared not smear the blood elsewhere, for Gallen's body was so battered and torn, he didn't want to hurt his friend. By hurting I heal him, Orick thought, and he dabbed the blood over a deep gash on Gallen's temple.

Maggie put a restraining hand on Orick's paw. Though she'd been sobbing uncontrollably, her voice when she spoke sounded calm. "Don't, Orick. You're only hurting him. Don't hurt him more. There's no time. Even with nanodocs, it will take weeks for him to heal."

Orick looked up at her. She's reconciled to her own death, he realized. "But, but—I'll fight for you, Maggie. I'll be your Lord Protector!"

Maggie held a glow globe lightly in her left hand. Its piercing light shone full on her face. She was pale as death, the freckles she'd had as a child standing out unnaturally clear. Maggie took several breaths. Gallen fainted, and she put one hand on his shoulder, then looked at Orick, as if he were far away.

"Orick, my friend, my dearest friend. There's nothing you can do for me now. If you fight in Gallen's stead, you'll die. You can't beat the Dronon. I won't have the weight of that on my conscience. Gallen wouldn't want it either."

Orick stared. She was right, yet he could not accept defeat. "No!" Orick cried.

"I'll . . . I'll . . . Will you listen to me," Maggie said. "Will you obey me, as if I were your Golden Queen?"

Orick's jaw trembled. "What? What do you want?"

"Gallen and I, we've had good lives. You know that we were both infected by the Inhuman. We remember life. We cherish it. We've both lived—far longer than any person should rightfully live. It's time for it to end. You have to let us go."

"No!" Orick roared.

"But I think I speak for us both," Maggie added, "when I tell you that of all our lives, this one we've spent with you is the one we treasured most. You've been a great and good friend."

"No!" Orick shouted.

"Leave us, now," Maggie begged.

Tallea came up behind Orick, nuzzled his ear, and whispered. "The Waters of Strength. We could still save him."

Orick looked up to the Dronon who had addressed Maggie, and shouted, "Where will the battle for succession take place?"

"At the great palace, the seat of government for this world," the Dronon answered.

Orick turned to Maggie. He promised, "I'll get the Waters. I'll be back. I'll bring it for you."

Maggie nodded, biting her lower lip, unbelieving.

Orick and Tallea made their way to pass the Dronon messenger who stood before them, to pass through the chamber.

"Halt!" the Vanquisher ordered.

Maggie stood, letting her arms hang loose at her side, a pose of dignity under the circumstances. "You will let them pass. I'm still Golden Queen on this world, and you'll not interfere with my servants on their errand."

The Dronon stood warily, then raised itself up to its full height in a defensive posture, its battle arms poised to strike, and stepped away. Orick scampered past the Vanquisher, then into the darkness beyond, where several more Dronon lined the wall.

Tallea held her glow globe in her teeth. In moments they were running together, shadows bobbing in the darkness.

Gallen's path ahead was easy to follow—trampled by Dronon tracks. The Dronon had apparently found his trail, taken Gallen from behind in an open chamber. Even a Lord Protector cannot withstand six dozen Dronon when he's outgunned.

Orick came to a broad bog, silent and cold, and had to swim across. After that, Gallen's tracks became confusing. He'd spent hours exploring various passages, backtracking, climbing up and down tree trunks, looking for the road.

Zeus's tracks followed Gallen's. In one place, Gallen had followed a false trail, and Zeus had gone after. Orick imagined that it was under such circumstances that Gallen had returned from his trip, passing Zeus, who had gone chasing a false trail. Indeed, Orick found the precise spot where the Dronon had met Gallen's trail, bypassing Zeus. And Orick followed the false trail a few dozen meters, found Zeus's tracks in the dirt, plastered around a little side chamber.

Zeus must have hidden here, watching the adjoining tunnel. He must have heard the Dronon coming. In fact, Zeus may even have spotted Gallen from this hiding place.

So Zeus was headed to the city, Orick reasoned, not searching for Gallen at all. Zeus had gone questing for the Waters of Strength to suit his own ends.

This information filled Orick with a terrible sadness.

Orick had little choice but to follow Gallen's trail—a long and winding way through the tangle. For three hours he picked his way—twice losing Gallen's trail in boggy ground, once taking a false track.

Gallen had returned to one great chamber on three occasions—taking several trails that all connected, and Orick had to follow each trail to its conclusion, for the scent and footprints in this chamber were so jumbled as to be impossible to read.

At last, he and Tallea found a broad tunnel with timbers shoring the walls in places. At its juncture he found several dead sfuz.

Four times over the next few hundred meters, Orick found dead sfuz and Dronon. Gallen's trek had been neither easy nor uneventful. The hacked bodies, bleeding gore both green and purple, bore evidence of Gallen's proficiency in swordsmanship. If Gallen had won his way back to camp, this journey would have been the stuff of legend on Tihrglas.

Orick was acutely aware of the fact that he and Tallea were mere bears, without the weapons Gallen had mastered. If they met any sfuz or Dronon, they'd not be able to win their way so easily.

Fortunately for Orick the road was quiet. No sfuz whistled through the tunnels.

Yet as Orick proceeded, to his terror he heard marching feet, the clacking of carapaces against the ground.

Ahead, the tunnel curved. The great timbers shoring it up looked for all the world like the ribs of some great fish. Bright lights shone. A Dronon war party was marching his way.

He looked to Tallea for suggestions. If a Dronon saw two bears down here, what would they do?

They'd fire, never knowing what they'd killed.

"Run!" Orick shouted, and he turned. Together he and Tallea raced back down the tunnel, away from Teeawah.

Forty-two

Maggie followed the Dronon in a daze, stumbling through the tangle. It was not a long journey—the Dronon guided her to the nearest shuttle, only a thousand meters from where she'd found Gallen, but it was a difficult journey.

Gallen couldn't walk, even with Maggie's help, so a single Dronon Vanquisher lifted Gallen in its battle claws and carried him, while Maggie walked beside, cradling Gallen's broken leg. He seemed so light and frail. At times a misstep jostled him, and Gallen would cry out like a child.

Maggie found no weapons beside Gallen, none but his mantle. She wore it now, knowing in all likelihood that it would avail her nothing in the battle to come. She had no hope of beating a Dronon, but Maggie would not give up.

Could not give up.

As Gallen had protected her so many times, she'd struggle to protect him now. She wondered how the Dronon would react to a Golden Queen who fought, instead of relying on her Lord Escort.

All through the journey, she marveled at the Dronon. She saw dozens of their dead, sprawled along the road. One Vanquisher lay headless from a sfuz's snare, another with a burning hole under his abdomen where, Maggie assumed, he took a hit from friendly fire.

Such a waste of life in this magnificent display of force. The Dronon could kill Maggie anytime, could have done so months ago when she and Gallen first defeated the Lords of the Sixth Swarm, but they had to carry on their farce, had to hold to their ancient formulae for succession.

So they marched till they reached a wedge-shaped cruiser deep in the tangle. Inside, the Dronon escorted Maggie to a holding bay, a veritable prison with white ceramic walls. The room had no windows; one dim light glowed red as the sun on Dronon.

The Vanquisher unceremoniously dropped Gallen to the floor. Gallen landed on his side with a yelp, then curled into a ball.

Maggie knelt over him, took her canteen, and wetted the tips of her long hair, then began cleaning his face. It was a mass of bruises, his nose broken and skewed to the side. In the darkness she'd thought all his teeth missing, but saw that only two of his top teeth were knocked out. The others were darkened by blood.

Gallen winced from her ministrations, opened his eyes, stared at her, pain showing in every line of his face, in the swollen bruises. Maggie bent and tenderly kissed him. "It will all be over soon enough. Don't worry."

Gallen shook his head. "No," he gasped. "It doesn't end. It just goes on without us."

"Close your eyes," she begged. "Rest now."

"I'll rest when I have to," Gallen said. "Let me look at you."

Maggie smiled at him, tears filling her eyes.

"So pretty," Gallen whispered. "So pretty. The best in all County Morgan, or anywhere else I've been, for that matter."

She kissed him precisely in the center of the forehead. "I needed to be. You wouldn't settle for less."

Maggie wondered as she kissed him. The people of Tremonthin bred him to be a Lord Protector, and Ceravanne had said his seed was spread across the galaxy on backward worlds. Maggie wondered if somewhere in a place she'd never imagined, a woman held another Gallen, a man with the same face, and kissed him with such passion as she did now. She hoped so. She hoped he'd live on in some form. She didn't want Felph to resurrect him. Gallen wouldn't want to live without her. But he deserved to be treasured.

The floor of the shuttle began to quiver as it lifted gently from the tangle. Maggie got the vague floating sensation one does at liftoff.

She held Gallen's hand. "How can I make you comfortable?"

"Escape," Gallen said.

Maggie laughed softly, not really amused, simply wanting to humor him. "All right, I will, if you'll come with me."

Gallen whimpered, and closed his eyes.

"I love you," Maggie said as he rested. "I want you to know, that lately, when I dream, sometimes I dream of the other lives that the Inhuman showed us. I dream we're Roamers out on the veldt, squatting in the limbs of some sprawling oak tree, and I remember old mates. But in my dream, every husband I've ever had, when I dream of him, it's you I think of." Maggie knew she sounded crazy, but she wanted Gallen to know, that of all the loves she remembered, of all the mates whose presence she still craved, she loved Gallen most.

Gallen grinned, a relaxed upturning of the lips. Maggie held his hands for the twenty minutes it took to reach Felph's palace. He fell asleep, and though Maggie yearned to wake him, she didn't have the heart to. She merely hunched over him, her face pressed so close she could taste his breath, and she tried to memorize his face, every detail of his face. Some priests back on Tihrglas, those who recognized the Tome as canonical, said men and women could marry for eternity, so in the next life they'd still be one. Maggie wished it were true. If God had any sense of justice, she told herself, if He had the slightest notion of right and wrong, He'd make it so. He'd let them be together in the next life.

As she told herself this, it helped soothe the sting of watching Gallen sleep the last few moments of his life away.

When he was fast asleep, she took off the black robe she wore, the robe of a Lord Protector, and wrapped it around Gallen's broken leg. Then she ripped strips from her dress, bound the thing. Perhaps it would do some good. Perhaps the robe would protect him one last time, saving him some little jarring pain when they reached the killing fields.

Gallen slept as she bandaged him, and he still slumbered when the cruiser reached Felph's palace and landed in the great court before the gates.

The Vanquishers came for them; one lifted Gallen in its great claws. Maggie took Gallen's hand, held it as the Dronon carried him from his cell to the top of the gangplank.

Maggie wasn't prepared for the sight before her: it was just dawn, light beginning to break over the far mountains.

In the fields before the gates of Felph's magnificent palace of pink sandstone, the Dronon warships circled. Black, squat, adorned with armaments, bristling with weapons. Clinging to every surface of every vehicle, and scattered on every inch of ground, were Dronon Vanquishers and technicians, a vast sea of black-and-tan carapaces. In many places, Vanquishers climbed atop one another's backs, creating black walls, forming a great arena made of chitin.

Yet behind them were the glorious towers of Felph's palace, the thundering waterfalls all backlit by thousands of footlights.

The Dronon had set pavilions at seven corners of the arena, pavilions of red, each covered with the evil-looking designs of various Dronon Swarms. Beneath these languished the Golden Queens, with countless dwarfish workers attending, white as grubs.

Around the great circle, millions of Dronon chanted, mouthfingers clacking over their voicedrums, while Vanquishers shook incendiary rifles in the air. Maggie did not know what they shouted. She was past caring.

Mustering her dignity, Maggie walked down the gangplank beside the Vanquisher who bore her husband's limp body. Gallen roused enough to crane his neck, surveying the battlefield. When they reached the edge of the open field, the Vanquisher gently set Gallen in the grass.

Maggie looked across the field for humans, anyone at all. Lord Felph was not here, but on the left side of the field, Hera and Athena broke into a run, rushing toward her, tears in their eyes, faces pale.

Athena rushed up and grabbed at Maggie's left wrist, pawing her, shouting, "What's happening? What are you doing?"

"Everything will be fine. Go on, now. It's not you the Dronon are after. You'll be all right," Maggie found herself trying to calm Athena. She wished the girl would calm herself, not force Maggie to be strong.

Maggie kept pushing at Athena, trying to get her to leave.

Hera saw the determination in Maggie's eyes, pulled Athena back, retreated to shadows thrown by the ship behind Maggie.

At the far side of the field, a Golden Queen began to heave herself onto the battleground, her pale attendants struggling beside her, pushing her bloated body forward. For one moment, Maggie saw the Dronon queen not as an emissary of her death, but as a huge balloon being pushed and shoved on the shoulders of children, and the image seemed somehow comic and somehow painful.

Beside the Golden Queen strode her Lord Escort, the black chitin of his exoskeleton gleaming in the afternoon light. Lord Kintiniklintit was, frankly, the largest Vanquisher Maggie had ever seen. Good, she thought. At least I'll be killed by the best.

Beside him, in a dark brown robe, walked a husky man in a golden mask. Lord Karthenor.

Maggie's right leg shook as she walked. She halted, willed it to stop trembling, tried to show no fear.

Let them come to us, she thought. So she stood and leaned her head back, closed her eyes, trying to excise these images from her mind.

A cool dawn breeze blew; through partly opened eyes she saw clouds on the horizon.

Clouds! Here in the desert where Felph told her it had not rained in ages. Maggie wanted to taste the fresh air, to feel warm rain on her cheeks, to bask in sunlight.

She closed her eyes fully, shutting out the images, inhaled deeply. She knelt and took Gallen's hand in her right hand, squeezed tight. "Gallen," she whispered, "if you try, you can smell Felph's rose gardens from here." The aroma came, distant and sweet.

In moments, Lord Karthenor and his Dronon master stood before her, their shadows falling over her.

"Closing your eyes will not make us go away," Karthenor said.

Maggie opened her eyes. He was fatter than she remembered. The golden mask he wore, shining with its own wan light, made his face gleam like some round moon. She wished she had a gun. "The avaricious we have with us always. Just because I wish you dead, does not mean I think you will vanish."

"I'm happy to see you again, too," Karthenor laughed. "Who would have thought that when I captured a silly girl six months ago, it would lead here, to the green fields where you will die?"

Maggie didn't want to speak to Karthenor. He wasn't worth it. She found herself shaking with rage. She knew Gallen had a translator in his pack that would let her speak to the Dronon, but she did not want to look foolish, digging it out now.

"Talk to your bugs," she said, nodding toward the Lords of the Seventh Swarm, just behind Karthenor.

"Gladly," Karthenor said, and he fumbled to switch on the translator pinned to his robe.

"Tell them," Maggie said, recalling the words to the ancient Dronon ritual, and she shouted, "You are my food, nothing more! This land is mine. All land is mine! A Great Queen comes among you. Prostrate yourselves in adoration. Prepare to do battle!"

She yelled the words so Karthenor would not say them. The translator on his lapel shouted the words in Dronon, so their clicking tones carried over the field.

To her astonishment, Lord Kintiniklintit halted and bowed to her, crossing his battle arms before him in proper obeisance.

It was an unnecessary gesture, a gallant gesture. She didn't deserve it. By Dronon custom, Maggie had dishonored her entire swarm. No Golden Queen ever refused a challenge. None dared run from battle. The Dronon were uncertain how to handle such behavior, thinking it madness. And on Dronon, the mad were destroyed without remorse.

Maggie smiled at this Lord Escort, the greatest of all Vanquishers. Ah, I like this one, Maggie found herself thinking.

She stepped forward, shouting the ritual, "I am Maggie O'Day, Golden Queen of the Sixth Swarm. For five months I've ruled my swarm. Our children shall eat your corpses! Our Vanquishers shall claim your domain. Your royal children shall fertilize our fields! Your hive shall submit to us!"

Maggie shook with rage. In her nightmares, in her dreams about this confrontation, she'd never imagined being angry. But they were going to kill her, damn them!

"Your Golden Queen will submit to inspection!" she shouted.

Cintkin, Queen of the Seventh Swarm, crossed her front arms in obeisance and bowed. Maggie made a great show of walking to her so the white workers, like fat lice huddling in her shadow, scurried away.

Maggie searched the queen's carapace, looking for scars or wounds, anything to give her an excuse to back out of this fight.

Though she played the bold one, her eyes kept straying to the Dronon surrounding the fields, searching for Orick—or, or anyone who might save her. Maggie looked behind her to Gallen, and involuntarily she gasped. Gallen had recognized their predicament and pushed himself to a crouching posture. He tried to stand on his good leg, precariously balancing.

Maggie turned and ran back to him, held him so he wouldn't topple. The wind blew through his long blond hair, and Gallen balanced himself by leaning against her. It took all his strength. He grunted in pain, and his lower lip trembled.

Maggie's heart pounded, her mouth felt dry. She looked at Gallen, at his lips purpled and bruised, and wanted to kiss him one last time, but dared not. Somehow it would be demeaning to share that one last intimacy with the Dronon.

"Are you ready?" she asked Gallen.

"Yesh," he said through swollen lips.

Maggie nodded, mind numb, and called to the Dronon. "I find your Golden Queen worthy. Let the battle begin!"

She paused as Karthenor's translators relayed her message. She expected Lord Kintiniklintit to attack immediately.

But Karthenor's eyes gleamed, and he shouted, "Wait! Lord Kintiniklintit must first inspect Maggie O'Day, to find if *she* is worthy." Karthenor did not even try to hide the gloating tone of his voice. He stared at Maggie. Her heart pounded.

Don't make me do this, she whined within herself. Don't do this to me.

But Lord Kintiniklintit parroted Karthenor's sentiment. "I demand right of inspection on this Golden Queen." She did not blame the Lord Escort. He had no way to know what he asked. He didn't understand human modesty, didn't know the humiliation his "inspection" would cause.

The Lord Vanquisher stepped forward to remove her clothes, to inspect Maggie's flesh for signs of scars, for any impurity that would make her unworthy to participate in combat. It was the one last rite, the way for her to prove she was truly the Golden Queen of her hive and had not lost her title.

But as the Lord Kintiniklintit approached, Karthenor stepped forward and smirked. "I'll help you disrobe her, My Lord."

Lord Kintiniklintit really had no gentle means of disrobing Maggie. She'd have been forced to do it herself, but as Karthenor stepped forward and grabbed her tunic, ripping it off so he exposed her breasts, Gallen came alive at Maggie's side.

With blinding speed Gallen slammed a fist into Karthenor's throat. Gallen's black battle gloves, with hardened selenium chips at the knuckle of each finger, made the blow deadly.

The Lord of Aberlains staggered back, eyes flying open wide, gasping, and clutched his throat. The blow had landed squarely on his esophagus; the instant swelling of his trachea began the slow work of strangling Karthenor.

He dropped to one knee, gagging and retching, lips turning blue as his life ebbed, then recognized his dilemma.

He fumbled inside his robe, tried to pull a pistol.

Lord Kintiniklintit saw the move, slapped the human with the back of one great battle arm, dashing him backward on the ground some five meters off.

There, Karthenor lay choking until his miserable life ended.

Rage seemed to rouse Gallen. He pulled off his own pack, pulled out his translator, put it on his own lapel, then glared up at Lord Kintiniklintit.

"You object to the examination?" Lord Kintiniklintit asked Gallen. "This is your right, but in doing so, you relinquish your swarm."

Maggie drew a breath in surprise. She wanted nothing more than to relinquish her right to control of the Sixth Swarm. She'd sought to escape her role as its leader ever since she'd won the position. But if she relinquished leadership, Kintiniklintit could simply kill her without a fight. That's what Dronon did to human leaders who succumbed. They threw them away.

But perhaps Kintiniklintit was different. Perhaps he would merely mark her, give her back her life. He seemed a noble sort.

And yet, and yet, even if he offered that boon, Maggie could not accept it. To do so would be to betray mankind.

She could not admit defeat. She needed to let the Dronon know, to make them understand, that mankind would never suffer their domination.

Gallen said it for her. "No, you have the right of inspection, but I won't let men like Karthenor touch Maggie. He was not worthy to touch the Golden. It was not his place."

"Agreed," Lord Kintiniklintit clicked.

The great Vanquisher stepped forward, and Gallen unfastened the back of Maggie's dress, pulled it away for the Dronon to see. Maggie wished she had some scar, some recent cut. A blemish, even the smallest one, might save her life. But her skin was flawless.

Gallen worked his way around, struggling to keep his balance on one leg, revealing her bit by bit to the Lord Escort, until Lord Kintiniklintit had verified her worthiness.

"I find this Golden Queen to be without blemish," Lord Kintiniklintit said at last. "I find her worthy."

It was done. There was nothing to do now but fight. Maggie still wore Gallen's mantle, wondered if she should give it back, if he could put up any fight; he made no move to take it.

Lord Kintiniklintit backed away. He held his arms in the air, in sign of the temporary truce that would end only seconds from now, when the battle began.

Gallen didn't move, stood leaning against Maggie, looking into her face, holding her right hand with his left. In his right hand he held up a scrap of her torn dress. She felt the warmth of his breath on her neck. He bowed his head; some of the long hairs of his head tickled her shoulders.

She looked into his blue eyes; he stared through a mask of bruises; she imagined from his eyes he would not fight, and she'd not fight. Instead, they'd die like this, holding each other.

Thirty paces across the field, Lord Kintiniklintit dropped his battle arms and buzzed his wings, taking to the air for the attack. A tide of voices rose with him, a million Dronon clacking their praise in unison.

At just that moment, the sun cracked over the horizon, shining over the field. It lit Kintiniklintit so that he seemed to have risen, gleaming blackness made alive from the shadows, and it lit Gallen's upturned face, white like a flower petal. Clouds were racing in from the North, but for a few moments, the sun would yet shine.

The Lord of the Seventh Swarm circled the huge field once, his wings rumbling. The swell of Dronon voices thrilled Maggie somehow, despite the fact that they came from her enemies. Maggie looked across the field, saw the morning sunlight shining on the Golden Queen and her little white attendants.

Kintiniklintit circled the entire field, and as he passed over each Vanquisher, they each raised their incendiary rifles in the air and shook them, so that it almost appeared as if each arm magically kept the great Vanquisher aloft.

As he circled once, he built up speed, then came round half a circle again until he lined up with the rising sun, then veered toward them.

Maggie had been watching Kintiniklintit's progress from the corner of her eye; now she turned to Gallen. She wanted Gallen's face to be the last thing she saw.

"My love," he whispered.

Forty-three

*T*homas gripped his pulp pistol with both hands. Dozens of sfuz scampered along the ceiling, whistling a strange, frenetic call, issuing from a wide passage that led lower into the city. Their purple-black eyes gleamed in the light of Felph's glow globe.

Felph dropped into a crouch and fired rapidly. Black gobbets of gore blasted from the sfuz. Felph screamed in fury, as if possessed, "Back me, back me!"

Thomas stood at Felph's back, firing over his head. Something heavy hit Thomas, knocking him forward, and a searing pain in Thomas's ribs told him he'd been stabbed.

He fell into Felph, knocking the lord headlong, but Thomas had the presence of mind to spin as he fell, firing twice.

A sfuz stood over Thomas.

The creature's lower jaw disintegrated under the force of the gunfire.

Thomas whirled again, opening fire on a sfuz on the ceiling directly above.

The thing exploded, dropped like a bag of warm mud, knocking Thomas backward, so his head slammed into the floor.

Everything went dark for a moment, and he woke to Felph shrieking, shrieking, firing his weapon. Thomas pushed a dead sfuz off his face with one hand, rolled to an elbow.

Felph stood, ringed by four sfuz. One had tossed a sticky net over him, so

Felph's left hand lay pinned to his body. Felph screamed, desperately fired his weapon. His gun was empty.

Thomas snapped a shot at the nearest sfuz. The shot hit the floor and exploded into shrapnel. Perhaps that saved them. If he'd hit the sfuz directly, the shell would have exploded within the creature. As it was, the shell sent fragments into two sfuz, so they dropped to the floor.

More importantly it sent the last two racing out of view just as Thomas fired again, only to find his pulp gun empty.

Thomas stood taking stock of himself. His back hurt. The wound felt deep. Blood ran down his spine, and that frightened him. He couldn't see the wound, and he was so much in shock, he could hardly feel it. It seemed he stood outside himself, recognizing something was wrong, not knowing what.

Lord Felph, who crouched on the ground, did not glance at Thomas as he reloaded his pistol. He pulled off the spent clip and dropped a full one in reflexively, then charged forward.

Thomas wanted to ask Felph to turn around, to examine his wounds. He wanted to know if he bled badly, but his Guide would not let him speak.

So he staggered onward woodenly, impelled only by his Guide. Damn it, Thomas thought. If Karthenor doesn't free me, he'll use me up without knowing it.

Thomas imagined clutching Karthenor's throat, imagined the revenge he'd extract—when he got free.

Lord Felph clutched his glow globe so tightly, it lit like a star, and he rushed forward, excited, darting from side to side, glancing down each adjoining passage. He found a path that corkscrewed deeper into the city, till at last it opened onto a wide landing.

Here, a great battle had occurred. Dozens of dead Dronon littered the floors, some with their carapaces split and spilling vile fluids. Sfuz lay among them, some crushed under Vanquishers' battle arms.

But most corpses showed no external sign of damage. The limbs were horribly twisted and clenched, as happens when a creature suffocates. The air here was choked with smoke. Even now, hours after this battle, Thomas could hardly breathe. The corpses so cluttered this corridor—in many places stacked three or four deep.

In this battle, no one had emerged victorious.

Felph clambered over the bodies, forging down a long corridor whose sides rose up like canyon walls. Identical images had been carved in bas-relief on both stone walls: a birdlike creature, flying through flames, writhing in agony.

At the end of the corridor, the sfuz corpses lay piled so deep they blocked the passage ahead. Felph ran to them, climbed to the top of the heap, and pulled several dead sfuz away.

Thomas began clambering over the bodies, his feet sinking into the soft flesh, his hands punching into the warm fur as he dropped to all fours. The bodies shifted beneath his weight, making his feet sink in deeper, as if he climbed up sand.

Felph moved several bodies, enough to reveal a passage. Behind these corpses, in a darkened corridor, Thomas glimpsed a curtain of green light, green raindrops that glowed with their own light, falling into a vast pool.

"Here! Here!" Felph shouted. "The cisterns are here!"

Felph dropped his glow globe, pulled more sfuz aside.

Thomas suddenly felt as if he were being watched.

He spun, saw nothing but sfuz corpses, all lying so quietly. They terrified him. The sfuz, with their soft dark fur, felt warm to his touch. Thomas knew they were warm because of fires that had burned here within the past hour or two. Marks from incendiary rifles scored the walls.

Yet Thomas feared that the sfuz would leap at his touch. He couldn't bear to pull at the corpses as Felph did. He felt trapped.

He whirled again, thought he caught a movement from the corner of his eye—the wispy gray shape of a sfuz, leaping away. But this shape had no body, only a shadow.

I'm imagining things, Thomas told himself.

Thomas shivered, looked down at his hand. His hand was on the belly of a sfuz, its legs curling helplessly up, like a dead spider's. Its four eyes stared at him, undimmed in death. Perhaps this bothered him more than anything, to see these eyes, still glowing with life, even in death.

Up ahead, Felph finished pulling corpses away, began climbing down the bodies on the far side of the corridor. "Come on!" he shouted.

Thomas followed unwillingly, a human machine, scrambling over sfuz corpses, till he half slid, half tumbled down some bodies to stand beside Lord Felph at the opening of a vast chamber.

The green rain showered in a thin curtain before them, baffling his eyes so that Thomas could not see well beyond the opening of the chamber. Instead, his eyes were drawn to the curtain of dancing lights. The falling droplets made no sound as they dripped to the floor, nor did the huge droplets of light bounce on the stone and splinter under the impact.

Beyond this curtain of liquid light, Thomas could see an enormous cavern. The green rain did not fill the chamber. Instead it only showered along the walls, in a great irregular circle. From this, Thomas guessed that the far wall was back a quarter of a mile or more; the chamber rose hundreds of yards to the ceiling.

A vast dew tree filled most of this cavern, its trunk at least a hundred yards wide, rising up and up till it met the roof, then proceeded through the stone. The hoary roots of the tree splayed from it in every direction, like twisted fingers emerging from a purple hand, and among the roots were knobby pale growths, like knuckles.

Felph just stared. This tree, here in the stone cavern, was totally unexpected. And it was so huge. Everywhere its dark roots seemed to wriggle across the floor—veins and arteries. Something large, like an anteater, with an enormous snout, trundled along the ridge of one twisted root.

Wings flashed in the darkness around the bole of the tree.

Life. With the green rains and the unexpected forest, the movement of animals within that room, Thomas got the impression of abundant life, everywhere beyond that veil.

"Of course, of course there would be creatures here," Felph said. "There can be no death in that room."

Felph glanced up at the top of the chamber, far above, and Thomas followed his gaze. A machine covered its roof—vast and hoary. Thomas saw huge piping carved in the stone, engines whirring silently overhead. He could not guess the purpose of this great machine, but he could guess part—all along its edges, the green rain fell. As if the rain dropped from this machine.

Lord Felph seemed reluctant to enter the room, to pass through the veil of green light—or perhaps he was merely curious. Experimentally, he held out the butt of his pulp pistol, so sheets of rain fell over it.

The green drops seemed not to spatter the gun, but merely to pass through.

In wonder, Felph said, "Well, I've never seen anything like this, nor heard of it." He glanced at Thomas, as if to ask his opinion on whether they should proceed. Thomas could tell him nothing.

I am but a simple man of Tihrglas, he wanted to say. What do I know of such things?

Surprisingly, Thomas's Guide let him speak. "Och, man, let's tuck our tails between our legs and scurry out of here," he said. Then he could say no more.

Karthenor had told Thomas to protect Felph. Perhaps a word of warning fulfilled that commandment.

Felph frowned. "It's an energy field of some kind. I've heard of physicists who've tried to create stasis fields—holes in the universe where time ceases to exist, but they always collapse. Anything stored in such holes is destroyed. But . . . see—" Felph pointed to his left, to a corner away from the tree, in an area of the vast chamber where Thomas had not even looked. There a mass of white bones lay in huge piles. Among the bones were strange, dusty, birdlike faces, staring out at them. "Qualeewoohs died there and rotted. Over the centuries, their bones fused." Felph shook his head. "If the corpses are fossilized, time exists beyond this veil. So I wonder what the veil accomplishes?"

Lord Felph regarded the fossils thoughtfully. "And the bones make me wonder. Qualeewooh legend says that if one drinks the Waters of Strength, the Waters give eternal life. But if that is true, why is this room little more than a grave?"

Thomas shivered as he began to understand what treasure Felph sought. It frightened him to follow a man so obsessed.

"Tell me," Felph said. "Do you think it could be true, that the Waters let some part of you—your spirit—travel to another dimension? If that is so, it may be that this energy field is really the portal, not the Water. Or perhaps the Water acts as a catalyst for a physical change that can occur within this room."

Felph laughed giddily. "After six hundred years of seeking this end, I find myself frightened to enter this chamber."

"Do not enter," Thomas warned.

Felph ignored him, began talking rapidly. "You know, I have studied Qualeewoohs for centuries. They say ideas have life. The seeds of ideas exist outside us, and are planted in our minds by gods. The Qualeewoohs wear spirit masks to make that task easier.

"But they say in time, thoughts grow and take flight on their own." Felph gazed past the barrier. "Most human biologists seem to believe that the Qualeewoohs' sayings are a metaphor, a nice way to say we must not simply follow our heart, but should give it wings."

Felph muttered under his breath. "I have sometimes wondered: could it be a metaphor for what happens when one drinks the Waters of Strength? Could the thoughts and intents of your heart take flight, transform into something else, some more pure and lasting form of life that exists beyond this dimension? The Qualeewoohs say their ancestors fly 'between the stars.' I've pondered that. Space. Empty space. Could they mean their ancestors exist in a realm without matter? Or in a world human science cannot yet weigh or measure. And if that is true, what would be the advantages of transferring one's consciousness to that realm? And what might be the penalties? And would it be wise?"

"Do not go," Thomas said one last time. He meant that Felph should not go into that new realm he spoke of with such glassy-eyed wonder. The notion terrified Thomas.

But Thomas's words jarred Felph. He spun, gazing at Thomas as if he'd never seen him. "Of course I'll go. This body is but a clone. This life one of many I can spend as I want! If the Waters kill me, what does it matter? Why shouldn't I go?"

Thomas could give no reply.

Lord Felph turned and strode through the green rain, passed through, turned and stared back at it in surprise.

Thomas could only follow.

He touched the green veil with one hand, felt something cool, like a cold wind washing through him, like a million icicles piercing every fiber of his being. As he passed through the wall of shimmering rain, he felt a tug, as if he'd just pushed through a tangle of vines only to find something, something insubstantial, left behind.

Thomas, too, turned to look back, for he feared he'd see his body dead on the floor, on the other side of the veil.

But the corridor he'd just passed through was empty. Felph chuckled nervously, then turned and marched over the ground.

In the distance, among the folds of roots about the great tree, Thomas heard strange, hooting calls. Something made a noise like breaking glass, and Thomas thought he glimpsed shadowy movements, as if small animals scurried, but he could not see clearly in the half-light. The green shimmering rains did not give much radiance, not enough to see well by.

The ground crunched oddly beneath their feet. The floor was littered with white stones. Thomas hiked through the chamber as if by moonlight, and Felph raised his glow globe till it flooded the path at their feet with piercing whiteness.

At Thomas's feet, an ancient purple skull stared at him from shadowy sockets, silver lines engraved over every surface. Around the skull were bones, white bones of ribs and wings. These made the odd crunching. Thomas leapt aside in horror, jumped on a tangled mass of rubbery root instead.

Felph began breathing heavily, as in fear. "I'll do this," he whispered. "I will walk between the stars!"

He climbed a rubbery root, began jogging, waving his hands as he tried to balance. He followed the roots toward the great tree. "Dew trees always set their roots in water," he explained as he ran, his shadow writhing behind. "The Waters must be just ahead."

Thomas followed more clumsily. Something whistled over his head, and he felt beating wings, looked up to see some batlike creature with translucent wings flap past his shoulder.

It was not a long journey, but an arduous one. As the roots increased in thickness, Thomas found himself walking higher and higher above floor level, until he was dozens of meters up. Creatures scampered into hiding as they passed—long-snouted furry things that had bored holes the width of a hand into the roots of the dew tree. From some of these holes the dew tree exuded a sweet-smelling liquid; shrimplike insects in hundreds of sizes and colors huddled around these holes to feed, each waving a dozen small pincers at Thomas as he passed.

As Thomas ran, he saw a large, eyeless beast, like a lizard, quietly clinging to the side of a root below him. It gaped its mouth wide, showing row on row of teeth as pale as quartz.

The air here was richer, somehow more invigorating than anything Thomas had smelled before. It was neither warm nor cool, and carried no scent of the smoke that had choked the corridors of the warrens above.

Everywhere, wild creatures fled at their coming. Eden, Thomas thought, I am in Eden.

Lord Felph kept darting to the side of the trunk now, holding out the light as far as he could, looking down for water. They were still far from the bole of the tree, but suddenly Thomas heard a splash as something plunked into the pool at their approach, almost at their very feet.

"There!" Felph shouted. "Down there!"

He held his light high. The root they stood on was perhaps a dozen meters above water, and it shot wriggling tendrils down.

The light reflecting off the water's surface showed gleaming patterns of ripples over the dark tree roots. Yet the pool below was clear and dark. Thomas could see minnows darting deep beneath its surface, some larger eel shape wriggling at a leisurely pace farther down—then blackness.

Lord Felph pressed the glow globe into Thomas's hands. "Hold the light for me as I climb down."

Thomas did as ordered. Holding the lamp would protect Felph, keep him from slipping. Thomas's Guide allowed the action.

Felph began scrabbling down the slope of the root. He used the round holes burrowed by creatures as handholds. When he got near the bottom, he called to Thomas. "Throw down the glow globe. I can't see handholds in this dark."

Thomas hesitated a moment, unable to move, until he decided Felph would be safer with the light. He tossed the glow globe. Felph caught it deftly.

Felph squeezed the globe to brighten it. The waterlogged roots were dark and slippery. Felph carefully tested each step, and his journey took well over two minutes as he sought a path around various roots, climbing down in one spot, learning he'd found a false trail, then climbing to another.

Thomas began following in Felph's trail, but in the shadows it was too difficult. He managed only to climb down partway, then crouch in a hollow, holding to a twisted knot.

Felph found a path down to one root that dipped at water's level, providing a platform so he could reach the clear pools.

Thomas's heart pounded. Everything had gone silent, the animals around them. No scurrying creatures. No hooting cries. It was the quiet of a forest, when wolves are on the prowl.

Sfuz, Thomas thought. He backed against a root, hid in a dark crevasse. If sfuz were coming, he didn't want to be standing in the light, in full profile.

So pervasive was the quiet, Thomas found himself glancing up, watching roots above Felph. The globe shone its brilliant light down around the roots of the great tree, but Thomas could not see beyond that paltry circle. Everything else was in the shadows.

Thomas heard Felph grunt, followed by burbling sounds. Felph crouched on a twisted root, and dunked a canteen underwater, letting it fill.

Suddenly in the darkness, on the huge root on the far side of the pool, Thomas spotted movement. Shadows separated from a stump and moved into the light.

Thomas pointed his weapon, expecting trouble.

A young man stepped from behind a wrinkled knob of root. Thomas's heart was pounding. Thomas considered calling out a warning, but his Guide would not let him. He'd been told to be quiet. Then Orick stepped out of the shadows behind the young man. Was this young man a friend, then? Thomas relaxed his guard.

The young man drew a pulp pistol, aimed at Felph.

Thomas would have opened fire, but his Guide forbade it. If the young man pulled the trigger in his dying throes, then Felph might get shot. Thomas would have failed in his charge to protect Felph.

Holding the pistol forward, the young man said, "Father, don't touch that."

Forty-four

C ooharah and Aaw sat in a rock pile in the starlight just before dawn. Cooharah watched a line of thunderheads approach, bringing the grumble of distant thunder, the first rain so far south in a decade. The bone years were ending. The light of Brightstar was warming the land, melting the great ice floes in the north, as the teachsongs said would happen.

It should have been a wonder. This should have inaugurated an age of hope, a new beginning for Cooharah.

Instead, he felt dismay.

Aaw preened her wings, as if discussing some minor thing. She cooed, "We must atone. Two lives for one. This is law."

Last night, still unsure of the extent of their wrongdoing, it had been relatively easy to deny the voices of the ancestors, easy to flee. But Cooharah and Aaw had lived the laws since they were chicks. To disobey them would have been madness. The ancestors would cry through the spirit masks, over and over, a litany of guilt.

"I will go," Aaw whistled. "I will take the egg. We shall atone for the oomas."

"Negative to the fourth degree," Cooharah whistled. "I will not live without you."

Aaw quit preening, looked up at him, eyes bright in the starlight. "Then we give three lives for one. Our atonement will be generous."

It seemed so easy for her to speak of death. Sometimes, Cooharah thought the ancestors spoke more clearly to her than to him. But he knew it was not true. He was the one who had stayed up at night, vainly clawing his spirit mask, trying to silence the voices of the ancestors. If he'd managed to unmask himself, he'd have become outlaw. His life would have been forfeit, should other Qualeewoohs see him.

Now he realized how impetuous he had been. It was true he heard the voices of the ancestors more strongly than Aaw. Such was the make of her spirit mask, that she heard them only distantly. But she had a firmer mind, a more obedient nature.

"Your atonement is generous," Cooharah whistled. "Mine is not. I give my gift grudgingly." With that, he flapped his wings, took to the air, heading south, toward the aerie of the oomas. Aaw followed. Behind them, the distant thunder snarled.

Forty-five

G allen held Maggie tightly, never wanting to let go. Kintiniklintit swept overhead, finishing his great circle over the Dronon Swarms, having built up his wingspeed. Gallen had seen Dronon do this before, and he didn't fear attack in these first few seconds.

Maggie was shaking. He'd never seen her show such fear. She trembled like a child who has had a nightmare. She stared into his face.

Everywhere all around them, the swarms of Dronon Vanquishers drummed their mouthfingers over their voicedrums, till the sound was a rumbling storm. Six Swarm Lords had gathered to the killing field, each with nearly half a million Vanquishers, workers, and technicians, so that now literally millions of Dronon raised their voices in unison, cheering the Lords of the Seventh Swarm.

Gallen knew such meetings must be impossibly rare on Dronon. Battles for succession would attract only two pairs of Swarm Lords. But there had never been a battle like this, a battle where the fate of two species hung in the balance.

Above them, Lord Kintiniklintit finished his great circle, veered to attack from far away. Gallen pushed Maggie aside. His head felt clearer. Perhaps it was the nanodocs from Orick's precious blood, but he felt less dizziness; his wounds were less swollen. Still, his leg was broken, despite Maggie's binding. Even with a full course of nanodocs, it would have taken days or weeks to heal. Gallen could hardly stand on his one good leg.

"I have to fight," he told Maggie.

"You can't win," Maggie said. "Not with your leg."

Gallen closed his eyes, as if the very thought of fighting pained him. "I can't win, but I can fight. That's what I do." He needed this. He needed to know he'd done all he could.

"Then I'll fight with you," she said.

Maggie wore his mantle. She began to remove it, place the net of black rings on his head. But he knew it would be no use. He couldn't leap about. Couldn't kick. The mantle could do nothing for him.

"No," Gallen said. "You keep it. You're in better physical shape than I."

Lord Kintiniklintit's wings rumbled, a slight shift in tone that indicated he was picking up speed, Gallen looked up. The sun was just rising, and in the northeast, a line of thunderheads loomed. Ruin's dark sun did not give much light, as red and distant as it was. With the clouds obscuring it, it gave even less. Still, Kintiniklintit made his first run from that direction, choosing to fly in out of the sun, blinding his opponents.

Gallen hobbled to Maggie's right, held her shoulder lightly, balancing on one foot. The grass here was part of an open field, somewhat barren. Gallen knelt and pried up a large rock from the ground, held it in his right hand.

"When Kintiniklintit comes in, he'll expect you to split left, me to split right," Gallen whispered. "Don't do it. Fall right. I'll be in front of you."

"What if he spits acid?" Maggie asked. She'd once told him that in all her dreams, it was not dying from wounds inflicted that worried her, it was the painful burning from acid first.

"I'll feint right," Gallen said. "I won't really move. If he spits, I'm hoping he'll miss." And if he doesn't miss, he thought, I'll be shielding you with my body. You've done so much for me, so much to help me, that this is the last service I can offer.

Maggie nodded. She shivered, terrified. Perhaps she wanted to turn and run, or to curl into a ball and hide, but Gallen needed her to stand beside him, to prop him up. He wasn't sure she could do it. Gallen feared that when Kintiniklintit attacked, she'd simply remain standing, too frozen to move.

Gallen squeezed her shoulder and squinted up into the light as Lord Kintiniklintit completed his great circle and veered at them, full speed. He raised his serrated battle claws over his head as if to attack.

At one time that battle stance would have struck terror in Gallen, but he'd heard how Kintiniklintit fared in other battles. His great arms could chop a person in half like a cleaver. Death would be instantaneous.

Kintiniklintit rushed toward them, wings humming, carapace sullen in the dawn light. Gallen recalled how he'd fought the Dronon before, his incredible leaps, his diving and weaves.

He wished Maggie could move like that. Perhaps she could have, months ago. But not now, not with a child in her.

When Kintiniklintit was a hundred meters out, Maggie tensed as if to run, but Gallen held her shoulder stiffly. Everything seemed to slow. Kintiniklintit was coming in low, too low. It was a killing run. He didn't plan to spit his acid on them, as other Dronon would have. He planned to split them in halves, give them a quick and merciful death.

I should have known, Gallen thought. He's a gallant one. Kintiniklintit plans to kill us. I shouldn't have told Maggie to fall right. He'll come straight through us!

There was no time to warn her now. He could only hope she'd see the danger.

Suddenly he felt her shift, spin away as if to dodge left. Gallen feinted right, and Lord Kintiniklintit spit, his stomach acids exploding out, frothing white, hurtling over Gallen's right shoulder.

But instead of dodging, Gallen hurled his stone with all his might, catching the Dronon Lord in the right front eye cluster. In surprise Kintiniklintit turned his head defensively. Gallen dropped and rolled right.

Kintiniklintit's battle arms swatted the ground as the great Lord passed, hitting the precise spot where Gallen had stood. Fortunately, Maggie had ignored Gallen's advice and dived left. The maneuver saved her life.

The Dronon hosts suddenly quieted, surprised.

And yet Gallen did not feel relief to see Maggie alive and unharmed. Instead he felt only dismay, for as the Lord Escort had passed him, Gallen had seen Kintiniklintit's left sensor whip sail by, within easy grasp.

Gallen had bulldogged a Dronon that way, jerking the sensor whip down so hard that the Dronon flew headfirst into the ground. It might not be enough to kill Lord Kintiniklintit, but Gallen realized, to his dismay, he could have struck a blow against the Lord.

As Gallen struggled to rise on his broken leg, he heard Maggie grumble. "If I'm going to be in this fight, I'm in all the way. I'll not be just a lamppost for you to lean on!"

Maggie fumbled on the ground, pulled up a rock as Gallen had done before. Then she came to Gallen.

Kintiniklintit hurtled through the air, redoubling his speed. Maggie helped Gallen to stand. He groaned in pain as he tried to put weight on his leg. He had retrieved a rock.

"I don't think it's legal to use these," Maggie said.

"I don't care about the rules anymore," Gallen said.

Lord Kintiniklintit had reached the apex of his climb. He veered and streaked toward them. The thunderheads behind him were moving fast, so that even as the sun rose, the darkness deepened. He flew now not in sunlight, but in shadow.

"Same tactic as before," Gallen whispered.

Maggie glanced at him fretfully. "Are you sure?"

"I never used exactly the same tactic twice in my other fights," Gallen said. "He'll know that. He won't expect this."

Gallen considered dropping his stone. If this was to be a replay, he knew what he had to do. He had to grab that sensor whip and yank down with all his might, though the force of it rip his arms from their sockets.

But this would not be a replay.

Lord Kintiniklintit came in lower, and from the left. The front edge of a Dronon's hard wing could slice a man like a saber, and by aiming his attack at Maggie, Lord Kintiniklintit showed that his gallant overtures had reached an end.

If Maggie could not dodge him, Gallen would have to leap between the two. The Dronon expected him to do so.

Maggie remained steadfast as Kintiniklintit attacked. "Go right," she shouted, and at that moment she threw her rock.

Perhaps she'd imagined Kintiniklintit had enough eyes left in his right eye cluster that he would see the rock coming, try to dodge. She'd imagined wrong.

The Vanquisher flew straight on, taking a hit to the head, the rock bouncing harmlessly off his exoskeleton. Maggie tried to drop beneath his wings, too slow.

Gallen threw himself in front of her, blocking the attack with a fierce blow to Lord Kintiniklintit's wing. The sturdy wing cracked under the impact, but the edge of the wing caught Gallen in the temple on its upstroke, slamming his forehead.

Gallen felt himself falling, saw nothing but bright flashes of light in the darkness.

The next Gallen knew, he lay on his back, not knowing how long he'd been down. He opened his eyes, felt blood in them, saw red. Blood gushed from his brow, had pooled in his eye sockets.

"Gallen, get up! Save me!" Maggie screamed. She slapped his face, tried to rouse him.

Gallen vainly tried to recall where he was, could not remember. But he rolled to his knees, in tremendous pain. Only Maggie's screams seemed to penetrate the fog in his mind.

He stared at the ground for a moment, tried to focus. All around a great din arose—the clacking cries of Dronon. He stared dumbly at his gloved hands, saw hot blood spattering on the ground, his blood. Maggie screamed and grabbed his shoulder, tried to pull him up.

He grasped her arm, tried to struggle to his feet.

"Where—what's happening?" he asked. "Where's Orick?" He didn't know why that question came to mind. He had a sense that if Orick were here, Orick would fix everything. But as Gallen glanced around, he could see no bear— only the red pavilions, only the millions of dark bodies.

The air around him smelled acrid—the scent of Dronon stomach acids. "Oh, Gallen!" Maggie cried, and she was holding his face up, trying to look into his face, but blood spilled down onto her hands. The shock on her face, the fear in her brown eyes, told him he did not look well.

"What? What?" Gallen asked.

And suddenly amid the clamor and the tumult, the million voices crying out in a furor for blood, suddenly in the slow wind, Gallen looked out toward the sun, saw Kintiniklintit winging toward him, flying out of the sun, low to the ground, battle arms raised.

"Got to go," Gallen said thickly, tried to push Maggie away. The Dronon Lord was flying toward her unprotected back. But Gallen's muscles had all gone rubbery, his movements felt disjointed.

He tried to push her away, and felt as feeble as a child. She held him, tried to hold him upright. She glanced over her shoulder at the Vanquisher.

Gallen tried to push her, tried to get in front of her, but realized numbly that she held him tight, that she shielded him with her body.

"I love you, Gallen," she said.

The Vanquisher was coming, and Gallen struggled with Maggie in a clumsy dance. With one great heave, he shoved her back, just as Kintiniklintit struck.

Gallen only had time to half turn to the monster thundering toward him when he heard battle arms whistle downward. One of them struck him on the right shoulder, cleaving through the collarbone, ripping down through his right lung and the rib bones, exiting from his belly.

The blow totally undid Gallen, ripping him nearly in half. He dropped backward to a sitting position from the force of the blow, was thrown sideways so that his face hit the dirt.

He lay there, unmoving, unable to move—yet still strangely conscious. He felt no pain, sound was but a dim rushing in his ears, the delighted cries of Dronon Vanquishers sounding like nothing so much as the sea.

Maggie got up from the ground, stared at him in dismay. Her lip was bleeding, and though Gallen struggled to breathe, he found himself choking and knew that in seconds his life would bleed from him. He felt no sorrow for himself, only for her. He so wanted to reach out, to comfort her.

Gallen saw Kintiniklintit turn sharply, double back, and the roaring of the sea grew, filled his ears. When a Lord Escort came to kill a queen, it did not move so swiftly as when it killed her protector. The Dronon considered the combat to be over. Golden Queens, with their bloated bellies and feeble arms, could not protect themselves.

Maggie touched Gallen's cheek, stroked it, and glanced over her shoulder as Kintiniklintit made his final assault.

To her credit, Maggie raised her fists and assumed a combat stance. The mantle she wore must have shown her this stance.

But Maggie was no Lord Protector.

Kintiniklintit dived toward her, and by now, Gallen's hearing had gone dim. He coughed uncontrollably, his life hacking from him as he struggled for breath. Distantly, he saw the Dronon Vanquisher stoop, battle arms raised high overhead, mouth opened so that its terrible teeth, like the yellow teeth of a horse, gaped at her.

Orick, where are you? Gallen wondered. He remembered now that Orick was seeking the Waters of Strength, that Orick would drink from them, was supposed to come save him. If the Qualeewoohs had conquered time, then Orick should have been here by now. But Orick was nowhere to be seen.

As Kintiniklintit neared, Maggie leapt in the air and kicked.

But Maggie was no Lord Protector. She did not leap high or fast enough. While carrying a child in her womb, she could have done neither.

Kintiniklintit's battle arms swung down with alarming speed, slashing Maggie at the midriff, slicing her nearly in two.

Blood sprayed in the air—dark droplets that seemed to fall in slow motion, and Maggie's head and torso dropped backward, thudded next to Gallen.

Her head was toward him, face upraised, as if in her last moment she'd tried to turn to him. Her eyes, her deep brown eyes with their flecks of gold, stared at him vacantly, unmoving.

Gallen's mantle lay in a pile beside her red hair, the gems in it shining. It had slipped off.

She did not breathe, did not cry out. Gallen felt—nothing. So empty. Why did I bring her to this? he wondered. He could feel nothing, no pain or despair, no love or hope.

Instead, he simply stared out over the crowds of Dronon in their millions, saw them raising their arms, crying out in triumph. In the distance, across the field, Hera and Athena rushed toward him.

Go back, he wanted to say. They could do nothing now.

The ground felt cold on his face, and he imagined that the smell of blood came from the soil, that blood was somehow rising from the earth.

The earth bleeds, he thought in wonder, just as we do.

He stared off at a line of clouds rushing toward him, lightning flashing at their crown.

Thunderheads.

Everything nearby had gone out of focus. Before the line of clouds, two dark forms winged toward him—hazy, indistinct.

Angels, he realized. Black angels coming for me.

Forty-six

*O*rick raced desperately down the tunnel beside Tallea, fleeing the Dronon Vanquishers. He needed to find the Waters of Strength, and soon, yet found himself running away from Teeawah, dashing through the smoky corridors, leaping over the bodies of dead Dronon and sfuz.

They had run perhaps six hundred meters, when Orick realized he had missed his turnoff. With the smoke so thick, his sense of smell was going, and he hadn't smelled his own scent.

Here, in these dark corridors, where the shadows lay so thick on the irregular walls, he hadn't noticed the narrow hole in the tunnel wall.

He only knew that he'd reached unfamiliar territory, that they'd run for a moment without his recognizing any landmarks.

Tallea came to a halt, dropped her glow globe on the ground. "Where to now?" she asked.

"I don't know!" Orick said. He glanced back. The Dronon were not far behind. Their light reflected dimly from around the bend. They were marching fast, and Orick dared not keep running ahead blindly. What if they met another Dronon patrol? Who knew how far it might be till this tunnel intersected another.

"Orick, over here!" Tallea hissed. She lifted her glow globe in her teeth, bounded toward several dead sfuz, over near one wall.

When she reached them, she dived behind the nearest corpse, and Orick stared in surprise. The sfuz had fur of dark, dark, purplish hue, but Tallea, with her black fur, looked like just another dead sfuz. If the Dronon didn't study the corpses closely, they might just pass her by.

Orick rushed to a pair of dead sfuz near her, then nosed under one of the hairy bodies. Orick didn't have the six long legs to make the disguise complete, but he stuck his rear paws in the air, hoping it might fool the Dronon.

He did not have to wait long. In only a couple of minutes, the Dronon Vanquishers came surging through the tunnels.

The point guards consisted of six Vanquishers, side by side, each carrying a pulp gun and a light, so that as they came marching down the hall, the Vanquishers filled the tunnel with light. Behind them, the others marched in files of three.

Orick watched them from squinted eyes. The Dronon moved swiftly, in an eerie silence. Unlike humans or bears, who would swing their heads from side to side as they listened for enemies or sniffed the air, the Dronon marched with heads fully erect, facing perfectly forward. With their numerous eye clusters, the Dronon could see everywhere ahead and behind.

The Dronon marched over him, and one of the guards near the far wall actually stepped on Orick's belly, never paying attention to the bear.

Then he was gone, and the others marched past.

Hundreds of them marched together, but most scurried in darkness, and would not have been able to discern Orick's form.

Somehow, Orick felt terrified that they would recognize him as a bear, but after the first hundred Dronon had passed, he began to wonder. Did the Dronon even know what a bear was?

Only the Lords of the Sixth Swarm had ever been to the human-occupied worlds. These other Dronon might never have even laid eyes on a human, much less a bear. If they noticed that Orick wasn't a sfuz, perhaps they imagined he was just some other local varmint.

So it came as no surprise when the last Dronon scrambled past.

The Dronon had not checked the corpses. They've probably all heard that Maggie has been caught, Orick realized. They're just retreating to their ship, glad to be quit of this place.

When the last Dronon footsteps had echoed away, Tallea got up. "Let's go," she said.

She picked up her light. Once she put it in her mouth, it began glowing softly. Orick rose, and together they ran, galloping at full speed, fearing time was of the essence.

In five minutes they reached golden cliffs of carved sandstone, and the tunnel that ran along beside the cliffs, climbing uphill. Here, a tremendous battle had raged. Sfuz and Dronon lay dead by the thousands and tens of thousands; fires still burned dimly among the humus.

Oval holes along the cliff face showed where Qualeewoohs had nested once, ages ago. Orick's heart leapt.

This is it, he thought. This is Teeawah.

Tallea climbed into one of the first holes, bounding through, and Orick followed her into a room full of bones and a few dead sfuz, looking for all the world like dried spiders. This room led them into a wider corridor, and the air here felt clogged and unhealthy, almost unbreathable, as if someone had just cleaned a chimney.

Yet, here Orick made a remarkable discovery. Rushing down a wide corridor he caught familiar scents: the florid essence of Lord Felph's bath perfumes, along with Zeus's distinctive lotions, accompanied by . . . someone Orick recalled—the aroma of pipe tobacco, and a wool coat. And . . . that old blackguard Thomas Flynn!

Just as Orick began to recuperate from the surprise, up ahead, along a stone corridor, he heard the pop, pop, pop, of a Dronon pulp pistol.

Orick halted, wondering what strange news this portended. Zeus he had anticipated might be here—but Felph and Thomas Flynn? He'd left Thomas months ago, back in the Milky Way. Thomas could only have gotten here by a world gate—in company with the Dronon.

Tallea dropped her glow globe, whispered, "What's wrong?"

"I'm not sure," Orick said. "Plenty, I think."

Orick stood, wondering. He'd never been a hero. That was Gallen's job, standing in the midst of the battle. But though Orick had the heart for battle, he lacked Gallen's appendages.

Normally, such minor things wouldn't bother him, but he was on the path of three men, all of them probably armed, none of whom he trusted. One of them was blasting away, at something.

"Let's take care," Orick said.

He and Tallea stalked slowly, sniffing, eyes forward. Orick could smell Zeus most strongly. The young man had come in just moments ago, not far behind the others.

The path led down, past the bodies of several sfuz who lay, still bleeding, in their death throes. The smell of explosive was heavy in the air.

Tallea dimmed her light, and Orick hurried forward. Somehow, he felt odd—as if every side passage contained sfuz, as if something watched him.

The corridor turned twice, headed down, past a pile of corpses—both sfuz and Dronon, until at last a pile of sfuz corpses nearly blocked the passage, hundreds upon hundreds of them, all lying in a great heap, their legs twisted horribly, bright black eyes shining in the darkness, white fangs gleaming in Tallea's dull light.

Felph and the others had merely crawled over the corpses, crawled up and over through a narrow passage, where a faint green light shimmered dimly.

Tallea stopped and studied the dead sfuz, somehow as unnerved by them as Orick was. Orick couldn't help but remember that Felph had said that these things would reanimate a few hours after death. All of them looked—so alive.

How long had it been, anyway, since the Dronon had fought here? Orick estimated that it had been six or seven hours since the Dronon first made it into the tangle, and a dark line of thought occurred to him.

These sfuz might waken soon. Not just some of them, all of them. This whole place would be crawling with them, and if Orick didn't hurry and get to the Waters now, he'd never make it out alive.

"Come on," he told Tallea, as he charged toward the pile of sfuz, bounded up, climbing over the bodies. He had to be careful. Even in death the sfuz were dangerous—fangs gleamed everywhere, and each leg had sharp climbing spurs on it, dangerous things as sharp as any knife. And Lord Felph had warned that these creatures used poisonous weapons. Orick feared that those climbing spurs might be deadly.

Just as he reached the narrow opening at the top of the pile, and glimpsed the green curtain of light farther down the tunnel, something came alive beneath his feet. A warm black body twisted, long spidery legs slashing out with their spurs, trying to disembowel him.

Instinctively Orick tore with his paws, bit down. A sfuz that had lain in the pile squealed in pain, stabbed as it tried to free itself. The monster was impossibly quick, striking three blows to Orick's chest for each one of his to the monster.

Orick grunted in pain at the blows, trying too frantically to counterattack to make any display of anger.

Just as he began to realize he was in more trouble than he could handle, Tallea darted in, grabbed one of the sfuz's long legs in her teeth, and pulled. The distraction gave Orick enough time to bat the thing in the head, and the sfuz fell still.

Orick stood panting, his chest heaving. He felt blood oozing out his chest, winced in pain. The wounds were deeper than he would have liked, closer to vital areas. He only hoped that his nanodocs would keep him together.

Yet more frightening than this attack was the fact that one of the sfuz had apparently come alive.

If this one revived, why not others? It might be only a matter of minutes before they all arose.

Orick squirmed over the dead sfuz, down the far side of the pile, and did not slow as he rushed through an icy veil of green light, sniffed something strange: a great dew tree filled this room, its twisted roots splaying in all directions. The lights all about them, the green curtains of light that felt so cold to the touch, let him see well enough for a bear.

Up near the base of the great tree, a white light shone among the roots. Someone was climbing down from the tree, and the light dipped behind a root like a star falling beyond the horizon.

Tallea had dropped her own light on the ground, let it dwindle completely. Orick could smell Zeus now, his scent strong. He'd been here only moments before.

"That way!" Tallea said, nodding toward the distant light of the glow globe.

Orick didn't feel so confident. "Tread quietly," he whispered.

For the next several moments they ran, surefooted over the twisting roots, moving faster than any human could in the same circumstances. Ahead, the light continued to dwindle and descend, so that now it lit the roots as if it were a campfire in a grotto.

When he neared this circle of light, Orick slowed. Up ahead, on the root they trod, Zeus stood in the darkness, sneaking toward the light, gun drawn.

He shouted some command into the darkness, gazing down toward the light. His face was a pale mask of anger. Orick and Tallea scampered into the shadows to watch.

Lord Felph squatted down near the water, a glow globe in one hand, a canteen in the other. Zeus waved his gun at his father. "I said, put it down. Now!"

Felph looked up, startled, and smiled nervously. "Zeus, so glad to see you made it," he said, trying to sound casual. "Is the Lord Protector with you?"

He peered about, trying to find Gallen.

"Throw me the canteen," Zeus demanded.

"There is plenty for both of us," Felph chided, waving expansively to the Waters before him. "Plenty for this whole world."

"Throw me the canteen!" Zeus shouted, firing a quick burst that whipped past Felph's brow and exploded into the roots, behind him, down at water level.

Orick breathed deeply, found his heart pounding. So that scoundrel Zeus was trying to steal the Waters.

Lord Felph tossed the canteen up. Zeus grabbed it, while his gun pointed steadily at Felph. Zeus shook the canteen.

Felph said, "See, I was bringing some back for you. Plenty for us all."

Zeus smiled wickedly, waved his weapon at Felph. "Drop your gun, now, into the water. Slowly."

Felph did as commanded. When he finished, Zeus nodded toward the shadows. "Tell the slave to drop his weapon."

Lord Felph glanced back into the shadows. "Do as he says."

In the shadows, Orick could discern only the smallest of movement. Thomas Flynn stood there, frozen, unable to move. Orick could see the gleam of silver on his graying hair—a Guide.

"Throw down your weapon, slave, or you might both die," Zeus repeated.

Thomas tossed his gun. It clattered over the roots, dropped into a crevice.

Zeus said, "Thank you," nodded at Thomas. Then addressed Felph. "Really now, Father, you don't think I'd let you drink from this, too? You don't think I'd let *any* of you have this."

"Why not?" Felph asked.

"Because I don't have to," Zeus said. "You're here in the tangle, so far from home, your Controller can't transmit a signal back home. If I killed you now, you'd awaken in a few days, knowing you'd gone into the tangle and never returned. You'd never discover what had happened down here."

"Come now, after six hundred years of searching, you wouldn't deny me this?" Felph said. "There is plenty for both of us."

Zeus chuckled, laughing easily. "You made *me* to be the ruler," Zeus said. "You made me to hold the power. I . . . I don't need any equals."

"It is true, I made you to crave power," Felph said. "Perhaps I was mistaken in that."

"So, my life is a mistake?" Zeus asked. "That's what Arachne told me."

"When?" Felph asked, his face suddenly clouding with doubt.

In answer, Zeus fired his gun. The blast caught Felph in the belly, and the charge from the pulp gun exploded, carving a ragged hole in his gut. Felph sat down backward, then let the glow globe in his left fist roll from his hand.

It bounced once on the root, dropped into the water, and dimmed as it began to slowly, oh so slowly, sink from sight.

Lord Felph fell backward, lifeless.

"Just before I killed her," Zeus answered. He gazed over at Thomas, a frown on his face.

"You want to kill me, don't you?" Zeus asked.

Thomas did not answer.

Zeus glanced down at his father, waved his gun. "He's not dead, you know. In a few hours, he'll be strutting around the palace. I haven't really hurt him, have I?"

Thomas said nothing.

Zeus chuckled. Apparently killing his father's clone was not a major crime. He waved his pulp gun at Thomas, and Orick knew that the young man pondered whether he should murder Thomas.

"You could kill me," Zeus said. "I see it in your eyes. You want to, but you're a slave. I know what it is to wear a Guide. I know what it's like to want to kill someone, and not be able."

Zeus stared at Thomas. "I give you a present: you shall be my audience."

Zeus uncorked the canteen, brought it to his lips, and sipped. Orick found himself holding his breath, watching Zeus, watching to see what the water bought with so many lives would do.

Zeus blinked a moment, as if in surprise, then he pulled back the hood of his cloak and stood, looking into the sky above as if staring at something far away. "Ahhhhh!" he sighed in wonder.

Zeus raised his hands upward, placatingly, almost as if trying to pull himself into the sky.

Orick could not see well in the gloom. Zeus stood, arms wide, as if in greeting, and Orick saw something strange: a purple light in Zeus's eyes, as if reflected while he focused on something high above.

"I see, now!" Zeus breathed in wonder, in rising excitement. He shouted, "We are gods! It is finished. I can lay down my life, and take it up again. I see how!"

Zeus began shaking with excitement, and to Orick, his face seemed unnaturally pale and bright. His dark hair was combed straight back. Orick could see all of Zeus's face, the strong lines of his mouth drawn back, the skin so pale he looked bloodless.

Orick realized Zeus's face wasn't just pale, it glowed with a dim violet light. The green stars dancing in his eyes burned like flames, and Zeus trembled, gazing upward.

"I go now to my fathers." Zeus closed his eyes, exhaling in a ragged shudder. Orick thought Zeus would die, thought by the way he totally relaxed, the man would simply collapse.

His knees wobbled drunkenly, but he remained standing, and the glow globe below him had almost extinguished. The glow globe, drifting down in the water, had become so dim it looked like a pearl sinking into the sea.

Zeus leaned back his head and opened his mouth, as if to emit a silent scream, and Orick could hardly credit his eyes: for a shadowy form began to break free, struggling from Zeus's mouth, oozing out like a jellyfish—a shape of shining darkness, a horrible black form shot through with purple lightning, a creature that wriggled on dark wings.

Orick's heart pounded, for he thought some strange beast was ripping free from Zeus's body. But as the hideous form surged out, Orick realized he was witnessing a birth, a child struggling from its womb.

The black form put two hands on Zeus's head—one on his forehead, one on his chin, and twisted as it brought its hips through the narrow cavity of Zeus's throat, tussling, then suddenly it broke free. For a moment, it sat experimentally on Zeus's upturned face and spread its dark wings, watching them flap.

Zeus's body dropped with a sigh, a skin sloughed off, and the dark creature took to the air, wheeled overhead in a tight circle.

The creature leaned its head back, opened its mouth wide, and in Orick's mind, he imagined that he heard a great cry of triumph. But the beast made no sound. It remained utterly silent.

Yet its body language spoke volumes. It wheeled and whipped through the air in dizzying circles. It flapped joyously and soared upward with abandon, then dived as quickly.

Orick imagined that Zeus would leave, that he would take flight and never return, but suddenly, a green spark erupted in the sky overhead—a spark or a sheet of flame.

In seconds, another blazed, then a third.

Orick gazed up, and saw an emerald form—pale emerald light in the shape of a great bird. For one second, it dived through solid stone, and then it soared upward again.

Half a moment later, six or seven birds of light dived back into view, stooped toward Zeus's black wriggling form, threatening.

The creature that was Zeus darted and weaved, studying the birds above, dived toward a great root and sat, cowering.

One green bird dived toward him, and Zeus emitted a keen wail and raised his hands to cover his face, folding great black wings behind protectively.

Orick gaped in astonishment. He recognized those birds, had thought only hours ago that one of them was the holy spirit, descending in the form of a dove.

And he recalled the green pool he'd drunk from when he licked the water from Tallea's lips. And he remembered the feeling of something stirring within him, and the terrifying sense of doom he'd felt as the birds of light swooped over him, the sense that he was being judged.

And the truth of what had happened struck him to the core.

The pale birds now drew into a tight circle and wheeled above Zeus, flying faster and faster, like the lip of a whirlwind. Zeus could not take to the air, could not hope to escape them.

One bird dived like a hawk, raked Zeus's head with its claws, then rose again soundlessly, blazing fiercely bright.

Renewed. The bird was renewed. Orick could only imagine that the bird of light had somehow fed upon Zeus, taken energy from him.

More birds came, here and there, up near the ceiling, appearing to fly through the stone—dropping like some fiery and magnificent fruit from the great dew tree.

Zeus huddled in fear, scurrying back from the bright beings above, and only now did Orick see that this dark being was but a shadow, as incorporeal as the birds that flew above.

Zeus flew a short ways, tried to reach his own corpse, the body he had sloughed off a moment before.

The mouth was wide-open, as if in a silent scream, and the black form sought to struggle back into it, as a hermit crab will take up an old shell.

I can lay down my life, and take it up again, Orick thought. Zeus had laid his life aside, now he wanted it back. Yet it was not an easy fit. He writhed and twisted, struggling to reenter his body.

But as Zeus worked to take up his life, a bright bolt of green shot down, raked its claws over his head, gouging deeply.

Worms of purple light bled from Zeus, and a ragged wound formed.

The emerald birds seemed to take courage from this attack.

A second form swept down on flaming wings.

It grasped Zeus with its talons and pulled at his dark soul, opening more wounds, so that the black skin of the creature seemed torn wide, spilling light.

The bird clung to him, bit deeply.

In pain and terror, the creature that was Zeus raised its hands, protecting its shadowy face, and tried to beat its attacker back.

A third bird of light descended, blazing like a green furnace, grabbed Zeus's wing in its beak, and tore.

Purple flames of light erupted from the joint at Zeus's back.

He turned and pummeled vainly at his attackers, striking with all his might. The birds of light flapped their wings, retreated to the air.

Zeus's black form bled purple light that erupted from a dozen major wounds, yet Zeus struggled on. For half a moment, the black thing drooped, as if weary, as if it would simply die.

Yet in that moment, the shadowy form surged back into Zeus's body, flowing like something molten, sliding into Zeus's throat.

Zeus lay on his back, his mouth gaping wide, purple light shining from it as if he'd swallowed a glow globe. His eyes, too, glowed purple.

He breathed raggedly, struggling, and gave a choking sob.

The birds of light dived now, redoubling the attack, as if furious with Zeus.

Zeus raised one hand, as if to hold them at bay, and a bolt of lightning cracked the air, splitting the sky.

For half a second, the bird of light glowed brilliantly, caught in its arc, and then veered away. The others also swerved in their flight, suddenly wary.

"Damn you!" Zeus shouted. And he began laughing, a throaty croak. He struggled up to one elbow. The green birds of light became frantic, one swooped near.

Zeus threw another lightning bolt, cracking the sky, and for half a second, Orick was blinded.

Then Zeus began to shriek. Orick blinked, struggled to see what was happening.

Zeus was shrieking, rolling on the ground. All around him was a confusion of green light, emerald brilliance that baffled the eyes. Zeus held up his hand, as if to shoot off another lightning bolt, but none came. He was out of energy. The flock of birds seemed to be ripping him, dipping their beaks into his body, tearing away flesh. Yet Orick could see no physical damage, no bloody wounds, no gaping rents. Instead, the birds were dipping their faces down deep, below the level of flesh, tearing away something more essential.

For nearly a minute the birds took him, ripping at him, and Zeus's cries diminished. He stopped rolling, stopped trying to fight them at all.

Until one by one, the birds of light rose, ascended back up through the stone roof, back up past the odd stone pipes and hoary machinery.

Orick ran to Zeus, more from curiosity than from any desire to help the man.

Zeus took labored breaths. The light in his mouth and eyes was dimming, fading so that Orick almost wondered if he imagined that he saw the purples. Tears slid down his cheeks. Orick knew he would die, that he could not last much longer.

Nearby, Thomas was climbing down a root to see if Lord Felph, by some miracle, remained alive.

Zeus gasped. "Help me! Help!"

Orick could not help him.

Zeus looked up, imploringly. "They . . . stopped me. Almost, almost I was one of them, but they fought me."

Zeus acted as if he wanted Orick to pity him.

But Orick felt no pity. Zeus had taken the Waters of Strength, and would have withheld them from Gallen. Having entered the gates of heaven, he would bar the way from all who would follow.

"Water!" Zeus begged, desperate. "Give . . . more."

Orick dared not. Perhaps the Water would heal Zeus. To let such a monster live just didn't seem right.

Orick backed away, as Zeus sagged, his last breath coming out with a rattle.

Down by the water's edge, Thomas checked Felph's corpse, found it dead.

"Go and protect Lord Felph," Thomas said aloud, "then return."

He got up woodenly, and began climbing through the tangled roots of the great tree, heading out of Teeawah.

Orick would have argued with Thomas, told him to stay. It would be dangerous for one old man to wander off alone, with the sfuz waking.

But Thomas wore a Guide, and right now, there was nothing Orick could do to stop the old fellow from leaving, short of biting his pants and hanging on.

Tallea whispered urgently in Orick's ear, "Orick, we have to get the Waters for Gallen and go—if you still want it. If you think it will do any good." The hour was growing late.

Orick didn't know how long ago Gallen and Maggie had reached Felph's palace, did not know if they had battled.

Yet, somehow, he imagined that the hour was past. He was too late.

Orick wondered. The Qualeewoohs claimed to have conquered time, space, nature, self. What would that entail?

Do I have such powers? Can I reach Gallen?

More importantly, what good would the Waters be, if Gallen met a fate like that of Zeus?

And yet, and yet—not everyone met Zeus's fate, Orick knew. The Qualeewoohs had judged Zeus, found him lacking.

Orick looked down at the pool, shimmering velvet in the darkness. His heart pounded. From distant reaches of the caverns came a frantic whistling.

Forty-seven

G allen woke to the sound of rain battering the tall windows of Felph's palace, and so fierce and incessant was the pattering, that for a moment he thought it was an anxious neighbor rapping at the windows.

He opened his eyes slowly, recalling the night he'd first met Veriasse and the Lady Everynne back on Tihrglas, a night when it rained madly, as it did now.

He lay in an unfamiliar bedroom, decorated with rich teak paneling and a central hearth all made of white marble, with a brass grill to hold the logs. A cheery fire burned therein—the smell of blazing cedar filling the room with its spicy aroma.

He felt cold, terribly cold despite the fire.

Along the wall, service droids awaited his commands. Gallen could not recall how he'd got here. His last memories came from the tangle, of running back through the dark tunnel from Teeawah, where he'd come so close to the gates of the city. He'd seen the *cloo* holes, like dark eyes, and the golden sandstone, and he heard an enormous firefight within the city, the Dronon discharging weapons, the whistling hunting cries of the sfuz. He'd run out of time to hunt any longer, so he'd been hurrying back to Maggie, to bring Maggie and the others, when the Dronon suddenly ambushed him.

He recalled discharging his weapons, a great battle of sword upon chitin there in the tunnels. Whirling like madness, kicking, punching, till the blows of the Dronon beat him down. He remembered his mantle sliding off.

Nothing more. Nothing thereafter.

I've died, he decided. I've died, and Felph brought me back.

Beside the bed on a chair lay his clothes—a new white tunic, with the black robes of a Lord Protector folded neatly beneath, and under them all, his battle gloves. To the back of the chair were strapped his weapons—the vibro-blade in its sheath, his incendiary rifle in its holster. At the foot of the chair lay his boots, black and polished.

All the clothes seemed too clean, too fresh.

Gallen got up, examined himself. He felt . . . odd. He pulled on the white tunic, wondering what kind of world he'd awakened to. What now, now that the Dronon had won? Which worlds would resist Dronon rule; which would succumb? Worst of all, who would embrace the Dronon?

Obviously, the Dronon had begun building their own world gates, sending ships through. Otherwise, they could not have reached him here on Ruin, not so fast. It had only been a matter of time before the Dronon developed such technology. Now all the human-occupied worlds would be within the Dronon's grasp.

But what of Maggie?

If I died, Gallen feared, then she must be dead, too. He'd been so close to her hiding place when the Dronon took him. They'd have found her.

It takes six weeks to grow a clone, Gallen realized. She's been dead for six weeks. And Maggie had never had her memories recorded. She was dead, and would remain so forever.

Gallen did not want to live under Dronon rule, in a world without Maggie.

Though he could not bear the thought of living without her, Gallen knew he would go on.

He would fight. He'd continue fighting, and fighting. A hundred lifetimes, a thousand.

So the struggle continues. He felt heartsick. Perhaps already, a new Lord Protector from the human worlds had defeated Kintiniklintit. Someone would have to step into the role. Gallen did not envy that person.

Gallen stood a moment, slipped on his new tunic. A new tunic they give me, he realized, because the other is torn and bloody. He gazed down at the chair. Beneath the tunic lay his mantle—the black rings polished and free of rust, the memory crystals gleaming wildly. A small thing, so beautiful—yet so powerful.

He picked it up, turned it over and over in his hand. Should I put it on?

He did not want to. Orick had criticized him for his hardness, for his willingness to take on every battle, for his desire to right all wrongs.

Balance and perspective. He'd lost that once. Perhaps because he'd lost it, he'd lost Maggie in the bargain.

Though the mantle brought him power, it did so at too high a price.

Gallen sat back on the bed, hung his head, and wept.

It was a long hour later when he felt well enough to put on the rest of his clothes, slipping the mantle into the pocket of his robe.

He wondered where Orick might be, if at least the bear had come out of the tangle alive. He doubted it. Orick would have fought the Dronon when they came for Maggie, Gallen thought.

So Orick would be dead, too.

Did Lord Felph revive Gallen simply to finish his quest, to go back in search of the Waters of Strength? Possibly so. A job left undone.

A meaningless job.

It seemed unfair.

Gallen got up, stretched, and looked out his window. He recognized this wing of the palace. The north wing. The rose gardens lay beneath him, the great peacock fountain glistening black on a small hill among the throng of roses—sapphire and peach, flame and saffron.

Though rain pummeled the windows, he considered going out for a walk. No, for a rose. A blood-red rose. Something beautiful, that you can touch and smell and hold.

He stood watching the gray clouds sweep over the valley in waves. The roses seemed to beckon him, the golden ones a reminder of sunshine among the deep gray.

As he stood gazing out the window, they came to him.

The great wooden doors behind him swung open, and Maggie swept in, ran across the room, and as he turned, she leapt into his arms, hugging him, kissing his eyelids, his forehead, his lips.

She tasted the same as ever, her lips so sweet. She smiled hugely, weeping for joy. "You're awake. You're awake. It's been days!"

Nothing had changed about her. Her eyes sparkled when she looked at him; her womb seemed a little larger, a little more full. Gallen stared at her face in wonder, holding her head in the palm of his hand, wanting to kiss her, wanting to just hold her in his sight.

Orick and Tallea bounded in behind Maggie, and the bears kindly kept their distance, staring up at Gallen shyly.

Like a floodgate, the questions poured from Gallen. Maggie and Orick told a story that was remarkable—as joyous as it was improbable.

"How did I die?" Gallen asked, hoping he had died well.

"You didn't," Maggie said. "You were wounded by the Dronon, wounded so badly, we carried you to the battlefield here before the palace. We fought Kintiniklintit, and just when we thought all was lost, the Qualeewoohs came and saved us—Cooharah and Aaw."

"The Qualeewoohs?" Gallen asked. "Saved us. How?"

Orick said, "The Qualeewoohs you freed, they came back to pay for Herm's life—to give their lives for the one they took. They challenged Cintkin and Kintiniklintit for Right of Charn."

Gallen listened to him, incredulous. He could recall nothing—no battle, no ride to the palace.

"Don't you remember anything?" Maggie asked.

Gallen shook his head.

Maggie said, "The battles were magnificent. The Qualeewoohs fly twice as fast as Dronon, and they fight in pairs, while the Lord Escorts must stand up to them alone. The thunderstorms swept in just as the battle began, bringing in a heavy mist and fog. Kintiniklintit never knew what hit him. The Qualeewoohs attacked from behind, like starlings harrying a crow, and drove him into the sky. He spit acid, but the Qualeewoohs wheeled and spun at such dizzying speeds, he never fazed them. When he got high enough, they ripped his wings so he tumbled to earth. His head split under the impact of the fall. Then they went after the Golden Queen, marked her with their talons."

"I saw this?" Gallen asked.

Maggie nodded, so calm, so self-assured. Of course it had happened. Gallen recalled the Qualeewoohs from the wild, so beautiful, regal, faintly ridiculous in their spirit masks.

Lord Felph had discounted them, thinking them nothing, impotent. But the predators on this world moved so swiftly, had evolved so differently from anything on Earth—or on Dronon—that in aerial combat, the Qualeewoohs had distinct advantages. No, Gallen didn't doubt that the Qualeewoohs could have won. He only doubted that he could have seen any such thing and forgotten so completely.

"I—don't remember anything like it," Gallen said.

Maggie smiled at him gently. "You were delirious. The Dronon beat you so badly. Perhaps the memories will come back in time." She reached up, stroked his face. "And Gallen, there's more.

"The Qualeewoohs challenged the lords of the other five swarms, defeated each in turn, humiliated them."

Gallen could not believe it. It seemed a dream come true, too good to be real. He looked to Orick for confirmation. "It's true, lad. The Dronon have fallen and shall never rise again. The Qualeewoohs won control, and Aaw has commanded the Dronon to return to their home world, and never leave again. She's destroying their world gates, removing all records of the technology. Yet she's done more.

"The Qualeewoohs are painting spirit masks on all the Dronon. They don't believe that the Dronon have a total lack of compassion. The Qualeewoohs hope someday to train them, to prepare them to join the rest of the galaxy in peace. They'll never trouble us again."

Gallen looked at them all, suspicious. He found the whole story so implausible, he didn't know how to respond. " 'Never' is a long time, Orick."

"Never, Gallen," Maggie said firmly. "Never! We have the Qualeewoohs' promise."

Gallen felt startled, uneasy. "How can they keep that promise?"

"Cooharah and Aaw have drunk from the Waters of Strength," Orick said. "I found it, but too late to do you any good. The Dronon will never beat them in combat."

Gallen considered. Qualeewoohs that would never die. Conquerors of time and space, nature and self. He wondered at what it all meant.

Glancing from face to face, he settled upon Orick. "You found the Waters?"

Orick nodded slightly.

"And you drank from them?"

Orick shook his head, looked down at the floor. "I didn't dare. They weren't made for the likes of us. Zeus tried to drink from them. What happened to him was too terrible to tell. The Qualeewoohs' ancestors came to judge him, and they killed him."

"But what of the sfuz? They drink the Waters, and derive some benefit."

Orick shook his head. "That's debatable. Lord Felph has a theory. He believes that the Waters create a construct based upon your consciousness. And while the sfuz show some signs of intelligence, they don't seem to be fully self-aware. So they don't get the full benefits from the Waters of Strength, and the ancestors don't feel the need to put them in judgment."

"In judgment?" Gallen asked.

Tallea spoke up. "The caverns where the cisterns lie are full of bones, Qualeewooh bones, from those who were destroyed for drinking the Waters. Not everyone who drinks is allowed to enter their heaven."

Gallen studied his old friend's face, then scratched behind Orick's ears. Gallen had dozens more questions, but asked none for the moment.

The answers he heard left him unsettled. He knew that Orick was hiding something.

So he celebrated that night with his friends, a grand feast in Felph's palace. Felph's latest clone led the celebration, with Hera and Athena in attendance, along with the servant Dooring and all the others in the household staff. To Gallen's great surprise, Thomas Flynn showed up. Orick had met him in the depths of the tangle, and Thomas played his latest songs on the lute.

One of the songs he sang was a ballad, which told how he had followed Felph into the tangle, and what he saw in the depths beneath Teeawah, when Zeus drank the Waters of Strength. And he sang of his journey out, how Orick and Tallea had fought the horde of sfuz that had begun to revive, that sfuz that barred his way back to the Dronon's shuttle.

Of all the strange tales that Gallen heard that day, Thomas's fascinated him most. To lose a companion on one world, and find him in another galaxy, seemed marvelous beyond the telling.

So he partied, and he celebrated the fall of the Dronon empire, and in his heart he wondered, and worried.

It was not until four days later that the rains broke for a bit, and then Gallen insisted that he and Orick go for a walk alone in the fields in front of the palace.

The fields were green, new grass sprouting in abundance. Everywhere lay signs of the Dronon—great holes in the ground where their ship had set down, the trampled fields where their millions had circled the killing field.

Gallen surveyed the field a bit, then walked over to a spot on the ground, a spot dark with pooled blood. Two pools, side by side. Over the past seven weeks, the blood had first dried black, then soaked into the ground, killing the grass.

Gallen went to the spots, gazed down and touched them with his toe. They told the story that Orick would have hid, and Gallen asked, "Where did you bury us, Orick?"

The kindly bear gazed up, licked his lips, considering what story to tell now.

"Where did you bury us?" Gallen asked. "I want to see Maggie's grave."

Orick nodded toward a slight rise, where three hawthorn trees trembled in the breeze. The ragged clouds whipped overhead, so that the trees stood first in sunlight, then in shadow, their leaves rattling softly.

Gallen went to the unmarked graves—two small plots, mud mixed in with the new tendrils of growing grass.

"Maggie's here, on the left," Orick said, his voice choked from emotion. "And you're on the right."

Seeing the graves did something to Gallen, filled him with a nameless ache he'd never imagined, an ache too large to either hold or express. He wanted to cry out, but that would change nothing. He wanted to deny it.

So this is what I come to, he told himself as he knelt above Maggie's grave. He brushed his hand over the new grass, as if it were hair, felt the water tickling his palms.

This is what I come to.

Orick had warned him. Gallen knelt on the grass and sobbed for a long time, until the pain gave way to emptiness, enough emptiness that he could speak again.

"Maggie doesn't know about this, does she?" Gallen asked.

Orick shook his head. "No. We checked her memories. She doesn't really want to know—just as you didn't want to know. She wants to go back, for everything to be like it was. She wants to live with you, have the baby you planned together. We can't undo the past. This is the best we could give her. Felph cloned her body. She was wearing your mantle when she died, and she knew her death was coming. The mantle downloaded her memories into a crystal. Yours were already stored in Felph's AI. They'd been radioed ahead."

"How can she not know that she's died?" Gallen asked.

"In the end, Felph edited her final memories of the battle. He just altered some of them so that Maggie didn't recall her final wound being so serious. The Dronon took holos of the fight. It was easy for Felph to get images of the Qualeewoohs coming to the rescue. Maggie just doesn't know they came too late, that they stood over your corpses and fought like—like dragons."

"I learned the truth easily enough," Gallen said. "I knew we were dead. In time, Maggie might figure it out, too."

"How? How could you know?" Orick asked. "Felph duplicated every mole, every scar. He . . . he even cloned Maggie's baby from her womb, let it grow inside her. That was a task, mind you!"

"Oh, I look the same," Gallen said, "But I don't feel the same. The knife scar on my right wrist—it always used to ache when it grew cold, when the rains came. The scar there now looks much the same, but it doesn't go deep enough. Some scars go too deep."

"But—you won't tell Maggie?" Orick asked. "We went through so much work!"

Gallen considered. "It was kind of you," he said at last. "I won't tell her. I think she'll be happier not knowing."

He sighed, reached into his pocket, and pulled out his mantle. It kept a record of every battle that its wearers had ever fought, recorded far more than perhaps Orick knew. Gallen had not worn it since reawakening, for he had not been sure he wanted to know how his last battle had ended.

Now, he donned the mantle, pulled its familiar weight over his head, felt an easy tenseness fill his body, as always happened when the mantle made connection, assuming partial control of his neural system.

Then, he sat beneath the tree and asked Orick, "Will you excuse me for a few minutes. There's something I must do."

Beneath the shade of the hawthorns, gazing out over the green valley that had filled with Dronon warships only weeks before, he whispered to his mantle, "Show me my death."

Gallen felt the familiar lurch as his viewpoint shifted, and he saw these fields as they had been, the grass much shorter, less alive, with the Dronon circling in their millions.

The sight awed him, the Dronon queens beneath their crimson pavilions, the sounds of their cheering, the warships in the background.

He watched the entire battle from Maggie's eyes, felt her love for him, her burning desire to defend him to the last moment, felt how she craved his kiss and his touch, her horror at watching as the Lord Escort slashed Gallen nearly in two.

He watched her bravely kick one last time, trying to strike a blow against the Dronon, felt her surprise as Kintiniklintit sliced her nearly in two. For half a second she had looked down, seen her own gut spilling into the grass, and then fainted.

The mantle fell from her head, disengaged from her consciousness.

In that last moment, Gallen had crawled to her, looked into her face, his own visage a study in sorrow and despair. He was beaten and bruised, blood running free. A frothy red foam boiled from his mouth, and his breath came in shallow pants.

In the distance, lightning flashed and thunder shook the earth as a great storm rolled in. Gallen had glanced toward the storm, whispering "Angels," and then turned suddenly.

In that last moment, he grasped the mantle that had fallen to the grass. With one hand he pulled it over Maggie's head and whispered the command: "Save her."

The recording went blank for several long minutes as the mantle diverted all its energies to downloading Maggie's memories. It was an odd moment, a tremendous wrench in consciousness, for Gallen suddenly saw the world not as himself, but as the mantle saw it. All external sensors were turned off, and the mantle sent electromagnetic pulses through Maggie's brain, firing all neurons.

Though she lay dying, the mantle was able to draw out her memories, like wispy fragments of vivid dreams, and shoot them through its programs, reconstruct the pathways and scenery of her mind, manipulate it into a sequential tale, till it formed a coherent whole.

The process should have taken three minutes, but Maggie expired before the second minute finished, and her mantle had to assume some of the autonomic body functions, force her severed lungs to breath, her fibrillating heart to beat, just long enough to finish its download.

When the mantle completed its duty, it turned its external sensors back on, began recording.

Kintiniklintit was in the process of defiling Gallen's corpse. The Lord of the Seventh Swarm had decapitated Gallen, chopped him into several pieces, and was parading the headless corpse past cheering Vanquishers.

And in that moment, the Qualeewoohs landed in the midst of the battlefield, eyeing the Dronon in that stupid-looking way that birds have. Lightning flashed from the advancing storm, and its light reflected from the silver in their spirit masks.

Even the Dronon recognized that something odd was happening.

Cooharah and Aaw began bobbing their heads, whistling loudly, and Athena was forced to run into Felph's palace for a bit to fetch a translator. It took nearly half an hour for her to return, for the Qualeewoohs to grasp what was happening, and then to issue their challenge to Lord Kintiniklintit.

By then, the storm had come in full upon them; the towering thunderheads turned morning into a mockery of night. Rain pounded the ground, and thunder shook the skies. Raging winds whipped across the battlefield, blowing the crimson pavilions down.

And in the driving storm, the Qualeewoohs took flight with Lord Kintiniklintit. Across the fields, the Dronon jeered the ungainly Qualeewoohs, who were so much smaller than a Dronon Lord, so much more slender and less powerful.

Yet when the Qualeewoohs took to the sky, they were a marvel! They swooped and soared through the pounding rain, and while Kintiniklintit began to circle in an effort to get up to battle speed, the Qualeewoohs swooped in from behind, began pecking out his rear eye cluster.

The great Vanquisher redoubled his speed, seeking to escape. The labored sound of his buzzing wings came as a weary drone, and on the fields below, the Dronon hosts fell silent, their cheers forgotten.

It was apparent from the opening seconds of battle that Kintiniklintit could not win.

He tried to turn, and maneuvers that had seemed sleek and deadly before now looked ungainly beside the Qualeewoohs. They stooped in behind him, began attacking his wings, ripping off the back edges so that they fell away like scales.

Those wings had been deadly to a human. The reinforced cartilage along their leading edge could chop a man in half. But the Qualeewoohs were attacking from behind, ripping the wings apart at their weakest point.

Kintiniklintit fought madly, trying to slap his wings backward, strike a blow in flight. Twice he smashed Aaw in the face, knocking the little Qualeewooh backward, nearly felling her from the sky. Gallen's heart went out to her.

But the Vanquisher's tactics only enraged Cooharah, so that he fought more vehemently.

In a last effort to dodge his opponents, Kintiniklintit veered upward, as if trying to escape in the clouds. Climbing toward a wisp of fog, Gallen thought he'd almost make it. He imagined that the Dronon could then swoop down, playing hunt and hide in the mist.

Till lightning struck, a blinding flash that blew the Dronon lord from the air, so that he tumbled in flaming ruin.

This astonished Gallen, for the manner of Kintiniklintit's death was nothing like the story told by Maggie. But then Gallen had to remind himself, Maggie wasn't really there to witness the battle. She bore false memories.

Afterward, Cooharah and Aaw had swooped low, clawing Cintkin so that she lost her right to rule as Golden Queen.

Then, with some coaching from Hera, the birds realized that they had to perform the same feat over and over again.

Five times they challenged the Dronon Lords, and Gallen watched as the Lord Escort of the First Swarm crashed to the ground, just as Maggie had described.

He watched the magnificent Qualeewoohs battle, saw Cooharah get struck down, wounded in his third skirmish, so that Aaw had to fight on alone.

Not all their victories were convincing. Not all the battles pretty. With each victory, the surviving Swarm Lords were forced to fight with greater desperation, greater cunning.

The final Lord Escort did not even leave the ground; he instead opted to fight on land, his great battle arms poised, batting almost blindly at Aaw as she swooped time and again, too fast, too fast for him to react, till she left him blind and crippled. She could not finish him. She didn't have the strength to pierce his thick chitin. So he lived, in shame, as she went after his Golden Queen.

It was, perhaps, an unprecedented move. Gallen knew from his mantle that Lord Escorts were never spared in battle. If a Lord Escort chose only to wound a Golden Queen, leaving her alive, then he would become her mate. But a living Lord Escort, one horribly wounded and disfigured, could serve no purpose in Dronon society. It would only be killed by workers, used to fertilize the fields.

So for Aaw to leave this useless Vanquisher alive was the ultimate insult.

When at last Aaw struck the final Golden Queen, the Dronon Swarms fell silent. Indeed, they were more than silent. They were unmoving, statuesque. Gallen wondered if they had died. He'd never seen a Dronon in shock.

But now the entire Dronon worlds stood astonished, as Cooharah and Aaw landed in the midst of the field, growing muddy from the pounding rain, and sat panting, preening their feathers.

Through all this, Orick did not arrive.

And when Maggie's body had grown cold, and at last the Dronon swarms had begun to recover from their shock enough to prostrate themselves and offer obeisance to the Qualeewoohs, then Orick's shuttle came, through the pounding rains, and the poor bear rushed out onto the battlefield, checked Maggie's body, sorrowed over Gallen, then bore a canteen of water to the two bedraggled birds.

Gallen took readings from the clock in his mantle. Two hours. Orick had come to the rescue two hours too late.

When Gallen removed his mantle, he sat for a long moment and rubbed his eyes.

So, there was truth to Orick's tale. The Dronon were defeated. Perhaps forever.

Gallen talked with Orick for a long while, until clouds blew in and it began to rain anew. In the shelter of the hawthorns, Orick related much of what had happened—how he'd gone into the tangle, retrieved the Waters of Strength, and escaped back into the tangle with Thomas, fleeing to the ship that Karthenor had loaned Felph.

Cooharah had at first rejected the Waters. "This life is not given to us for our own use," he had said. "We exist to serve one another, nothing more. You cannot purchase my life. I give it freely."

Yet in the end, he had agreed to accept immortality, commune more deeply with his ancestors.

"But why didn't you drink the Waters yourself?" Gallen asked. "It could have been *you* fighting the Dronon."

"Och, man, after what happened to Zeus?" Orick said. "You couldn't have paid me! Besides, I'm not one to spend eternity lording it over a bunch of Dronon. I've got better things to do, thank you."

Gallen asked, "What of the canteen, the one filled with the Waters? Surely the birds did not drink it all?"

"No," Orick said. "They didn't. I sold it to Felph. He didn't have a recording of what had happened when Zeus drank, so he wanted to try it himself. I sold it to him cheap. I just asked him to give you and Maggie the rebirth, pretend that nothing had ever happened."

"And what happened to Felph when he drank?" Gallen asked.

"He hasn't, yet," Orick answered. "He's just held on to it."

"For seven weeks?" Gallen said.

"I think he's debating," Orick grumbled. "If he drinks it, he won't have a sample left to analyze, see if we can duplicate it. But if he keeps testing the stuff, he soon won't have anything left to drink. . . ."

"I see," Gallen said, satisfied. He got up from under the tree, stood thinking for a long time. "Orick, you once told me that I should not fight, that I should cease to struggle. You said I could run from the Dronon, or hide. In effect, you said that if I quit fighting, God would fight my battles. The world would go on without me."

"I did?"

"You did," Gallen said, grateful that he remembered anything at all from the past. "Maybe your god didn't fight for me, but the Qualeewoohs fought in his place. Maybe you were right."

"Are you certain it wasn't God who fought for you?" Orick asked. "I've been thinking on it. Maybe the Qualeewoohs were just His tools, in the same way that David and Joshua were His tools."

"You think?" Gallen asked.

"And if that's true, maybe you were right to fight, Gallen. Maybe God needs people like you."

Gallen shook his head, uncertain. He affected his old brogue accent, putting it on now as if it were an old, favorite cloak. "Orick—right now, I don't think I ever want to fight again. It's a long rest I'm wanting. Certain I am, I don't want to expose Maggie to more dangers."

"Och." Orick sighed. "Well, if anyone ever deserved a rest, it's you."

"But I doubt I'll rest easy," Gallen said. "In a few months, maybe a year, I'll hear of some outrage, and I'll want to go right to it. The Lords of Tremonthin made me that way. It's in my blood. We are our bodies. I can't be any different. I'm afraid that sometime in the future, you'll just be burying me again."

"Maybe," Orick said, "maybe not. You say you are your body, but I've a feeling there's more to you than the Lords of Tremonthin know. I'd say that you're *also* your body. You're a being of spirit, too.

"Gallen, you and Maggie are good friends. I managed to win you back from the grave once, but I don't want to see you there again. I want you to live forever. If not here, then in the Kingdom of God.

"And if it's a fight you're craving, then fight the pull of your flesh, Gallen. You'll find a sweeter victory than you'll ever win out here in the killing fields!"

Gallen gazed down to the circle below, where the grass lay untrampled, where his body had finally succumbed, and felt that perhaps Orick was right.

He whispered, "Damn, you'll make a handy priest someday, Orick."

"Not a priest," Orick said. "Just a missionary."

They went home then, walking to Felph's palace in a miserable, pouring rain. Gallen leaned his head back, caught droplets in his mouth, while Orick sermonized to him.

Forty-eight

O ver the next eight weeks, everyone took their ease. Gallen found that Orick was serious about his missionary work. Tallea kept her snout in the Scriptures for days on end, sitting at Maggie's side. But Tallea wasn't his only convert.

Orick baptized Athena in the fountains outside the palace, and even Lord Felph seemed to listen to the bear with something of an open mind, though he made no formal declarations of conversion.

And Orick began traveling about Ruin, preaching to all who would listen— poachers, scientists, madmen. It didn't seem to matter. He made a few converts in his first two weeks, and chief among them was Felph's personal body servant, Dooring, who came in tears and begged Gallen and Maggie for forgiveness. He admitted to being the one who'd notified the authorities as to their location. The Dronon had found them because of him.

Gallen frankly forgave the man, and after that, Dooring accompanied Orick on all his trips, flying him about by florafeem. With Felph's beautiful daughter Athena in his retinue, and Thomas to lead in singing the hymns, Orick "the baptizing bear" got a reputation for putting on quite a show, and he endeared himself to many, though he made few converts.

In his preparations to leave Ruin, he ordained Dooring to the office of High Priest, setting him in charge of all the spiritual affairs on Ruin.

. . .

There was one woman Orick despaired of converting: Hera.

He spoke to her passionately and often, yet Hera remained distant. She'd asked about the manner of Zeus's death, had heard the sad tale, and then thanked him, coldly. After that, it was as if she never really listened to a word he spoke.

Hera dared not tell Orick what so disturbed her: it was that she loved Zeus still. Despite his infidelities, despite his greed, she had loved him as a wife for many years. Would always love him.

Orick swore that Zeus had been killed by his own wickedness. And yet, and yet—how could that be? Hera wondered. Zeus was a created being. He was what Lord Felph had made. If Zeus had faults, they were not of his own creation.

It was unfair of the Qualeewooh ancestors to have judged him so harshly.

And there was another secret that Hera dared not speak: the belief that the bear was lying to her. If Orick and his friends were to be believed, then her husband had killed Arachne, had confessed to the deed just before his death.

She couldn't imagine that. Arachne had been her closest friend, her closest advisor. Zeus had never trusted the woman, thought she was too wise, yet he'd never hated her, either.

No, Hera imagined that someone else had killed Arachne. Gallen, perhaps, or even Orick. She could think of no good reason that they would commit such a murder. She could hardly admit to herself that she harbored such notions. Yet the uneasy feeling would not go away.

So Hera became distant, seldom speaking to the others.

She cleaned out her room, removing all reminders of Zeus, disconsolate. She folded his clothes, pressing her nose into them to catch a trace of his scent, before tossing them into a garbage chute. She got rid of his combs and brush, his razor and lotions. She kept only a sheaf of love poems that he'd written to her, and these she placed in the bottom of her dresser.

And when she'd finished removing all traces of him, she decided to do the same for Herm and Arachne.

Herm's room was not much of a room—an aerie high in the palace with a door that had been permanently locked from the inside. He'd always entered the room from an ancient cloo hole. He'd even installed a perch outside his room.

It took a service droid nearly half an hour to gain entry, and once Hera opened the room, she wished that she hadn't. Herm's room was such a filthy mess, she could never have imagined it. In every corner were twigs and leaves and tufts of grass, a pile of hay to sleep on, loose feathers in everything.

The twigs were often nailed to the wall—as if, as if Herm had been fascinated by their shapes. Indeed, Hera looked at one slender twig on the wall, and it reminded her very much of the stream that flowed beneath the palace, the silver stream with its tributaries running through it. She wondered if this was what had mesmerized Herm, the way the branches must look like rivers from the air.

But no, many of the twigs were just scattered on the floor, thrown into piles, as if, over time, Herm had become careless with his prizes. Here and there among the twigs were other things—bits of a broken blue pot, pieces of shiny metal.

Herm had little in the way of possessions. There were several odd combs—some for hair, some for his feathers. He had a long woodwind flute sitting on pegs on one wall. Hera remembered that years ago, sometimes, in the evenings, he would play that flute, and the eerie music would drift over the palace.

But he'd never learned to play human songs. His woodwind only echoed the breeze as it sang through rocks and glens, or sighed over a field. Never a tune, just a mournful howling.

And everywhere in the room were the small white-and-brown feathers from his wings. It looked as if Herm had preened in here for years and never cleaned the place. Bits of himself were everywhere.

As Hera surveyed the place she realized that it did not look like a human room at all. It looked like a nest.

The sight of it nearly broke Hera's heart.

She'd never known that Herm had so much of the bird in him. Never known how truly alien he was. He was not human at all, she considered, looking at the room.

He was my brother, and I never knew him. He must have been so lonely. So lonely.

Yet he'd seemed so normal.

It was the Guide, she realized. He'd never been free to become anything but what his Guide had made of him. If he'd been free, perhaps he would have flown away, made a life for himself in some mountain aerie.

Hera left the room, taking only the woodwind, and ordered the droids to dispose of the remaining junk.

Afterward she hurried down to Arachne's room.

Arachne, her dearest friend and counselor.

The room was much as she'd remembered. A huge wall filled with bobbins of bright thread made from silk and wool, the vast loom filling most of the room, the small bed in a corner, where Arachne hardly ever slept—for she'd worked night and day at the loom.

It was just as Hera recalled from nearly four months ago, on the day of the invasion, when she'd come searching for Arachne at Lord Felph's request.

Except that on that day, she'd only been looking for Arachne. She hadn't really *studied* the room.

Now, Hera gazed down at the loom, at the images that Arachne had been weaving before her death. There, on the last portion of the tapestry, in a lower corner where it was plain to see, Arachne had woven a picture of herself. In her right hand, she held Gallen and Maggie, and a horde of Dronon Vanquishers were appearing on the horizon behind. Arachne knelt, hunched, as if shielding Maggie with her body.

Standing over Arachne was Zeus, a bloody knife in hand, making a stabbing motion. On Arachne's chest was a small, bloody puncture wound.

So it's true, Hera realized. Zeus murdered her, just as she knew he would. Hera bit her lower lip. And I was too blind to see it.

Hera spent the rest of the day in her rooms, weeping.

That night, shortly after dinner had passed, Lord Felph came to Hera's bedroom.

He stood just inside the door, under the cluster of purple lights. The mellow scene of cypresses outside the evening pools went well with his dark green tunic.

"I don't mean to disturb you, but we missed you at dinner," Felph said. "I do hope you've ordered the droids to bring you something."

"I'm not hungry, Father," Hera said, rising from her bed. She turned her back to him, went and looked out the window. It was early evening, and the day had been mostly clear. But she could see more golden clouds, waiting on the horizon, out above the fields.

Felph's vineyards and fields looked lush and green. Inviting.

Hera had an odd memory, from when she was a child. She'd often longed to run in those fields outside the palace, to explore the stream, or play hide-and-seek in the hawthorn groves. But in those days, there had been giants in the land: purple giants that each carried a huge club. She remembered them clearly, the rotting furs they wore, the single huge horn in their foreheads.

"Father, whatever happened to the giants?" Hera mused.

"Giants?" Felph asked.

"The ones outside my window, in the fields. I used to see them hunting."

Felph laughed softly. "Ah, those. They were only images programmed into your Guide. I didn't want you straying from the palace, you see, so the Guide showed you the giants from time to time, to keep you here."

"I see," Hera said. "When I was a child, you used to say that I wore a Guide because I was a princess. You said all princesses wore crowns."

Felph laughed. "I'd forgotten."

"Am I still a princess?" Hera asked.

"Of course you are," Felph said. "You'll always be my little princess."

"And when you die, what will I inherit?" Hera asked.

"What would you like?" Felph asked.

Hera just looked away, shook her head. He's already dead inside, she thought. And all I've inherited is . . . desolation. He wouldn't let himself pass away permanently.

No, I'll get nothing from him.

"What do you want?" Felph asked again, more loudly.

Freedom. Love. Love. Love. Freedom.

Hera shook her head, unwilling to speak. In consternation she finally answered. "You're the one who should have died in Teeawah, you know. You're the one who made us what we are. You should have drunk the Waters of Strength."

For a long moment, Felph did not say anything.

"You think so?" he asked.

"Yes, I do," Hera said firmly.

"Then I will, tonight," Felph pronounced. "And you shall be there to watch."

So that evening, Lord Felph finally drank the Waters of Strength. He'd wasted most of it, trying to analyze the stuff. He'd found that though it was clear like water, it contained strange amino acids in numbers far too large and in sequences far too complex to be adequately catalogued. Beyond that, he found mixtures of suspended elements, along with nano devices for assembling them into something which he just couldn't quite grasp.

So it was that he gathered his friends and family in one of the lower plazas of the palace late in the evening. Brightstar shone like a brilliant moon, upon the circle of palms.

Felph had everyone get back, then he unstopped a small flask, and touched only a single crystalline drop to his lips. Hera saw it fall in the night, like a gem, into Felph's mouth.

Then she watched in fascination and horror as Felph underwent his transformation.

It happened precisely as Orick had described: the purple glowing eyes, the manic exclamations from Felph describing how he felt tremendous power, the dark-winged beast that struggled to emerge from Felph's mouth, tear free forever.

Then the emerald birds of light appeared, wheeling under the stars, like a whirling, flashing tornado.

They came not in ones or twos, but in dozens and hundreds, until the heavens filled with them.

Then as one they stooped to slaughter the winged beast that was Lord Felph.

He wriggled like a bat, flying through the heavens, seeking escape. Unlike Zeus, he did not try to take shelter in his body once again. Instead, he darted and veered.

But there was no escape. The birds of light caught him, tore into him, by the dozens, fighting for the honor to kill the beast. And high above the tiny group, Felph exploded into a ball of purple light that hung like a glowing cloud for several minutes.

Hera thought it was as pretty as any firework she'd ever seen.

Hours later, a new Lord Felph emerged from the revivification chamber, bearing the recorded memory of how the Qualeewooh ancestors had judged him unworthy.

This newly born Felph seemed a much more subdued, more thoughtful man.

I t was a scant five days later that Maggie gave birth to Gallen's son, a whopping large child with eyes of a darkest blue and dark hair with a tinge of red.

Gallen wanted to call him after his own father, but Maggie insisted on calling the babe Orick, and Gallen felt that it, too, was a fitting name for the boy.

If it seems that peace came easily to Gallen and his friends after the Dronon, know that it did not come easily to all.

For Tallea loved Orick as a woman loves her husband, but Orick still felt torn by the issue.

Two days after Maggie gave birth, as Tallea pored over the Scriptures at Maggie's beside while Maggie lay propped on some pillows suckling her son, Tallea mentioned her problem to Maggie.

"Orick's a fine bear," Maggie said, "and certainly he'll never find another she-bear like you. Everyone wants you two to marry, and I think you should. It only makes sense."

"But Orick won't marry me until he feels God has freed him from the vow of chastity he took in his heart," Tallea said.

"You need a miracle," Maggie said, then Maggie got the strangest faraway look in her eye.

"What are you thinking?" Tallea asked.

"I think . . . Tallea, may I borrow your Scriptures for a day or two?"

"Yes . . ." Tallea said, unsure.

She did not see the Bible again for three days. It was a busy time, as they packed their things and prepared to leave Ruin. Gallen and Maggie wanted to return to Tremonthin, to build a home in a glen they'd seen in the mountains east of Battic.

In truth, the days were not busy so much from packing. Most of the time was spent saying goodbyes, for by that time, Orick knew everyone on planet, and all were sad to see him depart.

Tallea found that as for her, she'd become most closely attached to Hera and Athena. After Tallea had returned from the tangle, she and Orick had reached the killing field only moments after the Qualeewoohs faced the Swarm Lords in their deadly battle.

The Dronon were still on planet, trying to make sense of the Qualeewoohs' orders. Felph was dead, and his AI didn't know yet to revive him.

Hera and Athena had been forced to take charge. They'd taken the first cell cultures from Gallen's and Maggie's bodies. They'd freed Thomas from his Guide. They'd acted as liaisons between the Qualeewoohs and the Dronons, and revivified their own father to help give some direction.

If it had not been for Hera and Athena, everything would have fallen apart. Tallea imagined that literally, the fragile accord that was forged between the three species would have foundered.

Felph had created his daughters to be leaders and counselors, and they fulfilled their role admirably.

In those few brief days, Tallea had grown to depend on the young women, and upon Thomas and Orick.

So she found it difficult to say goodbye to these people. Tallea moped about the palace, in company with Hera and Athena, and none of them broached the subject of departure until the last few hours after the ship was fueled and packed.

Lord Felph had a formal luncheon for his guests, during which he gave each of them a few small gifts to show his gratitude. To Gallen and Maggie, he gave seeds from his gardens and orchards, along with a small vial filled with water. "The Waters of Strength," he told Gallen. "The last few precious drops, in case the need is ever great, and you dare risk drinking them."

Tallea thought the gift inappropriate, considering what she'd seen happen when mere humans drank from those waters. She didn't think it was safe for humans. But Orick had a theory. He firmly believed that the effects of the water varied not by species, but by individual.

If that were the case, then Gallen might drink safely. If he dared risk it.

To Thomas he gave a selection of several fine new instruments.

Beyond those few gifts, to Orick and Tallea he gave some exotic fruits for their journey and copies of ancient philosophical manuscripts that he felt Orick might find entertaining—the writings of Buddha and Mohammed.

And when he had given these things, Felph said, "And I have one final gift for those who have been my guests."

He turned to Hera. "To Hera and Athena, I bequeath my love, and my best wishes for a long and fruitful life."

"What . . . do you mean by that?" Hera asked.

"I've already spoken to Gallen and Maggie," Felph answered. "Their starship is small, but they can easily carry you—anywhere you want to go. Both they and I feel you should depart with them. I made you to fill large roles in the universe. This planet is too small to hold you." With that, he leaned across the table and presented each of the young women with a credit chip. "I know what you want from life, Hera. I'd give it to you if I could, but I can't. Out there, you'll find what you need—yourself, a man to love you. But I want you two to have an inheritance: each of you will receive one-third of all that I have. Believe me, it is far more than you will ever need."

Hera took the chip, and stood, breaking into huge sobs.

Felph slipped close to her, caressed her cheek with one finger. "I hope that sometimes you will think kindly of me. I promise that if you ever come to visit, you will find no monsters guarding the premises. And, hopefully, you will find no monsters within."

Hera hugged him then, and held him for a long time as she wept.

Tallea wept openly at her friends' good fortune, and for herself, for it meant that she would be able to spend some few more days with Hera and Athena. And she wondered at the change in Felph, wondered if perhaps Orick's preaching wasn't having its effect even on that cynical old crust of hardbread.

So it was decided. That night, they boarded the ship and began the journey first back to Cuzzim, where they would return the *Nightswift* to its proper owner.

From there, they would take the world gates back to Fale, a planet where Thomas wanted to renew an old acquaintance, a planet where Hera and Athena might build a new life.

And from there Tallea, Orick, Gallen, and Maggie would depart for Tremonthin, to make their own homes.

So Tallea felt little sadness when she left Ruin, watched the planet shrink on the *Nightswift*'s viewscreens. Much had changed on the world. When they'd come a few months before, the planet had been a red, angry-looking orb. Now the whole world seemed white, swathed in clouds that turned rosy pink at the terminus.

Tallea watched the planet recede, till it became a cloudy pearl that shone on a field of glittering diamonds.

T hat night, Orick and Tallea slept on the floor of the ship's hold. Maggie and Gallen used one stateroom with the baby, Orick, while Athena and Hera slept in another. Thomas had passed out on the couch in the ship's lounge, and so the bears were forced to make do.

Thus it was that Orick woke in the hold, disturbed by a strange scent—a mixture of blood and urine and something more. It seemed out of place here, among the strange odors of the *Nightswift*'s hold, but he recognized it at once, and something in him stirred.

Tallea was in heat.

Orick lay on his belly and put his paws over his nose. Trapped. He was trapped here on the ship, at least a week out from Cuzzim. Trapped in a closed space with a she-bear in heat.

It shouldn't have happened. Orick didn't know Tallea's chronological age. The Lords of Tremonthin had grown her in a vat, forcing her to reach something near maturity before downloading her memories into the bear's body. But still, Tallea was small. Orick imagined she would be no more than a year old, though it was hard to tell with bears. A small two-year-old was not much larger than a one-year-old, and a two-year-old could go into heat.

Still, Tallea seemed too young.

But Orick couldn't gainsay what his nose told him. Perhaps the Lords of Tremonthin had some esoteric reason for making Tallea small and fertile. Perhaps they'd given her maturity while sacrificing size. Whatever the reasons, Tallea was in heat.

In other rooms of the ship, Orick could hear the sound of Thomas snoring, of Gallen tossing on his bed.

Yet Orick lay alone, sniffing the scent of Tallea.

Oh, God, why do you do this to me? Orick wondered. Is this a test? I promised You—never again, never again. . . .

Orick's prayer escaped his throat as a whimper, and for a long time he just lay still, trying to control his erratic breathing, trying to still his racing heart.

Tallea lay close enough so he could hear her own deep breaths, watch the rise and fall of her chest. Her rear legs were toward him, her nose pointed somewhat toward his tail. She absently pawed with her hind leg, then moaned in her sleep. Discontent.

Even in her slumber she knew what she needed.

Orick's own glands responded to her craving. I could just crawl over there on top of her, Orick mused. I could straddle her and deliver the goods right now, while everyone is sleeping.

The thought aroused him further, and Orick raised his own muzzle in the air, half-involuntarily, and sniffed again. The smell of her was growing stronger. Here in this closed atmosphere, such scents tended to become overwhelming— the scents of fur, of Tallea's sleek fur, and of her need.

The smell made Orick dizzy. His heart pounded so hard, the blood thundered in his ears. It seemed that his brain was afire, burning, and his tongue felt thick and dry in his throat. He whimpered.

Eight more days of this, he considered. Eight days of estrus in these tight quarters. Does God want to drive me mad? Is that it?

Yes, that was it. God would punish Orick for his impure heart, his unclean thoughts, his—Orick had a sudden vision of himself, climbing on Tallea's back.

The very notion sent shivers of anticipation up his hairy spine.

Sister Tallea. She's Sister Tallea now, Orick reminded himself. She's been baptized. She's my sister in the gospel. That's it.

Now that she'd accepted the gospel, Satan was tempting Orick. It was the perfect trap! The old dark angel could lure the two of them away and secure both their souls in one fell blow!

Ah, the pity of it! Orick considered. She loves me. She yearns for me like no she-bear should. It was unnatural for the Lords of Tremonthin to do that, to give life to a she-bear who loved as deeply and firmly as any human woman could. Now the devil would use that love against them.

Orick imagined Tallea as she had been a few weeks before, rising up out of the waters of baptism, the light of God shining in her eyes—those beautiful brown eyes, that sleek dark fur, those shining claws, those inviting legs, those eyes so full of love.

Calm down, Orick told himself. You have to calm down. If thine eye offend thee, pluck it out.

But of course that Scripture didn't apply here. If Orick were to pluck out his eye just because he envisioned himself succumbing to temptation, he'd be eyeless in thirty seconds. But it wasn't his eyes he needed to pluck out. It was that other thing. It had hardened in an uncomfortable position.

Like a dog, Orick thought. You're no better than a dog.

Orick lay there, perfectly miserable, praying.

At length, Tallea rolled over, looked up at him, sniffed the air. "Something's wrong!" she whispered. "I smell blood!"

Orick didn't dare speak. In a moment she recognized the source of it.

"I'm sorry, Sister Tallea," Orick whispered. "I—I don't know what to do."

"Oh, Orick, your vow!"

"Yes," Orick whispered. "God has chosen to punish me, or test me. Or maybe it's Satan, I don't know."

"It's not just you being tested. It's both of us. We should pray."

"Good idea," Orick said. He picked up his Bible in his teeth and Tallea commanded the ship to turn up the lights in the hold. Orick had the ship close the door to the hold, so that the sound of their voices would not disturb anyone else. The air was so thick with Tallea's odor, closing the door only made it worse.

Tallea let the Bible flip open at random, and began to read:

"And from the rib, which the Lord God had taken from man, made he a woman, and he brought her unto the man.

"And Adam said, This is now bone of my bones, and flesh of my flesh: She shall be called Woman, for she was taken out of Man.

"Therefore shall a man leave his father and mother, and cleave unto his wife: and they two shall be one flesh."

Orick perked up, surprised at the Scripture she had picked to read. "Wait a minute!" He said, "Try another one."

Tallea closed the Bible and flipped it open again, near the end this time. She read:

"But from the beginning of the creation, God made them male and female.

"For this cause shall a man leave his father and mother, and cleave unto his wife.

"And they twain shall be one flesh: so then they are no more twain, but one flesh.

"What therefore God hath joined together, let not man put asunder."

Tallea looked up at Orick, her snout wrinkled in surprise. "Oh, Orick, do you think God is trying to tell us something?"

Orick frowned. "Wait a minute. Let me see that thing!"

Orick closed the Bible, closed his eyes, then flipped it open at random and opened his eyes. In the dim light, one passage seemed illuminated above the rest—a holy glow, shining down on the paper. He read:

"Marriage is honorable in all, and the bed undefiled."

The hairs raised on Orick's back. To open the Scriptures three times and find such passages, it seemed more than pure coincidence could claim. Surely this was a message. He squinted up at the ship's lights, saw that they were not brighter. He looked back down on the page. Surely that verse stood out more than all others. He gazed at it for a moment, saw the difference—the paper behind those words was whiter than the rest, somehow highlighting that verse. It was a miracle!

"But what of my vows?" Orick asked.

Tallea looked about warily. Gallen and the others were all still asleep. She whispered, "Perhaps this is God's way of telling you that it's all right for us, that this is more important to Him."

Orick didn't like the idea of taking spiritual direction from someone like Tallea. She hadn't been baptized for more than a few months. Her fur was hardly even dry, and here she was expounding the will of God to him.

"One more. Let me try one more!" Orick said. He flipped open the Bible and read silently:

"Doth not even nature itself teach you, that, if a man have long hair,
it is a shame unto him?"

Orick frowned. This had something to do with prayer—Paul spouting nonsense about the virtues of baldness, something Orick sincerely doubted he would ever experience firsthand. But then he saw it, the brightness three verses higher on the page, and he read aloud:

"Nevertheless, neither is the man without the woman, nor the woman
without the man, in the Lord."

Orick's heart pounded, and he could not think straight. Surely the Lord willed that Orick take Tallea to wife, and Orick could think of no commandment he would rather keep at the moment, yet somehow it saddened him.

He felt, in a way, that God rejected him.

Orick set the Bible down.

"Tallea, will you take me to be your lawful husband?" he asked. It was a simple vow, the kind poor folks who could not afford donations to the church would make back home. Yet all his life, this vow had been treated as sacred by everyone he knew.

"Yes," Tallea said, not knowing the more proper response. "Will you take me?"

"How can I not?" Orick whispered. "God commands it."

"Then I don't want you," Tallea said, turning away. "You can just go off and do whatever. I won't have you as my husband!"

"What?" Orick asked, shocked at the anger in her voice.

"If you're marrying me only because He says so, then I won't have you. When you're hungry and I haven't got dinner fixed, I don't want you getting mad at Him. And if someday you do get mad at Him, I don't want you taking it out on *me*. If you want me, then take me because you want *me*."

Orick did not speak for a moment, simply gazed into Tallea's eyes. In that moment he forgot she was in heat. He forgot to feel that he was inspired to make this decision. For one brief time that seemed both infinitesimal and eternal, there was only Tallea crouched on the floor of the hold before him, the woman who had given her life for him fighting the giant Derrits in the tunnels of Indallian; Tallea who had given away her dreams so that she could join him when the Lords of Tremonthin gave her back her life in the body of a bear. She'd given her life for Orick, given all her dreams for him. Certainly Tallea deserved only the best, and Orick wished he could give her all she deserved.

"Every breath I breathe from this day forward," Orick said, "I will draw for you. Every dream I dream, I will dream for you. Now I know why God so seldom gets involved in matchmaking: because there's only one she-bear like you."

"Good," Tallea said. "That's the way it should be. Now will you say it in public?"

Orick agreed, and together they woke the others on the ship, and as captain of the ship, it was Maggie who married them, and all of it was recorded by the ship's AI.

So Orick and Tallea took their vows that night flying amid the stars, in the quiet of the ship's lounge, and Orick would always remember how Tallea's eyes outshone the stars.

No woodland chapel could have been more beautiful, more reverent, or sacred.

Fifty-one

A few days after the wedding, once the travelers had landed on Cuzzim and made their way through the world gates to Fale, when Tallea and Maggie were alone feeding the babe while the men were off introducing Hera and Athena to civilization, Tallea asked Maggie about her part in the wedding.

"You had my Scriptures for those three days," Tallea accused. "And now those verses on marriage are permanently stained."

Maggie didn't deny it. "It doesn't take much for a Lord of Technicians to figure out how to train a Bible to open to certain pages. Simply crack the spine and add a line of liquid at the base of each page, so the paper thickens. If you want to highlight some verses, a little acid will bleach the paper enough so that some words stand out more than others. I did nothing wrong."

"But Orick thinks its a miracle!" Tallea said, her heart sore. She loved being married to Orick, but she couldn't rid herself of the feeling that she'd done something sneaky.

Maggie merely shrugged. "Orick wanted God to tell him to get married. He could have figured it out earlier, if he trusted the Tome completely, but he wanted to see it in the Bible. All I did was show him the verses in the Bible where God already commanded him to get married."

"What if he finds out that we tricked him?" Tallea asked.

"Did I?" Maggie asked. "God is the one who made you go into heat. Orick believes that God is the one who put those words in the Bible in the first place, and I won't argue the point."

So it was that Tallea accepted Maggie's maneuver, and the next day, Maggie, Gallen, their son, Tallea, and Orick took their leave of Hera, Athena, and Maggie's Uncle Thomas, none of them ever to meet again.

In that last meeting, more than a few tears were shed, and Hera surprised everyone by making a present to Orick. "There is something more you deserve," she said, producing a small crystal vial from behind her back.

"What's this?" Orick asked.

Hera undid the stopper. "A children's toy: we called it the Wind of Dreams. A scent to make you feel like a hero, a conqueror. Zeus and Herm used to make bets with one another for the right to take a whiff of it."

Hera undid the stopper, and the sweet scent of gardenias filled the air, but it was more than that, more than all the flowers in the world. It was a feeling that filled the air, a sensation that made Orick feel he could stride across the clouds, a feeling that he owned the universe, and the universe felt unbounded gratitude to be in his possession. A feeling that the day had been long, but the labors all well worth it. A feeling of love and acceptance.

It was a sensation heroic . . . an emotion a god would feel, resting in heaven.

"You deserve this, Orick," Hera said, "for all you've been through."

Orick looked at it in surprise. "I'm not sure anyone deserves that."

"But take it anyway," Hera asked. "To remember me by."

Gallen smiled broadly at Orick. "Take it, Orick," he said. "I swear: first Everynne, then Tallea, now Athena. I don't see why a hairy brute like you should appeal to women."

"Och, it's only because you're half-blind. Anyone ought to be able to see my charm." He gently licked Hera's cheek, kissing her goodbye.

When Maggie said goodbye to her Uncle Thomas, the last thing in the world she would have expected was a tearful farewell. He'd never been much of an uncle; had never offered a strong arm to lean on when she needed it.

But when she'd wakened after her battle with the Lords of the Seventh Swarm on Ruin, Thomas had been the one at her bedside, and he'd not left her night or day for the first three days.

She'd never expected the kind of gentle attention he'd shown her after that battle, and, frankly, she'd grown to be the kind of woman who no longer had much use for it.

Except for his songs. For he sang to her during those first dark and painful days, sang songs that were soft and sensitive and full of pain. Songs he'd composed himself.

She learned from Thomas that he'd been captured by Lord Karthenor, knew that the Aberlain had wrung information from Thomas, information that had led to Maggie's own capture. But she never did find out exactly what Thomas had to endure.

Maggie only knew, by the look in his eyes, that the old Thomas was gone, dead. Something had died behind his laughing eyes, a fire had sputtered and extinguished.

The evening before she said goodbye to him forever, Thomas came to her room on Fale with a mandolin and played for baby Orick in his crib. Lately, the lad could hardly be put to rest without Thomas's lullabies. So Thomas had told Gallen and Maggie to go for a walk by the starlit river outside Toohkansay while he cared for the child. Yet even after Gallen and Maggie returned, Thomas sang for long hours to the sleeping babe, as if hoping this gift of song would fill the boy's sleeping head, last the child a lifetime.

Maggie had listened, and when at long last Thomas fell silent and sat gazing out the window to the starlight shining on the river, Maggie said, "Your singing is more beautiful now than ever. How is that?"

"Och, I used to sing for myself," Thomas confided, "so that I could hear the praise of other folk. Now, I sing for the babies, and the children, and the young lovers in the back corners of the room, and for the old folks ambling off toward forever."

"Thank you," Maggie said.

"For what?" Thomas asked, leaning over with a grunt to put his mandolin in its case.

"For your songs. Maybe Orick won't remember, but I shall. And when he's old, I'll try to sing some of them for him."

Thomas's eyes misted at those words, and he gazed up at Maggie, then sat back in the deep rocking chair. "You're a good girl, Maggie. It's proud I am to be having you as a Flynn."

"Thank you," Maggie said.

"You were your mother's favorite, you know," Thomas said. "Three strapping boys she had, and when you were born, I told her she ought to toss you in the river—a worthless, skinny little girl, you know.

"But you were your mother's favorite. She said you were her reward for living a good life. The jewel in her heaven.

"I laughed at the notion," Thomas recalled, "but now, now I think maybe she had pegged it right. You would have made her proud. You've made me proud."

It was perhaps the only sincere compliment Thomas had ever given her, the only one she was likely to ever receive. "Thank you," was all Maggie could manage to say.

"Maggie," Thomas said. "I know I've never been much of an uncle to you, but I've been thinking: I'd like to go to Tremonthin with you. That babe of yours, he might need some kin to look after him, sometimes. . . ."

"I thought you liked it here on Fale," Maggie said. "I thought you had a woman to see."

"Oh, there are plenty of women in the galaxy, I'm starting to learn," Thomas said. "And Fale is a fine place, if you're after singing for yourself. But it doesn't matter where I am. Songs are needed everywhere. And I think that wherever I go, my songs will outlast me."

Maggie went and hugged him then, for she knew how much the offer had cost him. "There may be other women in the galaxy, Thomas," she said, "but I think there's one here on Fale that has a special hold on you. You were right all along. You've got your own road to follow, and I'll not have you dogging my steps just because I'm kin."

When she let Thomas go, he sighed; and though Maggie didn't doubt that he'd follow her to Tremonthin if she asked, she was happy to hear him sigh in relief, to see a bit of that mischievous gleam shining in the back of his eyes.

When Gallen, Maggie, their son, and Orick and Tallea took the final world gate to Tremonthin, they came to the land in high summer, when the fields lay ripe and golden. Because technology was outlawed over most of the world, Gallen and Maggie first went to the City of Life, where Maggie turned over her mantle of technology to the lords there, and Gallen laid his weapons aside for safekeeping.

They then took a brief journey to the Vale of the Bock, where they visited the Tharrin, Ceravanne, and told her of their plans to settle on her world, in the wild southlands, near Battic.

Ceravanne seemed surprised. "Are you certain you can do this, Gallen? My beloved Belorian, from whom you are cloned, could never have settled like this. He was forever seeking after adventure."

They were sitting on the lawn, beneath the shade of a portico up above the hot springs where the Bock wintered. It was a sunny day, and Gallen reached over absently, stroked the cheek of his son, Orick.

"I am more than just the clone of Belorian," Gallen answered her. "I won't repeat his mistakes. I think that loving a woman and raising a child are adventure enough for me, these days."

Ceravanne's eyes grew wide. "Why, Gallen, the way that you say that, I think perhaps you've found a peace that Belorian never knew."

Orick could tell that she wanted to say more. She merely stepped close, touched Gallen's chest shyly. "I wish you well. I only wish your father could have done so well, that I could have made him so happy."

And not for the last time, Orick wondered how a woman could love so deeply that even four hundred years after her husband's death, she could yearn for the man the way that Ceravanne yearned for Belorian now. It was so unbearlike.

Ceravanne wished them joy, and then they left, taking a slow journey by land through the ripening fields.

In the months that followed, they sailed over calm seas to reach their new home, then Gallen felled trees and let them cure for the winter, while they took apartments in the underground chambers of Battic.

By winter's end, Gallen's son could nearly stand on his own, and the child was delighted when Tallea delivered twin cubs.

That summer, Gallen and Orick built two fine houses in a wooded glen near Battic. They chose a peaceful valley filled with maple trees, where a clear river rushed through the rocks and formed small pools. It would be a good place for children and cubs to play and climb and learn to fish.

Both families lived side by side in that glen for many years. In time, neighbors began to move in, and a small village sprang up around them.

The village was a study in cultural diversity, there were over two thousand subspecies of humans about on the continent, and a full quarter of those sub-species built homes in the region. No one ever seemed to question Orick's and Tallea's origins, to wonder at talking bears. Nor did they worry about the origins of Gallen and Maggie, two seemingly normal humans in this land that had long been a stronghold for those who sported various genetic upgrades.

Gallen settled down to a life of farming, calling himself by the name of Farmer Day.

More children followed to Gallen and Maggie—two more boys, and two daughters, all of whom grew to be bright and strong. In time Maggie added enough room to her log home so that it could function as an inn, where travelers passing through brought news of distant lands. Gallen often teased her for this. As a girl she'd hated working at Mahoney's Inn—hated it so much that she'd rejected her home world. Now she seemed to love it, rising at dawn, falling down in a weary stupor at night.

The Day House, as it was called, became a favorite stopping point, known for its hospitality, and though Gallen and Maggie were considered close friends by all their neighbors, none ever heard the story of how Gallen O'Day became a Lord Protector and helped stave off the Lords of the Seven Swarms.

Indeed, though Gallen never talked of being a Lord Protector, in his bed-room he kept his mantle near his spirit mask. He seldom ever donned the mantle, and then only in great need. Many a petty thief made off with a local chicken and suffered no harm from Gallen, but once in a while, every few years, some new warlord would struggle to take control of a town, or some Derrit chieftain would bring his henchmen out of the mountains to feed on small children—only to find themselves impaled on the sword of a Lord Protector whose face shone like starlight, until a local legend arose of a just and deadly spirit, called "The Shining One."

On such occasions, Maggie hardly missed Gallen. A trip of a fortnight or two.

But at other times, Gallen would disappear for a month or more on "per-sonal business," and when the boy Orick grew old enough, Gallen would take his son with him, for the child had a knack for battle that surprised even Gallen.

On such occasions, Maggie would know that the Tharrin had sent their messages through Gallen's mantle, calling him to far worlds. But such occasions were exceedingly rare, and afterward Gallen did not speak of them, as if the killing he was forced to do shamed him.

And then one night, Gallen and the young man Orick came to Maggie, and her son wore the mantle and carried a packed bag. She knew immediately that he was going off alone. That he would never return.

"There's trouble, Mother," her son said.

Maggie nodded dumbly, knowing that the Tharrin would not have called him into service unless they had a great need. Somehow she felt relieved to find that the mantle would no longer weigh on her husband's shoulders, but she could not help worrying about her child.

When her son left that night, he walked off into the darkness, and Maggie cried until dawn. For months and months afterward, she could hardly ever speak his name.

But seven years later, he suddenly reappeared and brought a young woman with him, a ravishing thing with raven hair. A Tharrin woman. The two were married by Orick the bear, and they left days later.

From time to time, Maggie got offworld messages from them, but she never saw her son again.

Neither Gallen nor Maggie ever went back to the City of Life to have their memories downloaded. One life was all they desired.

One life lived well, together.

As for Orick, he gained a reputation as something of a wandering minister, preaching to small congregations. He somehow managed to wander far and wide, while never neglecting his wife and children at home. Indeed, his knack for showing up in the right place at the right time proved to be so uncanny, that Gallen finally forced Orick to admit that he, too, had drunk from the Waters of Strength in Teeawah.

When Gallen was an old man, in his sixties, he asked Orick to tell him about it. "What is it like, my friend? To conquer space and time, nature and self—to be a god?"

Orick stared at Gallen for a long time after the question was asked. They were sitting beside a deep pond, its surface unrippled by the wind, on a summer morning. Gallen had caught several nice trout for breakfast, and Orick could hardly wait to go eat them. By this time, both Orick and Tallea had lived far beyond the years that bears are supposed to. The first generation of their children had mostly passed away, and the second was growing old. Orick could not very well deny what he and Tallea had become.

"It's not what you think," Orick said. "The Qualeewoohs' ancestors judged me, and they let me live, but I'm not a god. I'm no smarter than I was, no wiser. I'm just . . . more powerful than before."

Gallen was smoking a pipe, the fumes of it curling through his grizzled beard. His face was deeply seamed, weather-beaten. But there were crinkling lines of joy around his eyes.

"I've often wondered," Gallen said, "if you've conquered time, why you didn't go back in time, give me the Waters before I ever battled the Dronon."

"It doesn't work that way," Orick said. "The Qualeewoohs defeated time by learning how to live forever. They defeat eternity one day at a time. We can't reverse time—just plod along with the rest of you. I reached the Waters too late."

"But you will live forever?" Gallen asked.

"I won't keep this body," Orick said. "There's too much to explore, out there . . ." he gestured with his muzzle toward the open blue sky. "Tallea and I talked about it. We'll stay until you and Maggie pass on, then we'll leave, too. I can lay down my life. I can take it up again."

"If you ask me, that makes you a god," Gallen said, somehow awed by his humble friend.

Orick shook his head. "Sometimes, lately, I've learned to leave my body in my dreams. Learned to control my powers better. I've seen real gods out there. I've seen—I can't even begin to tell you."

"You can't?" Gallen asked. "Or won't?"

"Can't," Orick said. "Can't, for now. Can't describe it. But when you die, I'll be the one to come to you. I'll take you out there, and show you. We can explore new trails together, just like we used to."

Gallen reached out and patted Orick's muzzle. Such a good friend, for so long.

"I don't know," Gallen said. "Are you sure I'll even be there?"

"Och, what do you mean?" Orick asked.

"Are you sure I even have a spirit? I am just a clone of a clone."

"Oh, you've got a spirit all right," Orick comforted him.

"I hope so," Gallen said. "But since I was killed by the Lords of the Seventh Swarm, I've never been the same. Knowing that I was a clone, knowing that I was supposed to live up to someone else's vision of what I should be— I've fought against it. In a way, perhaps it is the knowledge of what I am that's made me happy. But I've always wondered, did I get this way just because I wanted to change, or did someone change me?"

"No one changed you," Orick said. "Not that I know of, anyway. I think you wanted to change."

"I used to tell myself that it was pure stubbornness," Gallen said. "I always wanted to save the universe, but I figured that the most I could do was give my life for others. Once I did that, I felt . . . free."

"Do you ever talk about this with Maggie?" Orick asked.

"About us getting killed?" Gallen said. "Never. I've wanted to talk about it. I think she knows what happened. But . . . it doesn't seem to worry her, like it does me."

Just then, Gallen's granddaughter, Rebecca, called from down in the valley, telling him that he was to come home for breakfast. He and Orick disappeared up over a hill, through the pines.

That winter, when Gallen went outside to bring the milk cow to the barn during a storm, a tree fell on Gallen's chest, crushing him so badly that none of Maggie's prayers or ministrations could save him.

On that night, Orick kept his promise.

As Gallen lay on his bed, dying, holding Maggie's hand, he kept breathing harder and harder, the liquid so filling his lungs that soon he could breathe no more.

He heard Maggie weeping, calling out for him, but his hands went icy cold, and he couldn't feel her touch.

He thought he felt some coolness on his forehead, as her lips kissed him one last time, and he smelled her clean breath, her skin, her hair.

Then he saw a bright pulsing light, hidden within a fog, and felt a warmth in his chest as the light drew him near. He felt his body fall away, an unwanted husk, and he rushed to the light, thinking, I'm not leaving you, Maggie, my sweet. I'm only going before you, to prepare a place for us both.

And as he drifted up through the fog, into the light, Gallen met Orick, the old black bear waiting patiently.

Together they took one final journey.